Use Me or Lose Me

Also by Maryann Reid

Sex and the Single Sister

Use Me or Lose Me

a novel of love, sex, and drama

Maryann Reid

st. martin's press ✹ *new york*

www.stmartins.com

Design by Susan Yang

Library of Congress Cataloging-in-Publication Data

Reid, Maryann.
    Use me or lose me : a novel of love, sex, and drama /
Maryann Reid.—1st ed.
        p.   cm.
    ISBN 0-312-31437-X
    1. African American women journalists—Fiction.   I. Title.

PS3618.E54U84 2003
813'.6—dc21

                                        2003041414

First Edition: August 2003

10 9 8 7 6 5 4 3 2 1

To that brother who published my first article in that
major magazine . . . the story is just beginning. . . .

Acknowledgments

I want to give lots of love and thanks to my mother, Veronica Reid, the hardest-working woman in business.

To all the book clubs—thanks for the love and, in some instances, the home-cooked food! Talking about relationship drama is always better over a plate of catfish and candied yams. To all the radio stations, bookstores, TV shows and public access, Internet fans, and the New York Helmsley telephone operators who supported *Sex and the Single Sister* . . . thanks a bunch for your support and love.

Thanks to my agent, Richard Curtis—I like your style! Thanks to my editor, Monique Patterson, for belief in this book and its direction.

I can't forget Shawn for giving me a male perspective on things and for adding humor to my work. And my friend Latoya, who has the prettiest handmade curtains in her home, thanks for just being cool.

To all the other friends, you know who you are, thanks for your stories and gossip.

I want to thank my beautiful sister, Arlene; grandmother, Pastor Phyllis Brown; Matilda; Lucy; and Mami Gloria.

A special thank-you to the faculty at the University of Miami, especially Dr. Fred D'Aguiar, who helped me blend my MFA life and author life for the successful and timely completion of this book!

And most important, I want to thank God for another blessing.

Chapter 1 ♥ Farah

*F*arah dialed 1-800-FLOWERS. "Yes, I'd like to have a delivery tomorrow to five seventy-six Lincoln Terrace. Can you do it before noon?"

"Yes, sure, ma'am," the friendly operator said.

Farah gave the woman the information she had. She figured a bouquet of pink roses and some kind words would soften Judy Batista. After she placed the order, Farah thought about Judy some more as she got dressed for work. She wondered if she was suffering alone. She understood how it was to feel alone. *A single mom, with no crime or drug history, beaten and arrested by an off-duty cop?* She felt there was more behind the story. In the car on her way to the studio, she grabbed a pen. She jotted down some questions for the woman, but ended up throwing them away. The best interviews were those she hadn't planned.

Like every afternoon, Farah always had her identification card handy so she wouldn't fumble with it at the door. As she stepped past the security guards on her floor, she felt their eyes follow her shape. She avoided eye contact with all of them. It's not that she was trying to be rude, but she didn't want to waste her smile on men who were not options—old, middle-aged, and broke.

"Happy New Year, Ms. Washington!" sang the security guards as Farah sashayed past with her head held high. "You are looking fine as wine this afternoon," said the tall, skinny, gray-haired one. Farah smiled inside at his corny, outdated line. She mumbled New Year's greetings back to them and swiped her security card through the metal door.

Sailing through the doors, she collided with an overly energetic man talking to himself. It was Marty, one of the producers at the station.

"Marty! Good morning," she said smiling brightly, hoping he wouldn't start any small talk about how she spent Christmas and New Year's Eve.

Marty smiled back at her, running his pale, long fingers over his bushy, brown mustache. "I should say sorry, but I'd rather bump into a gorgeous woman any day than a grump like me," he said, holding the door for her. "I was just talking about you with Samantha. The changes you made in the script are fine for today. Oh, and Happy New Year!" With a wave, he walked through the door.

"Happy New Year to you, too," Farah said behind him. At least that was one less thing she had to worry about for today, she thought.

She walked quickly through the newsroom, her kitten heels announcing her presence.

"Farah, don't you get enough attention on air? I knew when I heard those clicking sounds it had to be you." Elizabeth, one of her favorite producers, laughed. "Every day. Click. Clack. Haven't you learned to wear sneakers like the rest of us? It's not like the viewers see your shoes."

Farah gave her a passing laugh and continued walking. She counted the doors to her office. She was almost there.

"I love that color on you, Farah! It looks so nice against your skin," said a production assistant as she walked past the break room.

"Thanks," Farah answered, acknowledging the reference to her purple-and-pink two-piece suit. It was her favorite and she liked that people noticed.

This was typical for Farah every evening. Since starting at Channel 7 News, an Emmy Award–winning news program, she had become something of a novelty. She was "the pretty black girl," or for that matter the only black person, everywhere she had worked for the last four years. And she wouldn't have it any other way. Her beauty got her male bosses to listen and her shrewd intellect got her the right assignments. In fact, while at Columbia she got an internship filing papers at a WABT-TV in Upstate NY. The news director took a liking to her since she was willing to travel the six hours every day from the city. He gave her a gopher job on the weekends. After she graduated college, she was offered a permanent weekend reporter position for a few years. At twenty-five, she was the only reporter, stepping over *20/20* and *Dateline*, able to interview the twelve-year-old boy in the nationally known Anniston case, who was accused of killing his father in Binghamton. The young boy said she reminded him of an older sister. Farah always found that funny since the boy was blond with blue eyes. Soon after, the WABT-TV news cast won an Emmy for that interview. After that, she covered the 1998 blizzard that disabled power and claimed many lives in Upstate NY. Her growing popularity reached New York City, where she was offered a job as an assignment reporter at WNBC and the following year quickly jumped at the newsanchor offer at Channel 7. At twenty-seven, she had her eyes on an even bigger scale.

She was almost to her door when she spotted Samantha, her producer. Sam was just walking out of her own office. Sam was in her late thirties, and had already had more cosmetic surgery than a rich L.A. housewife. Farah always noted that she was flawless, hair always glistening and nails always manicured. Her executive producer salary put her in the high-six-figure rank. Sam had her legs exposed under a knee-length skirt so everyone would notice her elegant, diamond-encrusted ankle bracelet.

"Happy New Year, Farah," Sam said as she and Farah gave each other quick air kisses on the cheek. "Can you get on the set now? We're having some technical problems and want to get you set up early. Okay?" asked Sam. She stepped back and inspected Farah.

"Sure," Farah said. "But can I—"

Sam gasped. "Oh, my God, where did you find those? Are those the new Jimmy Choo mules?"

Farah sighed. "I'll tell if I can use the bathroom first."

"Oh, I'm sorry." Sam giggled. "Hurry back, in case we get some breaking news on that cop-murderer trial decision. And I'm not going to forget about the Jimmy Choo info."

"Whatever," Farah joked as she walked down the hall to the ladies' room.

Her bladder now feeling more relaxed, she was ready to go on air. Farah walked onto the set, and for a moment stood there reveling in the explosion of activity. Technicians, producers, and camera crews hurriedly prepared for the six o'clock news. Farah smiled. If she couldn't have the effects of a real orgasm, her job was the closest thing to it.

"Farah, would you like some coffee?" asked Pete, the floor manager, as she sat down. Pete was five feet three inches, two hundred pounds and eager to please. No one really talked to him, but he did his job, and always managed to remain calm no matter what was going on.

"Thanks. Just remember I like a little milk in my coffee," Farah said, making Pete's fat cheeks pink.

A new production assistant, who Farah had never seen before, practically fell on her lap as she tripped handing her the show's rundown. Farah held her annoyance in check as the girl uttered a nervous apology, then remembered her days as a production assistant like it was yesterday.

"Farah, count to five for me, please," Sam ordered through Farah's earpiece.

"One, two, three, four, five. Okay, one, two, three, four, five," Farah said again. "Sam, it's a little too loud and picking up some background noise."

Pete walked over with the cup of coffee and adjusted Farah's mike. Then she went through the countdown again a few more times until it was perfect.

"Less than a minute to air," Sam said. The production assistant came back over with an updated rundown for Farah and the camera crew. Regina, the makeup lady, rushed in and powdered her cheeks because she was picking up some shine.

Farah's lips parted on a breathless rush as the opening music began to roll. This was the part she loved—all lights on her. The teleprompter lit up and she was now in the homes of millions of New York City viewers.

". . . And I'm Farah Washington," she said picking up after her co-anchor, newsman Scott Harrison. "Thanks for joining us this evening.

"Channel Seven is following a developing story. A shocker at the NYPD this evening. NYPD Commissioner John Bratt is denying claims that one of its top-ranked officers is accused of raping and beating a young woman in his custody. Commissioner Bratt defended his department in a press conference this afternoon. Wayne Miles is live now at One Police Plaza," Farah said with conviction.

While the tape played, Farah listened. This was usually a time to touch up her lip gloss. But she was convinced that the officer was hiding something and knew that the only person to reveal that would be Judy, the victim herself.

Scott leaned over to say something, but she looked straight ahead. After the segment, Scott picked up the next story.

The rest of the newscast, packed with stories about car chases, political shakedowns, drug busts, and new weight-loss fads went on without a hitch.

"Thanks, guys, that was great," Sam said through Farah's earpiece. After the show, Scott and Farah talked briefly about the segment and how smoothly it went, as usual.

"Thanks for getting me out of that jam. Couldn't tell if the drug bust story was for you or me. The rundown was screwed," Scott said.

"We're like Lucy and Desi. What can I say? We have to make each other look good," Farah joked.

Scott smiled back and left the set. The six-thirty people rushed in to do *Vince Kramer Live,* which was more of a talk-show format. Vince Kramer, a tall, gallant man with dyed black hair, was the show's veteran anchor. He had been on air for the last twenty years. Farah thought about sticking around and watching him in action, but she really needed to tend to some work in her office.

"Farah, wait up a minute," Sam called out to her.

"You're starting to look a little wilted," Farah said.

"I'm coming off of a ten-hour shift," Sam said, her voice raspy. "I just wanted to let you know that I heard Katie is tracking down that Bernedetti story like it's a hurricane. She's making all kinds of calls to get Batista on her show," she told her. "But you didn't hear it from me."

Farah looked at Sam, her heart speeding up. Katie, a fifteen-year TV veteran, was co-host of *Rise and Shine*, the station's bread-and-butter national news show. Farah thought about telling Sam her plans to scoop the Batista interview, but she passed. "Say no more," she said, winking at Sam. "I wish Katie luck." Then she turned and hurried to her office.

She called Lola, her best friend who she'd helped get a part-time job at CBS. She was an administrator in the newsroom and handled all the little details like petty cash, gathering messages from the news hotline, and returning viewer e-mail. Lola was happy with that because it was only three days a week and she could be home before Chris.

"What's up, Lola!" Farah said when she heard her voice.

"Were you able to use Judy Batista's address?" Lola asked anxiously.

"Of course I did. I'm having some flowers delivered to her. I know going into an anchor's Rolodex is not something you want to be caught doing. Thanks for getting that." Farah paused. "Even my agent thinks this story will get me more notice."

"I want to see you get this interview. And I know you can. You are young, black, and can relate to that young woman. They even sent some Hispanic reporters and the girl still won't talk to them," said Lola, whispering. "Damn, even Connie Chung was turned down by her."

"Everyone has their own technique. The flowers are not too much, but enough. And instead of calling, I'm just showing up at her door. I don't want to give her time to think about it. This story is extremely hot. It just broke this morning," Farah said with urgency in her voice. "Don't forget to stop by tonight. I have something for you." She hung up just realizing that she might end up doing what Connie Chung couldn't.

She dismissed thoughts about getting her boss, Ms. Meyers's, permission before she sought out the interview. She didn't want to wait on approval. Tony Bernedetti had been accused of viciously beating and raping a young Dominican woman in his custody. The cop's story had already made the pages of *The New York Times* and *USA Today*. She wanted to take a different angle and focus on the woman who had been raped. She recalled a Channel 2 reporter on television this evening banging on the woman's door for an interview and she refused to open it. Farah knew if she got the interview, Katie's embarrassment would be her reward.

♥

Sitting comfortably inside a black town car, Farah arrived at her high-rise condominium building in Fort Greene. She had bought her one-bedroom condo over two years ago when the area was undergoing an economic overhaul. The chauffeur came around and opened her side about the same time she opened it. She'd wait for a man to open a door for her to get inside a car, but felt silly waiting to get out of a car. The driver waited till she disappeared inside her building before he drove off.

Her apartment decor was understated and simple. A few white lamps sat alone, and a large, imposing painting of Frida Kahlo and Diego Rivera dramatized the bare walls. An elegant antique trunk given to her by her mom played the role of a coffee table. She took extra care to create a small nook in the corner, where she kept hundreds of magazine back issues and books on wooden shelves. They were organized in alphabetical order so she could easily find what she was looking for. It was the most used part of the condo.

Farah tossed her Jimmy Choos in the corner, where they joined a few others. She clapped twice and her state-of-the-art television system turned on to her news channel, where it was preset. Her clothes fell piece by piece on the wooden floor. Stripped down to her bra and panties, she strolled into the kitchen and heated up day-old Chinese food in the microwave. Then she sprinted into the living room, with her hot plate, when she heard Judy Batista's name.

Again, she saw a pathetic reporter banging on Batista's door. Farah ate as she immersed herself in thinking about what to do tomorrow. The loud beep of her doorbell brought her back. She remembered that Lola was stopping by. She quickly took her empty dish, rinsed it in the sink, and pushed her clothes that were on the floor to the side.

"I'm here to collect my reward," said Lola, walking in with her hair wrapped in pins after a salon visit. "Is that Chinese food I smell?" Lola twisted up her nose at the strong odor. "I would have brought over some fried fish if I had known."

"I have some left over, if you want some," Farah said. "Where's Arabia?" She stood by her friend who was comfortably dressed in loose jeans and sneakers.

"Everyone is downstairs waiting. Chris drove me by." Lola followed Farah into the bedroom.

"I hope you like these little Gucci booties for Arabia. They're to die for! No bigger than the palm of my hand!" Farah said, handing Lola the Gucci shopping bag that hung on the doorknob.

"How in the hell do you find those things?" Lola laughed, digging into the bag. She opened the box and her smile got larger.

"It's one of those perks you get in the industry," Farah said, waving her hand.

"So I guess Arabia can wear them when she is holding the Gucci bottle holder, too, huh?" asked Lola, reaching over to hug her friend.

"Oh, yeah, and I'm looking into getting her a little Gucci cap."

"My child the ghetto princess," Lola said, laughing again.

They talked some more, but Lola left within minutes. Farah was happy for the company, even though it was brief.

After making some ginger tea, Farah got ready for bed. She took her steaming cup into her bedroom and slowly sipped it while sitting in bed. She was hoping that it would help her sleep. She didn't like to linger alone in bed too long. The bed was cold and even colder when it snowed. The winter reminded her, more than any other time of the year, of her long-standing single status. She missed having a pair of muscular thighs and big biceps in her bed. This time, she didn't want it borrowed or leased from another woman. The only man in Farah's life was her career, and that was getting harder to predict.

What she wanted most was Katie's job—to be co-host of *Rise and Shine*. She'd played guest host a few times, but was getting bored with that. Ms. Meyers, the vice president of News, was the mountain standing in the way. Farah never had problems with her bosses, who were mainly white, but Ms. Meyers was different. Ms. Meyers was new at the network. She was part of a small following who felt Farah was too young and too popular. They joked that since she was so young to be an anchor, her publicity photos had to show off a "fierce" look to make people believe she was older than she was. Farah never understood why Ms. Meyers, who was also black and fifteen years older, showed her no "sisterly recognition." Farah wasn't looking to be best friends. She was just looking for the silent knowing that they were the only black people in executive positions and should stand by each other. She could accept Ms. Meyers being jealous, but not purposely ignoring her inquiries or calls about better stories and assignments.

Farah was at the point in her career where she was an asset to any news media company. She had won an Emmy Award at twenty-six, she kept reminding herself. Ms. Meyers should be after her to take on more assignments instead of the other way around. She wondered if Ms. Meyers knew more about her than she let on. What happened between her and Todd, her mentor and a former vice president at WNBC, was a secret that no one knew about.

Farah was brought back into the present when she sipped the hot tea too quickly and it burned her tongue. She set the tea on her nightstand and allowed it to cool some more. She remembered the day she told Todd she had gotten the anchor job at Channel 7. He had recommended her for the position and she knew he would be happy for her. He had invited her out for drinks to celebrate. They had gone to the bar downstairs from his office. As she sipped her cosmopolitan, Farah had been struck by how much the tall and rather slender Todd looked like Harrison Ford. And she'd had a crush on Harrison Ford since *Indiana Jones*. But it took her several more cosmopolitans to respond to Todd rubbing his leg against hers under the table. Then he slid closer to her and slipped his hand between her legs and cupped her warmth. She remembered. She'd had on her fitted black pants and a white halter. She had closed her eyes when he leaned over and whispered where he'd like his tongue to be. They were both a bit drunk and had spent much of the evening laughing at nothing in particular. Then they walked to Todd's upstairs office, and let their inhibitions go in the dark.

She had enjoyed every moment of their rendezvous. When would she have sex again with an old, rich white man? She shivered as she remembered all the things they had done to each other. The second time, Todd rented a room at the Mercer, where they had escaped—he from his wife and kids, and she from herself. She could be anyone else behind closed doors. Plush carpeting adorned the enormous suite where they shared a few hours of forbidden fantasies. Todd had been an animal with her and had filled every orifice of her body with his tongue, finger, or dick. He begged for her to wear the blond and platinum wigs he brought her. She loved seeing his white hands, fondling her brown skin. Thinking about it, she was turned on and embarrassed at her boldness at the same time.

After she finished her tea, Farah slid between the sheets, with a throbbing between her legs. But she tossed and turned. She didn't want people to get the wrong idea about her climb up the ladder. And the fact that Ms. Meyers worked with Todd didn't make her rest any easier.

A car alarm startled her from her sleep at 9:00 A.M. She rolled over and called the florist. They confirmed that the arrangement was already in transit and would arrive before noon. There was no guarantee that Judy Batista was going to be home, but she had to take a risk. She believed fate was on her side, and packed a sleek, soft yellow pantsuit in her bag.

From her Fort Greene neighborhood, she took a cab down Myrtle Avenue to Batista's building. She was dressed simply in sweatpants, a tank top, and a cap. She wanted to look like just another black girl from around the corner. When she approached the building, she saw a flower delivery truck. She passed by a small team of reporters in front of the building trying to talk to neighbors of Batista. The front door of the building was unlocked and she walked in. She waited around in the lobby rehearsing what she wanted to say in her head. She didn't want to appear overanxious for the story, but she was. A group of young Hispanic guys stepped off the elevator and looked her up and down. "*Ai, mami! Bella! Guapa!*" a few of them shouted as they walked by. One even touched her arm. She just brushed him off. Then a man wearing a shirt that said Gladys Flowers on it walked up to her and pressed the elevator button.

"Hi, are those flowers for Judy Batista?" Farah said to the disheveled-looking man who already looked like he'd worked a full day.

"Yeah," he said suspiciously. "Why?"

"Because I want to give them to her. I'm the sender."

"Look, lady. I have to get these flowers in on time. How am I supposed to know you are the sender?" he said with attitude.

"Just give me the damn flowers." Farah pulled out ten dollars from her pocket and gave it to him. She reached for the flowers. "Now can I have them?"

He let out a grunt and counted the money.

"Funny how who I am doesn't matter right now," Farah said, holding the beautifully arranged bouquet. She inhaled the perfumed scent.

"Sorry about that. I just wanted to be sure," the man said and left.

Farah pressed the elevator button again. She thought to herself that she spent nearly one hundred dollars on this arrangement and the man gave it to her for ten dollars. She laughed to herself. The elevator door opened. She stepped in and pressed five. When she got off, she noticed the face of a familiar reporter getting on with a camera crew. He didn't even look her way.

A few seconds later she was knocking on apartment 5H.

No one opened the door. Farah knocked again, a little slower this time.

A teenaged girl flung open the door, with a little girl on her right hip.

"Yes?" she asked, letting her eyes rest on the bouquet.

"I'm here for Judy Batista. I want to give these flowers to her," Farah said, handing the girl the arrangement.

She put the little girl down and smelled the flowers. "What is this for?" she asked.

Still standing in the hallway, Farah said, "I've seen these reporters treat Ms. Batista like an animal. Banging away at her door, disturbing her privacy. It's ridiculous. No one is showing her any respect. But I want to talk to her," Farah said, taking out her Channel 7 News ID.

"I knew you looked familiar, but I couldn't tell with that cap. Is that why you sent the flowers? To try to get in here?" the girl interrogated.

"Yes, I did think sending the flowers would help. I want to show that I care, but I have a job to do. I think I can help Ms. Batista get her story out before her name is dragged across the dirt any further." Farah was careful not to appear slick but compassionate.

The girl stood there tapping her feet. Farah peeked over her shoulders at the darkness in the apartment. She knew Judy Batista was inside.

"Well, you are the only one who has come correct. At least you are honest about yours, instead of like these sneaky reporters out there. Come in. But only for a few minutes." The girl stepped aside.

Farah entered the quiet apartment and heard the faint sound of something sizzling on the stove. She placed her bag down by the door.

"Judy! It's that black girl from Channel Seven for you!" the girl yelled down the narrow hall to the bedroom.

As soon as she did, Judy stepped out. She walked up to Farah and gave her a weak handshake.

"This is my sister, Sonia. She's like a watch dog for me, keeping away all those reporters out there," Judy said. Sonia gave Judy the flowers, who just stood there holding them. She didn't say thank you.

Farah didn't mind. She just wanted the interview.

"So whose side are you on? The police or mine?" said Judy, her eyes penetrating Farah. Sonia put the flowers down on a wooden stand and stood by Judy's side.

"I can't be on your side if I don't know your story. Nobody has heard anything from your end. How do you feel about that?" Farah asked, feeling Judy building a wall around herself.

Judy blinked. Her shoulders relaxed as she breathed in. She sat down on the floral couch, while Sonia went to the back room with the little girl. Farah took the space next to her.

"We at Channel Seven want to take a different angle with this case early on. Your voice needs to be heard. Personally, I'm tired of hearing the police department treat this like it's a nuisance. Please tell me you are, too." Farah reached for Judy's small, fragile hand.

Judy was dressed in bubble-gum stretch jeans and an oversized T-shirt. Her eyes were red and her lips chapped. But she had a luxuriant bundle of long, black hair that she tied to the side of her neck and a set of cheekbones that any cosmetic surgeon would want in his portfolio. "How do I know you are not on the side of the cops? And take my words to make me look worse? I want this to be done live," Judy demanded.

"We can do that. Today, as a matter of fact. If it's live no one can change your words. You can tell me whatever you want. I won't probe you. It's your stage." Farah hoped that reassurance would work.

Judy lit a cigarette and smoked it halfway down before anyone said another word. Farah hated the smell, but stayed put.

"I'll do it. But I will not do this with anyone else. Only you because you are honest." Judy wetted her lips and put out the cigarette. She shook Farah's hand.

Farah worked feverishly to get a technician team to her before the woman changed her mind. The news desk was eager to send a team down right away. She realized she had no other choice but to tell Ms. Meyers. She thought about how Ms. Meyers would react. She would sound happy, but be pissed, thought Farah. She reached for the phone and called her. Ms. Meyers's secretary transferred her right away when she mentioned the Batista interview.

"I got a live interview with Judy Batista coming in. It's an exclusive," Farah said. "The feed will be coming in at six." Farah held the phone tightly.

There was a short pause. "Good work, but you and I have to talk when you come back to the office," Ms. Meyers said and hung up.

Farah held the phone and wondered if she had made things worse between her and Ms. Meyers.

Minutes later, the cameramen arrived and immediately began setting up. A few of them complained about being harassed by competitor stations as they walked into the building, but Farah paid no attention. She was focused on getting Judy relaxed and prepared for the interview. In an effort to keep Judy calm, they talked about the latest movies, music, and weather.

A little before 6:00 P.M. Farah changed into her suit and applied her makeup. She heated her flat iron to straighten her frayed ends. Sonia helped Judy dress in a plain gray suit. They were ready before Farah was. When she walked out in the living room where everything was set up, she felt her adrenaline pumping. It was the same feeling she'd get in the newsroom. *Connie Chung, where ya at now?* she kept saying to herself.

The technicians adjusted the lighting at Farah's request. She complained it was too bright on her forehead. Judy agreed. After some changes, everything was ready to go.

"I'm here now, live with Judy Batista, the young woman who was arrested by an NYPD officer and accused him of rape and battery. You'll hear her story first on *News at Six.*"

Farah heard Judy exhale.

"Okay, when they come back from the commercial, it's us. Stay calm. Get your thoughts together. We're at the top of the hour," instructed Farah.

Judy kept her head down. Farah asked Sonia to bring Judy a glass of water.

By the time Judy took a second sip, they were back on air.

Judy began her torrid tale.

"I was at a local pool hall with a friend. Mr. Bernedetti came in, but I did not know he was a cop then. He and I started to talk and flirt. We exchanged numbers. I left the pool hall before my friend did. Mr. Bernedetti offered to drive me home since it was raining and he lived in the same neighborhood. Instead of taking me home, he pulls up to a motel. He said he had a family member there and had to make a stop. I got uncomfortable and asked to be taken home. He became all irate and tried to kiss me." Judy paused as she called to mind the details. "I tried to fight him off. He ripped my blouse and started showing me his penis. He wanted me to give him oral sex. When I refused, he showed me his police badge." Judy choked up. "He threatened to arrest me on fake charges if I didn't go down on him. We fought and he took a stick he kept in his car and started beating me on my arms and legs. I was bleeding a lot around my nose and was screaming in pain. That was when he arrested me. He put some adhesive on me to stop the bleeding before he took me to the precinct. He told me not to tell anyone. He told the people at the precinct that I tried to hurt myself. My family had to get bond money they didn't have to get me out," Judy explained. Her voice was tight as she held back tears.

"Can you show us what he did to you?" Farah asked. Judy's eyes opened at Farah's request. They hadn't discussed that.

Judy hesitated and Farah pointed to her eye while the camera sat on Judy. Judy reluctantly took off her eye patch and the camera zoomed in. Then Farah pointed to her arm. Judy rolled up her jacket sleeve and revealed black-and-blue wounds on her forearm. The camera zoomed in closer.

"How are you handling all this now?" Farah asked in her most concerned voice.

Judy began to cry. "I did not want any problems. I did not want this. I was just out to play pool that night. I'm sure I'm not the first girl he has done this to," Judy said, her shoulders shaking. "I can't even sleep at night or go back to work. My life is completely ru-

ined." Judy's voice was weak and had little strength. Her last statement was flat. It had no conviction. Farah took that as her cue to
end.

"Thank you, Ms. Batista. We will be following this story. You'll
hear the latest first on *News at Six*. Back to you, Scott."

After the interview, Farah consoled Judy and thanked her again.
Before she left, she offered a silent prayer for Judy and her sister.
She thought how Judy's life would never be the same once everyone
saw her face on television. A light wind of guilt flew over her as
she stood with her head bowed in prayer.

Farah arrived at work with the interview tape in her hand.
Nearly everyone in the newsroom, except Katie and Ms. Meyers,
welcomed her, dying to know how she snagged the interview every
network had been vying for. However, she was more interested in
what Ms. Meyers had to say. She knew there would be plenty.

She went into her office to get herself together. She was still
amazed about how smoothly the interview went. She knew it would
be played repeatedly on Channel 7's sister stations. When she
checked her e-mail, there was already a message from *Dateline* asking for a copy.

"Come in," Farah said when she heard a knock on her door.

"You were so wonderful tonight! I just wish I could have had
the camera guys with you from the beginning." Sam sat down.

"No, it just would have made a problem with Ms. Meyers. By
the time I called her there was no room or time for her to complain," Farah said.

"I was just talking to Ms. Meyers before I came down here,"
Sam said, glancing at the closed door behind her. "She said for you
to stop by when you had a chance."

"Why can't she just call me? Farah said, irritated.

"I'd just go up and find out," Sam suggested, rising from the
chair. "Just be cool."

Farah sighed, knowing that Sam was right.

Farah stepped off the elevator and faced the pristine glass double doors leading to Ms. Meyers's suite. She stepped through the doors and immediately heard the ringing of phones and animated voices coming from the small-screen televisions that lined the walls.

"Hi, I'm here to meet with Ms. Meyers," Farah told the secretary, an older white woman, who wore an embroidered sweater with Scottish dogs across the front.

The secretary looked Farah up and down, her mouth puckered as if she had a bad taste in her mouth.

"Good afternoon, Ms. Washington. Ms. Meyers is expecting you. Would you like some coffee?" she asked. Farah looked at her stubby, dry fingers around the cup.

"No, thanks. I'll just wait here," she said, and sat down, making sure her back did not touch the couch.

After a few minutes, Ms. Meyers came out. She stood at her door, all six feet of her. She was a slender woman. Her sandy-colored skin was blemished, and her face signaled she was past her prime. There were signs of once-high cheekbones that were now too round. Her big eyes, which were probably once considered seductive, were heavy with dark circles under them. Her hair was pulled back into a tight ponytail. She nodded for Farah to come into her office.

Farah walked in first and noted all the awards gracing her walls, some dating back to 1970. Farah hadn't even been born then. She guessed Ms. Meyers might be in her early fifties.

"Please sit down, dear."

Farah gritted her teeth. She hated the way Ms. Meyers called her dear.

She sat across from Ms. Meyers, who cleared some room on her desk. Her nails were painted a subtle brown. Her navy blue suit was pressed to perfection.

Farah decided to plunge right in. "I wanted to tell you about the story beforehand, Ms. Meyers. But I also wanted to be sure I would be able to get to her first."

Ms. Meyers finished shuffling papers and folded her hands. "You *should* have told me way beforehand, Ms. Washington," she said, her tone glacial. "I could have had some suggestions for the interview. You can't just go around here playing like you're Christiane Armanpour. You need to get *my* okay before you take a story like that."

"I have to say one thing, Ms. Meyers," Farah said, standing firm. "I find it a compliment to be compared to Christiane Armanpour. Though I'm nowhere near her accomplishments, I would do just about anything to get a story and to get it first for the station. Even if that means choosing between getting the story and telling my boss. The interview was one of those where there was no room for even my own suggestions. Judy Batista was very firm about how she wanted to do the interview and who she would do it with. That was the only way she would have done it. Nearly every newspaper is going to be quoting our station and the interview in the morning."

"And have *your* name all over it. Don't think I'm not onto you, Ms. Washington," she said glaring at her. "Next time I want my hand in this." Farah just nodded stiffly. "With that said, the interview was done well. Can you get the woman to come on *Rise and Shine* and talk to Katie?"

Farah shook her head. "She told me that it was her last interview. And besides, I did all the work to get the lady to tell her story. If Katie wants her on her show, then Katie should try to get her," Farah said, composed with a pleasant smile.

Ms. Meyers gave one of her false closemouthed laughs. "I see. We'll talk soon."

Within seconds, the distinctive clicking sounds of Farah's heels faded down the hall.

Farah returned to her desk, found a message from Sam, and immediately called her back.

Sam said happily, "It's time to guest host! At least for tomorrow. I just got a call that Katie will be out."

Farah nearly knocked over the empty crystal vase on her desk in her excitement. On the heels of her Batista interview, the timing couldn't be better.

"No problem, Sam. I'll be here bright and early," Farah said, grinning.

"You probably made Katie sick, since you got the story she was trying for." Sam snickered.

"It's her loss. Maybe she needs to get her act together," Farah said, glancing at the clock. "I'll see you in a few."

♥

After the 6:00 P.M. show, Farah waited in front of the building for the company town car. She checked her cell phone for messages, but there were none. The night air was raw and cold, and bit at her skin. The high from the *Rise and Shine* news had faded. That's how it usually was. When she got a chance to do it, she was happy. But then she found she wanted more. Not just in her career but in everything in her life. She thought about what she accomplished at work today and wished she could be celebrating with someone special. She thought about Lola and her marriage to Chris. When she slid into the town car's backseat, she instructed the driver to take her to Lola's. She didn't want to be alone tonight.

The warmth from Lola's home in Flatbush, Brooklyn, radiated from inside. When Farah walked through the front door, she just felt good. Everything had its place and was neat and organized. The living room was tiny, but comfortable. Farah gazed at the pale yellow curtains Lola had just finished sewing. She remembered Lola telling her about them last month. When she looked up, instead of a valance she saw a garland of dried fruits, herbs, and flowers wrapped around a gold cord at the top, gracing the living room with a pleasant scent. Her fingers traced the delicate ruffle that trimmed the yellow-and-white hand-sewn checkerboard couch pillows. An unexpected surge of insecurity crept inside her. She couldn't even hem a pair of slacks if she had to.

Lola brought out a fresh pitcher of iced tea, while Farah watched television with Chris and the baby. The baby sat between Chris's legs as he gave the baby a scene by scene description of the show they were watching.

"What is in this drink? It's delicious!" Farah said. "What did you put in here?"

"Just a little bit of ginger and lemon," Lola shouted from the kitchen. "It gives it an extra punch! It's not flat like that powdered stuff people use."

Farah didn't answer back because the powdered drinks were all she had time to prepare.

Chris got to his feet, holding the baby to his chest. "Here," he said, handing her the baby. "Watch this little monster while I make a kitchen run."

"Yes, baby. Yes, baby," she said to Arabia whose hair had a small pink ribbon in it. Her skin was light brown like Lola's, but even at eight months she had her father's temperament. Arabia kept squirming in her arms. Farah took out her scarf and wrapped it across her stylish blouse, to catch any drops from Arabia's bubbly mouth. Arabia began to whimper and twist her body even more. "I got something for you," Farah sang.

She reached in her purse and held out a small wrapped gift. Arabia's little hands patted the gift gently. Eventually, she managed to tear the loosely wrapped paper and immediately began shaking her new toy.

Chris came back into the living room and laughed when he saw what his daughter was waving around. "Oh, no! You got my baby a Gucci baby rattle. How in the hell did you manage that?" He sat his short, burly body back down on the couch.

"You can get these things made," Farah said, smiling at a now-happy Arabia.

"Soon she'll have the whole Gucci baby set," Lola said, finally joining them. "She's not even one yet and she already has more name-brand things than I do."

They all watched Arabia shake the rattle and chew on its end. Chris reached over and put Arabia back on his lap. As Farah watched them play, she couldn't help but wonder when she'd have her own kids. She was getting the "baby itch," but had nobody to scratch it. Lola moved closer to Chris and both of them played with Arabia, kissing her over and over again on her forehead. Farah sat by watchfully, as Lola's long tresses brushed over Arabia's face every time she leaned down to kiss her. Farah felt an ache somewhere in the region of her heart. Her parents had never showered her with this much attention. She had always played alone and sometimes ate alone, while her mother flitted from one party to the next, and her father, who had never lived with them, was home with his wife. Till this day, she still felt alone. She wondered if perhaps that was why it was so difficult for her to express affection. It was something her boyfriends had always complained about.

"Did you hear what I said?" Lola asked.

Farah snapped out of her thoughts. "Oh, no, I must have been daydreaming. What did you say?"

"I said thank you," Lola said gently, sensing what Farah was feeling. Then she smiled and changed the subject. "I saw that interview today, girl! You were tight. You had that girl pouring out her heart. She seemed to really trust you," Lola said, rocking Arabia.

"Yeah, it was nothing, though. Just doing my job. Would like to celebrate with a man and all, but you know," Farah said, feeling that her news was insignificant compared to what she saw in Lola's life.

"Talking about you want a man and your nails too long to roll a biscuit," Chris said, shaking his head.

Lola poked him with her elbow.

"If I want a biscuit, I'll go buy some at the bakery," Farah said, cutting her eyes at him.

"Man, I can spot a woman like you from miles away. Ya'll don't need men. Ya'll too busy being men yourselves," Chris said, not letting up.

Farah felt one of their many frequent debates about relationships coming up. "I'm just trying to take care of myself. What, am I supposed to play dumb and drop my career to get a man?"

"But don't wear your credentials all on your sleeve!" Chris said, animatedly. "I bet the first thing you do when you meet a man is tell him what you do. Right?"

"Yeah," Farah said. "So?"

"And then you tell him where you live and how hard you work. And what college you went to."

"Again, so? That is just part of getting to know someone. That's intro talk."

"That's the damn problem!" Chris shot back. "Sometimes you women talk too much, too soon. Just listen to the man, find out what he's about before you haul out your college degrees and job titles. If a man asks you what you do, then tell him what you do. And be humble about it. But don't launch the conversation with all that."

"Please, Chris." Farah sucked her teeth. "It's a lot deeper than that. I mean, I don't even get that far to tell men all that. They won't even *approach* me. Most of them recognize me from television."

"Men will approach anyone. It's your vibe. You just come off as a little stuck-up and busy," Chris said, looking at Lola, as if expecting her to back him up.

Farah looked at Lola, too.

"I mean, you do be all about your business. Even the times when we did hang out, you could have looked more friendly and approachable," Lola said, warily. "Then maybe they'll feel more comfortable."

Chris jumped back in. "When I met my baby, she was sitting with you. Now, granted you both are attractive. But I got a friendlier vibe from Lola. She was smiling, laughing. And you looked like you had better things to do," he said, while Lola's light skin reddened.

"That is just not my personality. I've always been a serious person. I'm not going to grin and laugh if it doesn't feel right. It can't be my entire fault that men don't talk to me. I am just not for every man out there. The man I want will see my 'busy' nature as attractive because he will be busy, too. I want a man doing something more than getting drunk after work at the lounge. Someone who is in his thirties and not dressing like he is in his teens." Farah stared at Chris's baggy jeans and oversized T-shirt that read Glock Talks, Bullshit Walks.

Lola grinned. "I've been trying to tell him, girl."

"Oh, I see now ya'll just going to turn this on me. I'm about to make myself *busy* with this remote," he said, laughing.

Farah and Lola left Chris in the living room with Arabia and they went in the kitchen.

"Don't let him get to you. He means well," Lola said, patting Farah's shoulder. She had never admitted it aloud, but to her, Farah was the lucky one. She wished she could have Farah's career, and would trade in her marriage chores any day. *I really would,* she thought.

"Maybe he has a point, because whatever I'm trying is not working," Farah said, reaching for a decorative bowl of grapes that sat on the table.

Lola hissed. "Girl, please. You have a lot more than a lot of us."

"Well, I *am* grateful. But I need affection and companionship, too. I want to hear a man call me his wife. My career titles are just too small for all I have in me."

"So what now?" Lola asked. "If I were you I'd just stick to what I know and let everything else come to you."

"That is exactly what I expect a married woman to say. Next time your car won't start, see who you go crying to. Oh, I forgot you have Chris for that."

Lola rolled her eyes. "All I'm saying is look at how you strategized to get that Batista lady to talk to you, and she did. Well, put that same energy into getting a man." Lola mumbled, "If you want one that bad."

Farah thought about how it would be to treat her love life, as she did her career, with careful planning and strategizing. "Remember when we were in our early twenties?" Farah said suddenly. "Partying, talking to this guy and that guy. Thinking it would always be that way?"

"Yeah," Lola answered in a reminiscent tone. "I remember all the Marcuses you had, too." She rose from her chair and put in the cabinet some dried dishes that were on the counter.

"Those were mistakes I made in the name of getting a man. I *can* control my career, but I can't control what happens with a man," Farah said, feeling down. She wanted her visit with Lola to make her feel better.

"So you're just gonna walk through life dealing with things you can control. What about risks? To really find out the possibilities in a relationship with any man, you have to take risks."

Farah breathed deeply as she felt her heart get heavy.

"I have been single for four years. Anybody I meet now *has* to want to marry," Farah whispered, practically talking to herself.

"Farah, you're different," she said, turning to face her. "And you 'different girls' always have to learn the hard way. God has plans for women like you. Women like me, I didn't finish college, and got married young. There are things I want to do, but can't. Girl, it's a catch-twenty-two."

"Yeah, but you got the thing that is hardest to grasp. What people write books and sing songs about. A family. A man who loves you. Here I am, almost thirty with no prospects," Farah said, taking a napkin Lola handed her.

"I am so tired of hearing you talk like you are one hundred years old. There are women getting married every day. Young and old. Damn, if I married when I was thirty, instead of twenty-two, maybe I would make some different choices, too," Lola said, turning back to the dishes.

Farah didn't want to touch that one. She thought if Lola wanted to expand on what she meant by "different choices" she would later.

She loved Lola and no one, not even her own mother, knew her as well as her best friend did. They both understood each other's unspoken words.

"Well," Farah said, "I've got to have something. If it ain't a man, then it's money. And I'm doing the money part all right."

"Thinking like a man again," Lola chided.

♥

The car company called at 3:00 A.M. to tell Farah that her car was on its way. She jumped into some jeans and packed her favorite stone gray Donna Karan pantsuit. She wolfed down a fried egg, a toasted waffle, and a cup of orange juice. As she chewed her food, she fantasized about a life sealed with bonuses and media spotlight if she got Katie's spot on the couch next to Adam.

The loud honk of the horn made her jump. She grabbed her bags and the suit, and headed out the door.

"Good morning, beautiful," Manuel, the driver, said as he opened the car door. "Check this out!" He handed her a copy of *The New York Times*. When she settled in the backseat, she didn't even have to open the paper. The top fold read, "Batista Talks, Channel 7 Listens." Her eyes flew across the page looking for her name. The article continued into the Media section. Farah smiled when she saw that her name showed up several times in the story. The article even praised her "exemplary ability" to snag the toughest interviews in the business. She slammed the newspaper down and clapped for herself. Now it was time to get ready for the show.

"Hi, there, Farah! Long time no see," Regina, the morning makeup person, said. "I heard those heels coming down the hallway. It's so early for that, don't you think?" she asked, her tone friendly.

Farah eyed Regina's new hair color for the month. It was orange. "I hate sneakers. Heels keep me on my toes in more ways than one." Farah went into a small room to get dressed. With quick precision, she slipped on her suit and stepped into her new strappy Manolo Blahniks.

When she was done, Regina directed Farah to the chair in front of her. "I love working on you. You have the best pores. Way better than Katie's," she whispered.

Farah "hmmmed," wondering just what people said about her behind her back.

"She's been rather quiet lately since you beat her to that story. Way to go on that Batista interview. I wish I could have been there to powder you up. You did look a bit shiny."

"It was *live,* Regina," Farah said politely. "Some things you can't prepare for. So, you say that Katie has been kind of quiet?"

"Yeah. I just think she's embarrassed. But knowing her, she's already on to the next thing." Regina started to dab some pink blush on Farah's cheeks, but Farah stopped her and pulled out her own makeup case.

"Oh, that's right!" Regina said. "You have your own equipment." She took the case from Farah, and looked into it frowning, as if someone just told her that her head looked like a pumpkin.

"And as you can see, there isn't much in there," Farah said, reminding Regina to go easy on her.

"What about the hair this morning? Do you want it straightened?" Regina asked, referring to her wavy, long hair.

"As usual," Farah said, somewhat disappointed since she liked her waves. The image consultants called the straightened look more approachable. "Just make sure every strand is in place. You know how my hair would stay wild if it had its way." She puckered up as Regina dabbed some dark pink gloss on Farah's pouty lips.

After thirty minutes in the chair, Farah walked to the set. She could feel the eyes of the cameramen as they watched the sway of her hips. Before she could sit down, Pete rushed over and pulled out her chair.

"Thanks, Pete." She gave him a bright smile. "Where's Adam?"

"He's in his office. He should be out any minute. Is there anything that you need?" He looked like an anxious student eager to please and it was obvious he was struggling to keep his eyes off her breasts, which looked round and full under her jacket.

Then she heard a boisterous voice come toward the set.

"Good morning, boys"—Adam looked at Farah and smiled—"and girl." Farah felt herself relax in the face of Adam's cheery mood. He waved a copy of the *Times* at her.

Adam had an Abercrombie & Fitch model look that topped his six-foot slim frame. He was always cordial with her. Adam was in his forties and began as host of *Rise and Shine* when Farah was still at WNBC.

Farah watched Adam and Katie every morning, until she got the guts to call Adam and introduce herself. They shared short phone conversations about the business and he offered tons of great advice on anchoring. When she came over to Channel 7 News, he specifically asked for her to guest host anytime Katie was out. That was a big deal when it happened and made it into a small column in the New York *Daily News.* It was then she knew that she could become a TV star if she played her cards right. But the network was standing by Katie and so was Ms. Meyers.

"Ms. Washington, I have to give it to you. You are something special. The *Times* rarely puts stories like that on the top fold. You're on your way, kid. We definitely have to talk about this on air," he said, waving the paper again.

Farah saw small stars in front of her eyes. "Thanks! I can't wait to talk about it," she said smugly.

"I had to make some changes since Katie's out, so here's the rundown," Jake, a producer, said. He handed Adam and Farah copies of the rundown.

Adam looked up from the sheet of paper, and asked, "By the way, how's she doing?"

"She says she'll be in bright and early tomorrow," Jake said.

Farah pretended not to listen.

When Jake walked away, Adam went over some fine points on the rundown with Farah.

Then she and Adam began to do the countdown at Sam's request.

"Roll music," said the director.

Farah's heart felt like a beating fist against her chest. As the music played, she looked over at Adam and he gave her a wink. She was ready for the stage, and this time, the entire nation was watching.

"Rise and shine, America!" Adam said into the camera. "I'm your host, Adam Lowell."

"And I'm Farah Washington, in for Katie Maury. Thanks for joining us!" she said, riding on Adam's energetic opening. For the rest of the show, she forgot who Katie Maury was, and made her own mark.

♥

After the show, Farah was left with a delectable high.

"Hey, Adam, hold on a minute," she said, catching up to him. She smiled. "We did it again. Another great show."

"Thanks, Farah. Like I said, you always do a wonderful job. The camera loves you," he said, touching her arm.

Farah took a deep breath and went for it. "Don't you think I'd be perfect for the *Rise and Shine* spot? I mean, the format hasn't changed in years and I think I can bring something fresh to the show."

Adam's mouth opened as if he wanted to say something, but he closed it and thought for a moment. "It's going to take a lot more than one story to show Katie up. But keep up the good work, kid." He patted her arm again, and said, "I like your style." Then he disappeared down the white corridors.

Farah stormed off in the opposite direction feeling a bit more than foolish. It was obvious to her that she had to get her hands dirty to get what she wanted.

*H*is last name was Whitworth. And his family lived up to the meaning of their name. The Whitworths, a respected Jamaican clan from Cherry Hill, were worth millions. But for Lenox Whitworth, each million brought a million problems. Underneath the Armani-clad exterior was a regular man, who preferred a shot of Hennessey to wine and canned tuna to seared swordfish. He also had a penchant for bad things, including bad women. He liked them, and they liked him—all six foot three inches.

Lenox was like a nicely wrapped dark brown candy that, when bitten into, dripped with sweet caramel from the inside. The type of caramel that you swirled around on your tongue and sucked from your fingertips. But too much of the sticky sweet stuff could lead to bad teeth.

And then there was the money. Not only was Lenox good to look at but he was financially blessed. His family owned homes in London, Jamaica, and the Cayman Islands. He spent most of his time at his prewar apartment on Central Park South instead of the family estate in Jamaica. And he was wise about his money. He could have had all his teeth capped with platinum three times, purchased fifty pounds of platinum jewelry, and had his cars custom made with rims and an interior that cost more than the vehicle if he wanted to. But Lenox wasn't into things that depreciated in value. Except the youth and beauty of women. Instead, his money was tied up in real-estate investments and exotic vacations. He could have jet-setted and lived off his trust fund, but instead he went to school and became a lawyer, like his daddy.

♥

It was the family New Year's celebration at the ranch and they had feted the horsy set and invited friends and dignitaries to celebrate. Malamander South was a multimillion-dollar facility Lenox's parents had built. It accommodated the show horses he had competed with as a child. Then at age seventeen, he had grown bored with horses, and tried his hand at race cars.

The servers circled the room with trays of skewered jerk chicken, coconut-crusted shrimp, imported caviar, and spicy crab cakes. Lenox stood tall in the middle of a circle of family "friends" as he recounted some story about his recent trip to the Greek Islands. Everyone noticed his dimples when he laughed, and the way he kept his left hand in his pocket, giving each person a bit of individual attention.

He invited Joanne, a sexual acquaintance of his for more than a year, to keep him company at the event. He liked Joanne because she never demanded too much. She was always there for him when he visited Jamaica, and accepted the way things were between them.

"I was looking for you for a half hour, ya know. Did you just get here?" Joanne asked, a little out of breath. Her hair was flat and her forehead was damp with sweat. She looked like she had put in more work at the party than he did.

"I've been here all afternoon. I told you I'd be at the center lawn. Didn't I?" he said, gently dabbing her forehead with a napkin.

"I guess. Usually I can just spot you in the crowd, since you almost always the tallest." She put the napkin in her purse in case she would need it later. "Can we go somewhere and talk? I'm feeling like I'm under a microscope with all these photographers."

"Let's take a walk," Lenox said, leading the way. It wasn't too far, but the grass on the slope was making it a trek. He didn't say much as they walked, leaving enough room between them to fit two people. He decided that this was a good time for him to break things off with Joanne. He wouldn't be coming back to Jamaica for a while and she wasn't necessarily someone he saw in his future. It was New Years and he wanted to start fresh.

When they got to the house, they sat on the swinging bench on the porch. The shade of the deck made it a comfortable place to sit. They looked like two eight-year-olds after school.

Lenox waited for Joanne to begin, but she just sat there swinging her feet. A slight wind lifted her already short skirt past her blackberry thighs. The white of her cotton panties showed and she crossed her legs.

He laughed, breaking the silence. "I already know what's under that skirt. I've seen it many times."

"I know," Joanne said shyly.

"So what's up?" Lenox asked becoming a little concerned at her suddenly insecure demeanor.

"I'm getting an abortion," Joanne finally announced, swinging a little harder. "I'm three months, but the doctor said it's not too late. So don't worry."

Lenox's let out an unexpected cough. He couldn't say the word "pregnant" either. He looked at Joanne and she looked like a completely different woman now.

"I have the money to raise a child. I don't want a dead baby on my conscience," he said. "I'm willing to give you a monthly allowance, but I can't marry you." It seemed as if offering to take care of the child was the right thing to him. He knew countless men who had children and just gave the women money. It didn't seem to be a problem. Even though he wanted children, fatherhood for him would be different.

She disregarded his last comment. As though she was talking about the season's new Gucci handbag, she said, "It's five hundred dollars now with Dr. Canon." Joanne still refused to look Lenox in the eye; perhaps one look would make her change her mind. "I have too many things to do this year then to sit and breed children."

"Then take it," he said, tight-lipped. He pulled out a checkbook, something he was good at, from the inside of his white blazer. It always solved his other problems. "I can't tell you what to do with your body, but I have a say. I don't want you going to Dr. Canon, because those people like to talk. Go to Dr. Irving." Lenox handed her a folded check for eight hundred dollars.

Joanne reached for the check and put it in her purse without saying another word.

"When are you going to do it?" he said, trying to maintain his coolness. As soon as he asked, he wanted to swallow the words, but it was too late. He knew he wouldn't be able to be with her.

"As soon as I can. I'm going to call Monday for an appointment. I have the Miss Caribbean beauty pageant next month. I can't represent Jamaica with a belly," she said with her beauty-queen smile. She touched her stomach with both her hands.

Lenox felt strange listening to Joanne talk about a baby inside of her, as though it was an ugly pimple that needed to be popped. There was no doubt the child was his. Joanne was very careful about sleeping around. Her reputation counted heavily in her winning pageants.

She had her back against the porch rail and was facing him. Her dangerously long legs were shapely. His eyes rested on her waist. He thought, *I have a child,* but quickly blocked the image. He decided to wait before breaking things off with her.

"So are you coming back for the pageant? You must!" Joanne said as she walked over to him and sat down again. It was the first time that she acted as if something mattered to her.

"I'm not sure," Lenox said, stroking her back. Joanne began pushing the swing with her feet for both of them.

"I really want you to come. I can do the abortion alone. But the pageant. I worked so hard for that." Joanne's voice cracked. "I want somebody there besides my mom and my cousins."

"You can tell me about a pageant months in advance, but you wait three months to tell me you're pregnant?" Lenox's eyes narrowed in on Joanne's stoic expression. But again, she maintained her poised beauty-queen demeanor.

"Keeping it wasn't even something I thought about. Telling you early on would have given us too many options. And if it ever got around to your overbearing family, it would make me sick for them to tell me what to do with my child," she said, rubbing the corner of her eyelid. She checked her finger for mascara.

"That was all you had to say from the beginning. Maybe this is the best for both of us," Lenox said.

Joanne laid her head on Lenox's broad shoulders. They sat there on the swing like that until she was ready to leave.

Lenox bumped into his father, who sat alone in the living room drinking a shot of brandy. He joined him. A shot of brandy was what he needed at the moment, too. Lenox and his father once had a tight, close relationship, but during his teenage years, he found out about his father's affair with their housemaid, and it had never been the same. To talk comfortably with each other, drinks had to be readily available. If not, their conversation was distant and forced. After several drinks, he told his father about Joanne's news out of guilt.

"You're a Whitworth man. You can't go around having sex without a condom! Joanne is a leech like her mother. She's a hotel worker in Kingston, for God's sake," he said dismissively as he took a swig of scotch.

"She's Miss Jamaica," Lenox slurred. But his father ignored that.

"Take this and give it to her. Write it out for how much you need." His father referred to his checkbook, which he, too, kept in his jacket pocket.

"I handled that already," Lenox said, surprised that his father assumed she was having an abortion.

"I wish you would have handled it before it happened, Lenox. I have a whole estate, lots of assets here and in London. I can't afford to have you screwing around and my life's worth ending up in the hands of some woman. You need a wife. There is too much at stake." Lenox's father's face was cold. His grandfather had given his father the same speech, when he married his mother after she told him she was pregnant.

Lenox didn't hear much except the word "wife."

♥

By early morning, Lenox and his parents were up and about in the house. The smell of fresh ackee, saltfish, and banana clung to the walls of the house. Lenox had already packed his bags the night before, as he was anxious to get back to his regular life.

He sat outside with his parents on the veranda overlooking the forty-by-fifteen backyard pool. The mangos in the tree next to it were ripe and gave off a sweet, warm smell. As his parents fussed over some mangos missing from the tree, Lenox sat back in the chair and thought about Joanne off and on.

With excellent timing, Elsa, the housemaid, who had been with the family for almost thirty years, brought out an ice-cold pitcher of sorrel. Just the way Lenox liked it, tart but sweet.

"Hey, Elsa. Good morning. You're still looking fine as ever," Lenox said, getting up to give her a hug. Gray hair was just beginning to crown her head. He looked at his mom over Elsa's shoulder and saw her cut her eyes away. Jealousy, Lenox thought. Elsa had been with the family since he was born. Lenox couldn't remember a time without her. She used to make him the best cornmeal porridge, smooth and sweet, early in the mornings before school. His mother credited his broad shoulders to it.

He also remembered Elsa as a big, fine, curvy sister with the smallest waist. Every part of her was accentuated—her dimpled cheeks, Asian eyes, dark skin, and thick hair always worn in a long, plaited ponytail. She was Lenox's first crush and his father's mistress. He used to be so jealous of his father and the smile she used to give him. She always showered his father with more attention than anyone else. And even though Lenox had been barely eight, he had noticed. Especially that time when he saw Elsa sitting naked on his father's lap. His mother and father had argued for days and sometimes his mother would leave. Then everything was back to normal. Everything around him *seemed* normal then, he remembered.

As they waited for breakfast to be ready, Lenox and his father listened intently as his mother bragged about her latest painting and the thousands it sold for. Lenox's mother was an artist in London, where she had met his father at an exhibit. Marrying Lenox's father made it possible for her to paint while she lived a life of luxury and comfort. His father even had a few of her paintings in his law offices in London. A few years ago, for a birthday gift, he opened a small gallery for her in the tourist part of Montego Bay. She sold her art exclusively there to dignitaries and out-of-town celebrities.

About the time an awkward silence was about to creep in, Elsa called them in for breakfast. The food looked like everything he remembered as a child. A fine white linen table setting, proper table manners, and the appropriate conversation. Nothing was out of place.

After breakfast, his father had offered to come with him to the airport, but Lenox insisted on driving alone. He wanted some time with his thoughts. But by the time he got on the plane, he blocked everything out. He and Joanne had made the right decision.

♥

When Lenox landed at LaGuardia Airport, it was already 2:00 P.M. He called the realtor to cancel his 1:30 appointment. He was looking into a new building for the Life House, a small organization he had opened for teenagers to have a place for positive reinforcement. The good he did with the Life House made up for his past or future wrongs, or so he liked to believe. He had been through a few reckless incidents in law school with his old friend Seht. Seht was him without a conscience. The Egyptian name for the devil was Seht and he fit the title to a T. The first incident was a cocaine overdose, after a party he and Seht attended. The second involved a car crash that left a young woman dead. Lenox was the drunk driver, but was sober enough to bribe the cops to forget the Breathalyzer test. He was injured and it was deemed an accident. Anything like involuntary manslaughter would have destroyed his career as a lawyer. It made the *Daily News* on page fifteen. His dad had to pull some strings to keep the young woman's family quiet. Her family used the money he gave them to pay off their mortgage. Till this day, the dead woman still visited him in his dreams.

The cabbie drove him directly to his apartment. He was already running late to meet his aunt, Joan Meyers, for lunch. She was now vice president at Channel 7 News. When she took the job, she brought him on as an entertainment lawyer for the network. For over a month, he and his aunt had been working closely negotiating deals to keep the best talent at the network and get rid of its losses. This was just one of his many duties he had performed for Channel 7 since coming onboard several months ago. For his first case, he led a team of lawyers on the last leg of an NAACP lawsuit against the network. The network was being sued for their "lazy efforts" to recruit minorities. He was a part of an elite counsel of lawyers spread evenly throughout the network. He was the only black lawyer, among mostly Jews, and he liked that.

When he got to his building, Jamal, the doorman, was grinning from ear to ear. Jamal was the son of one of his clients. Jamal's father had begged Lenox to get some gun-possession charges against him dropped. After he did, Lenox developed a liking for Jamal, and got him a job at the building.

"Man, you had this one woman coming in here this morning asking for you like the FBI! She was real tall! Nice long hair," he said, taking Lenox's bags.

Lenox couldn't imagine who he was talking about. He knew about four women who were tall with long hair.

"And she had this ass that stuck out like the letter *P*. Real nice," Jamal told him.

Camille, Lenox immediately thought. It was almost scary. He had hired her as an assistant at his law firm to "rescue" her from her old job. They met at the stripper's club where she worked. Rescuing women was something he often did. It satisfied his ego and his urge to be needed.

Jamal followed Lenox upstairs with his bags. Lenox thanked him and gave him an extra tip for the news.

When Lenox got to his door, he pushed the key into the hole. It wouldn't go in all the way. The hot Caribbean sun must have fried his brain, he thought. He forced the key to go in, but the lock had been picked. Camille must have made her way past the security desk. When he pushed his way in, the answering machine blinked insanely with over thirty messages. He didn't even check them. He dropped his bags, grabbed the papers he needed, and proceeded back out. As he closed the door behind him, the phone began to ring again.

♥

Lenox flashed his station ID to the security guard standing by the lobby turnstile. While he waited for the elevator, he called his aunt to tell her he was on his way up, but she wasn't at her desk.

Once he arrived on the seventy-second floor, his aunt greeted him. "Sweetheart, you're late! I have everything scheduled down to the nanosecond. This really throws me off." She looked at him from head to toe. "If you weren't so handsome, I'd really be angry." She grinned and gave him a hug.

"If only all the women were as understanding as you, Aunt Joan. Come on, we have three-thirty reservations." He slipped on her coat and they headed out of the building.

Peco was a small Portuguese restaurant in the West Village. It was in the ground floor of a four-story brownstone on Grove Street. If one walked too fast, one could miss it. The restaurant had been around for a while, and it had become their meeting spot since his trip to Portugal last year. The Portuguese chicken was Lenox's favorite meal. It wasn't too exotic and tasted like southern baked chicken. But he really went there for their selection of the finest Porto wines.

"You know, it's contract time, and things are very weird at the office," began Aunt Joan. "This year is particularly hard for some reason." She attacked her mashed potatoes with the white flakes from the salt shaker.

"Let me guess, too much talent, too little time," Lenox said. "It's every network's fantasy."

"Well, that's not our case. We're number one, but we have to stay there. And I'm afraid there are a few people who don't have the network's best interests in mind."

Lenox stopped eating. "Like who?"

"It's that girl anchor, Farah Washington. She's not good for the network's future. She's hasty and very ego centered. She went over my head the other day to get the Batista story everyone is talking about. She showed little regard for my input or anyone else who might have been working on that story. I was so embarrassed." The corners of her mouth went south.

"You're talking about *the* Farah Washington?"

"I guess so." Aunt Joan turned her eyes away. "I bet she didn't tell me because she was planning on selling that story to another network!"

"If we let her go, she'd probably get another job as soon as she walked out the door," Lenox pointed out. "The girl is known to be quite sharp since her days at Columbia. And since she's been on the air the last few years, Channel Seven News viewership among eighteen- to thirty-four-year-olds has jumped a whopping thirty-five percent. All the networks want a young star they can mold."

Aunt Joan slammed her fork down. "I want Channel Seven

News to attract a more sophisticated, older, loyal audience. That young audience is very fickle. Those ratings can change any day," she said, edgy.

"Well, they're your employees. You tell me what you want me to do," Lenox said, too tired to get into it with his aunt.

"Her contract is almost up and I'm seriously thinking about making some changes. I may want to move her around a little."

Lenox sensed a plot brewing.

"She is not ready for a national audience like *Rise and Shine*. She's too young," Aunt Joan said. She ordered another glass of wine. "But I'll figure something out. She's just too sure of herself."

Lenox suddenly understood where this resentment was coming from. His aunt felt upstaged by Farah, even though she had more power than her. He just wondered how far his aunt was willing to take it.

Aunt Joan continued, bringing the half-empty glass of wine to her lips. "I'm not giving that girl another chance to embarrass me. We are the only two black people there. You'd think she'd be more considerate about how things look. She's ambitious and manipulative."

"Sounds like somebody I know." Lenox sighed. But there was no response, just the sound of Fado in the background.

The waiter returned and filled both of their glasses with the rich, red wine.

Lenox stuffed his mouth with some of the crispy chicken. "I can't remember if this Ms. Washington is married."

"Hmmmp," she said, looking at Lenox. "She *is* single. No wonder."

Aunt Joan didn't like the look in Lenox's eyes.

"Lenox, just be careful with that girl. I don't think she knows we're related. But if she knew, she'd be all over you like syrup on pancake."

"And what's wrong with that?" Lenox asked with a boyish grin.

Aunt Joan shifted in her seat and asked the waiter for a refill. They ended the evening talking about his trip to Jamaica and his parents. And as they both left in their separate cars, all he could think about was how yummy pancakes tasted with syrup.

♥

When Lenox got to his apartment, the first thing he did was check his answering machine. "It's me, Nicole . . ." "Hi, it's Diane . . ." "What's up, it's Cindy . . ." interspersed with a few calls from Camille. Most of her messages were her sighing and hanging up or talking erratically. He decided not to call her back. She'd call again, anyway. For that matter, he wasn't calling anyone back. He barely remembered the names once the machine ended. But he remembered Joanne called telling him she made the appointment.

He yawned, satisfied that he had done everything he needed to do today. Then the phone rang. With a groan, he picked it up by the third ring.

"It's Camille," the low, tired voice said.

Lenox stayed silent and just listened.

"I'm sorry. I know they must have told you I've been looking for you."

She waited for a response. But still he said nothing. He knew Camille had a lot of explaining to do.

"And I hope I didn't ruin your lock. I just thought I heard you in there."

Again, he stayed quiet.

"And I forgot when you were supposed to be coming back," she continued, sounding more desperate. "I just missed you," she whined. "I want to see you."

"Is that right?" he finally answered.

"I can be there in ten," she said with liveliness.

He thought about telling her not to bother, but then figured that he might as well get some before he kicked her to the curb.

"Fine." He hung up.

Gradually he felt himself growing more tired of women in his life. He knew he was ready to cut dead weight and Camille was going to be the first to go. They had been seeing each other for about six months, but it felt like years. She was always reaching for something extra with him. She would go through his private things, break into his cell phone messages, and search his dirty clothes for lipstick stains. She exhausted Lenox and it was getting predictable. The reason why he began dating her in the first place was because she offered some excitement, some diversion from the bourgeois, uppity black women he'd been dating.

In exactly ten minutes the doorbell rang. He hadn't even showered, but Camille wasn't even worth that much effort. He just wanted to get what she was coming over to give to him.

The scent of Chanel walked in before she did. She was a tall woman, but had all the curves. Her trench coat fit her closely and drew attention to her behind. She let her slim arms go around him and pressed her warm body up against his solid frame. He did nothing. She tipped his chin down and their lips touched. His hands fell on the perfect P. She unbuttoned her coat and let it fall to reveal a too-short black lace dress. The dress was short enough to slip his hand underneath and squeeze the flesh of her behind between his fingers. She kept her ankle boots on and wrapped one leg around his waist. He dragged them back to the red leather couch and fell on it. In between her panting, he slipped his finger under her butt cheeks and let his thumb play inside of her wetness. She moaned. He placed his moistened finger in her mouth. She sucked his finger hard, making Lenox more excited. He reclined on the couch and she began to work her way down to his navel. She feverishly sucked him until he nearly came.

When Camille was done, she sat on the couch and began fingering herself. Feeling left out, he took over the job for her. He used his tongue and aggressively began sucking on the mound of flesh between her legs. She begged him to stick his tongue deeper inside of her. She came and then turned over on her stomach and lifted her hips in the air. Lenox entered her and began to thrust into her wildly from behind. The red leather pillows on the couch muffled her cries. He didn't call her the names she liked, but stayed silent. She struggled to raise her hips higher in an effort to gain more control, but to no avail. She bit his hand, which he put over her mouth. He pulled it away and grabbed her long hair back, bending her neck almost painfully. He sucked her perfume-scented shoulders and bit sharply into them. She let out a few yells and gasps. When he came, she did again.

He rolled onto the cool floor and tried to catch his breath. As soon as he recovered, he got up, put on his pants and fastened his belt. He walked over to the wall and turned on the bright chandelier lights.

Camille jumped up. She came hurling at him and started punching him against his thick chest.

"Please don't tell me to leave. Why are you acting like this!? I promise I won't try to come to your place again if you're not here. I didn't know," she cried.

Lenox held her wrists to keep her from hitting him again. He looked down at her and thought to himself, she had finally lost her wig. *Why do I always get the crazy ones?* He shoved her away from him. She stumbled back, almost falling on the couch. Crying, she picked up one of her spiked heels and charged at him again. To guard his face, he reached for her arm and snatched the boot from her.

"So now you want to fight me like I'm a girl in the schoolyard. You're pathetic," he said, walking past her. She stood there blankly. "Where are the fucking keys to my office?" Lenox demanded.

"You motherfucker! You wait! I'm gonna take your ass to court for sexual harassment!" she yelled, searching for her bag, still naked.

"As a lawyer, I would advise you to save your money and dignity. You've been a stripper for years. You have *no* credibility." He stood by the front door. "And you know what? I think it's best for you that you be fired. The head you gave me today was tired. You've been lazy in bed and disorganized at work," he said moving closer to her. "I want the keys to the apartment, too."

"So I not only lose my job but my fucking apartment, too?!" she yelled.

She sat back down on the couch and put her head between her hands.

"Fuck it! I'll get the damn keys," he said. He took her purse, which had somehow made its way under the coffee table. He emptied all the contents on the floor until he found both sets of keys.

"Please, Lenox," she said, reaching for his arm. But he gave her one look, and she sat back down. When he was done, she fell on her knees to put the things back in her purse. "I need this job. And I can't move back in with my mother," she said, pleading.

"I paid the rent in that apartment downtown. Don't forget that," Lenox told her. "You can tell your friends no more 'house-warming' parties," he said, referring to the several parties she'd had, none of which she invited him to, but heard about from her neighbors. "You've got two weeks to find another place."

She stared at him, distraught.

"Get dressed. It's time for you to go. Some of us have to work in the morning," he said. "If you come back to my place again, I'll have you arrested." He wanted to be clear that it was over. He had had enough of her drama.

He turned and walked down the hall to his bedroom, leaving her to gather her things and leave.

Damn, he thought. *Now I'm going to have to get a temp in the morning.*

Chapter 3 ♥ *Farah*

*P*aynard Patisserie was usually Lola's and Farah's final stop
after they hit all the stores on Madison Avenue. Lola wanted
to try Sylvia's Uptown for a change, but Farah was stuck in a French
mood. The quaint, dark brown wooden chairs and decor made them
feel like they were in a Parisian bakery. Their conversation competed with the chatter of other tired shoppers, tourists, and groups
of other girlfriends stopping in for dessert.

They ordered their usual: pumpkin crème brulée for Farah and
a banana tart with white chocolate mousse for Lola. When the
waiter brought Farah's dish, it was topped with a heaping spoonful
of whipped cream, while Lola had just a flimsy dap.

"Damn, looks like the chef gave you all the whipped cream,"
Lola said, picking at her banana tart.

"It's the waiter. I get the same guy all the time and he knows
how I like it. Plus, giving him an extra tip doesn't hurt." Farah
tapped the hard crème brulée topping with her fork and dove in.
Farah eyes rolled back in ecstasy as she ate the pudding.

Lola ate the whipped cream first. "So how's work life?" she asked. "Isn't your contract almost up?"

"Soon. And you know Ms. Meyers is the one working on the contract negotiations this year. That lady better not play with my money."

Lola was doing her best to stay attentive. She'd rather listen than talk about all the things she was going through.

Farah licked the edge of the fork. "I'm talking to my agent now to see the money we can get. I'm tired of talking about drive-bys and cop shootings every night. I know they can't just throw me on *Rise and Shine* tomorrow, but they've got to promise me something."

"But how will that work?" Lola leaned over and scooped up some of Farah's whipped cream.

"Well, my agent told me *Rise and Shine* and a lot of other programs are being reformatted. So I'm hoping within all that, I'll be included. Katie's contract expires around the same time as mine."

"And Ms. Meyers?"

"That is the problem. She is really paranoid about me. It's like whatever I want, she wants the opposite. Do you know she even tried to act like I was trying to embarrass her by not telling her about the Batista interview?"

"She's so petty. That lady's got it in for you."

"Thanks. That's exactly what I need to hear," Farah said, sarcastically. "If I get that *Rise and Shine* spot, I'll be national. Probably even make the cover of *TV Guide*." Farah sounded confident, but deep down she wasn't so sure.

They finished their desserts and sat in gaps of silence. Lola admired Farah's new lipstick color, which stayed intact so well as she ate. She took out her own lip gloss and carefully applied it to her mouth as they waited for the check.

"So you don't want to meet Alan, that real nice train engineer at Chris's job? The Transit Authority just gave everyone a raise,"

Lola said. She had been trying to get Farah to drop by the school and meet him for months.

Farah raised her hand. "If those are my options, shoot me now." She handed the waiter her credit card. "Let me put it to you another way." She leaned across the table. "A city worker? I don't want a man with a time card. I'm talking about my man and me taking trips to St.-Tropez. Trips you can't find in the budget travel section of the Sunday News," Farah said. "I need a Robert Johnson, or damn it, Donald Trump. Not Brian from the Records Department."

Lola let out a deep breath. "That shit ain't right, Farah," she said as they got up to leave. The other day, she and Chris had been looking at the four-day Bahamas special, but she kept that to herself. And the fact that Chris had been a city worker for the last ten years made Farah's comment sting even more.

"I didn't say that every woman has to have my criteria for a man. It's just right for me. You'd never wear a Hermès bag with a Kmart outfit, that's all I'm saying," Farah said.

"Farah, you're my girl and all, but you need to get realistic. I want to see you happy, really happy. You can save all that hard-up-TV-diva talk for someone else. You should see your eyes light up when you hold Arabia. It's like a whole different you. I don't even see you shine that much when you're on TV. And you love being on TV," Lola said, turning on the ignition in the car. She looked over at Farah for a response and saw her staring straight ahead.

At home, Farah thought about how much of her personal/love life she had given up in exchange for a career life. She was still young professionally, but she was getting old biologically. She thought about where she had messed up, and if women like her just weren't supposed to be married.

♥

The next day at work, Sam snagged Farah as soon as she walked into the newsroom.

"Hate to bust your bubble," she told her, "but it looks like they may be renewing Katie's contract for a few more years with some extra zeroes at the end," Sam said, overexcited.

"Good for Katie." Farah sounded unconcerned, but inside she cracked. Just then Katie and Ms. Meyers walked by laughing together like college roommates. That moment showed Farah that it would take a lot more than chasing big stories, but it was more about relationships.

She went back to her desk to be alone. Just before she immersed herself in answering e-mails, her phone rang.

"Ms. Washington, this is Lenox Whitworth, the station's lawyer," said a deep male voice with a light Jamaican accent.

"Yes. I can't talk to you until I speak to my agent first."

"I spoke to your agent a few minutes ago. Has he called you yet?"

"No, not yet," Farah said.

"Well, then call me after you speak to him. I have a personal message for you from Ms. Meyers. Speak to you soon," he said, hanging up.

Farah still had the phone in her hand, when her next line rang.

"Hi, Alex," she said. "What's up? The network lawyer just called."

"Jesus, I just hung up with the guy like forty-five seconds ago. Listen, they took most of what we put on the table. Sorry, but I can't get them to budge on the money. They stopped at four hundred fifty thousand dollars for a three-year extended contract," he said.

Farah huffed. "You know I'm being cheated here. Since I've joined the *News at Six* team, the ratings have shot up thirty-five percent and they have the younger viewers they were vying for," Farah insisted.

"Of course I mentioned all that and then some, Farah. But I managed to put in a clause for a salary review in about a year.

Perfect timing, since the word through the grapevine is that they are still revamping *Rise and Shine*. That Ms. Meyers really wasn't very flexible, unlike her boss. But since he left most of the negotiating up to her, she's pulling the strings here."

"Why am I not surprised?" Farah said, clenching her teeth.

"But they put a clause in there stipulating that you will play a 'major' role in any new programming. She and her lawyer seemed rather open to that."

Farah sighed. "Well, that sounds a bit better, but still vague. Now that I think back we should have taken that offer from WCBS a few years ago."

"May I remind you that they also wanted to put you on the 4:30 A.M. news team? That wouldn't have gotten you the face time you needed, kid."

Farah flinched. "I'm soon to be thirty, Alex. Give me a fucking break." She forced a laugh so it wouldn't seem like she was angry at that.

"I figure we'll go back to the table when the time comes. If they don't meet our demands then, we'll look elsewhere. FOX News has a slew of new programming coming up," he said.

"But they aren't number one like Channel Seven. Give me some time to think about all this, Alex. Fax me what you have," she said. "And thanks."

Their phone call ended. She hesitantly picked up the phone to call Mr. Whitworth.

"Ms. Washington, I take it you spoke to your agent?" he said rather cheerfully into the phone.

Farah turned around at the beeping sound of her fax machine receiving Alex's transmission.

"Yes, I did. I still haven't had time to digest the offer."

"Well, let me put it to you this way, Ms. Washington. There's blood on the newsroom floor right now. Big names like weatherman Eddie McGuire and executive producer Elizabeth Lunden have all been shown the exit. You've escaped Channel Seven's purge. And you're at the top of the list to be considered for any new programming that matches your expertise."

Farah snatched the fax from the machine and stared at the paper thoughtfully, but her focus of attention was on this Mr. Whitworth. He seemed self-assured and confident over the phone. His accent was definitely Jamaican as was Ms. Meyers's. She wondered if they knew each another. She'd make it a point to ask Sam when she got a chance.

"Mr. Whitworth, I'm signing this contract because I love this job and this network is number one. But I am going to have major concerns if it does not hold up its end, and fast," she said.

"There are no guarantees in this business, Ms. Washington. But I can guarantee that people are watching you, and your talent is not being ignored. We just want to find the right place to put you," he said.

"Sure," she said. But to her, his tone sounded rehearsed. It didn't sound like she could bet on it. She hung up, feeling stuck between a rock and a hard place.

The phone rang again, jolting her from her thoughts.

"Batter up! Katie's out working on a big story," Sam said, sounding annoyed.

"What big story? Am I missing something?" Farah asked, as she smelled an opportunity.

"Oh, I don't know. No clue here," Sam said, agitated. "Listen, I have to run. I have to get some tape edited."

Before Farah could respond, she heard the dial tone. Sam worked closely with Katie, and Farah knew there was more, but she let it go.

Farah gathered her script as she went out to the set. She saw Pete, who was standing by her chair cheerfully waving her earplug. As he got her ready for the show, her co-anchor Scott sat next to her.

"Hi, how's things?" Scott asked.

"What things?" Farah snapped.

"I mean things in general. Life. You do have one, don't you?" he asked, grinning.

Farah calmed down. "I guess it's okay. Just trying to do what I can," Farah said, trying to be as nice and as vague as possible at the same time.

"Things are changing around here. I can feel it," he said, turning his mike off. "This place is about to go for a tailspin."

Before Farah could get into it any further, Sam's voice came in through her earpiece, telling her that they were ready. In a matter of minutes, whatever gloom Farah was feeling had to be changed to glee. And whatever doom was approaching had to be sent away. Once on air, she turned into a woman her viewers listened to and depended on.

About ten minutes before the end of the show, a breaking news story came in, a botched robbery in Brooklyn that left two cops dead. New information was coming in by the second. Scott headed the story. While he was talking, Sam started giving information to Farah through her earpiece. Farah summed it up and made a smooth transition to a reporter live on the scene. She loved the feeling breaking news sent through her veins. It was exciting, unpredictable. She felt in control when she knew something most people didn't and they had to shut up and listen.

When they went off air, she went into the control room to see how it went.

"Thanks for going with the flow. I was trying to get the information to you and Scott as fast as possible. Sorry I kept yelling in your ear. How did you make out what I was saying?" Sam asked Farah.

"We've worked together too long. You can talk in sign language and I'll still know what you are saying," Farah said, standing by the director's chair. There was a whole new crew flying in for the next show, moving them out of the way.

"Farah, great job, kid," said Vince, passing by to the set to do his show.

"Thank you, Vince," she said smiling modestly.

"We'll talk later, I need to get ready for a seven P.M. show," Sam said. She disappeared back into the control room.

Farah stood around and talked to some more people. She blossomed in the circle of attention. She reluctantly withdrew herself from the group when she couldn't fight the urge to use the bathroom any longer.

She saw Ms. Meyers at the sink washing her hands.

It was too late for Farah to turn around. She didn't want Ms. Meyers to ruin her good mood.

"Hi, Ms. Meyers. Did you see the show?" Farah asked. She was hoping she did and could find something positive to say.

"I just came back from a lunch meeting," she said, drying her hands and not looking at Farah. "Was there a reason why I should have seen it?" Her tone was sarcastic and Farah knew she saw it because she never missed a show, according to insiders. She had TVs in her town car to catch everything.

"Just some breaking news." Farah said.

Before she could explain it, Ms. Meyers interrupted her. "I'm sure it went well. We'll chat later." Ms. Meyers barely dried her hands and flashed right past her.

"We sure will," Farah said shouting behind her, but she didn't think Ms. Meyers heard her.

Farah stayed in the office several more hours organizing her desk and files. She was trying to avoid spending too much time home alone. When the clock read 10:30 P.M., she figured it was time to leave. At least by the time she got home, she'd be ready for sleep, she thought.

"What are you doing here so late? You have to be up so early for *Rise and Shine,*" Sam said, walking up behind Farah, wearing a lush white cashmere coat.

"I'm meeting someone. So I decided to hang a little late, then go all the way back to Brooklyn," she lied.

They both stood at the elevator waiting.

"Let me ask you. Is it me or is Ms. Meyers a little off or something?" asked Farah.

Sam looked at Farah with her eyebrows raised. "It's something. I don't know if it's a case of bipolar or bitchaphrenia."

"She really comes off like she can't stand me. She seems angry," Farah said, adjusting her brand-new Birkin on the crook of her arm. The weight of the bag made it hurt.

Sam just shook her head and smiled. "I've known Ms. Meyers longer than almost anyone here. Now, I'm going to tell you something. It's not confirmed, but it's something being talked about in some circles." Sam looked around to make sure no one was standing by. "I had a colleague who used to work with Ms. Meyers. I heard she would try to intimidate women at her old job with her sexuality, since there were questions about her relationship with this one girl. Supposedly, she had a woman lover for years who she broke up with and it kind of screwed her up mentally."

Farah let out a howling laugh. "You can't be serious?!" The idea that Sam was making things up to feed her paranoia crossed her mind. "You knew all this stuff about Ms. Meyers and you didn't say a word to me?"

An elevator passed, which they both missed.

"Ms. Meyers brought that female 'friend' to an awards dinner last year. I heard the girl was some opportunist who used her. Her name was Michelle and she's married to a man now."

Sam went on and told Farah how Michelle was now working at CNN in Atlanta, a job Ms. Meyers helped secure for her. It was a high-end producer's job. At the end of hearing Sam read Ms. Meyers's card, she was nearly faint.

"Was Michelle black?"

"Yeah, she was black." Sam looked at her awkwardly.

They got on the second elevator. Farah wished she had never asked about Ms. Meyers.

♥

The next day, the two hours of *Rise and Shine* flew by like a race car in Daytona. Farah did a solo ten-minute interview with former president Jimmy Carter, a cooking segment with Adam, and joined him on several featured news stories.

After the show ended, everyone was complimenting her on her energy, which seemed to be especially on target this morning. But as the afternoon approached for her 6:00 P.M. show, she was running low on gas. Thoughts of whether it was worth jumping between *Rise and Shine* and her news show every time someone snapped their fingers crossed her mind. She was still taking home her anchor salary, but not nearly as much as she could if she was being paid for *Rise and Shine*, too.

♥

Rather than hang around after her show, Farah took a cab straight down Broadway to visit her mother. Not one of the most "motherly" of mothers, but she did have a knack for saying the right thing at the wrong time. Her mother was in love with Oliver, her soon-to-be-unmarried beau, and lived in his new apartment by Riverside Drive. At first, Farah made it hard on Oliver and had a one-to-one talk with him about her mother. She didn't want to see her mother alone, but not with anyone's sloppy leftovers either. She made that clear. But two years later they were still together and Farah couldn't ignore the change Oliver had bought to her mother's life and spirit. He also didn't flirt with her, which was a common trait in her mom's ex-boyfriends. She was just beginning to appreciate Oliver. And she never would have thought her single mother's love life would play out better than her own.

Oliver's building was immaculate. The floors were marble with fresh orchid arrangements placed in the corners. It looked like a grand hotel lobby. Farah walked in past the doorman. The concierge gave her a compliment about her looks. Too bad she couldn't understand him under his think Polish accent, she laughed to herself. When she rang their bell, it was Oliver who opened the door.

"Ms. Black Barbara Walters! How are you?" Oliver sang, his tall, lanky body embracing hers with a big hug.

"Great, Oliver. But Barbara Walters is a little too old to be me," Farah said, giving him a pat on his bony back.

He laughed and took her jacket. He pointed to the room where her mother was reading.

Farah walked down the narrow hallway, the walls decorated with the best black art on the Upper West Side, including a Jacob Lawrence original from his Migration Series. Black-and-white photos of her mother in her prime adorned the cream-colored walls near the living room. All the photos were of her heydays in modeling. Farah spotted her mother sitting on the living room couch like a princess with Gigi, her Yorkshire terrier.

"Nice to see you, baby," her mother said as she let her cranberry red nails run across Gigi's back. She was wearing a beige satin pants-and-blouse set. Her blond wig highlighted her mahogany skin. She always made Farah feel goofy and plain. One thing her mother was good at was glamour.

They kissed each other on each cheek.

"Could you please fix us a glass of wine, baby, while you're at the bar?" her mother asked Oliver, who was preparing a glass of Hennessey for himself.

"No, thanks, Oliver. I'm fine." Farah sat next to her mother and waited for her to begin.

"So are you feeling any better?" she asked as she sipped her glass of cabernet.

"Yeah, I'm fine. I've just been feeling weird working there now, since they got that new black lady running things." Farah had told her mom about Ms. Meyers before, so she knew the scoop.

"She probably needs to lighten up. She married?" asked her mother.

"Nope."

"Then that explains it. I've always found it easier to work for married women. Those single ones make you work all late because they don't have a man to go home to," her mother said sympathetically. Farah wondered if she would ever become that way.

"Hey, that reminds me, did I tell you, I showed your aunt Tracy all the tapes of your guest host spots on *Rise and Shine?* You know she can't manage to get out of bed so early. She couldn't believe how good you were!" Gigi jumped on her and tried to lick her face.

"Damn it, Gigi. I told you that mommy does not kiss! Stop that," she said, picking Gigi up and putting her down by her feet.

"Honey, you are smart, confident, and talented. Just play by the rules, sweetie. You know how that profession is." She looked around carefully to see if Oliver was around, then leaned in, and asked, "So, any prospects?"

"Mom, I just came over to relax. Not to get into all that." Farah got up and walked to the window overlooking Riverside Drive.

"Maybe that is what you need to wind *you* down a little. You just seem so stressed. You gotta get a life," her mother said shaking her head impatiently. She picked up Gigi and went over to pour another glass of wine. "Having a man makes things so much easier. Just look around." She took her hand and pointed to everything around her—the crystal chandeliers, the antique furniture, and the Persian rugs.

"He can kick you out anytime since you are living under *his* roof," Farah reminded her.

"You concern yourself with the details, honey. I don't. And all I'm saying is, I just want to make sure you are taken care of if something were to happen to me," she said, sitting back on the couch. She bent down to pick up Gigi, but the dog ran off to Oliver, who held a dog leash in his hands.

"I'm sure that's your only concern." Farah was a bit irritated. "Besides, I don't have a lot of time now. I'm working on getting that permanent host slot on *Rise and Shine*." She knew that would get her mother's attention.

"Yes, yes," her mother said, finally putting down her glass. "That's it. When you get that, you'll have arrived. Tell *TV Guide* I'll happily accept requests for interviews." She laughed.

*L*enox called George to make sure he was already in before he took the drive to Brooklyn. George was forty-six, married with three kids, and a former director of the Phoenix House. He was a man with almost everything, and seemed happy with it. George always spoke with passion. His eagerness and loyalty were the reasons why Lenox hired him for the job.

"When you coming down, man?" George asked. "I want to talk about things that have been on hold since the past two weeks," George said on the other line.

"In about an hour," Lenox said, stretching. I just got back in town a few days ago. How have the kids been doing? Any new stories?"

"Well, group five just finished their internships at city hall. They're writing their reports on that now. Their parents call me every day thanking us. One even sent a bouquet! It was addressed to you, of course."

"I'm glad they appreciate it. I'm very glad that they finished it without any drama. We need more of us in city hall. But we'll talk about that later. If I don't leave now, I won't get down there for another two weeks," Lenox said.

When Lenox got to Brooklyn, he parked his car on Vanderbilt Avenue and walked the extra block or two to the center. The freezing wind found its way inside his leather jacket and livened his pace.

Walking up the steps to the Life House, Lenox gave his good mornings to the landscapers, who were trimming the evergreens outside. George was at the door waving for him to come in.

He put his arm around Lenox and led him to his office.

"I really feel we're doing something here. The meetings are getting bigger. More kids are signing up for after-school homework and peer-counseling programs. It's blowing out the sky!" he said in his usual hyper manner.

Lenox knew what that meant. "Okay, how much money do we need?" he asked.

"Enough to get a bigger space," George said, waiting for Lenox to take a seat behind the desk.

"I've been talking to this realtor on and off about buying the building next door. I gave him an offer of nine hundred thousand dollars. He won't be able to get more than that for that dump." Lenox looked in his drawer for the realtor's business card to give to George. "Give him a call and he'll take you to see it. It just needs lots of gutting out and renovation. But once that's down it'll be worth double."

"I'll call today. Man, if we could get that building it would be perfect. I could even get some of my old friends from around the way to help fix it up. You know how those guys are always looking to make an extra dollar."

Lenox wasn't too crazy about that idea. "Run that by me beforehand so I can run a background check on them. Cheap labor is one thing, but I need the job done the right way. Not someone squeezing my job in with ten other jobs they have that day."

George stayed quiet.

"Anything else?" Lenox asked, checking his watch. This was the way they got things done lately. If Lenox had time he would stop by, check out the place, and tie up some loose ends. He barely had time to see the kids these days. The last time he did was at the Christmas party he threw for them catered with food and music. He spent nearly ten thousand dollars on Christmas gifts for them. He had authentic autographed basketball jerseys, several pair of tickets to Knicks and Giants games for the boys and generous gift certificates for the girls to shop.

Looking down at his list, George began checking things off. "How about a field trip? The older kids have been talking about doing something before school ends," he asked.

Lenox tapped his pen on the desk. "Give Randy a call at that ranch upstate that we used last year. Ask him if we can book a Saturday for some horseback riding lessons in the spring. If not, call Highland Country Club about golf lessons. We'll play that rap video with Puffy and Mase on the golf course to get them motivated."

"That sounds fine. But they were suggesting a party."

"We just had a party! These kids need culture and refinement, not another party," Lenox said, smiling. They both laughed because they both knew how much partying they liked as young men themselves.

"Let me know what Randy or Michelle say, and tell the kids. I just want to concentrate on that new building for now, and maybe we can do something in there once it opens."

George seemed to warm up to the idea. "Okay, no problem. Actually, Audry and I took the kids horseback riding and they loved it. Carlos has been taking golf lessons since last year," he boasted.

"That's why I love you, George. You got a real nice, well-cultured family," Lenox said, getting up from his chair. It was time for him to head back to the office.

"Well, you will, too, one day, Lenox." George had a hint of pity in his voice.

"Yeah, yeah," Lenox said, feeling uncomfortable. "For now, I have to keep making that money. Is there anything else?"

Before he could answer, Lenox said, "If there was, you could handle it, man. I trust you." Lenox patted him on the back. And in a way, he did trust him. He was almost like a younger version of his father, but more caring, and not ruthless.

"That's it. We'll talk later," George said. Lenox made his way down the hall and admired the way the place was kept clean, pristine, and organized. It was so important to Lenox to have a place like the Life House. As Lenox drove away, he couldn't help but feel good about himself for a change.

♥

"Mr. Whitworth, where would you like these? It seems like Camille didn't organize these files right. She has the Leighton-McDaniel case in the same folder as the Hamilton-Spear case." Margaret stood there with her round chubby face looking like somebody's grandmother. Lenox thought how much she looked like the old lady from *The Facts of Life*. She and the temp had spent the week picking up Camille's slack.

"Those cases are nearly five years old. Please put them in the archives," Lenox said, keeping his head down as he signed document after document in his in-box. Camille hadn't been very good at organizing files or much of anything for that matter.

Most of the documents he signed were from Alan, one of his best associates. Lenox had him working on the minute details with Channel 7 and the contract negotiations as Lenox played the front man. It didn't matter to Aunt Joan who was working on what, because she always called Lenox, anyway. Besides, Lenox was also busy drawing up contracts for their six new television shows this season.

After a few conference calls, Lenox left the office early to go to the gym. He left his coat open on a day that felt like the winter was beginning to submit to the gentler winds of spring. As Lenox walked across Central Park South, he counted at least three buildings Donald Trump owned, including the one he lived in. Lenox already owned one building, and hopefully would own another by year's end. His new-model Range Rover was safely parked down the street. No car payments, everything was paid in full on purchase.

Driving down Sixth Avenue, Lenox ran through a mental checklist for the charity event tomorrow night for the Life House. He had invited most of his client list and some of the city's socialites—black and white—for tomorrow's event. His aunt tapped the media world to come. Brianna Spencer, the wife of Carl Spencer, the city's legendary black congressman, brought in the more seasoned, old-money folks. Charity events were one of the many playgrounds of the rich and restless. Lenox's father always said it was a great place to find rich people who had nothing better to do with their money. The event was to raise money for the purchase of the building next door to the Life House, which Lenox thought was perfect for expansion. Lenox could have purchased it on his own, however he was saving his money for something bigger and better.

Once he did his self-prescribed hour and a half at the gym, he drove back uptown, navigating through the traffic-choked streets and bullying the smaller cars out of the way.

James and Nicole were going to be waiting for him at Tao in a few hours. It had been their regular spot since they could enjoy the nightlife and get business done at the same time. James and Nicole were also part of the Lyncs, the one hundred-year-old social club of prominent African-Americans, which Lenox headed regionally and for which he helped plan its special events. They handled everything from the invitations to the donations to the dinner menu.

Lenox got home in minutes and checked his machine. There were several messages, including one from Nicole confirming tonight. He turned on the Jacuzzi, and stepped in to soothe his sore leg muscles. He started to doze off when the phone rang. He reached over the sink to grab it.

"This better be good," Lenox said, his eyes only partly opened. "Can I come over and show you how good?" an unfamiliar voice said on the line. The voice intrigued him. He sat up all the way. "Who's this?" he said.

"How soon we forget?" He picked up that the voice on the end had an accent. A European one. However, he couldn't pin it down. He stood up, grabbed a towel, and walked into his bedroom to check his caller ID. He didn't recognize the number.

"You like your women tall, under one forty, white or black, and pineapples with your blow job." The woman's voice was very girlish but sultry. Only one woman knew how he liked his pineapples.

"And how have you been, Maritza? Staying out of trouble?" Lenox asked, remembering their last few encounters. He reclined on his neatly made bed and put his hand on his hardening dick.

"Those little incidents with the police were all misunderstandings. If it weren't for you calling a few people for me, I'd probably be in jail with a woman named Tony calling me her bitch." Her voice shook with a nervous laugh.

"Next time, be careful who you buy your coke from," he said. "Where are you?"

"Still in Amsterdam. I haven't been back to France in months. The best work is here anyway. I'm sure you know that." Her voice sounded like she was chewing on something. Maybe gum, he thought. But the sound her mouth and lips were making kept his dick stiff. Maritza was twenty-four, and had had a privileged up-bringing in France. Her family was from Guadeloupe. She was disowned when they found out she was dancing at the age of seventeen. Maritza was one of those women who were just like men when it came to sex—she couldn't get enough of it. Sometimes Lenox swore she was possessed. Lenox had met her on a "business" trip to Amsterdam last year. He had been visiting the facilities of one of his Dutch clients, Hagerfeld and Versheitz, who were in a litigation battle with their American manufacturer. Mr. Hagerfeld's son took him to the red light district, where Maritza was dancing at a club. From the back of the audience he watched her give men headaches as she popped and pumped her body in their faces. She was petite, no more than five feet five inches, but he remembered that she was shaped like a Coke-bottle. Her breasts were like a pair of Georgia peaches. He almost choked on his brandy when she gave him his own personal lap dance. She danced on no one else but him for the rest of the night. To Lenox, that was special.

"Lenox? You there, baby?" she asked.

"I'm here. I was just thinking about how good you looked the last time I saw you."

They both laughed as they talked about the sex and the last time she came to see him in New York.

"So how are you doing money-wise out there? Have you thought about taking up my offer to come to New York City? You have a place to stay." He knew Maritza was fiercely independent, maybe that was why he wanted to soften her sharp, headstrong edge. However, she had an air of vulnerability about her that he liked.

"I thought about it. But not right now. And you know money is never a problem for me. My brother Victor sends me money without my parents knowing. Do you believe I danced for one of his friend's birthday parties? But they had no idea I was his sister." She giggled like a little girl.

"And when will you take me up on the offer? It's still open," he reminded her.

"You know I think I've seen that video we made on our trip to Nice about five times already! You are incredible with your tongue, baby." That recollection was enough to make him drop the subject. They spent the next few minutes whispering all the nasty things they would do to each other on their next meeting. Lenox listened to her masturbate. He released the tension that had built up inside him since her call. After their call ended, he cleaned up with the towel.

Lenox realized it was about time to meet James and Nicole

to go over details for tomorrow. This must have been their third meeting so far this week. But Lenox was a meticulous micromanager. It was important that he control every minute detail and decision.

James and Nicole were seated at a table waiting for him. Lenox could see them shuffling papers and checking off some things. His chest tensed as he thought about any last-minute problems. He didn't have the patience for that, especially tonight. They had already done the planning and were basically reiterating what they had said the last few times.

"What's up, Ox? Look, man, everything is straight," James said, getting up and patting him on the back. He must have read the expression on Lenox's face.

Nicole was holding a red pen and was ready to get down to business. She hated these meetings with Lenox. He made her nervous even though they'd known each other since his days at Andover and hers at Choate. They'd had a love-hate relationship since they met. They'd go at it like enemies and then turn around and act like nothing had happened. She was fairly attractive, but he realized years ago, her personality was best suited for business, not pleasure. And she was now dating Derrick Roundtree, the son of the city comptroller who she'd met at a Lyncs party.

As Nicole and James both went over the plans, he realized that everything was set and he felt relieved. His Hennessey tasted better as he relaxed in his chair.

"It's our first charity event," Lenox said, shaking his head. "The Life House needs this. That's my name out there. I—excuse me— we can't afford for tomorrow night to look sloppy," he said to James and Nicole. He snapped his fingers. "We need a Page Six mention."

"I have that covered. We have all those gossip people there. Flo, Liz, Ana, and Michael. Your aunt Joan was really helpful with some of the contacts. She said she'd do anything for you," Nicole said. Lenox was pleased. He knew his aunt wasn't the easiest person to like, but she had really come through for him more than once.

Soon after they finished wrapping things up, Lenox left. He hailed a cab and took it down Fifth Avenue.

♥

When Lenox arrived at the Puck Building, there were already town cars and limos double-parked outside. He slipped in through the back doors to avoid anyone he didn't feel like seeing right away.

The ballroom was dressed up like a girl at a debutante ball. Chandeliers covered the ceiling all around, with warm tones of red carpet and mahogany furniture. It had a majestic feel to it and everywhere he turned the glimmering lights of the chandeliers looked like diamonds and ice. Making his way into the room, he couldn't help but notice everyone there was connected to him in some way. His clients needed his advice, his female friends were waiting for attention, and everyone else was waiting for him to add color to their stale conversations over cocktails.

"There you are!" Lenox heard Aunt Joan. "My God! I thought you had better things to do than come to your own event."

She gave him a kiss on the cheek and ran her hands down his tailored Prada tuxedo jacket.

"When were you going to return my calls, Lenox?" she said. "I have the president of the damn network breathing down my neck about the negotiations. We need to wrap this up. We have new shows coming up—"

"You do know that you look like a man tonight, Aunt Joan," Lenox said, looking over her men's style pantsuit.

"Well, everyone says I act like a man, so I might as well start dressing like one." She adjusted her tie, which was decidedly pink.

"It looks good on you. It gives you this androgynous look. I just thought maybe I'd see you in a dress for a change," he said, looking around.

"You can keep your fashion commentary to yourself. Now, what about the contracts?"

Lenox popped a cheese torta in his mouth. "Everything is almost done. I spoke to Charles last week. He may have forgotten to tell you."

Aunt Joan's jaw dropped.

Lenox continued, "Well, you know that I talked to Ms. Washington and her agent. She has looked over the contract and should be sending it back any day. She didn't sound too happy, though. She had questions about the word 'major.' "

"Good. That was my point. I wanted it to be vague. It gives me flexibility. And Katie?"

"We still have a ways to go with Katie about the money. For some reason we can't see eye to eye. She's asking for a damn lot," Lenox said.

"She's worth it. Let me talk to Charles and see what's going on. Maybe I can get him to be more accommodating."

Lenox grabbed another cracker from the platter. Then someone tapped him from behind, interrupting them.

"Lenox, we need you to take some pictures with some of the guests," Nicole said, anxiously pointing to the bar. "The photographer from the *Daily News* is here. He said he didn't mind waiting as long as there were martinis flowing with the ahi poki on crispy wontons."

Lenox gave his aunt a kiss and excused himself.

"Find Mr. Spencer, Mr. Selwyn, and anyone else you think we can include. Charles Dangle and the mayor are here already. Let's get them by the banner," Lenox instructed Nicole. He couldn't help but look down her blouse. She was wearing a plunging V-neck gold chiffon dress. He could see small beads of sweat on her cleavage as she talked on and on about the photographs. Lenox looked around and saw Derrick talking to some people from the mayor's office.

Nicole disappeared into the crowd. Before he could swallow another torta, Brianna walked up to him with Mr. Spencer.

"Young man, I have to say, you are one of the talented tenth," Mr. Spencer said as he gave Lenox his handshake. "Your father is an ace, and the apple doesn't fall too far from the tree." Mr. Spencer had one hand in his pocket as he held a glass of wine. He was moneyed and came from a long line of those rich Martha's-Vineyard-on-the-weekend black families. He'd always been good to the Life House.

"And handsome, too. You stay in such great shape," Mrs. Spencer said, blushing. Lenox could tell Ms. Spencer was a Dorothy Dandridge look-alike in her prime.

"Thank you, thank you," Lenox said, holding his hands up playfully. "I learn from the best. I wish more young brothers can experience what it is to give back to the community." All three looked around at the room of black, brown, and white faces drinking, laughing, spending money.

"And do you have a lady friend with you tonight?" asked Mr. Spencer. He and his wife looked on anxiously, as if he was supposed to snap his fingers and a woman would appear.

Lenox hated these moments. His mother always told him a man had everything once he's found a good woman. She was supposed to be the icing on the cake. Lenox had had all the icing he could want, but no cake.

"Come, let's all stand by the banner. Nicole is getting some people together for some *Daily News* photos," Lenox said as they followed him.

Mrs. Spencer jumped in. "And *New York Times* Sunday Society section, too." She smiled. She promised to arrange it and she did. "Emilio came with us. He's standing over there with the camera." She pointed to the doorway. Lenox looked in her direction and saw a small man, shooting away and bumping into people while he was at it. He seemed like he couldn't get enough photos. This was exactly the kind of attention Lenox needed. And the Life House, too.

It took them nearly ten minutes to get from one side of the room to the other. Old friends, clients, and even people Lenox didn't know were giving him pats on the back and handshakes for such a successful year with the Life House and his law practice. He managed to get near the banner, where the mayor, Charles Dangle, and Percy Selwyn were already having a good time.

They took the photos for the *Daily News*, the *New York Post* and *The New York Times*. Lenox made sure he was in all the pictures, standing next to the right people. Lenox reveled in being a novelty, with his color and youth, to the crowd of rich old folks. *Black, elite, and proud*, he told himself. Mrs. Spencer warned him that these photos, especially in the *Times*, would make him prey to New York single eligible women. More drama, Lenox thought. He just hoped he'd have a decent woman in his life by then.

After dinner, the event turned into a dance party complete with light music and hits from the '70s till now. Lenox was worn out talking about the Life House, and promising white rum cases and special favors.

As he walked to the back room to put some checks away, Derrick stopped him.

"Listen, man, can I talk to you for a minute?" he said. Derrick was sweating, but then again, he always looked sweaty to Lenox. He guessed an extra one hundred pounds could do that to a person.

"Problem?" Lenox said a little concerned.

"I may need a favor. There was this situation when I was back in law school. I was involved in some money laundering, that sort of thing."

Lenox counted his checks.

"Anyway." He sighed. "One of the guys, Jacob Richard, is being released from jail in a few days for good behavior. He has a beef with me because I backed out of the whole thing and didn't defend him. I know he didn't kill anyone, and I know the guy who did. He sent me a letter saying he plans to go to the newspapers with all this and fuck up my chances of winning the election. Somehow that Katie Maury did her own research and has been trying to reach him. And he if ever gets on that show . . ." He regained his composure. "I could forget about Congress or any political career."

"So what can I do for you?" Lenox said rather impatiently. He'd had no idea Derrick was involved in all that stuff in law school. That explained all the strange visitors he had at campus. *What an idiot,* Lenox thought to himself.

Derrick scratched his head. "You know I can't go to my father about this because he'll literally have a heart attack. I mean, he expects me to win this. You know my family has held the same seat in Congress for three generations. I need you. Could you please do something where you can get him back in jail? At least to finish out his sentence. And by then, I'd be nearly retired and he too old to remember anything," Derrick said, finally breaking a smile.

Lenox took a deep breath. It made sense why Derrick didn't want to tell his father. But now he wanted Lenox to put an innocent man back in jail to further his own pursuits.

Derrick's eyes looked watery.

"And if I do this little deed, then what?" Lenox asked. Lenox thought about how Derrick's whole career and life was on the line. He felt powerful and important. No one else could do this for him, without his father getting hold of it.

"Hey, man. Whatever you need. Like maybe Nicole?" Derrick said, laughing.

"Are you crazy? It's worth more than some pussy." Lenox wasn't smiling.

"I know, I know," he said, shifting his feet. "And I was just joking about Nicole." He gave Lenox a nervous look.

After a few seconds of silence, Lenox said, "Look, I have to get back outside. I'll take care of this, and I'll just consider you my friend and ally in Congress. Just in case I need *anything.*"

Derrick and Lenox shook hands. Derrick knew that Lenox had just saved his political career.

"Does this guy, the one you were talking about, does he have kids? Family?" Lenox had forgotten to ask.

"Yeah! He has a wife and four-year-old son. He's been in jail since his wife was pregnant," Derrick said, and disappeared through the oak doors.

All of a sudden Lenox's bow tie felt tight. A wave of guilt hit him about putting an innocent man back in jail, especially one with a young son waiting on the outside. He wished he had asked Derrick before he agreed. He couldn't back out because he had already given his word. He was tired of being the one people went to when they needed something, and each time, the stake was only getting higher.

The night ended with over a million dollars raised for the Life House. His energetic mood had dampened since talking to Derrick, but he was glad that he met his financial goal for the evening. Lenox stood at the door with George, who had arrived late, and thanked people for coming.

The empty wineglasses and food trays were all that was left. Aunt Joan stood by the stage and signaled for Lenox to come over.

"Darling, you were wonderful tonight. The speech you gave at dinner nearly brought tears to my eyes." Her attitude was a lot warmer than it was earlier this evening. Lenox hoped that she had forgotten about the network negotiations for a minute.

"Thanks, Aunt Joan," Lenox said, walking with her outside to the waiting car. The help staff and hostesses waved to Lenox as he left the building. They both walked and talked about the evening and all the media attention it got.

Lenox watched his aunt disappear in her car. He waited for the valet to bring over his Benz convertible from the lot. He thought about his aunt. In his family, everyone thought she was strange. No man, no kids, always had a short hair cut. His father swore she was a lesbian. His mother, her sister, never argued with that. And Lenox really didn't care.

Chapter 5 ♥ *Farah*

*F*arah stopped by Lola's house after work. It was Valentine's Day and she didn't want to be alone again in front of the TV. She called to make sure she wasn't interrupting anything romantic.

She rang Lola's bell and pushed the front door at the first buzz. Farah passed by a group of young men and women dressed for an evening on the town. One of the girls held a red rose. Farah tried not to look their way or listen to their giggles as they walked hand in hand. She thought to herself that the hardest part of the day was over. Roses and bouquets from husbands and boyfriends filled the reception area at her job.

"What's up, *mujer*! I was calling you all day. What happened?" Lola asked as she tightened her sloppy ponytail. She was standing by the doorway dressed in jeans and a sweatshirt. Farah thought that was a sign that there was nothing special going on inside.

They gave each other hugs and Farah walked in. "Girl, I am so nauseous from all those damn roses at work. I mean, it is so unprofessional to bring your love life all up in the office," Farah said, taking a seat in the kitchen. The kitchen was their favorite place to eat and chat.

Lola understood where her friend was coming from, but she wasn't about to agree with her. She just listened. She felt it was her job to make Farah feel better, not worse.

Taking a slice of the opened pound cake on the table, Farah noticed the house was terribly quiet. "Where's everyone?" she asked.

"Chris stopped by his mom's house. And the baby is asleep, but from those little whimpers I hear, she may be waking up soon." Lola got up from the kitchen table and tiptoed into the bedroom.

She came out with Arabia in her arms, dozing in and out of sleep.

"Ohhh, let me," cooed Farah. "I want to hold her. Why did you wake her up?"

Lola gave her the baby and she heated the bottle on the stove. Farah envied how much more womanly Lola looked since she married almost two years ago. The weight she gained around her hips looked good, but her chest was still as flat as a cutting board. Farah looked down and saw that Lola had on her favorite bunny slippers. At least some things stayed the same, she thought.

Farah rocked Arabia in her arms. She took her finger and gently traced her soft hairline. She swore Arabia was smiling at her. Arabia began playfully tapping Farah's big breasts as if she wanted to shake something out of there. She took Arabia's hands and started playing with them. She closed her eyes, imagining that Arabia was really Havelynn, her chosen name if she ever had her own child.

Lola took out a chilled open bottle of Champagne. She shared some for her and Farah in paper cups. Lola was about to take the baby from Farah to feed her, but decided she'd let her friend do it. She smiled to herself at how awkward Farah looked with the baby. After the baby fidgeted for a bit, Farah finally got the bottle between the baby's lips. Arabia sucked on it and kept her tiny eyes on Farah's face the whole time.

They both just watched Arabia drink the bottle and kick her feet around.

Arabia had had enough of the milk and began spitting some out. When Farah removed the bottle, she spit some on Farah's blouse. Lola saw Farah grimace and quickly hand her the baby.

"Sorry about that. Besides being cute, they can be moody, too," Lola said, wiping Arabia's chin. Farah felt a little embarrassed. She thought Arabia had liked her so far. She told herself that she had never been good with kids. Farah took a napkin and dabbed her blouse dry. She gazed at how relaxed and still Arabia was in Lola's arms.

Farah took a sip of the Champagne. "Damn. When was the last time you drank this? It's as flat as a bad note."

Lola looked away. "I drank it the last time Chris and I celebrated. I think it was about three months ago when he got his promotion."

Farah looked around the neat, white kitchen. She was looking around for chocolate Valentine's Day candies or crumpled wrapping paper, but didn't see any. She did notice a cute bouquet standing in a glass vase by the window.

"So what did you and Chris do for Valentine's Day?"

"He gave me some flowers this morning that he brought from the corner store. It still had the tag on it." She laughed. "Then I made him his favorite breakfast of egg-and-potato omelet. And that is pretty much it. He's supposed to stop at Blockbuster's on his way back." Lola poured some more Champagne in her cup.

"That is cheap! And you let him get away with that?" Farah said.

"Please, it's only one day. We have too much going on around here with Arabia to get caught up in those little things," she said.

"Are you convincing me or yourself? Sounds like Chris is slipping," Farah said. She immediately felt bad.

" 'Scuse you!" Lola said, covering little Arabia's ears. "Why come here with your misery and make me miserable?"

"Sorry, girl. I *am* miserable. If it wasn't for the smell of roses in the office, I wouldn't have even known it was Valentine's Day," Farah said, sucking a piece of sticky cake from her thumb.

Lola's phone rang. She picked it up and told the person on the other line Chris was not home.

"Who was that?" Farah asked, being nosy.

"One of Chris's friends." Lola sat back down at the table.

"Is this friend single?"

"*She's* single. It's one of his co-workers. Her name is Marlene." When she saw the look on Farah's face, Lola added, "I met her before. She's cool, Farah."

Farah almost choked on the cake. "A woman? A single woman calling your man at his house on Valentine's Day?"

"Yeah, what are you saying?" Lola asked with a tone of annoyance.

"What are *you* saying? It's fucking Valentine's Day! And she's calling him now?" Farah asked.

"Well, he ain't over there, obviously. That is why she called," Lola said, in a defensive manner.

"I hope you are not speaking about that hot-ass Marlene at his job!" The Champagne was flat but that didn't stop Farah from pouring her third cup.

Lola got up from the table to go to the sink. There was nothing to wash or get. But Farah had made her uncomfortable. "Yes, it's that Marlene. They run a football pool at the job. Plus, she's not even Chris's type. He told me."

"You had this conversation with him about her?"

"Kind of. He just sort of volunteered the info. He and Marlene are always running bets on the games. She's like a guy herself. They are just cool buddy friends."

"Buddies? I stopped having those in grade school," Farah said.

"Farah, please. Don't start bringing your paranoid ass in here. I don't have any reason to be suspicious or insecure. I have to trust my husband. He can have *friends*!" Lola insisted.

"Okay, whatever." Farah reached for her pocketbook. "If being married makes you dumb and blind, you can have it."

The writing was on the wall to Farah. It was obvious to her that Chris was fucking Marlene. Farah knew men well. She thought, what better way for a man to cheat on his wife than to tell her about it without really telling her. Plus, Marlene wasn't that bad looking either. She didn't care what Lola said about her not being Chris's type. She felt that a fat ass and long hair can be any man's type if there's some liquor involved.

"Listen, girl, I gotta go," Farah said, walking herself to the door. Lola stayed in the kitchen.

♥

It was almost 9:00 when Farah finally made it back to her place. She threw her coat on her sofa and fixed herself a real drink—a nice glass of wine. Drinking her wine, she listened to her answering machine with the same old stuff—hang-ups and wrong numbers, and a message from her mother. She unbuttoned her blouse, took off her pants and her panties and let them lie on the floor. She walked into the warm shower, and massaged her skin with a brown-sugar scrub she'd bought at Sephora. The water ran down her head and straightened her hair. She let the powerful pressure of the water beat on her back and sides. She opened her mouth and let the water run down. She felt rejuvenated.

She let her body air dry and lotioned her skin. She slipped on her favorite nightie from Victoria's Secret. It was short, flowery, and flirty. She had bought it last summer knowing she'd have someone to wear it for, but so much for plans.

Farah felt ashamed admitting to herself that she was glad Lola's marriage was experiencing problems. She thought that maybe Lola didn't want to tell her because she was ashamed. She talked about Chris all the time as if he was a saint and really the man was causing her pain. And they'd just had a baby daughter. Farah shook her head in disbelief. She told herself she'd try to listen more and not be so accusatory next time.

♥

The first thing Farah did when she got to the office in the afternoon was sign her contract. She then messengered it over to her agent, who would handle the rest. She couldn't help wanting to rip it up first and then send it.

She returned to her desk and threw herself on the chair. She did absolutely nothing for ten minutes. She felt empty. Besides feeling alone, Farah felt her faith in God taking a beating. She said a silent prayer.

She heard her phone ring.

"Hello, there," sang a man's voice on the phone.

"Hello, Mr. Whitworth. Don't worry, I signed the contract. My agent should have it by this afternoon." She leaned closer to the phone cradle to hang it up.

"That's not all I called about. How about lunch one day? Do you like Indian food?" The way he asked sounded almost as though he was sure she'd say yes.

Farah's antenna immediately went up. She thought that it was rather unprofessional for him to ask her out.

"From your silence, I take that as a no?"

"I'm not the biggest fan of Indian food. But I was silent because I was caught a little off guard."

"Don't worry, the network hasn't sent me to spy on you or pull any further commitments from you besides what's in the contract. I'm just hungry," he said, trying to persuade her.

"How can you ask me to lunch when I don't even know your first name?" Farah said. She did know his first name, but she just forgot it.

"Lenox," he said simply. Farah heard the slight Jamaican accent in his voice again.

"Give me a call later this week because I'll have a better idea of my schedule," Farah said, only to shake up his smugness.

"Fine," he said calmly. She heard his other line beep. "I'll call you soon."

Farah knew what kind of man Mr. Whitworth was, and to him getting women was easy. She imagined him having tons of smart, gorgeous women pursuing him. She wasn't about to be his little catch of the day, she told herself. She had too many things on her mind for that. However, a small voice in her head threatened to kick her for not accepting his invitation. *It was just lunch,* it kept saying.

Unlike most days after her show, she rushed home for some reason. When she got inside, she dialed her answering machine at work. She felt giddy like a little girl, checking to see if Mr. Whitworth had left a message. And he had.

"Ms. Washington, just letting you know that I checked *my* schedule. And it seems like I am going to be hungry about every day during lunchtime. So remember to give me a call after you've checked yours. Take care."

Farah hung up the phone not listening to the other messages. She was flattered by his aggressiveness. But the contract was her only priority.

♥

She called Mr. Whitworth back when she arrived at work in the morning, but he wasn't there. She left a message that she was just returning his call. She didn't mention lunch because she was still unsure if she should go.

Then the phone rang. "Okay, maybe you're not a lunch person. How about a drink today after work?" Lenox asked when she picked up her phone.

"Not only are you hungry but you're thirsty," Farah said, referring to his comment from the day before. The invitation for drinks really made her believe that Mr. Whitworth had more pleasure than business in mind. But as the network lawyer she was going to be dealing with him for at least three years. She wanted to be careful not to look bad.

"Forget drinks, then. How about dinner tonight at Shukran? No big deal. Just two people taking a break from a hectic week?"

Farah thought that she did need something to relax her. And it had been so long since she'd been out with a new man, she didn't know how to act.

"I've heard of that place. Where should we meet?" she asked.

"*Meet?* Isn't that what people eat?" he asked, laughing at her. "I'll pick you up in a black town car. Be downstairs at about seven o'clock. Is that okay?"

"That's fine. I'll see you then," she said, hanging on to his deep, throaty voice. Then it occurred to her that she was at work, with her work clothes on. There was no time to go shopping, however. She looked in her desk drawer and pulled out an old pair of beaded Manolos that could transform her skirt suit into an evening look. And that was all she needed.

She waited in front of the building on Broadway, holding her turquoise blue pashmina wrap to her chest. Its fringed edges kept blowing in her face. She managed to hold it down under her arms. She didn't worry that Ms. Meyers would see her with Mr. Whitworth, since she was out of town.

Just before 7:00, a black Lincoln car pulled up. Farah was waiting for him to get out of the driver's seat, but he got out of the backseat. He held the door open for her. She rushed inside as the beeping horns serenaded them.

"Thanks for picking me up," Farah said to Lenox as she scooted next to him. She couldn't even look him in the eye. He didn't fit the small word of *fine,* but he was excruciatingly handsome with full, suckable lips and a dark brown complexion that Hershey couldn't get to look so edible. She felt him suck up her own presence with his and it made her feel self-conscious.

"I wouldn't let a woman like you walk these mean, crowded streets now," Lenox said, twisting his body to look at her. She still didn't meet him eye to eye, but she felt him taking in her own very good looks.

"So this is the life of a lawyer?" Farah asked teasingly to break her silence.

"When I'm coming from work and the traffic is like this, I use a company car. The last thing I want to deal with is the stress of traffic," he said, extending his long legs.

"Feeling hungry?" He glanced at her bare knees, but made his eyes travel back to her face.

"Yes," she said, feeling a shiver of excitement. His powerful presence had taken up every inch of the car.

"I think you'll like Shukran. It has a nice ambiance and great views of the city. Real cool place," he said, sounding happy. She looked over at him dressed in a gray suit with a navy blue shirt. His tie matched the color of his suit. His legs were open wide and she could see the outline of their shape through his full-legged pants. He definitely had an athletic, strong body. Farah made her way to his Rolex watch and his Italian leather shoes. He was well manicured and taken care of with a short, even haircut.

They both sat back and watched the vibrancy of the city through the car window. She began to relax. It felt good to be going out to enjoy the evening instead of going home. But this was business, not pleasure, she reminded herself. It was the only way she could cope with being dateless in three years.

When they finally got to the elegant restaurant, the hostess rushed them to their table. Farah recognized that it was the best one in the house.

"So what do you think?" he asked pulling her chair out. "Have you been here before?"

Farah looked around at the elegantly beaded curtains.

"I've only read the great reviews." She stretched to look out the window. "I can see Central Park from here." They both peered out the window, which showed a sweeping canvas of the evening sky.

"Listen," he said, reaching over the dimly lit table to open her menu. "Take this as a good gesture from Channel Seven."

She nodded. They both perused the choices of Indian delicacies.

When the waiter came, Lenox ordered a bottle of red wine and a platter of appetizer samplers, which he made sure included samosas.

Farah cringed at his choice. "What are samosas?"

"It's like little patties. They're good. I feel honored to be the first person to introduce you to it," he said. He was surprised that a woman as sophisticated as Farah never ate Indian food.

"Oh, those things! I think I have seen them somewhere before."

"So you've had Indian food before?" he asked, laying the napkin over his lap. She did the same.

"Dana Murray brought homemade samosas for us the day when she was on the set. I heard they tasted pretty good. By the time I tried to get one, they had already been eaten."

"I can see why. Dana is like the ultimate housewife. She can cook, decorate, and run her own business. She's amazing." The waiter poured their glasses of wine.

"Do you know her?" Farah asked, curious at his familiarity.

"She's my client," Lenox said. Farah knew that Dana Murray was worth millions and had a slew of celebrity friends. She was bigger than Martha Stewart, Farah thought. She was becoming more and more intrigued by this man.

Farah took a sip of the wine and savored it. The wine had a nice long finish. It was one of the best burgundies she'd tasted in a while.

She held up her glass. "Nice choice."

Lenox nodded and sipped his, too.

"So tell me, are you Jamaican?" Farah asked.

"I was born there, raised there and go back every chance I get," he said. The waiter came and placed the appetizer sampler in front of them.

Lenox served the spicy samosas on her plate, then his. She sliced hers in half. "What part?"

"Cherry Hill," he said.

Farah remembered a girl from Cherry Hill who used to work at NBC. It was where the elite of the elite lived. But she hid her growing interest. She dipped her samosa in the small bowl of raita. "This raita tastes good with it."

"Let me see," Lenox said, reaching for her hand. He took the samosa she had bit into and bit into it again. Some of the raita stuck to the corner of his mouth. Farah looked on, aroused at him chewing the samosa she had just bitten into.

"I think the only Jamaican I've worked with was this girl from NBC," she said in between bites of the Biryani chicken and rice that the waiter brought to their table, "and Ms. Meyers. I think she's Jamaican, too."

"She's my aunt," Lenox said, patting the corner of his mouth with his napkin. His etiquette was almost out of a book, she thought. His elbows did not touch the table once.

Farah nearly dropped her fork. "Your aunt?" she gasped. "Did she send you to try to get some dirt on me?"

Lenox chewed his food while keeping his eyes on her face. Almost as though he wanted to catch every second of her reaction. "Now, hold on a second, Farah." He felt the gates rise around her.

"Yes?" she said, her lips tightly closing.

"This has nothing to do with my aunt. She doesn't even know we're here. And frankly, if she did know I'm not sure she'd be too happy."

She put her feelings in check. "I could see why she wouldn't be too happy. Her nephew eating dinner with the woman she loves to hate."

Lenox did not acknowledge her assumption.

"I'm always surprised at what a small world this is," Farah said, picking up her fork again.

Inside her heart was racing. She was taking a liking to him in more ways than one. The way he ate, sat, and talked all signaled something different about him. The fact that he was Ms. Meyers's nephew was sounding off in her head like a green light.

They went through dinner talking about current events and their own ambitions. By the end of the evening, they had finished a bottle and a half of Rioja.

Farah didn't want the evening to end with just a handshake and on with business the next day. She saw this evening as another opportunity she couldn't let slip through her hands.

The black town car was waiting for them outside. And like the perfect gentleman, Lenox opened her door, and got in after she did. They were sitting much closer to each other this time.

"Did you enjoy dinner?" he asked, putting his arm around her shoulder. He brushed a strand of her hair away from her eye, which made her blink rapidly.

"I loved it. Thank you so much for such a nice evening," she said, as he touched his lap.

"So next time I'll let you pick the spot?" he asked, sounding as if date two was already secured.

"Maybe," she said with a grin that said yes to a second date. She imagined how it would feel to kiss his thick lips.

"Where do you want to be dropped off at? It's still pretty early, come to think of it," he said.

"Well, where do you live?" she asked, looking him in the eye. She moved closer to him.

He smiled. "I live in Trump Parc. Three blocks away." He told the driver to take him to his building.

When the car pulled up in front of his building steps, Farah barely noticed. Lenox was tracing his fingers up and down her thighs. His lips brushed against the scented skin of her neck.

The driver knocked gently on the window and they got out.

When they got to the elevator, the ache between Farah's thighs got heavier as he stood behind her. She was surprised by her reaction to this man. His scent stirred around her as she inhaled deeply. She stepped back into him, until she felt his hardness pressed against the small of her back. He squeezed her closer. Farah tilted her head, inviting his lips to her neck. He lightly kissed her.

Farah didn't want to control her urges as she was used to doing. She stood against his door unbuttoning his shirt while he searched for the right key. She discovered his chiseled chest with strands of unruly hair at the top. She started nibbling each one. He finally got the door opened, hustled them inside, and kicked it shut. He held her face with one hand and kissed her opened mouth. She felt as if he was drinking in her soul. His other hand unbuttoned her skirt and let it fall to the floor. They both got on their knees and he laid her on the floor. He was on top of her sliding off her panties as he kissed her breasts. He cupped her pussy and squeezed the fat in his hands. He brought his fingers to his mouth and spread her legs and began to work his way down her body.

Instead, Farah rolled over and got on top. "I want to make you want me more," she said softly, with her breasts hanging over him like chapel bells. Wearing nothing but her heels, she undressed him with slow precision. She landed kisses on each new part of him that was exposed. She looked down on him as his eyes rolled back in his head.

"I want you to remember this feeling," she whispered in his ear, letting her lips linger around the edge.

She stared down at him. His fitted black boxers did nothing to hide the treat she'd be receiving soon. She ran her long, gold nails through the hairs of his chest, and then leaned down and nuzzled his belly button with her nose. Her excitement was building up. She had waited so long to be with a man like Lenox in this way. She slowly peeled his boxers off as he lay there with his fists clenched at his sides. Farah smiled to herself at the tense feel of his thigh muscles. This man was not used to giving up any control. She traced her name on his dick with her tongue. He groaned and every time she would trace a letter his dick would flex. She took him entirely into her mouth, a little too eager, and sucked him until her jaw ached. But she couldn't seem to get enough of him.

She finally pulled away because she was ready for more. Lenox grabbed a condom from his wallet on the floor and the next thing she knew, he had her riding him like a wild horse. He turned her so she was facing away from him. She felt a surge of energy rise through her, but she wasn't ready to come. She eased off him and reached for him to go inside of her again. But he put his face between her wet thighs and sucked on her like a peppermint. She moaned and opened her legs wider. When she went limp with delight, he settled on top of her. He reached places inside of her that never opened for another man with his thrusts. Their eyes met and they both refused to close them as they stared into each other. The sweat on his face started to drip into her eyes. But she refused to look away. She refused to submit. Instead, she reached over with both of her hands and cupped his ass. It was when he put her on her stomach and entered "Sheila" from behind that she surrendered.

When they both lay there panting, she glanced around his apartment for the first time and noticed the theme of passionate reds. One wall was painted a dark red. It was hung with a chilling Basquiat painting of a distorted face. There were four Chinese red upholstered chairs in the dining room. She looked to her right and saw the opening of his bathroom and the edge of what looked like a Jacuzzi. Lying there, she felt as if she was in a scene from a movie in which she happened to have the starring role. One day she was moping around her apartment, and the next, she was in bed with a man in one of the ritziest addresses in the city. Dinah Washington's song was true, she thought to herself. A day did make all the difference.

Finally, they both drifted off right there on the crimson-carpeted floor. When Lenox woke up some hours later, he asked, "How about spending the night?"

"You must have read my mind," she said, smiling.

"I had no idea this would happen. I didn't plan this," he said, his dark eyes wide with seriousness.

Farah believed him. "Neither did I." She felt a lump in her throat.

"What did you think this evening would be like?" he asked, his face relaxing.

Farah hesitated. "I don't know. I thought we would just have a good time. I just didn't know it would be in this way." She played with the edges of his trimmed goatee to distract him.

He didn't say anything, but Farah sensed a change in him. She just couldn't tell what the change was.

"Let's take a shower," Farah said, playfully climbing on top of him.

Lenox carried her into his bathroom. It was neat for a single man. She admired the soft, sandy shade of the room and how well all the towels and furnishings blended together. His bathroom was vastly different from her own, which was overcrowded with beauty products. He had three different kinds of shaving cream, and his razors were all neatly hung over a porcelain sink. The shower had four heads, one from each corner. He got in first, and turned all the heads on. Farah stepped in behind him. He pushed her up against the tiled wall and started kissing her breasts, was even a little wilder than before. So was she. They ended up in a corner of the shower discovering each other all over again.

In the morning, Farah woke to hear Lenox calling his office to tell them he would be late. She lay still in bed to observe his morning routine. He threw on a pair of boxers out of a drawer and strolled out of the room. She heard a refrigerator door open and shut.

Farah climbed out of bed and walked, still naked, over to the large windows that lit up the room. She looked out at Central Park and early-morning joggers across the street. She hugged herself, feeling as if she was in *Arabian Nights*. His bedroom had an exotic look, with warm, spice-colored curtains and covers. She walked out into the living room and saw him sitting on the windowsill.

He turned around as she sauntered over to him.

"So do you walk around naked in your own house?" He grinned, pulling her close. He placed a big juicy kiss on her lips. "We could wait for Luisa to cook breakfast, or we can get something to eat downstairs now."

"Luisa?"

He moved away from the window and went back to the bedroom. He came back in with a clean T-shirt.

"She's my cook. She comes only two, three times a week." He handed her the shirt. "My father recommended her to me. She just came from Jamaica." He walked into the kitchen and fixed himself and Farah a glass of orange juice, which she didn't ask for but took anyway.

He continued, "She's a real nice older lady. Makes the best stew peas ever!" he said. This time his Jamaican accent was potent. "And she comes with all her own stuff. I don't have shit in those cabinets," he said, pointing to them.

They decided to go downstairs to the busy diner after they freshened up. She wore the same skirt, and the men's shirt he gave her. Her blouse from last night was wrinkled and smelled of sex. Farah thanked God her coat covered up the bad ensemble.

Farah asked, drinking her coffee, "So, when is your aunt, I mean Ms. Meyers, coming back in town?"

"Sometime this afternoon. Why?" he asked.

"I just want to know if you plan to tell her about us. It would make me feel awkward at work. That's all." The waitress arrived with her Belgian waffle and his eggs and toast.

"Do you really think you have anything to worry about now?" He looked up at her. His dimple stood out from his face as he waited for her answer.

"What do you mean?" She was hoping it was what she thought.

"After I talk with 'Ms. Meyers,'" he said, jokingly putting her name in quotes, "you'll be feeling a lot better about the two of you." He slapped a generous amount of jam on his toast.

Farah didn't say anything.

"What I'm saying is, I know *Rise and Shine* is what you have on your mind. I can help with that," he said. "And what I want is a beautiful woman, who's smart, can be a bitch when she wants to, and is almost as ambitious as me." He paused. "We're two young people trying to do our thing. We're made for each other."

"How do you know I can be a bitch?" Farah said with a sly look.

He grinned. "Just something I picked up on."

"And what do you get out of helping me?"

"Let's not get into details. All I know is I want to be with you and I *know* you want to be with me." He chewed hungrily on his toast.

His left knee brushed hers under the table.

"You know right," Farah said, cutting her waffle and feeding him a bite. "But next time you'll be feeding me."

*M*r. Whitworth, Ms. Meyers is on the line for you, sir," Margaret said.

"Sure, put her through," Lenox said, taking a deep breath.

"Aunt Joan, before you say anything, we have to talk."

"Shoot," she said, sounding perky.

"Look, a lot has happened since you've been away—"

"You fucked her!" Ms. Meyers yelled through the line. "You fucked my anchor!" Her whole tone changed. *Her anchor?*

"Oh, now all of a sudden you have an affinity for Farah?" he said.

"Oh, my God! She's slept with everything from NBC to Channel Seven!" Ms. Meyers said. "Did you know that?"

Lenox didn't know and he didn't care.

"Farah and I fucked. However, I like her and there's more to it than just that. I also would like it if you can be a little easy on her. From what I've learned, you've been a thorn in her side."

"Damn it, Lenox. That is so unprofessional. You've put me in an awkward position. If the higher-ups find out about this, they'll raise hell. You are supposed to work on the network's behalf. The anchors are only thinking about themselves."

"Let me worry about that part. Just be easy on Farah and everyone will be happy," he said with a more rigid tone.

"Yes." Aunt Joan held in her anger. Lenox had her wrapped around his finger since he found out that she was lesbian. He had heard the gossip in the industry and confronted her about it. She admitted that she had been a lesbian for ten years and begged Lenox to keep it to himself and not tell the family. They never talked about it again.

"And another thing. Her contract does say 'major' role in any new programming. We stuck it in there just to hold her, but see what you can do about *Rise and Shine*. She is talented. You can't deny that," he said.

"I'll have to see about that. I have a boss to answer to, you know."

Lenox laughed.

"If you want to be used by her, then go ahead. She fucked you hoping that you'd do what you are doing now. The girl is so transparent. Even I thought she'd be smoother."

"Are you done now?" Lenox asked, bored.

"Go ahead and be the fool, then." She paused. "Then again, knowing you, maybe she's the fool." She sighed. "All right, I'll see what I can do."

When Lenox hung up he called the district attorney, who he'd happened to go to Harvard Law with. He requested that Jacob Richard stay behind bars. He'd be sitting out his remaining eight years. He thought that hopefully by then Derrick would have accomplished something.

♥

Lenox left work early for the Life House. Before reaching the Life House, he called Farah to meet him. He knew she was still at home and lived close by. He had told her about the Life House, but she hadn't seen it before. When he arrived an hour later, Lenox sat on the steps and waited for her. None of the after-school programs had begun since school wouldn't be out for another hour or so.

"What's up, baby," she said, walking up to him and giving him a peck on his dimple. Lenox leaned back and looked at her from top to bottom. She was wearing a lace top that accentuated her breasts and a skirt that hugged her thighs. He licked his lips, satisfied with what stood before him.

She looked up at the building. "So this is your thing, too?"

"Yeah, and we just purchased that building next door. We want to build an auditorium for concerts and performances," Lenox said, boasting a little. He pulled out the article in the Sunday *New York Times* Lifestyle section, which he had been walking around with for the last few weeks. There were pictures of him, the mayor, city officials, and other important people. She took the article from him and examined each photo like an excited kid.

"I can't believe all this," she said. "I mean, what else is there about you I need to know?" She put her arms around him.

"I'll show you." They climbed the white marble steps to the building.

Once inside they went to his office, where Lenox checked his messages. Farah walked around to better acquaint herself with this other aspect of his life.

Lenox had a few messages from the firm and his contractor. The last message was from Camille. He picked up the phone.

"Ox, it's me. We need to meet." She paused, and said, "Today."

"Lenox, did you talk to Ms. Meyers today?" Farah called from the hallway.

"I did. And everything is straight. I think she'll put away her claws." Lenox hung up the phone just as Farah walked back in the office.

"Lenox, are these your kids?" Farah asked pointing to a picture on his desk.

"Those are the kids who were here last year. Every year we get a new group of kids from different parts of Brooklyn. We have programs, events, and trips for them. Anything to broaden their scope on life.

"I have to take care of some things in here," Lenox said, sounding distracted. "There's a display with the kids' work on the second floor. They played journalist and interviewed a prominent figure in the community. I did the hard part, trying to get those folks to participate, but it went well." Lenox took out a notebook and started to look busy, hoping she'd get the hint. "Look at it and tell me what you think," he said.

"Sure. Are you going to be long?" Farah asked, puzzled by his sudden businesslike manner. It was something he turned on and off like a light switch. When they were together, he'd better learn to keep it off, she thought.

"No, I just have to write down some things to do before I forget."

"Make sure you make me first on that list. Especially for tonight." She winked and left.

Lenox waited a few moments until he heard her footsteps fade, then quickly dialed Camille's number.

"What is it?" He barked into the phone as soon as she picked up her cell.

"I need twelve hundred dollars or my mother is going to kick me out. She says she needs the rent, but I haven't been able to pay it for months." Her voice was shaky. "I'm sick all the time, I don't have any energy—"

"And just why should I give you any money?" Lenox asked.

"I can't collect unemployment for some damn reason! And I just got my last check from the firm. I'm broke. I used up all my savings!" she yelled. "We got to meet today or I'm going to come by tonight."

"Stay away from my house. And let's get something clear. I've moved on. Way on," he said, thinking about Farah.

"This is the least you can do after firing me. Don't even get me started, Lenox." Then she started crying.

Lenox felt the bite of guilt. He had fired her and she had lost her apartment.

"Listen," he said, his voice low and intense. "I'm going to give you the money because of how everything went down. But after this, I want to forget you ever existed." He slammed the phone down.

Farah knocked on his office door. Her eyebrows rose when she saw his expression. "What happened to you?" she asked coming into the room.

"What?" he said agitated. Then he shook his head. "It's nothing." He loosened his tie and got up to open a window. "Did you like what you saw up there?" Lenox asked sincerely interested. He took great pride in what the Life House produced.

"Yeah, especially this one. This young lady really has talent." Farah handed him the written report. "I'm sorry. I sort of took it off the bulletin board. I'll put it back." She leaned on his desk. "Her use of language is impressive for a twelve-year-old. Her writing has a sleek conversational style. Perfect for television!"

Lenox smiled at Farah's enthusiasm. "You should come down and talk to the kids. Some even watch you sometimes on the news. They think you're a celebrity or something."

"Soon." They both agreed on that one.

Just then George came in and Lenox introduced him to Farah.

"A priceless beauty," George repeated over and over as he shook Farah's hands. His eyes resting on her breasts turned Lenox on a little, instead of making him uncomfortable. George was used to him bringing fine women around. And if another man didn't look, then the point was all lost to Lenox.

After Lenox introduced her to a few more folks, he dropped Farah off at the G train station. He thanked God it was time for Farah to go to work.

"I'll call you later." Farah grabbed her pocketbook and coat. "If you start to miss me, turn Channel Seven on at six o'clock."

"I always do," Lenox said, bending down to kiss her cleavage.

"Later, baby," he said, as she got out of the car. Lenox waited for her to disappear down the train station steps before he drove off, heading toward Camille's mother's apartment farther up in Park Slope. She lived on the top floor of a two-family house on Seventh Avenue.

When he was about two blocks away, he called her on his cell, and said, "Meet me downstairs."

She just hung up. Sometimes he really thought Camille was crazy. Her erratic behavior made her difficult to control. It was as though the rougher he got with her, the crazier she acted, he thought.

Of course, she wasn't standing out there when he pulled up. He beeped his horn a few times and saw her mother peek out the window. Then he saw Camille walking down the steps. She was wearing heels and a black satin mini and white frilly blouse. Why she needed heels in the house at three in the afternoon was beyond him. *She looks good . . . as usual,* he told himself. Watching her, he compared her to Farah. Lenox had always thought Camille "had a body built to fuck." Her legs were shiny and muscular, one of her best traits. Farah had a more exotic look—softer, Indian-type features, which was more to his liking. While Farah's light brown hair was long and naturally wavy, Camille's was bone straight with the help of a weave. Lenox liked his women's hair long, even if it was fake.

She got in on the passenger side and sat there pouting.

Lenox took one thousand dollars cash out of his glove compartment. He normally kept about three thousand dollars on him in case of emergencies. He knew Camille could manage to get the rest.

She took it from him and counted it, not saying anything about the missing two hundred dollars.

"I'm moving to Chicago next week. A friend from college is offering a room." She stuffed the money in her bra.

"Oh, so I guess you plan to use that money to buy a first-class ticket. Do you think I'm stupid?"

"I said I needed it for the rent! My mother wants her money before I leave," she said, looking at him big-eyed. He hated that look.

The muscles around his jaw tightened. He didn't want to get into another argument.

"Anything else?" he asked, starting the engine and turning up the music.

When she didn't respond, he turned to look at her. He glanced at her skirt, which rode all the way up to her thighs, and wondered if she was wearing any panties. She had often gone without. He imagined how the fold of her ass would feel if he touched it. He wondered where she was going dressed like that. Maybe she had a show tonight, he thought.

She crossed her legs when she caught him looking. "You can treat me like shit, but you would still fuck me. All you men are the damn same!" Camille got out of the car and slammed the door shut. She walked up the steps counting the money again. Another problem solved, Lenox said to himself.

He thought about going down to the office, but he needed a mental break. He left a message for Farah about meeting in a few hours at Lotus. The Lyncs were throwing their regular Thursday after-work party there. As little as Farah knew about him, he wanted to show her all his good sides, all his good parts. He didn't want her to find anything out on her own. He thought about how she could come out tonight, meet a few of his friends. It would also be a good way for him to assess how she was around others and around other women.

Lenox took the car for a wash, and while he was waiting, Farah called back.

As soon as he answered, she blew a big kiss through the phone. He blew one back. She made him feel like a schoolboy.

"Can you meet me tonight at Lotus?" he asked. "Around 8."

Farah grunted. "I have to hang around and transcribe a tape."

"Get an assistant to do the transcribing. I want you to be with me tonight," he said with firmness. "I already told a few people you were coming."

"Well, I didn't know *I* was coming," Farah said, with a hint of attitude. "I have work I want to get done."

"Just get to work early tomorrow. You have a man now and gotta do things a little different."

Farah was quiet for a while. "I know you lawyers tell people what to do all the time, but don't let me come over there and spank your ass," she said, her tone light and teasing. Then she reluctantly agreed to be ready at 8:00 P.M.

Lenox put his cell phone away shaking his head. The woman had been single for so long, she had forgotten how to behave with a man. He was running the show, but he was sure she'd get used to it.

♥

Farah and Lenox walked in to Lotus a quarter after eight and Nicole, Derrick, James, and a few other familiar faces were already there. Nicole hurried over to them.

"Did you see *The New York Times* story and Page Six!?" She held the two articles in her hand. "I think I deserve an extra bonus," she said, practically giddy.

"I saw those when they came out weeks ago," Lenox said, as if it was nothing. "You deserve something, but that was your j-o-b. I don't know if you need an *extra* bonus." Lenox gave the hostess their coats.

"It doesn't hurt to try," Nicole said, looking at Farah.

Lenox put his hands on Farah's waist. "Nicole, this is Farah." The ladies gave each other friendly, quick handshakes.

"And what do you do for Lenox?" Farah asked, smiling. She slipped her arm through his.

Nicole looked at Lenox and then back to Farah. "Oh, he didn't tell you, I see," Nicole said with a half smile.

Farah felt her face tighten as Lenox stood beside her. "Tell me what?"

Nicole burst out laughing. "Geesh, relax girl. He ain't going nowhere," she said, patting Farah on her shoulder. Farah looked at her shoulder, then back at Nicole as if to say "Oh, no, you didn't."

"I'm his special-events coordinator/publicist/friend from way back," Nicole said, stressing the word "friend."

"Lovely. I'm the anchor for evening six," Farah said.

"I knew you looked familiar!" Nicole yelled. Lenox gave Nicole a look, knowing she could be ghetto when she wanted to. "I just didn't want to say anything, you know. You look a lot older in person." Derrick was calling Nicole to him from the bar, so she left them alone. "Girl, we'll talk later," she said, walking away. But Farah wasn't looking forward to it.

"Ready to meet some more people? Don't mind Nicole," Lenox said, as they walked through the club.

"If they are anything like your *friend*, I need to be drunk to pull off that phony act she gave me. I need a drink," she said. He walked her to his table near the stage. He brought her a drink and made some rounds without her. He could tell Farah hadn't been out to a club in a long while. She felt a bit strange, but glad she was with a man instead of looking for one. She was mildly surprised to see Lenox in this sort of atmosphere, as she was just thinking earlier that he was too business oriented.

As Lenox made his way across the crowded dance floor, the club manager approached him.

"Hey, man, let me know if you want to make this twice a week," Lenny said, holding a cigar. "We make the most money when the Lyncs come through. You people can spend!" He pulled another cigar out of his pocket for Lenox.

"I'll let you know," Lenox said, lighting it. "Volume is high now, which is good. But we may be ready to move on to a larger place."

Lenox watched him from the corner of his eye as he puffed on the cigar.

"Whatcha talking about, moving to a larger place?" Lenny asked with a puckered brow. He frantically waved away the smoke standing between them. "This is Lotus. It's a celebrity place. You can't find any place like this, with the deal I gave you," he insisted.

Lenox looked over to his right and saw Farah take her gaze off him. That women had eyes like a hawk, he thought.

"Le Cipriani just offered us their space on Thursdays. I'm still thinking about it. They were willing to even give us the twenty percent of the bar on a seven thousand dollar guarantee," Lenox lied.

Lenny thought to himself. They both stood there amidst the R Kelly and Jay Z blazing their latest in the background.

"Listen, Lenny. I got a couple of things I need to do. I'll let you know what I decide," Lenox said, taking a long drag from his Cuban cigar.

"Okay, okay," he said, putting his hands up. "Fine. Have twenty percent of the bar on your three thousand dollars guarantee. Which I must say always goes over limit. Just promise me you'll at least stick around for a few months." Lenox had been in business with Lenny for years. Lenox followed him all over, but he didn't want Lenny to get too comfortable making more money off black folks than he did.

"Good. And from the looks of things"—Lenox eyed the door with herds of people spilling in—"I'd like to start tonight. James will follow up with you." He left Lenny sitting by the bar. It always amazed Lenox to see Lenny's stubby, middle-aged body try to kick it to the beautiful sisters. And it amused him more when they'd fall for Lenny.

Before he could go back to his table, a Spanish-looking girl stopped him on his way. "Lenox Whitworth?" she said, putting a hand on his chest. She was wearing a short, skimpy pink dress.

He looked at her hand on his chest, which she still didn't move.

"Yes? You know me?" Her nails were long and orange. Almost as orange as her shiny lips. She looked in her early thirties.

"Do you remember me? I was one of your hostesses for those parties you used to throw at that SoHo loft in '99." She inched closer, looking up at him.

Lenox could tell by the way her eyes grew small that she wanted to get better acquainted. She was so close her breasts were nearly touching him.

He looked over at Farah, but she was gone. That made him a little uneasy.

"What's your name?" he asked, backing away from the dance floor, which left him too much in the spotlight.

"Mona," she purred.

"Lenox?" He turned around, relieved to see Farah, though a little annoyed at her sneak attack.

Farah came up beside him and put her arm around his waist. "I'm Farah Washington, and you are?" she asked, holding her hand out.

Mona took her hand slowly. "Mona. I just was congratulating Mr. Whitworth on his accomplishments." Mona smiled, obviously flustered. "If you'll excuse me?" Then she turned and walked away.

"You could have waited for me at the table," Lenox said, now putting both his arms around her.

"Waited for what? For that woman to climb all over you?" Farah asked, playing with his goatee.

Lenox took her hand. "Come on, I want you to meet some people."

He introduced Farah to James and Derrick. They both recognized her from TV. Farah even promised Derrick an interview before Election Day. Channel 7 catered to an audience that Derrick desperately needed to win.

Farah and Lenox finally had some time to themselves and sat by the bar. She had two more Cosmos and Lenox had his shots of Hennessey. Lenox was relieved when Farah didn't bring up the

Mona incident. Lenox thought that the other women he knew, like Camille, would have dragged that on all night.

"Oh, we've got to dance to this." Farah got up and danced onto the crowded floor. Lenox sat on his stool, watching her.

She swayed her hips to the new Mary J. Blige tune that was pumping in clubs everywhere. She teased him with a little booty dance that called Lenox to her like a little puppy. He put his drink down and moved up behind her. As they danced, he felt the dampness of her blouse and gingerly kissed the back of her neck. Then a reggae hit came on and Farah began to pop her hips as if she had no bones in her body. Lenox just held on for the ride.

They didn't leave Lotus until 1:00 A.M., when a spring shower came down on them as they left. The rain slicked them salty-sweet as they walked down the winding, empty street to the car. In the backseat, Farah dug her nails into Lenox's back as her hips danced, to his beat this time.

♥

Lenox woke up at about 5:00 A.M. to do some work on his laptop. Farah was still asleep beside him. He watched the way she slept peacefully in a fetal position all night, not bothered by his abrupt twists, kicks, and turns. She gave him the impression that she would be in his corner no matter what. He had every intention of being a good man, but knew being faithful was another story. Men like him had options. Lenox loved women . . . all women. He was in his prime. Damn it, his photos were featured in *The New York Times* society pages. Then he sobered. A part of him wanted to settle down as he approached his midthirties, and he wanted a solid relationship with a woman for once in his life. He wanted to fit into the shoes that were made for him by his family. They had a lot of expectations for him, such as prominent political positions like the prime minister of Jamaica. He wasn't trying to hear that one, though. He wanted good relationships with people, but it seemed as if he was just an easy target for a favor or a first-class ticket to Chicago. He wished he could be detached from women like his father. But he wasn't his father.

One thing he knew for sure was that Farah wasn't like Camille, or anyone else he'd dealt with, for that matter. He knew Camille would suck the corns off his toe if he asked her to. Farah had a backbone to her. She was also manipulative. He knew that. That was the only way he could explain her sudden affection toward him on their first date and ever since then.

*F*arah noticed that lately things had changed with no direct intervention on her part. The biggest change was that she was doing more stories of national interest. Ms. Meyers had given her the green light to cover the slew of local sniper attacks that were making headlines across the country. Katie was also working on the story, but had less time to contribute to it than Farah. Farah saw it as another chance to rise to the occasion. Instead of anchoring, she was doing live shots from the latest sniper shooting scene, in the thick of the media frenzy. On the scene, they all had to wear bulletproof vests. Lenox and her mom warned her about the dangers of such a story, but she welcomed it. Since the assignment, gossip that she had been receiving special treatment, and the motives behind it, spread like the flu throughout the newsroom. She felt Sam was behind the rumors, but covered up her hurt feelings of isolation and focused on her work and Lenox.

Farah had been spending so much time at Lenox's place that she had decided to sublet her condo. His lifestyle was somewhat intimidating to her with its flashy, fast pace, but it made her feel alive. Before Lenox, she stayed home on the weekends and the closest she got to getting drunk was taking too much Robitussin. They had dinner the other night at Nobu and were seated near Robert DeNiro and a date. They got courtside seats to every Knicks games. Last night, they sat next to Jack Nicholson. Getting tickets to sold-out Broadway shows was effortless. Lenox was able to get backstage passes for every big event in the city. Farah was not ashamed of riding on a man's coattails for a change. She saw it as a new and more entertaining way to gain prestige.

When they went to parties together, she felt like a princess. Anything and everything she needed was attended to. People were overly accommodating and solicitous. Sometimes too nice, she thought. When Lenox was away, some would come up to her and ask her what his latest venture was, giving her phone numbers for him to call or try to get her to persuade him to take on an investment. His power had given Farah her own power. She took pleasure in that, but was still learning how to wield it. She had just wanted to sleep with the man, and now she felt like the black Blaine Trump.

As Farah rested in Lenox's bed, her mind was crammed with thoughts of him. She decided to call Lola to divert her attention.

"Hey, girl, why don't you come over with the baby? I'll buy some McDonald's for breakfast?" Farah said.

"All right," Lola said, sounding a bit down. "It's a little short notice. But yeah, we can do that. I need to get away from here anyway. Give me about an hour."

"Is everything okay?" Farah asked.

"Yeah, but we'll talk later. Let me go so I can get ready," she said, and hung up.

Farah called McDonald's and ordered her favorite cheese biscuit meal, a steak-and-cheese biscuit meal for Lola, and pancakes for Arabia. In Lenox's neighborhood, they were kind enough to deliver and it was one of her number-one places to indulge.

She opened a window and let in the spring breeze. Just when she sat down to do some work, the bell rang. Farah smiled when she saw Lola and Arabia standing there looking like twins in a set of matching sweaters.

"Damn, I could eat two of these biscuit things," Farah said, biting off a piece of the hash brown. She opened the pancakes, and cut it into baby slices. "Let me feed Arabia."

"Farah, I don't feed my child McDonald's. She's not even two. I don't know what they put in those pancakes. This is a little baby," Lola said, protectively reaching for her child. "I have a bottle in here, just in case. But trust me, she is not hungry."

"I was just trying to be nice." Farah took a bite from her biscuit sandwich.

"I can't believe you would feed a baby who barely has teeth McDonald's. Girl, it's better you don't have kids anytime soon, until I give you a sit-down lesson."

"This is your first child." Farah grimaced. "You are learning like everybody else in your shoes. And just because I bought some McDonald's doesn't mean that I don't know how to take care of kids." She went back to eating her biscuit.

"Just stick to what you know," Lola said, while bouncing Arabia on her lap.

"Don't worry, baby, soon you gonna be calling Auntie Farah to come pick you up from your strict-ass mommy," she said, taking the baby's hand. Arabia screamed.

Farah pulled away and moped in her chair.

"So where's that new man you met?" Lola asked. "If he looks as good as his apartment, you've got something to hold on to."

Farah's face brightened. "He's out of town. He's in Amsterdam now visiting one of his clients. Then he's stopping in Jamaica for a few days," Farah said, wishing she was with him. "I would have gone, but I have too much work to do."

"What work? Please! If you married that man, you wouldn't need to work."

"Lola, men like Lenox are used to women trying to get a ring on their finger. I want to be different. I want him hooked. For instance, he wants me to stop by the Life House. Lenox wants me to tell him what I think he should do about the decoration of the new auditorium."

"If you do that, your influence will be all over that building if he ever met anyone else. Sounds like he's serious. When will I meet him?"

"Maybe on Monday. He does this network event at Spa. As a matter of fact, I'll call you when I leave work so you can meet me there. Can you leave the baby with Chris?" Arabia was dozing off in Lola's arms.

"I have to see." Lola's demeanor changed. "If not him, then my mother. He's been acting strange lately." She got up and put the baby down on the couch, and Farah followed her.

"Is it that Marlene thing?" Farah asked.

Lola's forehead wrinkled as she concentrated. "I don't know if it is Marlene or someone else. I don't even know how he would find the time in his twelve-hour shift." Lola cleared her throat. "I even went through the garbage last night to see if I could find anything he threw away. The only thing I walked away with was grimy hands and an aching back."

"Did you check his pants, jackets, e-mail, or cell phone?"

"Yeah, all that. I know all the numbers in his cell phone. I did see one I hadn't recognized that he dialed a few times. But there was no answer." Lola massaged the side of her head. "I swear I cannot be like these single moms and raise Arabia all alone. I hope that man ain't tripping!"

"All right, calm down. You know I believe a woman's instinct always should have the last word, but that cannot prove that he is cheating."

Lola took a blanket out of Arabia's Gucci baby bag that sat on the coffee table and covered the baby.

"Have you ever told him about you and Hamilton?" Farah asked, knowing she was venturing into sensitive territory.

"Yes, like a fool," Lola said, throwing her head back. "I told him that it was a mistake. When we had that big argument last Thanksgiving and he spent the night at his mom's house, I just kind of spit it out." She sighed loud enough to almost wake up Arabia. "I was going to tell him anyway, but not like that."

"What did he say?" Farah asked, sitting at the edge of the couch.

Her voice grew small like a whisper. "He called me all kinds of dirty names, but I kept telling him it happened before we were married. That was the only thing that seemed to save me."

"Did you tell him about Arabia?" Farah asked. This time Arabia's eyes opened. Lola picked her up and rocked her back to sleep.

"I couldn't go there. But every time we fight, he asks if Arabia is his or not." Lola put Arabia back down on the couch.

Farah held up a finger. "Wait a minute. You've got to tell Chris about Arabia!"

"I will. After I get pregnant." Lola said.

Lola looked weak and tired. This was a side to her Farah hadn't seen since her mistake with Hamilton.

"You're putting yourself through all this because it's catching up with you now. That is why you are looking through the garbage late at night. You're scared he'll hurt you just as much as you hurt him," Farah said.

Lola put her chin in her hand as she gave a small, sad laugh. "That is why I like you, Farah. As much as I try to go around like everything is perfect, you put my shit under my nose and force me to smell it. And I was really trying to forget about things. But you are right. I need to get it over with."

Farah stroked Arabia's hair and wondered about the little girl's future.

"Do you love him?" asked Farah.

Lola just kept her eyes cast down.

After an hour of *The View* and a carton of cookie-dough ice cream later, Farah dropped Lola off in Flatbush and then went downtown to the Life House in Lenox's Range Rover.

She quietly thanked God that it had been a few months into her relationship with Lenox and there was still no drama. Usually, the curtains came down on week three of most of her relationships. She liked calling it the three-week stand. It just seemed like things would fall apart. But today, as she sailed down Dekalb, she felt as if she was flying, her hair flowing behind her.

She parked in the lot and took the Life House keys out of the glove compartment. She opened the door to the new building, which had been under construction until about a week ago. When she walked through the door, the quiet, empty space seemed to engulf her. She slowly looked around her. The room seemed to be waiting for someone to come along and dress it up. Excitement cruising through her, she dug her notepad out of her bag and went from room to room scribbling notes. The place needed color, but Lenox didn't want it to look too gaudy, she told herself.

While she stood at the doorway of the auditorium daydreaming, Farah realized that she had to meet her mother for brunch. She stuck her pad in her bag, shut off the lights, and locked up. Farah hadn't seen her mother for several weeks and she had yet to tell her about Lenox. She wanted to hold off saying anything until she and Lenox had been dating for a while. This time, however, she thought to herself as she started the car, she'd be the one chirping about her love life.

They met at Awkwaaba, an old mansion-style restaurant in Brooklyn. When she went in, she saw her mother seated by a painting toward the back. Farah noted that she looked striking as usual. She had on a short, fitted orange dress that showed off her petite frame, and a matching wide-brimmed straw hat. She made Farah feel dumpy in her designer sweatsuit.

"Where are you coming from? Jogging?" her mother asked with a look of distaste. She watched Farah sit down.

"It's Saturday and I spend every day of the week in a suit. I deserve to be in a sweatsuit once in a while," Farah said, smiling.

Her mother gave a delicate cough. "And to what do you attribute that glow?" her mother asked, twirling her straw around her lemonade.

"I'll have a lemonade, too," she told the waiter when he asked. She was going to keep the lady guessing. "Come on, let's get some of the pancakes, before they finish," Farah said, pointing to a group of people standing around the buffet.

"Not until you tell me what's going on with you!" she squealed. She sounded like a teenager about to get the latest gossip.

Farah got up from the table and her mother followed her.

"Where should I begin?" Farah said, filling her plate. "I've been seeing this man for almost four months now."

Farah's mother stared at her, stunned. "A man? I hope there's more."

"He's a lawyer, single and lives on Central Park South." Farah took a scoop of the fresh berries and placed some on her mother's plate.

"Why did you wait four months to tell me?" her mother said, outraged. "You usually tell me everything."

"I wanted to wait until we passed the three-week mark and developed something. He is not the average single lawyer living in the city. He is pretty well known. He was in *The New York Times* society pages a few months ago," Farah said, taking the last salmon croquettes. She knew her mom read the Sunday *Times* religiously.

"I read the *Times* every Sunday! Is he black?" By this time, her plate was sprinkled with fruit and a few pancakes, but Farah's was stacked.

"He's black and very successful," Farah said. Then she walked over to a side table for extra butter. She left her mother standing by the salmon croquettes. "I'm surprised you don't know him," Farah said, walking back to her. This time she took a spoonful of hot macaroni and cheese. Her mother looked at her plate disapprovingly.

"Is he feeding you?" She watched as Farah reached over another lady and scooped up some whipped sweet potatoes.

"In more ways than one." Farah walked back to the table with her mother not far behind her.

"Give up?" Farah asked, sitting down. She took pleasure in watching her mother do a mental rewind of every issue of the Sunday *Times* for the last three months.

"I remember seeing some photos about a charity recently with some black folks," she said, gesturing with her fork. "Then again, there are usually black folks in those society photos. Even if it's just one." She broke down. "Baby, you better tell me who this man is!"

Farah laughed. "His name is Lenox Whitworth. Partner of Whitworth, Seagel and Scott, and president of the Life House and president of the Lyncs," Farah said proudly. She knew her mom would be impressed. She'd been dying for her to get together with a "man of worth" since she graduated college.

Her mother's whole face beamed. "You mean you've snagged one of New York's most eligible black bachelors. And he's not a rapper or athlete?"

Farah stuffed her mouth with a croquette to hide her dislike of the surprise she heard in her mother's voice.

"He was into me way before I was into him," Farah said defensively. She poured some more syrup on her pancakes. "It's not like I had to convince him of anything."

Her mother clapped her hands. "Well, you've made the first steps. Next you've got to get him to put a ring on your finger," she told her.

"Yeah, well, I didn't even tell you the best part."

Her mom looked on with wide eyes.

"He's Ms. Meyers's nephew!" Farah whispered.

Her mother nearly choked on the piece of fruit she just put into her mouth. When she stopped coughing, she said, "Baby, that is the *best* part! You'll have the old witch eating out of your hands now."

"Well, she's giving me much better assignments."

Her mother pursed her lips thoughtfully and Farah knew she

was going through her mental archives of *The New York Times.* "You know, I do remember reading about him. My, he's handsome and built!" They had the same taste in men. "And he's extremely rich. And that Whitworth name . . ." she said, bringing a finger to her chin. "I think I met his father years ago when I was a legal secretary. He was worth millions."

"I know that," Farah said, trying to sound informed. She was slightly bothered that her mother knew as much about him as she did.

They stayed at Awkwaaba for almost two hours. At the end of their meal, Farah's mother asked again if he was feeding her. Farah hit the buffet table a second time and took a little bit of all the same food she had the first time.

Farah dropped her mother off and when she got back to the apartment, it was nearly dark. She glanced at her watch and realized Lenox would be calling any minute.

Even still she jumped when the phone rang.

"I've been trying to reach you. I thought you'd be done with the Life House earlier," Lenox said. She could hear music and people laughing in the background and wished she were there with him.

"I met my mother for brunch, then I had to drop her back home," Farah said. It had been a while since she had explained her whereabouts to a man. "I just got in."

"The interior decorator called me today and I wanted her to talk to you before she went to Highpoint to buy fabrics and furniture."

"If you give me her number, I'll call her on Monday."

"Don't worry about it," he said, irritated. "I'll call her Monday myself. I had wanted you to talk to her *before* Monday. That's why you had to go to the Life House today."

"Look, if I had known—" she began.

"I gotta go now. Say hi to your mother for me." Then she heard the dial tone.

She felt guilty, angry, and confused all in the same moment. Here she was running around taking care of his business and he had the nerve to call her with an attitude? "Well, he can handle his own damn business from now on," she said out loud.

♥

Farah was standing in the lobby waiting for the elevator when she heard Ms. Meyers say, "Hello, Farah. And how is my nephew?"

"Oh, he's fine. He'll be back today," she said, turning to face her. Her heart nearly sank at the sight of Ms. Meyers standing there with her phony grin plastered on her face. It was the first time they had stood face-to-face since Farah and Lenox had become "official."

Farah felt it was her responsibility to break the ice.

"I know this is awkward for both of us. But I'd really like to start fresh with you, Ms. Meyers," she said. "I'm falling in love with Lenox, and I don't want to hide that." Farah felt the sting of the word "love." She felt the word was a bit too loaded for her new feelings, but she wanted to convince Ms. Meyers that her intentions were sincere.

"Of course, dear," she said, keeping the grin on her face. "And for the record, I never hated you, I just didn't like you," she said. "I'm not sure if I like you now. But you are my beloved nephew's girlfriend, and there's some value in that."

Farah respected her honesty. "And I'm very excited about my new contract and plan to give it my all here at Channel Seven. Wrapping up the sniper story after three weeks was incredible and a relief. I'll be happy to give Katie my notes on the story."

"I'm surprised Katie wasn't able to follow through on that story. She's very good at those things. I think she was just too busy," Ms. Meyers said, shaking her head. "And I did promise Lenox to let you have more . . . opportunities."

"He's very supportive of my career. I couldn't ask him for more than that."

"You'll be asking him for a lot more than just that, dear. And so will he," she said in her usual cynical tone. "Oh, and I'd watch my weight if I were you." And with that she walked into the elevator as soon as it opened. Farah stepped in last and could feel the heat as she stood in the front.

♥

After work, Farah headed across town to Spa to meet Lola. She still hadn't heard from Lenox. She worried that maybe he was running late, too.

When the cab dropped her off, there was already a line at the front door and it wasn't even 8:00 yet. She pressed through the crowd of men in suits and women in heels. Tony the bouncer needed her to okay a few people who weren't on the RSVP list.

"Sorry, but we're over capacity tonight. Maybe next time," she said to a group of guys and one girl. They mumbled a few words and turned away in separate directions. Lenox was notorious for keeping his crowd exclusive, she reminded Tony.

She walked in and settled down at Lenox's table. Nicole brought her a drink when she saw her.

"I thought you weren't going to make it," Nicole said as she handed Farah a martini.

"Why would you think that?" Farah was annoyed at her assumption. "The party is just getting started."

"I know. I'm just used to Lenox being here on time."

"Well, get used to new things," Farah snapped back. Farah played hostess and made her rounds around the room. She greeted all the VIPs she had invited personally, such as Rick, the senior VP of Entertainment at HBO and celebrity publicist Tina Rosenbaum. She made sure their needs were met and she instructed Nicole to take care of any special requests.

Farah then welcomed Lenox's legal and political friends. This was the easy part for her, she thought. All she had to do was smile a lot, nod, and move on. Lenox called this "good business" or "the art of making Lyncs" with prominent folk.

Then she spotted Lola. She was wearing a thigh-length leopard-print skirt, a stretchy black V-neck tank top, and ankle boots. Farah looked in awe at Lola's bare legs.

"Girl, I don't think I have seen your legs in over a year!" Farah said, hugging her friend.

"I know! Breast-feeding all day doesn't exactly make you feel sexy." Lola tugged her skirt as she followed Farah to the bar. "And I didn't know you had thighs, girl. I always was a bit bigger than you."

"Oh, please. This is nothing. I can work this off in a week. It's only a few pounds," Farah said, leading the way to the bar. She ordered a ginger ale for Lola, since she wasn't much of a drinker.

They sat down at Lenox's table.

"So where is he?" Lola asked.

"He's on his way. I think he's stuck in traffic. Is the baby with Chris?"

Lola sipped her soda. "Nope, she's with my mom. I don't want to talk about him now, Farah. I just want to have a decent time."

"Oh, okay. Let me introduce you to some people." Farah took Lola around to meet some of the same faces. She figured by the time they were through Lenox would have arrived. She was dying to know what Lola thought of him.

It was nearly 9:00 and there was still no sign of Lenox. Farah was getting tired and her three-inch heels were starting to hurt her calves. She was also getting a little damp under the arms. She was grateful her black minidress hid the damp circles. The room was getting warmer as the crowd increased and the music got louder. Everyone was dancing, even Lola. Farah knew it took bourgeois black folks a good two hours into a party to unwind, and "truth serum" really loosened them up.

At last, Lenox showed up at a quarter to ten. He walked in majestically and was dressed in black, too, from the shirt to the suit to the tie.

Before she could even walk up to him, Nicole rushed him. They stood at the door and Farah watched Nicole talking animatedly to him. Lenox and Farah's eyes met over Nicole's head. He walked around Nicole, who was still talking, and headed toward her.

He bent down and grazed her lips with his. She tilted her head up, as he stuck his warm tongue in her mouth, sucking on her lips, as she did to him. She could feel some eyes on their mouths as they indulged.

She ran her hand down his neck, and he withdrew slowly. He licked his lips for any remaining lipstick.

"Everything is running smoothly this evening. You can see for yourself that this place is packed and filled with happy spenders!" she said, holding his hand.

"Of course it is. That's why I didn't bother rushing. I knew you'd handle it," he said, glancing at Lola, who was sitting expectantly.

"I want you to meet my friend Lola," Farah said. "Lola! This is Lenox."

She and Lenox shook hands. Lola would not let go of Lenox's hands. Farah had to literally break her hand away.

"Are you in any way related to Morris Chestnut?" Lola said, flirtatiously.

"No," Lenox said, smiling and putting both hands in his pockets. "But if I had known my girl had such gorgeous friends, I would have brought someone to introduce you to."

"Oh, she's married," Farah said. Lola grunted.

Lenox laughed. "Sometimes a woman likes to be reminded how special she is. Isn't that right, Lola?" he said, his dark eyes glimmering.

Lola shook her head, charmed.

"No friends for Lola, Lenox. She's fine with her *husband* and *child*," Farah emphasized over the piercing music.

"If you change your mind, Lola, give Farah a call," he said, flashing a devious smile. "I'll be right back, ladies."

Lola fanned herself as she watched Lenox walk away. "Did you see that sinful smile he has? He is a fine specimen. I think he is the best I've seen you with in a while."

"Oh, trust me, he is. But I can tell he's a little scandalous. Trying to set a married woman up on a date," Farah said.

"He knows how to make a woman feel good, though," Lola said, searching for the last of her ginger ale with her straw.

Lenox came back. "Are you ladies enjoying yourselves tonight?"

Lola peeked at her watch. "Actually, I think I'll get going. I do have responsibilities." She sighed.

"Here, take a cab and call Farah when you get home." He peeled off sixty dollars.

"Thank you," Lola said as if she had just been touched by the pope.

"And you?" Lenox said, turning to Farah. "I know you've been here all night waiting for me." He kissed her on the forehead. "Why don't you keep those covers warm for me at home?"

Farah scanned the room and noticed that the women in the place outnumbered the men five to one. She stood up and put her arms around him. "No, I'll stay."

*A*s Lenox got ready to drive down to the Life House, he caught a television commercial of the Ms. USA pageant. It reminded him of his last trip to Jamaica to see Joanne win the title of Ms. Caribbean. He was almost close to ruining it for her, too. A shady pageant official dug up some records of Joanne's abortion. Lenox knew that it would stain her career and reputation, since the Caribbean was still very conservative. When Joanne told him about what had happened, he didn't hesitate to pay the pageant official five thousand dollars so that she wouldn't run to the press with the information. He smiled when he remembered the smile on Joanne's face when she won. They agreed to stay friends, despite their history. But every time he thought about her, the image of the baby that never was popped up. He wished things could have been different. But things never came easy for men like him.

He drove his car up to the Life House building and parked his car in the driveway. A few of the boys were outside playing basketball. Lenox watched them from the sidelines, until one boy threw a ball in his direction. He stood there holding it, not sure if he should join them since he was dressed in slacks and street shoes.

"Come on, Mr. Whitworth! Just a couple of shots, man. Don't tell us you are six feet three inches and can't shoot a ball in a hoop?" shouted a tall skinny boy with a long neck, who looked like the leader in the group of teenage boys.

Lenox dribbled the ball in their direction. The boys cleared the pathway as Lenox made a shot that was all net. He even surprised himself. He took out a pair of old sneakers from his car trunk and played a full court game. When the game was over, he had scored the most points. No matter who was on the other end, Lenox loved competition.

Sweaty and tired, Lenox went inside to meet with George, his real reason for coming to the Life House. Though he enjoyed hanging with the kids when he could, his legal work and parties were consuming his time and all Lenox had was money to give to the Life House. George was his source of communication with the Life House.

"Good afternoon! I saw you out there giving the young ones a beating on the court. Lord, if I had the back I used to, I would have been out there, too. I miss playing some ball," said George. He sat down in front of Lenox, who was looking through some receipts.

"I hear you, man. Tell me about the dude ranch," said Lenox, his tone dry and serious.

"The kids truly loved it. Some of them did the horseback riding and the others took swimming lessons. And that course on etiquette you arranged for them was hilarious. I mean, they did well, but I don't think I ever saw so many left-handed children in one place! And they're clumsy, too. But old lady Johnson was patient and they figured if an eighty-year-old woman can remember which fork to eat with, they could, too. After that, the kids cooked dinner and practiced their etiquette. The whole trip was a blast. Wish you and your pretty lady could have joined us," said George, sounding pleased with the results.

"Good," Lenox said, still looking at the receipts from the dude ranch. The exorbitant bills overwhelmed him. He hadn't expected the weekend at the dude ranch to cost nearly ten thousand dollars for fifteen kids.

"George, what is up with this bill? It's way over what we both agreed the trip would cost. This is way overboard," Lenox said, exasperated.

"Oh, yeah, well. Here's the deal. I thought it would be a good idea that the kids took some of the optionals. Like the canoeing, the horse race, and the sailing. You would think a dude ranch would offer nothing but horses, but there are other things to do." George frowned, not understanding Lenox's concern.

"I know what they have at dude ranches. But we agreed that it was just horseback riding lessons for the weekend. Who approved these optionals?" Lenox asked, holding the papers up at George.

"I approved them. You know, you're not the easiest person to get a hold of," George said in his own defense.

"Then you can call Farah. She'll then get in touch with me. I've told you that before." Lenox looked at the bill again. "Who the hell ordered a lobster dinner?"

"Come on, Ox. It was one lobster dinner Saturday night. Some of those kids haven't had lobster in their lives."

"I know what you're saying, but we're not running a resort here for these kids. We have to keep the budget tight and stay focused. I'm pretty disappointed, man. I count on you to look after these things." Lenox shook his head at George. "This can't happen again."

"I guess I get a little excited when I see the smiles on their faces. I'm sorry." George took his file folder and left with his head down.

Lenox called Nicole when George closed the door. He asked her to plan the summer Lyncs trip to St.-Tropez in the next two weeks. There was already a fund set up for these types of things, so collecting money from people was not an issue. He knew Farah would be excited about St.-Tropez. Just when he was about to call her, his cell phone rang.

"How about snow crab legs tonight?" Farah asked when he picked it up. She was cooking a special dinner for the two of them. He wanted to stay at the Life House late, but he loved snow crab legs.

♥

When Lenox got home that evening, his apartment smelled like cooked food. When he walked in the kitchen, all the pots were cooking on high with the fire turned all the way up. He remembered Elsa saying that was a sign of a bad cook. He thought it was just a symptom of Farah's impatient personality. Farah looked as good as the food smelled, standing by the stove in three-inch heels stirring the gravy. She had on a short purple night dress that kissed every curve of her slim frame.

She smiled when she saw him and gave him a full wet kiss, the kind he always waited to get from her at the end of the day. "I was just heating the gravy, but everything is done. You want potatoes or rice?" she asked as she held the pot open. Lenox placed the bottle of Rioja he'd bought in the refrigerator and opened the pots on the stove. However the kitchen was spotless.

"Give me everything." Lenox eyed the crab legs, greens, rice pilaf, mashed potatoes, and smelled something baking in the oven.

As she heaped their plates, Lenox took off his shoes and loosened up in the living room.

"Baby! We're having dinner in the dining room tonight," she yelled from across the kitchen.

He heard the clicking of her heels as she entered the living room and he eyed her outfit again. "Where'd you find this little number?" he asked, mischievously slapping her backside.

She turned around with her mouth open. "This is La Perla. You picked it out for me when we were in the Village together last weekend," she said, her head tilted to the side. "You do remember?"

"I buy you a lot of things, baby. I can't remember them all," he said, stroking her thigh.

She heaved a sigh. "Come on, let's go eat," she said, grabbing his hand and pulling him to the table.

"I bet you never knew I could get down in the kitchen, too," Farah said as Lenox picked up a snow crab leg. She remembered how he liked them. Or at least remembered what he said when they had them at the South Street Seaport.

"Everything looks too good to eat," he managed to say as he ate his crab leg. He then opened the bottle of Rioja and poured them each a glass as he watched Farah gnaw on a crab leg.

"I'm planning a Lyncs trip to St.-Tropez. Think you'd be interesting in joining us?" He asked.

"St.-Trop?! Wow, pretty good choice. I would love to go back to France. Especially with *you*."

"Well, it's in two weeks," he said, sniffing the wine. "We'll probably do a week out there or something. Depending what Nicole can work out with the travel agent."

"Let me take care of planning St.-Tropez. I've always wanted to go there. I went to France, but didn't get past Paris."

"Nicole already started planning," Lenox said, drinking his wine.

"I really want to plan it, Lenox. I promise it will be fabulous. Just say yes." He didn't respond. "You know I find Nicole to be unprofessional and lacking in social skills. When I got to Spa the other night, she seemed to barely be handling things."

He flashed a quick smile at her. "I'll see."

Farah thought it was a good time to change the subject. "So, any *Rise and Shine* news? My agent said something about them canceling the reformatting of *Rise and Shine*? He said they're having a ratings problem since *Good Morning America* hired that young female anchor."

"That's just a rumor. I haven't been told about anything being definitely canceled. Plus, I don't feel like discussing that now," Lenox said, falling in love with the mashed potatoes.

"Remember we talked about me having a 'major' role in any new programming? And that will count as new *if* they are reformatting it! You still are looking into me getting on that?"

"I'll see what happens. I'm not in charge of programming, but I can and have told Aunt Joan what to do with you."

"It'll probably happen a lot quicker this way anyway. I know for sure Ms. Meyers is the one who handpicks talent. She sure as hell kept me on the *News at Six* unusually long while the other female anchors moved on to bigger shows."

"Did it occur to you I have other business I need to take care of, besides getting you a promotion? Plus, I need to talk to Aunt Joan. We both should talk to Joan. It's not going to happen overnight."

"Do you have an idea?" Farah asked.

He just wanted a relaxing evening with his girlfriend, but he was losing his appetite and patience. "What is this? Some type of business meeting or dinner?! What else do you want to know? Or need?" Everyone always needed something.

"I was just trying to start some small talk, baby. That's it." She reached over and touched his wrist. "Did something happen today at the Life House?"

He thought about telling her about George, but he resisted. And she didn't ask twice. They ate the rest of their dinner in silence.

Lenox took a quick shower. When he got out, he heard his cell phone ringing. Then it stopped.

By the time he got out to the living room, Farah had the phone in her hand. She was saying "hello" repeatedly into the mouthpiece.

"I was going to take a message," she said as he went up behind her and snatched it away, but the person had already hung up.

He went into the bedroom with the phone and slammed the door. Farah took off one of her shoes and threw it against the door. She yelled something behind him that he couldn't understand.

He brought up his list of received calls and stopped when he came across the last number.

"How are you?" Lenox asked, happy to hear from Maritza.

"Did I call at a bad time before? A woman picked up and said you were busy. But she was nasty about it."

"Yeah, I was in the shower," Lenox said, and reached for a toothpick on the nightstand. "So I may be in France soon. St.-Tropez."

"I heard. I'll be back from Holland during that time. I can meet you," she said in her sweet French accent, which tickled Lenox.

"I was hoping you would since we didn't exactly plan this. But listen, we'll have to talk tomorrow," he said, alarmed at the crashing sounds he was hearing in the kitchen. It sounded like dishes breaking to him. Maritza agreed.

He hurried into the kitchen. "What the hell is going on?" He looked down at a shattered plate and a broken bottle of Rioja on the tiles. Farah's clothes were all wet as she stood at the edge of the sink.

Lenox grabbed her by her arm. "What are you, fucking crazy? You haven't paid for shit in here to go tearing up my place! You gotta start cleaning this shit up." She abruptly pulled her arm out of his.

He grabbed her arm again. "When are you going to start talking to me like I'm your man? Instead of hounding me about your damn career every time we sit down?"

"Don't try to flip this over on me! You think I'm blind. Everywhere I look or turn, there's somebody or some woman asking for you." Farah voice was firm and loud. She refused to let one tear fall.

Lenox stood confused, because from what he knew, she'd never caught him with another woman. In all his years, Lenox still hadn't figured out how women knew these things.

"I should have known from that first night we were at Lotus

and you were all up in that girl Mona's face. It was embarrassing. Everyone was watching you. While I was there!" she yelled. "And who were you just talking to on the phone?" she asked breathlessly.

"Look, calm down," he said, lowering his voice. He approached her and put his hands on her trembling shoulder.

"Who was it?!" she yelled.

"Shut the fuck up!" Lenox exploded. He didn't want to make things worse, but he felt as if he was starting to lose it.

Farah sat down at the table. "I don't know how I can deal with you about other women. Whoever called was blowing kisses on the phone. That is downright disrespectful to me."

Lenox grabbed the keys to the car and decided to go for a ride. "Look, I want that cleaned up. Those are imported ceramic tiles in there."

He drove around for about an hour. He needed to vent. His mother never asked his father any questions like that. Being with other women was just sex, nothing personal. If only women understood that and stopped reading those bullshit women's magazines, he thought. He believed variety was the spice that saved his own parents' marriage. If his father hadn't had a chance to roam, he would have left. At least that's what he told him. His father roamed, but came home every night. Lenox respected his mother for seeing the importance in that. Farah's reaction and her constant focus on her career instead of him made him look forward more to seeing Maritza.

Farah was asleep when Lenox got back home. The kitchen floor was spotless and so was the sink. Lenox was sure Luisa would probably clean it all over again anyway.

Lenox lay down next to her. He wanted to touch her. But he didn't. Instead, he savored the quietness of the night, until he drifted off to sleep.

Lenox was running from people with no faces. A group of men and women chased him until he climbed a fence. But the fence got shorter and shorter, making escape impossible. The group jumped over and chased him to the end of a dead-end street. He looked up and saw the Life House on fire. Then schoolchildren joined the group. Everyone jumped on him, some punching him. He started fighting. He heard gunshots. Then everything faded.

He sat up in bed drenched with sweat. His gold chain felt stuck to his wet throat. "Catch your breath, baby," he heard the voice in the background say. Farah wiped his face, but he knocked her hand away. Her one hand felt like dozens of hands. Farah's voice sounder clearer, more distinct. "Catch your breath, baby." He threw his head back on the pillow and tried to breathe. "Go back to sleep," he heard her say. She gave him a kiss on the check and put her arms around him.

He felt suffocated. Lenox got up from the bed. He picked up a stack of documents on the nightstand and knocked over a full glass of water. Farah looked at him in bewilderment as he walked out of the room. He just needed some space to breathe.

He turned his laptop on in the living room and sat down to do some work. He stayed up for the next three hours with a headache, paperwork, and a bottle of Hennessey.

♥

Farah used their fight a few nights earlier to finally convince Lenox to let her arrange the entire excursion to St.-Tropez. His guilt made him agree. Nicole was left to do the mailing of the itineraries. Lenox did nothing but pack. He arranged for Maritza to meet him in St.-Tropez. He booked her a room at La Grande Belle, where the group would be. He didn't think it was a big deal to put her in the same hotel as he and Farah were staying. He felt the easiest way to let a woman know you were cheating was to hide it from her. He knew that he couldn't do anything too out of the ordinary because Farah was always one step ahead of him, and never behind.

When they landed in St.-Tropez, the day couldn't have been more perfect. It reminded Lenox of the last time he was there. The consortium of outdoor cafés where people hoped to be seen and the huge yachts lined up in the port was a scene out of an old French movie.

When Lenox walked into their suite, it was exactly like the one he stayed in before. It had a Jacuzzi, living room, two bathrooms, minibar, patio sofa beds, and a complete, underused kitchen. The master bedroom had a soothing view of the little white boats at the dock and shimmering turquoise water. It didn't matter to Lenox about what kind of room they had, but since Farah had her hands in everything she insisted that they get the nicest suite in the hotel.

Lenox stood by the bedroom window and watched the promenade filled with artists with little market stalls and local fisherman selling their new catch.

Farah was unpacking her bikini from the bag, bobbing her head to a hip-hop tune that was coming from one of the yachts below.

"Sounds like some of us are out there already," Lenox said, still by the window. Farah walked up to him wearing a thong bikini and no bra.

"Can you help me put this on?" she asked, holding up the stringy material.

He pulled the curtains and went over to her. "You don't need to put anything else on." He took his thumb and moved the thong string to the side.

She bent over the love seat and pulled her thong down. He could see from the wetness between her thighs that she was ready. He entered her with a force that nearly made her hit her head on the wall. She placed her hands against it as she pushed back. He grabbed her by her hips. She pushed back harder. He reached for her shoulders and pulled her toward him. She rotated her hips until he found her spot. She began to moan so loud, Lenox joined her. He pulled her hair into a bun and squeezed it tight as he came.

It was a quickie. When they were done, Farah's thong was now hanging off her ankle. She laughed and threw it at him.

"Are we just gonna sit around all day?" she asked. She got up and reached for her guidebook. He didn't even know they made guidebooks for St.-Tropez.

Lenox had very little energy left in him. He had come twice in an hour (the first time was on the plane, when she jerked him off under the airline blanket). All he wanted was some sleep and one of those sandwiches from the café downstairs. Lenox knew he had a long night ahead and needed the rest.

They took a shower together, and headed outdoors where the salt water gave the air a crisp, fresh smell. Lenox's head was beginning to throb as he thought about the interior decorator and whether she would be finished before he got back. And that Alex would be able to finish the Channel 7 contracts without him. And that Seht missed his plane to St.-Tropez. Hopefully he caught another one.

Farah stopped by an ice-cream stand for a sundae with 'extra' chocolate sauce. When they got to the beach, it seemed as though they were the last ones to arrive. James, Nicole, Derrick, and everyone else was out there. Farah and Lenox had to squeeze in between a couple who were lying naked beside each other. The woman, who was speaking in Italian, showed no inhibitions, lay on her back as she spread her legs. Farah gave Lenox a shove when she saw him looking.

Twisting up her face as if she smelled something bad, she said, "I don't think I can sit here and watch people turn red under the sun. Look at that," she said, pointing to a fat man in a thong strolling by. "He looks like a fried pork chop!" Some people turned around to look at her.

There wasn't enough room to spread out their blankets, so Farah used the hotel towels. Lenox sat down and opened a can of beer.

"Let's go in the water. I'll race you." She got up and shook sand off her thighs. "Come on," she pleaded, pulling on him.

"I have some calls I have to make about tonight. Go ahead. Look," Lenox said, pointing to a few people they knew in the water, "Go have some fun. I'll meet up with you."

"I hate that bitch Nicole." Farah looked at Nicole and Derrick in the water. "Have you talked to her?"

Lenox glanced around and spotted Maritza sunbathing with two of her friends. Their eyes met, which said they'd meet later.

"Lenox?"

He looked back up at Farah standing in front of him in her graffiti-print bikini. He got the feeling that Maritza would be a welcome distraction during this trip.

"I was looking for James. I'll be there in a few," he said. He watched Farah step over person after person on her way to the blue foamy water. She was such a beautiful woman, he thought. It was something that helped keep his temper down in those heated moments.

Lenox gave Maritza a wink in her direction. She threw Lenox a kiss as she rested on her elbows. Her breasts were hanging loosely but covered by the towel underneath. Before he could indulge any further, Nicole walked up.

"You mind walking with me to get some sodas?" She wore a plain purple bikini bottom and a matching bra top.

"Where's Derrick?" Lenox asked, squinting against the sun's glare.

"He said he had to go back to change his swim trunks. Ever since he's lost weight, he think he's hot shit now," she complained.

"I need to talk to you for a minute, Nicole."

"All right. What is it?" she asked, taking Farah's spot on the towel.

Lenox watched Maritza in the water wetting her hair. She was standing just a few feet away from Farah. He and Farah saw each other and they waved.

"I don't know how you can stomach that girl. She's so manipulative. I can't believe you let her plan this trip. I could have gotten us at Le Meridian by the coast. This place is saturated with tourists," she said, looking around.

"How would you like a job at HBO, doing publicity for their

original-series department?" Lenox didn't want to get her started with complaints.

"You know how I feel about working for those big corporations, where I have to take orders and push all kinds of paper," she said. "That's why I like working for you. You let me make my own decisions. You also inspire me to have my own business one day."

Lenox felt a jolt of surprise. He'd never thought he was an inspiration to anyone, besides the kids at the Life House. It made it harder for him to tell her what he wanted to say.

"Thank you. But the reason I'm asking is that I'm thinking about changing some things. And I may not be doing these parties and events anymore. I just want to make sure you have a job. So what do you think about HBO?"

"Are you firing me?" she finally asked. "Or is Farah?"

"It's me. Not that I don't think your party planning expertise is important, but Farah could do that for me and I don't have to pay her."

She looked at Lenox shocked. "*You're* firing me?!"

"We've been doing this for like three years now. You gotta move on anyway," Lenox said. He didn't feel good about just firing Nicole. Giving her another job offer was the best he could think of. "A high-profile position like this at HBO would take people years to get to. They'd at least need agency experience. And you can skip all that with one phone call from me."

She still didn't respond.

"At eighty thousand dollars a year?" Lenox made sure she heard that.

Suddenly she looked intrigued. "My own office?"

"Your own office. Your own window. Your own stationery," Lenox said, counting on his fingers. "So it's a deal?" Lenox put out his hand for her to shake.

Instead, she gave him a peck on the corner of his mouth. "You know how to take care of a woman," she said, then got up.

Lenox looked up and saw Farah walking toward him, dripping wet and already a shade darker from the sun.

"What was that about?" Farah asked, picking up her towel. "Were you firing her or giving her a raise?" She started toweling her hair.

"Both. I got her a gig at HBO. Listen, find James for me. We need to confirm the jet for tonight to the villa. And he has to arrange the bottle service for at least one hundred people," he said. "I've been calling his cell, but it's off."

"Okay, okay. I'll find him." Farah put on a matching tank top to her bikini and made her way back to the hotel. Lenox knew James was probably sleeping to gain his energy for the night. Something he should have done, he thought.

His cell rang with Maritza on the other end. As they talked, Lenox could see her in the same spot she was in earlier.

"So that's how you like them now? Big breasted with wild hair," she said.

He grinned. "She's only wild in bed, like you."

"When can I show you my wild side again?" she asked, her voice low and sultry.

Lenox watched her lick her shiny, lacquered lips.

"Tonight. We'll be at Le Savoy, the villa on the bay. You can get on the helicopter with the second group." His dick hardened just thinking about getting his hands on her later.

"Ditch the girlfriend . . . unless she wants to join us."

"Farah's not into that threesome thing and she's very territorial," Lenox said, thinking that the idea would have been good with someone else.

"I saw Seht. He's around here somewhere. I think he's looking for you."

Lenox sighed. "I don't think I can handle both you and Seht without at some point ending up in jail this weekend. Just make sure I get you before he does." Lenox was aware that she and Seht had slept together several times before. But they were all open about that. However, Seht and Lenox didn't share exact details about what Maritza was like. Lenox, like most men, liked to believe women yell and scream a particular way because of something they are doing, not for just anyone.

They hung up after making plans for late that night. Before Lenox could finish his second beer, Farah came back with James. He confirmed with Lenox that everything was arranged for the night and went off about his business on the beach.

Farah cozied up next to Lenox, letting her long hair strands mix with the short fine hairs on his chest. He zoned out all the techno music and European accents as he listened to Farah steadily hum to the music on her CD player. It sounded like a Dinah Washington tune, his favorite jazz singer.

After a quick nap, they hit the water together. They must have stayed in the water for hours jet skiing and just being silly. Farah had more energy than any other woman Lenox had been with. They were like two bubbly teenagers. In the water, Lenox got a little frisky and Farah ended up losing her bikini top. Lenox was glad that she was definitely blessed. The peaches and grapes walking around were no comparison to her cantaloupes.

Night fell on the beach. It left Farah and Lenox and a few other couples under the bright lights of the clubs and restaurants getting ready to open. They got back to the hotel, and slept until it was time to board the helicopter for Le Savoy.

♥

Lenox had reserved Le Savoy for the Lyncs only. It was a wide-open space that offered a variety of different environments and nooks for those private moments. Though the party was for the Lyncs, some uninvited but welcomed visitors from nearby villas stopped by. There were mostly young chic Parisians, who seemed to relish being part of a hip black party. Farah and Lenox lounged around in the chamber room, which was already filled with some guests, including Seht.

"Can you believe that one of those white French chicks just asked me if I was Puff Daddy?" he said to Lenox, sounding pleased with himself. Seht had a permanent, gaping mouth, like Puffy, which showed his plentiful teeth, and with his shades on it was hard to tell the difference.

"Yeah, I can. To them any black man with enough money to come here has to be Puffy Daddy," said Lenox, eating a sardine. "What did you say?"

"I said, 'Mo' Money, Mo' Problems,'" Seht said, laughing. His eyebrows were thick and connected in the middle. When he smiled, he looked like the devil incarnate. "She's standing at the bar right now waiting for me."

They all waved at the French girl wearing a white bodysuit and neckline that led to her waist. Her hair was long and jet black and covered both her nearly exposed breasts.

"I see your type hasn't changed at all." Lenox put his arm around Farah's shoulders. "I want you to meet Farah, *my* type of woman."

"The pleasure is all mine." Seht took her hand and gave it a kiss. His eyes slid down her body in its little black see-through dress. She looked edible and she knew it.

Lenox saw in Farah's eyes that she was uneasy with Seht's flirting.

"So nice to finally meet you," Farah said, pulling her hand away from him.

"I've been in D.C. for months working with Senator Taylor. You do know him? He's the Republican from Alabama."

"Yeah, I sure do. I think we did a story on him—"

"For the Republican fund-raising party at the Waldorf in New York. I know, I was at the party," he said, his eyes glued to Farah's thighs.

"Well, I'll let you and Lenox talk your guy stuff," she said.

"Don't go too far. I got a little medicine for later," Seht said, reaching in his pockets. He looked at Farah to see if she knew what he was referring to.

Lenox gave Seht a sharp glance and waited until Farah wandered to the other end of the room.

"The only thing Farah knows about coke is the drink," he told him. "Don't show that stuff around her. I don't feel like hearing her nagging tonight. She can ruin a wet dream when she wants to."

Seht grimaced. "Why bring a woman to St.-Tropez? I mean, she's fine and everything, but . . ." Seht looked at Farah sitting awkwardly by the door. He stopped before he said the wrong thing.

"I got my hands full tonight and I'm not interested in any more than that. Sorry, man," Lenox said.

"Fine," Seht said, and danced his way to the bar where the French girl was still waiting.

"What are you two planning?" Farah asked when Lenox walked back to her. She looked in Seht's direction. "I can tell that man is about no good."

"Don't worry about Seht. You should be worrying about mingling, talking to folks, and making sure people are taken care of," Lenox reminded her. He held her body close to him and kissed her forehead.

She backed up. "I hate it when you kiss me on the forehead like I'm some little girl."

"Okay." He kissed her on the lips. "How's that?"

"You know, I came here to have a good time like everyone else. But now you want me to disappear into the crowd."

Lenox closed his eyes and inhaled. Farah was beginning to suck his energy. He ordered some drinks for the two of them. He wanted Farah to have a good time, too, but he wasn't in a "people" mood. Schmoozing and grinning was something he hated. And he knew Farah was used to that at work, talking about endless stories she probably cared nothing about. As they waited for the drinks, he said, "Baby, you're a lot better than me when it comes to dealing with folks. If anybody needs me, come get me." Lenox read the look of surprise on his face. He never admitted she was better at anything than him.

"All right, all right." Her cheeks relaxed and the air around them lightened. "I'm going to talk to Darius and Michele. They're sitting by themselves, and I'll check with James." She stopped as if she was trying to think of what else to do. "And I'll see if I can get that DJ to play some DMX in here!"

"Good, I'll be around. You'll find me." He kissed the place between her eyes.

Lenox watched as Farah glided around the room just as Maritza walked in. His pulse raced when he saw her petite frame showed off in a tight stretch dress that showed nothing but legs.

Without asking any questions, she sat right down next to him. Lenox acted as though he didn't notice. He didn't want to catch Farah's attention, but if he did, he knew exactly what lie to come up with. Then Maritza whispered something dirty in his ear and he had to smile at her.

"You like the dress you bought? It looks good on me," she said, crossing her legs.

"It's nice," Lenox said, not keeping his eyes on her thighs too long. His headache was coming back. He finished his drink, as he needed something to loosen him up. He was unusually tense. Lenox didn't even look in Farah's direction, but he felt her glances. Any other man's impulse would have been to sneak away with Maritza, but he didn't want to feel that Farah was chasing him away.

Maritza didn't seem to notice. She kept on whispering nasty scenarios in his ear. "I want to suck you so bad. I played with myself in the tub tonight. Just thinking about seeing you again." She kept moving closer until she ultimately sat on his lap. Her seductive, sleepy eyes scanned his face. Lenox looked to see if Farah was still in the room, but she was gone.

Maritza ran her delicate, painted fingers along his goatee. "I miss that Jamaican yagga-yagga fuck you give me. You make it hurt. These European men are too good to me in bed."

Lenox forced a smile. Then a song came on and threw the club into a loud roar.

Then she went on to her second-favorite subject. She reached into his pocket, and asked, "You have any candy? I know Seht has some. He better not have any of that Spanish tutti-frutti shit like last time," Maritza said, looking at the crowd in the next room. Her French accent made "shit" sound more like "chip."

Lenox got Seht's attention and called him over. His French friend followed him.

Seht placed the weed-and-coke mixture in a piece of rolling paper. Lenox took out his share and rolled it up, as Maritza and Seht's friend did the same. They burned the end of the joints and got higher with each inhalation.

There were tables everywhere doing the same thing, some snorting coke and popping ecstasy out in the open. But Lenox wasn't into hallucinogens like ecstasy. He just needed something to quiet the chatter in his head.

Lenox's headache was easing away, and he was feeling a rush. Doing this reminded him of what Seht and he used to do back in college. But now he wanted to get high to escape, even if for a few moments.

The night was getting louder as more people arrived. Flickering lights danced over the outlines of the faceless. Now and again, they passed over opened mouths of laughter and grins. Some revelers danced by and spilled their drinks to get to the dance area. Lenox could define every note of each instrument being played. He was immersed in his high.

"Ox!" Maritza called out. "Come on, I want to do all those things I said. I just want to go off!" she pleaded. Maritza got on top of the table and started doing a striptease and lifted up her dress. He looked up and he could see her thin panties. Seht was busy searching the French girl's mouth with his tongue.

Maritza kneeled down and tried to pull his shirt open with her teeth. The heat of the club was getting to Lenox, as he began to sweat. He took out a white handkerchief from his back pocket and wiped his forehead. As he was wiping, Maritza was kissing him.

Lenox took her to the bedroom upstairs. The thought of bumping into Farah and seeing the look on her face slightly excited him. His heart was beating so fast it became one with the music. He shut the door and kept the lights off. He pulled Maritza's dress up and let his linen pants fall to his ankles. Maritza was so wet she made it difficult for him to last inside her. She hiked one leg up on the bed and reached underneath to play with his balls. The sex wasn't the same as he had with Farah. It felt different, cold, mechanical. But he had no room for sentiment.

"Lenox! Lenox!" he heard a woman's voice call from far away. He pushed deeper inside Maritza with Farah's image coming into his mind. High or not he couldn't shake his nagging conscience. He heard the woman call his name again. Then the voice faded.

When Maritza bent over to touch her toes, Lenox came—finally.

Anxious and out of breath, Lenox quickly put on his pants and Maritza pulled her dress over her head. She pressed her lips against his as she asked for some more. But he gave her some money to spend on drinks for her and her friends, knowing that would keep her busy for a while. She walked down the stairs first.

A few minutes later, he followed. He saw Farah standing alone by the food table. He walked up to her from behind and surprised her.

She turned around with her eyes piercing him.

"I was looking for you. Where were you?" she asked.

"I just came back from the bathroom. There was a little line," he wiped his forehead.

Farah gave him a hard look.

"I was using the bathroom," Lenox said, looking down on her. He didn't know how else to explain it. He just wanted to be close to her suddenly.

"Well, you don't look the same. Look at you! You're sweating like you're high on coke or something," she said, both hands on her hips.

"What are you saying? You sound like you're high on bullshit." The pitch in his voice grew uncomfortably loud. It was beyond him why she would assume the worst thing. But it was the last thing he wanted to admit.

She stood there chewing on her thumbnail, which she unconsciously did when she was studying something.

His nose began to itch a bit so he wiped the sides. She was making him nervous with her interrogation.

"What's up with your nose? Allergies?"

"I guess. Maybe it's all the greenery around. I have some sinus spray at the hotel," he said, shaking his pockets for his room key.

"Lenox, everybody here is high on something, except me. You're either high on coke or drunk off Hennessey. Or damn both!" She kept rambling, but her voice was fading as the music played.

"Are you listening to me?" She stepped back to let some people walk in between them.

His head was starting to throb again. "*You know* I like my Hennessey," he said dramatically, wiping his face again. "You want a drink? Let's go by the bar and relax." He hoped a drink would make Farah drop her charges.

She reluctantly agreed. They moved to one of the bars and squeezed next to a wrinkly old French man in a tank top and booty huggers. Farah and Lenox looked at each other. "Only in St.-Tropez," they said.

Lenox got himself a Hennessey and her a gin and tonic. He was on the last run of his high, but still feeling nice.

Playing with the straw in her drink, Farah broke her silence. "We haven't danced all night. That was why I was looking for you," she admitted in a sad tone.

"I thought you'd never ask," he said, grabbing her hand. They both left their drinks on the bar. A New York favorite was playing and seemed to bring the whole club onto the floor, even the old man. They found a small space near the chamber room to dance. Farah put her hands on her knees and did the booty dance Lenox liked. He loved the way she danced. She used every part of her body and teasingly put her fingers in her mouth. He held her by her head and ran his fingers down her back. He kissed her and sucked on her bottom lip. The fact that he just kissed another woman about fifteen minutes ago aroused him. He was getting hot, but this time it wasn't the coke.

"You want to go upstairs?" she whispered in his ear. Her hot breath sent chills down his leg. She flicked his lobes with her tongue.

Lenox saw Seht with the French girl and some of her friends. Seht gave him a nod and raised his drink in salute when he saw him. It looked to Lenox as if they were all going to end up in bed next.

Between dance moves, Farah tugged Lenox's arm. "You want to go?"

Lenox still hadn't seen Maritza. He wanted to meet with her again later.

"Not yet. The party is down here, unless you want to go back to the hotel."

"*Not yet*," she said, pinching his ear.

They stayed on the dance floor for about another three songs, and then Lenox wandered about. Farah stayed dancing with James and a few other people who gathered around. Everywhere he turned, there was someone he knew patting him on the back. He couldn't even recognize people's faces. Brianna and her husband were there and he politely talked to them for a while. By now, his high had deflated, and he wanted to be left alone.

Lenox was exhausted. The music was sounding like the same tune over and over. He sat outside to get some air.

"Let's run away to the room again," he heard Maritza say behind him.

She sat down next to him on the wooden bench. Outside was crowded, almost as bad as it was inside. People were smoking, sitting on cars, and some coming back drenched from a night swim.

Lenox watched Maritza kick off her heels and light a cigarette. She placed it between her glossy lips. A light breeze came through and knocked it out of her hand.

She lit another one, and asked, "Where's the girlfriend?"

"She's still inside, waiting for me. I just need a break," Lenox said, with both hands in his pockets. He looked at Maritza's tanned legs stretched in front of her. Lenox let his eyes take him from her painted toes to her round hips.

She read his mind, and rubbed his leg. Maritza offered Lenox an excitement that Farah was starting to lose.

"If I was her, I'd be giving you a blow job in some dark corner, taking care of those needs," she said, touching the bulge between his legs. "We only have a short time together," she whined.

Lenox reached in his pocket and took out his wallet. "Do you need any more money?"

"Yeah, for tomorrow and the next day. I do plan to buy more than drinks in St.-Tropez," she said, shamelessly putting out her hand. Lenox gave her a few hundred dollars.

She took a strong pull from her cigarette as she counted the crispy bills. She usually smoked after her high faded. She thought it made her coming down a lot easier to handle.

Lenox said, "We can meet later. Like seven A.M. I've already given up trying to get any rest."

She laughed with her sleepy eyes brightening. "Who sleeps in St.-Tropez any old ways?" Then she stubbed out her cigarette.

Lenox walked back inside to the chamber room. Finding Farah was easy, since she was sitting in between a row of people. She was telling a story and had everyone engaged. She was animated, using her hands to emphasize whatever point she was making.

"Baby, remember the time I was telling you about what happened when I was on air? When I was reading and the teleprompter blanked and I had the wrong script!?" she asked.

He forgot, but he told her he remembered.

"Brianna says she saw that show!" Farah yelped.

Everyone started talking at once about how Farah did such a great job. How she had a way with words. Lenox just sat there and agreed. But he gave her a cue.

"Okay, I guess we're ready to go. I'll see you all tomorrow." She reached for the new Fendi clutch he had brought her from his last trip to Holland.

"Good night, everyone." Lenox shook some hands and tried to get to all the folks sitting around. On their way out, Seht whispered something in his ear about a ménage à trois with the French girl.

As Farah and Lenox left, they passed Maritza sitting by the bar. She reached out and touched Lenox's back as he passed. Lenox didn't know if Farah noticed as she was walking beside him.

When they got to the room, Lenox headed straight for the bathroom, without saying a word. He stripped, turned on the showerhead, and let the cool water beat down on him.

He yelled at Farah to bring him a towel.

"Why did you just rush like that to take a shower?" she asked, setting the towel on the rack. "We usually take one together."

"I was just sweating so much in that place. I felt dirty," he said, still in the shower. But really, he didn't want to have sex with Farah while Maritza was still on his dick. He did respect Farah as his woman.

Before he could get out, Farah got in. She playfully pushed him against the shower wall away from the running water. He knew she was about to pull a trick for him out of the bag.

She got down on all fours and started kissing the length of his legs. She took her hands and held them around his thighs. Using her tongue, she formed little circles around the back of his legs. She then let her tongue slip inside his ass, and nibbled at his balls.

She switched to the front, still on her knees. The water was coming down on both of them, and stuck Farah's wavy hair to her face.

With his hardness standing at attention, she opened her mouth and used her tongue to caress his dick with its warmth. She sucked him into her mouth as far as possible. Lenox leaned against the shower wall, and watched her head move up and down, up and down. He guided her head as she got more intense. Then the muscles in his legs stiffened, and she knew it was almost time. Lenox backed away a little, but she moved forward with him still in her mouth. Then she started sucking him harder. Lenox came with enough strength to bring him to his knees. He was pleasantly surprised that Farah didn't flinch the way she usually did when he came. His juices still lingered on her lips. That morning, she surrendered her inhibitions.

Later on, Lenox joined Maritza in her bed.

*L*enox and Farah had a huge argument before they got on the plane about his disappearing acts in France. When they got off the plane, she and Lenox took separate cars. Farah was going to the apartment, while Lenox went to the office. Farah suspected he was cheating on her on the trip. Half the condoms they brought with them were missing. He was being outright about his affairs. Farah still didn't know who he was running around with because he had been so good at cleaning up after himself.

When she walked in the apartment, she went straight to the bedroom and threw herself on the bed, without bothering to undress or unpack. How much longer could she put up with this? she thought to herself. The nightmares, the temper, the cheating, his discomfort around people were all becoming too much for her. She didn't know what was coming next. She wondered how much of this situation she had created.

The phone rang.

"Excuse me, but can I speak to Ms. I Got a Man Now and Don't Know Nobody?" asked Lola on the other end.

"What's up, Lo, I just got in." Farah was hoping she'd call back later. Her tears were still stuck in her eyelids.

"How was France?"

"It was interesting," Farah said, not wanting to elaborate.

"I told him," Lola said.

Farah didn't respond.

"He said he knew from the day Arabia was born she wasn't his, but he didn't say anything. He said he loves me to death, but he's had a hard time forgetting."

"No one can forget that. That is asking for a bit much," Farah said, with her eyes closed.

"Anyway, he said he's trying to forgive me . . . but I still don't know."

"Did you ask him again about Marlene and his so-called strange behavior?"

"I did and he asked me how in the hell could he find time for that in his twelve-hour shift." She laughed lightly. "I should have probably known that myself."

"So, good, things are fixed now," Farah said.

"I don't know, though . . . I mean, I had so much fun going out the other night with you. I'm tired of being up in the house all day, doing the same things. I think I want something different, some excitement."

Farah opened her eyes. "Please! Would you just stop the bullshit? As many of us out here trying to get husbands, you want to play games with yours! You have a good man at home! Recognize that."

"Okay." Lola sighed. "What happened with you and Lenox?"

"He's cheating on me and he's practically throwing it in my face. It's like whatever I try to do, it's not enough for him. A few weeks ago, I made him a nice dinner. Something I never do because we always go out to eat. I wore a sexy outfit, cooked snow crab legs, mashed potatoes, and even baked a damn cake. And after all that he got the nerve to take a phone call from another woman and lock himself in the bedroom!"

"You cooked for him? Now, you know your ass must have picked that up from some fancy-ass restaurant and threw it in a pot."

Farah couldn't deny the truth. "Well, he didn't know the difference. He ate it up like it was homemade. I never told him I was Julia Child."

"And what about this chick he was talking to? Who was that?"

"That seems to be the million-dollar question around here." Farah took a deep breath. "When we were in St.-Tropez, he was acting very sneaky. All of a sudden he was breaking out on me at like seven in the morning and coming back at like two in the afternoon!"

"So he was creeping with some French chick down there?"

"I don't know if this woman is part of the Lyncs or what. But if she was I'd know. I do have a feeling it's one woman. And it's even more dangerous when there is just one. And get this!" Farah sat up. "Every time he came back to the suite he would take a shower."

"Red flag! That right there is a dead giveaway."

"Then he'd fall right asleep for the whole afternoon."

"And wherever he was there wasn't much sleeping going on," Lola said. "Why do you put up with it? Chris is my husband and the only father Arabia has known. It's not like you need this guy."

Farah felt cornered. "I *do* need him. Since we've been together my life at work has been a lot easier. I'm certain now that Ms. Meyers won't pass me up for *Rise and Shine*. I'm practically part of the family." She tried to smile. "Plus, I like being somebody's woman. I like being part of a couple."

"But you've gotten so far on your own, why do you *need* his help now?"

"I'm tired of fighting my way up the ladder. Not only do I have a man in my life but he also has an interest in furthering my goals. I can appreciate that and overlook some things. Especially things I cannot prove." Farah shrugged.

Farah stopped for a moment as she thought if she should tell Lola about the coke. She was getting upset all over again as her throat started to tighten.

"But two seconds ago, you were all hot and bothered about him cheating? Are the two of you playing some kind of game? You gotta ask yourself if it's all going to be worth it."

"I can get angry, but doesn't mean I am ready to do anything about it. It's all worth it now. He'll fall out of this shit. Maybe it was the whole vacation thing that got him worked up," Farah said, convincing herself. "People do act funny on vacation."

"And so the denial begins."

Farah huffed. "I just got in from a six-hour flight. Let's talk later. And I'm glad things between you and Chris are cool." They promised to chat later.

Farah listened to her cell phone messages, then decided to go out. She didn't know why she wanted to go. Maybe she'd visit her mother, she thought. She knew once she got back into the office tomorrow, it would be all about work as usual.

Farah got off the 1 train at Seventy-second Street. Most times, she called her mom before she dropped by. Her mother hated surprises, but she didn't feel like calling. The street was brightly lit with the sun casting shadows on the white buildings. She walked quickly, her Louis Vuitton bag bouncing against her hip. It was nearly 11:00 A.M. on a weekday and the streets were teeming. Every other minute, someone's shoulder cut off her path, forcing her to dip in a new direction. She finally made it to the building, and gave Tim, the building doorman, a nod. She hesitated at the concierge desk. She thought about calling before going up. Instead, she greeted the familiar security guards and walked by. She was hoping her mother would be home.

When Oliver opened the door, he smiled and gave her a warm hug.

"Hey, baby! Nice to see you. How was St.-Tropez?" He was clad in a very expensive Ralph Lauren robe. His face was a healthy bronze that highlighted his salt-and-pepper beard.

"It was interesting, to say the least," Farah said. "Never knew so much partying could go on in a town no bigger than a quarter."

"Enjoy it. That's what being young is all about," he said, putting his arm around her shoulders. "Did you bring your boyfriend with you?" Oliver looked behind her.

"He's at work now," Farah said flatly, walking ahead of him into the living room.

Oliver just nodded and called for her mother.

"Oh! I was just taking a nap," Farah's mother said, shuffling into the living room. She gave Farah a light hug and a kiss on the cheek. "Why didn't you call first?" she asked.

"I was in the area," Farah said, hugging and kissing her in return. "I just wanted to stop by. Daughters can do that, can't they?"

"Of course, sweetie. But you know how I hate surprises. And I forgot you were coming back today from St. Thomas."

"It was St.-Tropez." Farah cut her eyes at her mother. They both sat down on the sofa.

"So, how was it?" her mother asked, folding her legs Indian style.

Farah took a drink of the ginger ale Oliver handed her, just to wet her throat. She was still upset, but didn't want to look too obvious. "It was an experience. The food, the weather, everything was well planned," she said.

Her mother blew Oliver a kiss as he disappeared behind the wooden doors leading to the den. He knew Farah needed some private time with her mother.

"Well, what about details? Did you meet any rich European men? Or better yet, any rich European men for me?" she joked.

"Not really." Farah said, already thinking she shouldn't have come here.

"Where's Mr. Society Page? Did he have a good time, too? I thought you would have brought him with you. When am I going to finally meet that man?" she asked. "Did you lose him in France?" She giggled.

"Kind of," Farah said, her shoulders slumping slightly.

"Sweetie, the energy around you is awful. Your mood is blacker than the leather on this couch!" she said, looking at Farah's long face.

"We had a good time, I guess, according to who you ask," Farah muttered. "He's just starting to be a handful. I didn't know where he was half the time on the trip."

Her mother shifted her weight. "It sounds like you're talking about a hyper five-year-old," her mother said knowingly. "Look, men like Lenox are awfully busy. They're always stressed out and even moody. They keep a lot of things to themselves. They need women who are agreeable and are going to be a partner. Not dead weight."

Farah listened patiently. She trusted that her mother was leading up to something big.

"Now, whatever you're thinking about this man, erase it from your mind. If you haven't caught him red-handed, there isn't much you can say without sounding like an old hag. There are women crawling around wanting men like Lenox. These women delight in putting suspicion in the mind of wives and girlfriends. They know suspicion is the first sign of demise of a relationship." She paused to stress her point. Farah just sat there like a lump staring at the painting in front of her.

"The bottom line is 'leave it alone.' I'm sure that man loves you, but may have a funny way of showing it. He is probably trying to make his own space. And as far as him not being attached to your hip, enjoy it! Because once you're married, you'll *wish* they'd go into the corner and play."

"So you're saying, just forget it?" Farah asked, her voice tight.

"Yes, at least for now. It could be all in your head. I mean, I didn't want to say this, but Lenox is a little out of your league." She stopped herself, bringing her hand to her chest. Then she continued. "I don't want to make your insecurity worse. But let's admit it. You both come from different breeds. I went to trade school. His parents went to Ivy League schools. So it could be that you are feeling a bit out of place. Loosen your grip on him, and make a place for yourself. Doing that will make him need you more than the other way around."

"I've been helping him with the Life House. Overseeing the decorating of the new space. I also planned this whole trip to St.-Tropez—"

"Good, good," her mother said excitedly. She took Farah's hand. "That's what you want to do. That's what all these 'society' ladies do. They may not go to work every day, but they use those managerial skills to push the buttons only women of successful men can."

She looked at Farah proudly. "Now, when can I meet him?"

Before she left, Farah's mother got her to promise to bring Lenox over for dinner the next night. She hoped she was free because her mother wasn't taking no as an answer, she thought, as she got on the train to head back to Lenox's apartment. It was times like these that she regretted giving up her apartment.

When she got off the elevator on Lenox's floor, his door was opened. She walked in and heard him on the phone in the den. She could tell from his voice that he was on a business call. He was sitting on his wooden chair, the one he always sat on by the window. She went over to him. He looked back at her with eyes that said what he couldn't.

When he hung up, he announced, "That was Aunt Joan. I mean your 'Ms. Meyers.' "

She stood up. "What did she say?"

Lenox opened the refrigerator door. "There's finally a new for-

mat for *Rise and Shine*. They should be coming up with a launch
date any day."

She waited for more. "Did she say anything about me? Did you
ask her about me?" Farah felt like a schoolgirl at the prom waiting
to be asked to dance.

"We talked about a lot of things. As for now, Katie is still staying
until we work out some contractual issues. She's considering you
for her spot and a two-and-a-half-million-dollar contract. I had to
throw the word "Auntie" in there a few times to get that one," he
said, somewhat smug.

"What! Oh, my God! Wait, is this definite?" Farah was feeling
faint. A spot on *Rise and Shine* and a two-and-a-half-million-dollar
contract?

"Not yet. We still have details to work out. My aunt said she
had a few other anchors to talk to who would also be good for *Rise
and Shine*. Fresh new talent."

Farah started at him. "What are you saying? You told me that
I was a definite shoe-in for that show. No matter what."

"Just don't worry about it, all right? I convinced her that you
are worth the money. But she wants to be fair to the other people
who have been there longer." He guzzled his beer down with fervor.
"It would have taken you years to get this far with my aunt there.
You should be grateful you're even being considered."

"I could have done it on my own. I hope you believe that, too."

"Sure," he said with a smirk. "But a little help from me never
hurt."

Farah just folded her arms and glared at him. *Smug bastard.*

He put the bottle in the trash and walked out. Farah followed
him in to the bedroom.

She came up behind him and slid her hands around his waist.
"Thank you, baby," she whispered. His body relaxed in response
to her hug.

"That's all I wanted to hear—a thank-you." He turned on the
TV. His bags were still unpacked, too. It looked like he started it,

but stopped for some reason. It ran through her mind that maybe a part of him was still in St.-Tropez.

He sat on the bed as he went through some documents in his briefcase. He put on his reading glasses that made him look studious but still sexy. Farah sat there on the edge of the bed admiring all his mannerisms. The way he fastened his papers with individually colored paper clips, each color noting its importance. The way his briefcase stayed organized with pens and pads neatly secured.

She was about to make a move to break his attention and show him how happy she really was. But there was something distant about how he was acting. She thought, at least, they'd go out to celebrate after the news.

Farah rubbed his legs and worked her hands up his sculpted thighs. He had on the striped Calvin Klein boxers she bought him a few weeks ago, dismissing her mother's warning about that. As Farah started planting kisses on his neck, he stopped her. He'd never stopped her advances before. She looked in the mirror to make sure she looked good. She patted her hair down smooth and reapplied her raisin-colored lipstick. She sat there with him and flipped the channels. He excused himself and went into the study.

After an hour of sitting alone in the room, she got restless. She walked into the den, and saw him crumpling paper after paper and throwing it into the trash. She stood there watching the trashcan fill up until he peeked over his shoulder at her.

She ran her fingers across his shoulders and gave him a massage. His neck rolled from side to side as he loosened under her touch. "Let's stop by my mom's house tomorrow evening. I'd like to tell her the good news then." Farah held her breath. He agreed and even offered to bring a bottle of wine. She reminded him that it wasn't a big affair. It was important that he knew that. When she was through explaining, he commenced the tapping on his computer.

♥

As soon as Farah got to her office floor she heard people buzzing about the new *Rise and Shine*. She tried to walk unnoticed to her desk, to catch up on any e-mails or memos about the new change. She actually wasn't sure what she was walking into. All she knew was that Lenox said the co-host job could be hers. *But did anyone else know?* she wondered.

"Good afternoon, Farah. I see the Mediterranean sun worshipped you well," Paul, one of the executive producers, said. Farah blushed and said "Thanks," and kept walking. Her office could not have seemed farther away.

She heard a few folks call out "Welcome back" as she passed the break room. She said her "hellos," but was waiting for more. She seasoned some of her short conversations with small talk before she told them she had lots to do. No one mentioned *Rise and Shine*.

Finally, making it to her office, she closed the door. There was no sign of Sam. Every ten minutes or so, someone would come in and say "Welcome back." She felt good to feel welcomed and missed. She figured no one knew about *Rise and Shine* yet. She just hoped that when the news came about her co-host slot that everyone else would be just as nice. Katie was like the mother hen of the newsroom and had the most seniority. Farah was ready for the couple of sourpusses that would be around.

Farah was gearing up for her 6:00 P.M. newscast when Sam knocked.

"Hi! How was St.-Tropez?!" Sam asked, peeking her head through the slightly opened door.

Farah motioned for her to come in. She told her the fun she had and the great food she ate, but she left out the other details.

Sam just sat there and nodded her head eagerly.

"Have you spoken to Ms. Meyers yet?" Sam asked cautiously. She was sitting with her legs crossed and hands tightly folded.

"No, I'm sure I'll see her this evening. We have to talk anyway," Farah said, studying her pensiveness. She stopped rummaging through her files, and asked, "Is something wrong?"

Sam began reaching for words. "How can I say this without sounding like the bearer of bad news? But your time slot has been changed to the eleven P.M. show."

Farah was practically lost for words.

"Starting tonight," Sam added, with a look of pity in her face. "Ms. Meyers thinks you can help the sagging ratings on the eleven o'clock newscast."

"Please," Farah said, disgusted. "I'm not buying that. Listen, I have to make a call. If you don't mind," she said. Sam apologized again and closed the door behind her.

Lenox's cell phone rang several times before his voice mail picked it up. She called back again. And again. Until he finally answered.

"What kind of games are you playing?" Farah asked.

"Hey, you told me you hated working on the six P.M. show," Lenox said. She could hear phones ringing, which meant he was at work, too.

"I said I hated local news because I wanted to be on *Rise and Shine!* I didn't want my anchor spot changed. Did you tell Ms. Meyers I wanted off the six P.M. show?"

Farah heard him talking to someone over his shoulder. Then there was complete silence in the background. "I don't have time to get into this. My aunt has her own reasons for doing things. If I were you, I'd just ride it out. I just told you earlier they are waiting for a launch date for *Rise and Shine.* Maybe they are just experimenting. Your raise still stands," he said, trying to minimize the issue. Farah still felt something fishy going on.

"Why didn't you tell me this earlier today, when you told me about the contract?" Farah was holding the phone so close to her ear it hurt.

"She said it was something she was thinking about. And I agreed the change would be good for now," Lenox said, sounding as if he really thought he did the right thing.

"Who the hell are you to make changes in my career?" Farah asked, trying to keep her voice low.

"I didn't hear you complain when I told you about that two-and-a-half-million-dollar contract."

He was right. She was fine with everything, up until now. Lenox was up to something and she had little control.

"I start the eleven P.M. show tonight. So what are we going to do about Tuesdays at Eugene's? We just started hosting that together."

He didn't say anything.

Farah continued, "I may not be getting home till after midnight and on football nights, closer to two A.M.! I'm going to be too damn tired to do anything! I've always made sure that I wouldn't get stuck on an eleven o'clock show."

"Listen, we'll talk later. I have a client waiting for me. Just calm down. I have your best interests always in mind. I wouldn't let my girl do anything that would make her look bad. Just believe me on this," he said. Before she could respond, she heard the dial tone.

Farah sat in her chair staring at the clock resting on her file cabinet. It was 5:00. Too early to prepare for the 11:00 P.M. show and too late to go home and cry herself into a nap.

Just when she was becoming absorbed with too many thoughts, Ms. Meyers called.

She sounded nice for a change. "Hello, Farah. Did you enjoy your trip?"

"Yes, I did. Too bad I didn't enjoy my first day back," Farah said. She was still highly strung and ready to give Ms. Meyers a piece of her mind.

Ms. Meyers's tone abruptly changed. "I know Sam told you the news and it's unfortunate you weren't told earlier. You know how this business is. Everything happens overnight."

Before Farah could respond she continued, "Plus, I thought Lenox would have told you sooner because I spoke to him about a week ago concerning this. I called him while you both were in St.-Tropez, about some documents we will need. I asked to speak to you, but he said you were busy."

At this moment, Farah wished she had a glass of wine to ease her nerves. *What documents? What call one week ago?* There were too many questions, and all the wrong answers.

"Oh, yes, I was very busy. Always out and about in St.-Tropez. He may have forgotten to give me the message." Farah tried to be gracious about it. She didn't want to badmouth Lenox to his aunt.

"Well, the eleven P.M. show is great. I'm sure you will be fine. There are a lot of other changes going on at the network and this is just one of them," she said. "I have to run to a meeting. Tell Lenox we'll talk later."

Farah was fed up talking to people who thought they knew more about her life than she did. She reached for the phone to call Lenox again. But she stopped herself. The last thing she wanted him to know was what she was thinking. She still had a job to do, and she wasn't about to lose control of her own future.

Calling him would be doing just that. And there was no game being played that she didn't know the rules to.

♥

The newsroom was bustling with anxiety and last-minute touches to the 11:00 P.M. show. Tired producers were pacing back and forth with their ties loosened and small white boxes of Chinese food in their hands. There were fewer people around at night, but the pressure was even more intense. Since it was the last news show of the day, producers had to scoop up all the day's events and be prepared for breaking new ones. Farah didn't recognize half the people running around and that bothered her.

She sat out in the producer's hub and ate her dinner. She was checking the wires, when thoughts of Lenox having a ball at their event at Eugene's filled her head. He hadn't even called to see how her transition was going. Her paranoia whispered to her that he was probably moving through the crowd like he was a damn star and talking to every gorgeous woman who strutted by. Anytime she was at Eugene's, she brought new faces and made everyone feel at home. She was glad that would be missing tonight.

"Hey, Ms. Washington, I'm your producer, Paul O'Nallie," said a tall, lanky white guy, dressed in a brown suit, with messy blond hair. "Wow, that chicken sure smells nice," he said, leaning over to see her food.

Farah placed the plastic cover over it. "Hi, nice to meet you. Anything I should know about?" she said, dabbing the corners of her mouth with a napkin. She was hoping he'd leave soon before her food got cold.

He responded, with his Australian accent leading the way, "Nah, it's the same ole thing. Just show that beautiful smile of yours and do what you do any other time."

Farah handed him a printout. "Good. Here's an update on that breaking story from earlier. The one about the car accident that injured seven pedestrians in midtown. It just came in."

"Marvelous! We've been following this all day." He stood there reading the update when another producer shouted across the room that they had an update on the same thing.

"Forget it. I've got it over here!" he said, waving it to a red-haired woman who rolled her eyes when she heard him.

"You can lead with this story. It's getting bigger by the hour." He paused and looked at her. She looked at her food.

"Most anchors come up here like prima donnas, waiting to be handed lines to recite. It's refreshing to see someone ready to dive right in." He patted her shoulder and walked off.

Great, she sighed. She wasn't digging for any further information. She went back into her office, to spend some quiet time alone until airtime. She felt that she was being isolated or pushed aside. It was lonely for Farah doing the late show. Sam was gone for the day, and there was no Pete waiting for her on the set. Her pity party came to an end when her name was called on the speaker. She rushed to the set to get prepared. She was taking another popular anchor's place and it was obvious. Her co-anchor, Brad Dunley, came out and politely welcomed her, but kept it short. When Paul asked her through her earphone if she was ready, she couldn't have been more ready. All her anxiety and anger had subsided. She was a little nervous, but knew once she heard the music roll, she'd be fine.

And she was. However, Brad and Farah didn't have the chemistry Scott and she had. Brad's ad libs were corny and rehearsed. It could have been that he was the nervous one, not Farah. She stayed in control and responded with a witty remark or two, to keep things flowing. But she didn't feel like going through this every night.

After the show, Brad called her to the side.

"I'm really sorry for fumbling. I wish we had more time to set up some rapport before air," he said, shifting his feet nervously. He couldn't maintain any eye contact. She wondered what his problem was.

"No worries. I wish I had more time, too. Trust me," she said.

"Great. Have a good night," he said as he went back to his office, a little embarrassed.

Farah left to go to hers, too, and tried calling Lenox again since she wanted to stop by the party. It was ten minutes to midnight and she knew he would still be there. But again, he was not picking up. She decided just to show up and see what the communication failure was all about.

When the cab dropped her off at Eugene's, there was a line as usual. She was exhausted from a full day, but she had to see how things were turning out. She was about as connected to these events as Lenox was. She heard the bouncer tell people he wasn't letting anyone else in. Farah watched as a few familiar faces walked away disgusted. Little by little, the line was starting to disperse.

Farah went up to Clyde, the club's three hundred-pound Asian bouncer. "What's the problem? Some of these people you turned away are here every week," she asked. He and Farah became pretty cool, since she started hosting with Lenox.

"Lenox said that the place is near capacity. It's his orders. By the way, what happened to you tonight?" he asked.

"I have to work late from now on," she said, not wanting to give details. She told him she'd chat with him later, and wearily made her way inside. Her chest was pounding because she didn't know where Lenox was. The last thing she needed today was more surprises.

She was stunned when she walked in. The place was half-empty. It was about two hundred people, to their usual five hundred. It was a Lyncs crowd, but a lot of the new faces she had invited over the last few weeks were missing.

Lenox was talking to the manager when he saw her walk in. He gave her a wink.

She waited for him by their usual table. From the looks of things, the party was still going on. People were swinging their hands and hips to the latest tunes. Some were laid out on the couches holding shimmery Champagne flutes and smoking the best "Cuban" cigars, which were complimentary.

Lenox came over to the table with drinks. He gave her a dry peck on the cheek, then lit his cigar.

"Glad you had the energy to make it tonight," he said, eyeing her straightened hair. He had always liked her waves better.

"Sure you are. You probably had my time changed on purpose," she quipped. She grabbed her glass of cosmopolitan and took a long sip.

"Think what you want. There's no reason for it other than what I told you. And I'm not arguing about this here," he said.

Farah studied the room to see if there were any wandering female eyes in his direction. There weren't.

"Nicole stopped by tonight. She says she loves her new job at HBO." He puffed his cigar smoke into the crowd.

"Yeah, well, that's nice. Sounds like somebody's better off," she shot back.

He pulled out his wallet and gave Farah a few dollars. "Here, why don't you take a cab home? You look tired."

"Another ploy to push me aside? I don't know what you keep looking for, Lenox, but you've found it. You just don't know it yet." She took the money and put it in her purse.

He turned his attention to the folks dancing.

"Face it, you need me in here to double this crowd," she said, getting up.

"I'm at a point now that I have a loyal crowd. A few missing faces is not the end-all. I can open my own spot with the crowd I already have minus *your* friends," he said.

"I'm tired. I'll see you later." She walked out and Clyde hailed a cab for her. Lenox didn't get home till 4:00 that morning. This time, she didn't care enough to argue.

♥

After dawn, she woke up to Lenox talking on the phone in the kitchen. She played as though she was still asleep. She didn't know how Lenox found time to sleep. Perhaps he was still on French time, she joked to herself. By the time her ears could make out what he was saying, the conversation ended. He dressed to leave for work, but Farah watched the time, noting that it was unusually early.

When she climbed out of bed, she read a note he left.

See George at Life House and new space.
Call Tavern on the Green for Friday.
Call me later.

There was a small blue box next to the note. She opened it carefully, hoping it was what every girl wanted. Instead, it was second-best. A Tiffany diamond-studded bracelet set in platinum. She put her hand over her lips as she let out a squeal. The bracelet felt icy as she wrapped it around her wrist.

The ringing phone jolted her from her indulgence.

"It's George! Hey, Farah." George's energy was unwelcome. She wanted to be left alone to lie in bed with her new gift.

"George, I'll be down there in an hour or two. How's everything going?" she asked, sliding into her satin slippers.

"Everything is going as scheduled. The space looks great. I think the interior decorator will be done in a day or two. I was wondering if maybe you can get Lenox to squeeze in some time to come down on Saturday," he asked.

"I'll try, but Lenox has been living under a pile of legal documents. He's at work right now," she said. "But I'm sure he'll try." She promised to stop by and see him later.

After they spoke, she took a shower with her bracelet on. Tonight Lenox was meeting her mom and she wanted to stay calm and collected.

She quickly dressed in vintage jeans and a blouse and slipped into her red stilettos. Her hair air dried back into waves. She called Lenox as soon as she got in the Rover and thanked him for her gift. He made it hard for her to stay angry. When she hung up, she called Tavern on the Green right away. Natalie, their contact there, assured her that their room was set for Friday night. Lenox was having a big soiree for the opening of the Life House's new building and Farah had to make sure everything was tight.

When she arrived at the Life House, she headed straight to the new building. Inside, she took some Polaroids to show Lenox. Everything was immaculate. It looked like a Carnegie Hall for kids, except the feel and colors were much more intimate. Most of her suggestions had been implemented, down to the color of the carpet.

George and Farah talked for almost three hours about activity plans for the Life House. They came up with a talent-show version of *Who Wants to Be a Millionaire?* and named it *Who Wants $3,000?* for opening night. George wanted it to be ten thousand dollars, but Farah thought that amount was ridiculous. He suggested that the seniors headline the talent show since many of them would be going out to college next month. They would do dance segments, skits, poetry, and could do various other performances. The winner was to get three thousand dollars for college. They called Lenox at the office to get his okay on the money, which he gave.

The next stop was her mother's. This time she called first.

As soon as she heard Farah's voice she asked whether Lenox ate pork. Farah told her neither of them did.

"I'm here preparing. Are you coming by now?" she asked, anxiously.

"Yeah, I'm on my way," Farah said, and hung up.

The traffic was thick going back into the city. It was balmy and humid. People were beeping their horns in unison. Farah wanted to disappear, but one look at her bracelet and everything else seemed worthwhile.

About an hour later, she was ringing her mother's bell. Her mother opened the door looking a little stressed.

When Farah walked in her mother had her best Waterford crystal set on the dining room table. Her maid was also there cleaning the bathroom and scrubbing the floors.

Farah gave a fake cough. "Who looks like the insecure one now?" she asked as she looked around. The place looked as if her mother was preparing for the arrival of a prince.

"No time for jokes. I just want everything to be perfect," she said, wiping her finger across the bookshelf for dust. "Remember, he's from good breed. I don't want to make you look bad in any way." Farah felt a little sad about what she said. This was her mother, and as annoying as she was, she had more class than most pretentious people Farah knew.

Carrying an empty tray into the kitchen, Farah's mother quietly observed her. "Your butt looks so big in those jeans. What are you eating?" She twisted up her face.

Farah unconsciously put her hands on her butt. She had gained twelve pounds since she had been with Lenox.

"I haven't been going to the gym like I should be." Farah sucked in her stomach.

She walked over to the couch and sat down. Her mother's constant nagging about her weight was beginning to wear on her.

"You know we Washington women are hippie, so be careful with that. Men like Lenox need elegant women. Women who can fit into a size four dress from a Chanel trunk show." Farah's mother was a size four.

"I've never been a size four. I was a six, now I'm a ten." Farah frowned.

"Then your boobs! It's too much. You don't want to get too big," she warned. "You haven't even had kids yet, for God sakes! If I didn't know better, I'd think you were pregnant."

Her mother always found something to pick on. "Lenox hasn't said one word about my weight. In fact, I think he likes it. Especially when—" Her mother interrupted her.

"Spare me the details, honey," she said.

They looked at each other and laughed.

"Is there anything you want me to do for later?" asked Farah.

Her mother held her hand to her chin and looked around. "No, no, you go, and just get ready." She checked the glass coffee table for streaks.

"Okay, I'm gone," Farah said, grabbing her fringe bag. "See you tonight." She walked herself out and closed the door. As she waited at the elevator, she heard her mother call out to the cleaning lady to clean the coffee table again.

♥

Lenox and Farah arrived at her mom's house right on time. He managed to come home and change and they left together, hand in hand.

Lenox was comfortably dressed in black cashmere sweater and

brown Armani slacks. It made his already dark complexion look warm and powerful. Farah had on the white version of the little black dress with the perfect Christian Louboutin high-heel sandals with the clear straps. But, she reminded herself that this was nothing big.

Farah was nervous as they waited for the door to open to her mother's apartment. Lenox seemed cool and relaxed and kept making fun of Farah's angst. She didn't want to be so obvious, but she was hoping her mother hadn't overdone anything. That would be too obvious.

Farah's mother finally opened the door. And she looked impeccable. She had on a plum-colored silk jumpsuit with a high-waisted gold sash. She looked elegant and regal.

"Welcome! So good to finally see the two of you together," she said, holding her arms open. She gave Farah a quick brush on both cheeks and gave Lenox a juicy kiss on his. Oliver stood to the side and shook Lenox's hand. Immediately, he and Lenox got into a conversation about the Eagles game the previous night.

Farah was still holding her breath and looking around for what her mother had prepared. When they walked into the living room, Farah stopped in her tracks. There were small platters of tiny roasted potatoes and caviar, crab cakes, seared tuna, and a rich chocolate cake drizzled with raspberry glaze.

"Sweetheart, are you okay?" Her mother asked resting her hand on her back. "You seem faint."

"Oh, I'm fine," Farah said, blinking rapidly. "I thought it was just drinks, you know." Lenox and Oliver were already in the living room.

"Come on, now, you really didn't think I was just going to take out a bottle of Asti Spumante and Ritz crackers. Did you?" She looked at Farah as if she was crazy. Farah knew better than to press the issue.

"It looks great," Farah said, shaking her head in approval. She gave her mother another kiss as they walked back into the living room. Farah realized that her mother must have gone through a few contortions to plan this. She wanted to make Farah look good. Or herself.

Farah decided to just make the best of it. The good part was that Gigi was in a room in the back. She could be quite the nuisance when she got ready to.

Farah sat next to Lenox and Oliver as her mother sat across from them all. She was scoping Lenox out from afar, his mannerisms, the way he spoke, the way he treated Farah.

Everything was laid out in front of them. Farah fixed Lenox a plate with a little bit of everything on it, and her mom did the same for Oliver. Farah just put a few extra crab cakes on hers.

"So what kind of clients do you have, Lenox? Anybody I know?" Oliver asked. He was particularly interested in Lenox's career, and Lenox loved talking about it.

Cutting into his crab cake, Lenox answered, "You know, just average folks. Madison Square Garden. The New York Giants. Exxon." He and Oliver laughed. Oliver was a retired judge and enjoyed legal talk.

"I'm out of the office a lot in client meetings or in the office signing letters. The best part about having such big clients is that it gets me the best table at any new restaurant in town," he said, with some arrogance. But by the look on Oliver's face, it was okay.

"So isn't there an awful lot of stress with such big clients?" Farah's mother asked.

"There is. But even with the smallest clients, people still expect the best. But I really don't deal with any of the clients on a day-to-day basis. Unless it's crisis time. Or a client happens to be family." Lenox looked at Farah, who knew he was talking about Ms. Meyers.

Her mother reached under the coffee table where there was an old *New York Times* article. Farah prayed she wasn't going to bring up that old picture of him from months ago.

She opened the paper, and said, "And how did you get involved with this? It's so wonderful to see young black men involved in such a good cause!"

Lenox blushed. He took the article from her. "Yeah, this was a good night. We raised a few million for the Life House. It helped me open up a whole new building next door in Fort Greene."

Her mother was glued to Lenox. She was hanging on to his every word. Everything he said, she followed with a smile or girlish giggle.

"Ms. Washington, can I say something without seeming foolish?" Lenox said. Farah watched him from the corner of her eye.

"Of course, Lenox. We're practically family!" she said clasping her hands together.

"You know, you look like a young Diahann Carroll. I know you must have heard that before."

Farah liked his comment. An attractive mother doesn't always mean an attractive daughter. But, in this case, it did.

"Oh, my! Thank you for that one. How much did Farah pay you to say that?" Farah's mother grinned.

"I gave him twenty dollars," Oliver said, jumping in. Her mother playfully nudged him in the side. The room lightened with laughs.

Lenox got up to walk to the window. "Is that painting a Jacob Lawrence original?"

Her mother adjusted herself as she walked over to Lenox. "Now, would Diahann Carroll be caught dead with a five-dollar copy in her house? Come on, let me show you around," she said, putting her arm in his. "Excuse us."

Gigi started barking furiously and Oliver left to calm her down. Farah was left alone. She smiled to think that her mother was putting the charms on her man. Farah was very much like her mother, though she hated to admit it. They both adored flirting with men, and adored the attention from men even more.

Farah cut a slice of the moist chocolate as she waited. She sucked the sweet raspberry juice from her fork when she heard her mom and Lenox come back.

They walked into the living room laughing like school pals.

"Honey, did you know Lenox has a love affair with painting?" she asked Farah.

Farah looked at Lenox unknowingly. "No, I didn't," she said, still chewing on the cake.

"My mother is a painter. When I was a kid, I was her left hand. And my mother is right-handed, so use your imagination."

Again, Farah's mother broke out in a roaring laugh. Farah laughed, too. *Who would have thought Lenox had the patience for painting?* she asked herself.

Lenox sat back down next to Farah, and wiped a small piece of chocolate from the corner of her mouth. He put it in his.

Farah's mother had her back turned as she took another plate of the potatoes.

"You two look so good together. Really. Farah, don't let this one get away," her mother teased. Farah was embarrassed.

She only smiled as Lenox looked in her direction for a response. She was waiting for him to say he wouldn't let her get away either, but he didn't.

"Lenox, dear. Honestly. Now, I don't mean to start anything. But don't you think Farah is gaining a little too much weight?"

Farah put down the cake. She started coughing and quickly grabbed the glass of Champagne, which made it worse. Then Lenox handed her a glass of water.

She got herself under control as she watched her mother wait for Lenox's answer.

"We do go out to eat a lot and we're always around decadent food at events," he said. "I certainly like the way she's filling out her pants these days. She has that Lisa Nicole Carson look. And the brothers like Lisa." He put his hand on Farah's thighs for re-assurance, but he was lying. Farah could tell. She had gained half of her added pounds since their trip to St.-Tropez.

"My main concern is that host job she wants on *Rise and Shine.*

Farah, you know those people want women who are perfect in body size. You have to fit an image. I don't want to see you get out of hand like that Star on *The View.*"

"Ma, please. Now you are getting carried away." Farah was trying to stay cool. Lenox was leaning forward with both his hands folded between his legs. He looked at her as she spoke.

"I'm only a size ten, and I'm five feet eight inches. That's perfectly normal. Jenny Craig would turn me away," she said, trying to hold her tongue.

Lenox busied himself with his drink. He and Farah never talked about her extra pounds. But she hated her mother for putting in his head the idea that she was fat. She was always trying to make Farah feel as if she was a dollar short. This time she had gone too far and Farah promised herself she'd give her a piece of her mind later.

Oliver offered them another round of drinks. The bar was always Oliver's domain. He took out the second bottle of Cristal, as they all held out glasses and cheered. He also threw on Miles Davis's *Kind of Blue* CD, which was the perfect buffer for those quiet moments. But they hadn't had any yet.

"I hear a slight accent in your voice, Lenox. Where are you from?" Oliver asked.

"Jamaica. I was born and bred there. I came here to go to boarding school." Lenox was enjoying the food, too. He was on his second slice of cake as he talked.

"Oh, yes, what part?" Farah's mother asked.

"Cherry Hill. It's like the equivalent to your Beverly Hills or Park Avenue here," he said.

Her mother began drinking her Champagne like juice. She came up for air, and said, "I'm very familiar with that area. What do your parents do?"

"Well, you know my mother is an artist. And my father has his own law practice in Jamaica and London. He graduated from Harvard Law in 1970," he boasted. Lenox knew that his credentials were reading off quite nicely and that Farah's mother was taking notes.

"Nice! I was in law, too," her mother chirped.

"Oh, really? What was your practice?" asked Lenox.

"I was a legal secretary." Her mother burst out laughing at her own sarcasm. Lenox and Oliver did, too. Farah wondered whether the Champagne had gone to everybody's head except hers. She was feeling out of place. Once again, her mother always had to be center stage.

"Women like you are invaluable. You keep the office tied together like a stitch," Lenox said.

The evening went on for another two hours, as everyone talked about everything from the rise of property values in Harlem to the decline of the family in America. The night ended with the last slice of cake.

Lenox and Farah had a quiet ride back to his apartment. Farah was the one who had the problem this time.

"Thanks for this evening. Your mother and Oliver really made me feel at home," Lenox said. He kissed Farah on the cheek.

"How do you really feel about the weight I've gained?" she blurted out.

His jaw clenched, moving the little muscles by his ear. She was waiting for him to say something.

"At what point exactly are you talking about?" he asked, turning right on Sixth Avenue.

"No. I think I should be asking you what you're talking about now," she said, glaring in his direction. She didn't want to start a fuss, but she needed to hear something to boost her confidence.

"I'm going to be honest with you. I'm indifferent about it. In bed, I love the way you look. Every part of you is soft, and feels good. But if you want to make it on TV you do have to lose a few pounds. About ten. And as far as I feel about it generally, I wouldn't mind to see you more toned," he added, trying to sound like a giver of good advice.

"I wish you'd leave the stiff-ass lawyer talk at work. I just asked you a simple question. I don't need ifs, ands, or buts."

He shot her a look that told her he was running low on niceness. It meant stop while she was ahead, but she couldn't.

"So, when were you planning on telling me how you felt about my weight?" she asked.

"I didn't see it as a problem, until your mother mentioned it. Baby, you still look good," he said, blowing a kiss in her direction. "Besides, you can come to the gym with me on the weekends. We don't want to give anybody at the network any reason to second-guess you as their pick for *Rise and Shine*."

"Fuck you and your gym. No one at work has said anything, and until they do, I'm not changing a damn thing," Farah said, folding her arms across her chest. "And by the way, I didn't hear you complaining about anything last night in bed when you were hitting it doggy style."

He beeped the car in front of him to let him pass. Then he asked, "Have you had too much Champagne? Because you are pushing it a little."

She didn't answer. They spent the rest of the drive in silence.

When they got home, Farah headed straight for the bedroom. She peeled out of her clothes and stood naked in front of the mirror. Lenox was on a phone call in the kitchen. She figured she'd see what everyone was all up in arms about. Her ass had gotten bigger and her waistline a little thicker. But her stomach was still flat, though far from toned. Her legs were meatier, but mostly in the thighs. One could tell by looking at her that she still had a slender frame. *What is the problem?* she thought as she turned back around. She felt good about how she looked, and agreed with Lenox on one thing: she liked the way she was filling out her pants these days, too.

She climbed into bed, trying to listen to Lenox's phone conversation. He had the kitchen water running so hard that the sounds were muffled. She flipped through an old issue of British *Marie Claire* until she felt Lenox's presence. He placed her magazine on the nightstand, as he raised his body over her. She caressed his back while he lost himself in her hair and neck. Her nipples hardened under the flicking of his tongue. He began to drink and dine on her body. No words were spoken. She lay on her stomach and gave him total control. He was particularly gentle and took his time. He couldn't tell her he appreciated her new look, but he showed it with each kiss from her calves to her forehead.

It was 8:00 A.M. when Farah woke up and Lenox had already left for work.

She dialed his office number to see if he had arrived, but his secretary told her she hadn't seen him. She decided against leaving a message.

One of Farah's old abs-buster tapes was sitting on the bookshelf. She hadn't used it for months. She rewound the tape and cleared a space in Lenox's living room. Luisa was off today and she wasn't planning on cleaning up. Farah lay on her back and followed the hyperactive instructor as he popped up and down demonstrating perfect crunches. After the first twenty minutes, Farah was out of breath and her hair was getting sweaty. She didn't want to mess up her hair, when she had a big night ahead of her. Turning the tape off, she got undressed and took a shower.

Lola called just when Farah settled down to eat breakfast. The kitchen was spotless, which showed her that Lenox didn't even make anything to eat or drink before he left. He usually found time to eat something in the mornings, she noted.

In between bites of crispy turkey bacon slathered in maple syrup, Farah listened to Lola on the other line.

"Meet me uptown on Ninety-sixth Street in a few hours," Lola said. "Chris took the baby and I have some free time. I know it's a last-minute thing."

Farah agreed. "Where do you want to go? I haven't been that far uptown in months."

"Prohibition. They have the best frozen cosmopolitans. I read an article about them in *The New York Times*, but I've never been there," she said, sounding out of breath. She was getting dressed and talking to Farah at the same time.

"Good. I'm game for any new restaurant. Tired of the same ole, same ole," Farah said in between glances of *The View*.

"That's my girl. You know how we do when we go out to eat. See you later."

Farah called Lenox at the office all afternoon. There was still no sign of him. Margaret told her he was in a meeting, but she knew his secretary was covering up for him. Farah remembered her mother used to do just that when she was working. She'd cover up for big-shot partners when their Long Island wives called while they were out cavorting with Manhattan whores.

Later arrived sooner than Farah expected. She met Lola at Prohibition on the other side of the park. While she waited, she tried Lenox's cell phone a few times, but no answer. The afternoon looked bright but rosy through her Chloe sunglasses. The bells of a nearby church made it difficult to listen to the phone. But she swore the last time she called someone had picked up and hung up. Farah blamed it on a possible bad connection. Then she saw Lola walking in her direction. A yellow cab was driving away alongside her.

"What's up, *mujer*!" Lola said, holding her arms wide apart. They gave each other a hug before they went inside. Lola's vibe was a bit shaky.

They stepped in the restaurant and were immediately seated by the tall hostess with thick-rimmed glasses.

"You weren't waiting long, were you? That damn cab took the long way. I told him to stay off of crowded-ass Broadway!" Lola complained.

"I wasn't waiting long. I was trying to reach Lenox. That's all." Farah put her cell phone away.

"You don't sound as good as you look, girl! Come on, where did you get this?" she asked, holding Farah's wrist. "That is a Tiffany diamond bracelet! What have you been doing to deserve that?"

Getting a little excited, Farah said, "Lenox bought it. I think it was after an argument or something," she said, shaking her head.

"I guess it pays to argue these days. And those shoes," she said looking down. "Did you order them, because I haven't seen those Manolos out yet!" Lola examined Farah's shoes, as she proudly showed them off. Two things they had in common were heels and meals.

They each ordered fried calamari strips to start, and four mini-cheeseburgers and shoestring fries, with two frozen cosmopolitans.

"What's wrong with you, though? You seem distracted or something," Lola asked.

"Funny. I was going to ask you the same thing," Farah said, meeting Lola's small eyes.

Farah decided to answer Lola first. "Everything is fine. How is everything with you and Chris?"

"I'm really thinking about leaving him. I need some time apart. I look at you and how you go after what you want. I want a man like Lenox who has nice things, can buy me gifts, treat me good."

"It's not as easy as it looks. You know I'm going through my own shit with him."

"True. But nobody is perfect," she said, chewing on the calamari.

"Don't follow my example. I know I'm not doing much about my problems with him, but I don't have a husband and child." Farah took Lola's hand and squeezed it. She could see that her friend was just confused.

"If you want I know a good therapist you and Chris can go see. I'll pay for it," Farah said, giving Lola a napkin.

"I'm willing to try that. Maybe it's just little growing pains. It's like we haven't had any time for ourselves since Arabia. I know he still loves me."

"I may be calling that therapist soon myself." Farah took a piece of bread.

"So, what is up with you and Lenox?"

"Lenox finally finished the Life House's new building. And all my little touches are in there. He's even having a big bash at Tavern on the Green tonight to celebrate it. And his firm just won a major case against that oil company that is always in the news."

"Okay." Lola tried to sound happy. "But what about the other stuff? Why are you on the eleven o'clock show now?"

"With all the changes and everything, they have to move people around," Farah said.

"But I didn't see anyone else changed from the six P.M. show," Lola said. The drinks came and the waitress placed two pink slushy cosmos down.

"All I know is I come home one day and Lenox told me the good news about *Rise and Shine* and a raise he negotiated for me. Then I go to work the next day, and my job is different."

Farah slurped her frozen drink. The cold iciness went to her head and gave her an immediate ache in her temples.

"Can you still be at all the parties if you are working on the late show?" asked Lola.

"No, I can't. I'm just plain tired or cranky afterwards." Farah finally put down her drink.

"That figures. He probably got you changed so he can be smiling up in all those women's faces at the parties! Maybe he's trying to squeeze you out." The waitress came back and put down their lunches.

"Squeeze me out? That man has made an investment in me." Farah showed off her bracelet. "He's not walking away that easily. I have no worries there." She wished.

"Farah, please. A man like that? He's definitely asking for some space. Something is up, though. He got your spot changed. I know he did!" Farah was surprised at Lola's excitement. "Do you know where your man is right now?"

"He's at a meeting. I think." Farah shrugged. Lola's persistence was becoming irritating. She was speaking all of Farah's own thoughts.

"If I were you—" Lola began.

"Look, fuck it!" Farah felt the nerve under her eye twitch. "Any bitch with him is getting the bone, while I'm getting the meat!"

Lola shut up and wrapped her short, polished nails around her cheeseburger. She didn't look Farah's way at all.

After a few minutes, Lola's eyes softened. "I just care about you. I would just hate to see you waste your time. He is stringing your career along as he plays with other women," Lola said.

"I can handle this, Lola," Farah said firmly. She really could, but she was just too tired to do anything about it.

♥

Late in the evening, while Farah was at work, Lenox finally called. He apologized for being "out of touch" the whole day, but was in Westchester at a meeting.

"I have some really good news," he said.

"Like what?" she asked, trying to appear interested.

"I have this interview for you. Derrick has a little dirty work that is coming back to haunt him. A few months ago, he had me put this dude back in jail while he ran his election. The guy threatened to tie him in to this murder. So lately, I've been thinking about letting the guy out."

"Why would you let him out if he's in jail?"

"He's innocent. And he has a family and it's been bothering me lately that fat-ass Derrick is walking around using his father's name to win an election and come off as a saint. If I arrange it, would you be able to interview Jacob Richard? I think everyone would benefit here."

"What about Derrick? It would ruin his career and he'll lose the election. And aren't you two friends?"

"I was Derrick's friend when it was convenient for him. But it's not convenient for me. And plus, his father did a lousy job in office, and personally, I wouldn't want a man who deliberately let an innocent man rot in jail as my congressman."

"Well, let the archangels sing! Mr. Whitworth has a soul. I had no idea you had that side to you," she said, laughing. "I'll happily do the interview. If it will make you feel better as a person." She smiled.

"And there's more. Katie Maury had already contacted Jacob Richard. So if you can break this story first, there's nothing else I need to do to get you on *Rise and Shine*. My aunt won't be able to overlook that. This is a big one," he said.

"Just let me know when."

"Good. I'll work on it. I'll have a car pick you up from the apartment tonight to take you to Tavern on the Green. See you later, baby."

Their phone call was over and Farah didn't have time to digest it all. After the news show ended at 11:30, Farah rushed home. The soiree had started hours ago and it would already be in full swing by the time she got there.

When she returned to the apartment, it was the same as she had left it. Lenox had not been home at all, she noticed. He must have called her from the office. Farah wondered what he could be wearing, if he hadn't come home to change. *Did he bring his clothes with him to work when he left the house this morning?* she asked of no one in particular. She didn't have time to waste worrying. Lenox was having his car pick her up at 12:30.

She quickly showered, and used her favorite scrub. While showering, she thought about how inconvenient it was for her to rush and get ready all in twenty minutes. There was no way that she could get used to her fast-paced lifestyle and the new 11:00 P.M. slot. And she was going to let Lenox know about it.

Everything she had planned to wear was carefully spread out on the bed. She slipped into an elegant black Calvin Klein dress with a plunging neckline. Her breasts were standing full and securely fixed with tape. Her hair still looked neat. She fastened her favorite gold choker around her neck and clipped on a pair of gold-plated earrings. The finale was a pair of gold leather sling-backs with a heel that could crack ceramic. Looking in the mirror, she thought it might be a little too flashy, but if she was going to be late, she might as well look good at it.

Before she left the house, she had a small glass of wine to calm her down. She was nervous for some reason, but she didn't know why. She felt strangely anxious about the Jacob Richard interview. When the concierge called about the car, she closed the door behind her. When she stepped out with her breasts, men and women stared. And it felt good. The night was steamy and all Farah was holding was a clutch purse. The streets were filled with couples passing by and some standing outside the building waiting for their own cars.

The driver opened the door, as Farah slipped in. As she sat back, her mind was relaxing. Then the car phone rang.

"Where are you?" she heard Lenox ask on the other end.

"We're driving uptown now. I should be there in like ten minutes. Traffic isn't too bad." She heard the hum of voices and music in the background. She felt like a late straggler.

"All right, there are some people who have been asking about you. Some folks you know?" he asked.

She thought about who he was referring to because she did invite people she knew as well. "Oh, yeah, those may be people from CNN and CNBC. Tell them I'll be there any minute."

"Yeah," he said, and hung up. She had forgotten to tell him she had invited folks.

When she finally arrived, the place was packed like sardines. There were way too many people. There was a Latin jazz band playing and people dancing. A man offered to take her jacket, but she told him she just came with "these," and pointed to her breasts. He smiled, so did Farah. She needed something to lighten her up.

Farah stood discreetly at the entrance and did a mental check of everything. The food looked good, the band was flowing, and all the important people who had to be there were. However, she thought again that she might have invited too many of her own people.

She entered the room and immediately people gave her their greetings. She heard some whispers nearby that sounded like gossip about her dress. But she didn't care. She was feeling confident and no woman in the room had anything over her.

"Farah, darling, look at you!" Brianna said. "You look so elegant, yet hot!" she said. "I was wondering what was taking you so long."

"With my new schedule, everything takes longer now." Farah gave Brianna's husband a hug. As usual his hand would rest a little too long on the small of her back.

"The food was marvelous! And this band. Ahh, I need their info," Brianna said, beaming. "I'm so proud of you and Lenox. That Life House auditorium looks amazing. We stopped by there the other day." Farah chatted with them for a few minutes and moved on.

"Excuse me, Mrs. Whitworth. My name is Matthew Levy. I was just in the other room enjoying dinner, when I heard Mr. Whitworth was doing something here. And I was hoping you can give him my card and tell him I have some property he should really consider. Word is, he is looking for a building in SoHo," the tall, well-polished man said.

Farah was taken aback. No one had ever called her Mrs. Whitworth. She hesitated before responding. "You will have to call his office and make an appointment. I can't take anything right now," she said.

"Sure, sure. I understand. Just tell him Matthew Levy will give him a call. I got a great place for him. It's fully renovated." He gave her his card anyway. "Thanks, Mrs. Whitworth. Enjoy your evening."

Before she could say anything, he was gone in the midst of the crowd. Farah just put the card in her purse. People were always trying to get to Lenox through her. In the beginning it was fun, but now it was old.

She made the rounds to a few more people, including those she'd invited. She had definitely made an entrance, with people throwing smiles and nods in her direction, especially the men.

Farah made her way to the back of the room, and saw Lenox from a distance. He was usually one of the taller men in the room and stood out. He was in the middle of a small group of folks. Next to him was a petite, very light-skinned young woman with cropped hair. Her mouth was blazing red, and her eyes were sleepy looking. She looked familiar to Farah because her eyes stood out. She looked at the young woman from head and toe, and she was dressed to the nines. She had on the latest Gucci baby-doll dress that Farah was dying for, but her behind had gotten too big for it.

Lenox caught her eye, and excused himself from the group. The woman with the red lips stared at Farah, while the others waved and nodded.

Farah watched as Lenox walked up to her and her insides started to waken. He looked good enough for a two-minute quickie in the coat room. She smiled to herself. When he kissed her, she inhaled his breath.

She put her arm around him and gave him a big squeeze. His body felt strong and thick against hers, through his Armani suit. He was wearing the Cartier cuff links she had bought him.

He took her hand and walked away from the band so they could talk.

"Listen, everything you did was great, but I wish I would have known about the fifty extra people you invited. The kitchen had to make extra plates and Natalie wasn't happy. They treated us well with this event being last-minute."

He didn't say anything about her dress or how she looked. Farah was waiting for some kind of compliment.

"It was last-minute RSVPs," Farah said, feeling guilty. "I was going to tell you, but I couldn't reach you all day."

He stood there with his hands in his pocket looking down on her. "And this dress? What's this about?" he asked, running his finger down her exposed neckline.

Her nipples responded to his touch and hardened. "I just wanted to look different. You know, sexy for you," she said.

He stepped back. "You do look fine. I mean, only you can wear a dress like that. Turn around." She turned around and posed like model.

He took a deep breath and gave her a real kiss this time. He ran his hand down her back past her ass. This turned her on even more.

"Come on, let's go home now." She played with his belt buckle. "I need help getting out of this dress."

"Soon, but I still have lots of mingling to do," he said, fixing his pants. His erection was starting to die down. He held out his hand.

"Is Derrick here," she asked, taking his hand.

"No. I purposely didn't invite him."

They walked back into the hall. The young woman was still standing at the same place with her eyes fixed on Farah and Lenox. It was almost as if she wanted to say something, but didn't.

"Lenox, who's that woman with the sleepy eyes you were talking to?" Farah asked, picking up the young woman's negative energy from across the room.

Lenox turned his head and looked at Farah with a serious stare, which made her nervous.

"She's a friend I invited from out of town. Let me introduce you."

He waved to the young woman to join them and she did. Farah was getting nauseus with each step the young woman took. Her head was beginning to feel tight. The closer she got to them, the more beautiful the girl was.

"Farah, this is Maritza," Lenox said, standing between them.

Farah stuck her hand out and gave Maritza a firm shake, but the girl's was light and weak.

"Nice to meet you. Lenox said you're from out of town?" Farah asked.

"Good to meet you, too. I'm from Lyon. Lyon, France."

"Oh," Farah said, looking at Lenox. "How did you and Lenox meet?"

"On a business trip," he interjected. "A few years ago, when I was in Amsterdam visiting one of my Dutch clients."

The last time Farah checked, Amsterdam was not in France.

There was some awkward silence as Maritza stood there next to Lenox. Farah felt uncomfortable with how close she was standing next to him. Maritza's style and mannerisms all dripped with sexiness. Farah could see Lenox being attracted to that.

"Quelle heure est-il?" Maritza asked Lenox.

"Il est une heure," answered Lenox, looking at his Rolex.

"I didn't know you spoke French, Lenox," Farah said.

"Please, baby. I think I told you that when we met," he said in a tone that suggested that she had carelessly forgotten.

Maritza had a little smirk on her face and looked down. Then she said, "He's a good teacher. Maybe he can teach you some things." Her eyes were on Farah's breasts, which was about the only thing Maritza was lacking.

"Excuse you?!" Farah stepped closer to her. Everything around Farah had blacked out as her adrenaline pumped through her.

"Listen, how about I call you a cab, Maritza?" Lenox asked.

"Oui," she said to Lenox, and kissed him on both cheeks. "It was nice meeting you, Farah." With that she walked away.

"Uhm, look, I don't know." Farah fumbled for words. She was trying to begin a sentence. She felt everything around had crumbled with the appearance of Maritza. A few people were looking at them. An older man was calling Lenox in his direction.

"Don't go making assumptions. There are too many people here to cause a scene. We'll talk about this later. I promise," he said, touching her cheek. All of Farah's suspicions had been confirmed. She felt detached from him. He walked away into the crowd. She ran to the ladies' room, and cried until her eyes became sore.

Maritza's arrival in New York City had a lot to do with Lenox. Her "career" as a stripper was beginning to lose its luster. With no other place to go to start over on a fresh slate, she called Lenox. And as always, Lenox was happy to help a lady in distress. He set her up in a comfortable, stylish apartment in a Lower East Side high-rise, the same place Camille once stayed. She had plans to become an actress, and within days of her arrival, Lenox arranged several auditions for Broadway shows. At first, his intention was only to help, but eventually he accepted Maritza's only way of saying thank you. He began leaving to go to "work" early in the mornings, when Farah was still asleep, to lie by Maritza's side. He was sleeping with two women, but in love with one.

*L*enox had it all planned out at Tavern on the Green. He was going to introduce Maritza to Farah as a casual acquaintance from his business travels. Farah would accept it with limited suspicion and he would convince her later. To have both women in the same room was a day at the spa for his ego. He enjoyed the interaction between Farah and Maritza. His father was always good at that between Elsa and his mother. Lenox had learned women will accept a lot from a man if he is up-front about things. And he couldn't think of any other way to hide his cheating than to show it.

That night he went home with Maritza. He would rather spend a short night with her than a long one with Farah. However, when Lenox returned to the apartment Saturday morning, Farah was still asleep. She didn't even wake up when he walked in the bedroom. He'd thought she would be up pacing or curled up on the couch crying. But from the looks of it, she had a better night's sleep than he did.

Lenox undressed. He sat at the foot of the bed and ran his hands up Farah's left thigh.

"Farah, let's talk about last night," he said.

She turned over and pulled the covers up to her face.

"Listen, I really don't want this to drag out. I'm no mind reader. So you need to tell me what you're thinking." Lenox believed his bringing up the topic first would give him more control of the situation.

"What am I supposed to do when you are throwing another woman in my face?" she asked.

"Maritza is a friend. She likes to flirt. It's nothing more," he said, stroking her leg again.

Farah sat up, careful to keep the covers from slipping.

"So where are you coming from now? It's sunrise. You always come home before then," Farah asked, staring at him with glassy eyes. Her tone was low and even. Lenox preferred it when she screamed and raved. At least then, she was getting it out. He knew what happened when women held things in. They exploded later and he didn't want to be in the way, if Farah did.

"Okay. I'll come clean," he said softly. "I was with Maritza. She invited me over because she knew things between you and me were shaky," Lenox said.

Farah's stared at him in disbelief. She knew it. She *knew* it. She massaged the area between her eyes.

"You had sex with her and have the nerve to come lay up with me now?" Farah said, her voice rough but still low.

Lenox didn't answer. He was about being honest, but not crazy.

Farah rephrased her question. Perhaps she didn't want to know either.

"You were with Maritza. Don't you feel the least bit uncomfortable admitting that?"

"You want me to lie, do you? You're being ridiculous," he said, taking off his pants.

"So tell me, Lenox. Just tell me, if you want to leave me for her. Don't string me along. That I can't deal with."

"Who said anything about leaving you? That never crossed my mind," he said impatiently. "We suit each other."

Lenox noticed that Farah's expression changed completely. Her lips parted as the corners of her mouth relaxed. He could tell he hit a note inside of her.

"Am I supposed to do a Jackie Kennedy and just turn my face every time my man enters a room with another woman?" she asked, not sure how long she could handle that.

"When we met you had a lot you wanted to accomplish. You were at a dead end at the network. Now you have a bright, secure future ahead of you," he reminded her. "I know that means more to you than *anything*."

"It sure as hell does!" she said, but she pressed down the urge to tell him how her feelings had grown more deeply for him, too. "I cannot have you disrespecting me in front of people like you did last night! And I don't know what that Maritza is about, but from the looks of her, I can tell she is bad news, Lenox."

Farah's words sounded more like an accountant warning his client about debt than a jealous girlfriend spitting fire.

He thought about what she said, but knew as long as Farah and Maritza knew about each other, there could be no bad news. The worst part was over, he thought.

Lenox crawled into bed next to Farah. It was 8:00 in the morning, and he wanted to catch up on the sleep he didn't get the night before. He snuggled up behind Farah, still feeling awkward. He couldn't quite put his finger on it as he lay there, but Farah still seemed a little too relaxed for what happened. He wasn't sure what she was up to. As soon as he got comfortable, Farah opened the shades, letting the white light of the sun hit his face. She closed the bathroom door behind her.

On the other hand, Farah had changed. Lately, he had begun tripping over her shoes in his apartment and had noticed her gradual but apparent weight gain. Being the Jamaican man he was, Lenox loved a womanly woman. He liked gripping the extra flesh on Farah's thighs, hips, butt, and arms. But it had turned into fifteen extra pounds. Sometimes he'd see candy wrappers and ice cream cartons in the garbage. He was relieved when her mother brought up the weight issue, and hoped she'd stop while she was ahead. He figured their problems were the cause of it, but he wasn't complaining. He did like her skills in bed and her pragmatic way of handling problems. Their relationship was built more on a power deal than anything else.

Lenox and Farah spent the rest of the day in separate parts of the apartment. He figured it would take some time for things to feel "normal" again. He made his place in the den and watched one football game after another. Farah busied herself trying out the new clothes and makeup she'd bought the other day. He could hear her chatting on the phone with a girlfriend, but wasn't sure what she was saying. He wished she could be like a real girlfriend and sit next to him on the couch as he explained the play-by-play. Or maybe even take a mop through the filthy bathroom, which she usually left wet and full of hair after a shower. He had Luisa for that, but she didn't come in every day.

He had been dozing off during halftime of the third game when Farah called him to the phone.

"The phone! Lenox!"

"Who is it?" he yelled back. He picked up the remote and began flipping through the channels.

"It's your mother," she said, coming to stand in the den's doorway. "She said she's been trying to reach you since last week. Something about your cousin's birthday?"

She handed Lenox the phone and left.

Before he had a chance to greet her, his mother started.

"Lenoooooooox," she whined. "You know Little Floyd's birthday is next weekend. What, you forgetting about your family? You know you have to come back home. Everybody is expecting you."

"I was just wrapped up with the Life House charity event. But I didn't forget. As a matter of fact, I'm going to have Margaret get two tickets for me. I'll be there in a few days."

"Two tickets? Who's the other ticket for? Seht?"

"It's for Farah. I want to bring her with me and introduce her to everyone. You should meet her, she's gorgeous."

"Well, so were Joanne and Paula."

"She's different. She's ambitious, focused, driven. A lot like me," he said.

His mother paused. "Well, she sounds like a nice girl. Where did you meet her? Andover? Harvard? Do we know her family?"

Lenox got up and closed the door. "Not exactly. She went to Columbia. And I met her mother. And she works with Aunt Joan. She's a local news anchor here." Lenox felt like a teenaged boy being scrutinized by his mother, but his mother was very concerned about class and status. Sometimes he felt like reminding her where she had come from.

"Oh! A reporter. Well, that's nice. And she had to go to college for that?"

"Come on, you haven't even met her and you're already throwing stones," Lenox said.

"No, baby. Whomever you choose I'm sure will be fine. Just make sure if she's nothing else that she's classy. Since you had that tramp Joanne around, I've been wondering about you."

"Leave Joanne out of this. You don't know anything but what you hear from your tea-party friends."

"Excuse me for breathing," she said uncomfortably. "Well, then let me just get to the point. If you are bringing her to Jamaica, I am assuming you are serious about her. Is that right? You won't be announcing an engagement or anything without telling me, will you?"

Lenox put his hand on his suddenly throbbing head. "Yes, we are serious. And I just want you and Dad to meet her. Don't read anything more into this, please."

His mother giggled. "Fine, but I'm sure Joan would be willing to tell me more than what you have."

"How about I call you when I get the tickets and we can take it from there?"

"All right, baby. I can't wait to see you and Sarah."

"It's Farah, mom. And say hi to my father for me. Love you." He clicked the phone off and smiled at what he knew Farah would think was good news. "Farah, baby, come here."

She hopped in trying to button some khaki pants. "Damn, I hate these stretch things!"

"Okay, well, just have a seat for now. We need to talk."

"Look, I can't take anymore 'talks' right now. And I just got three other pairs of godforsaken jeans to try on. I already have to return two that I swore looked good in the store," she said, taking them off.

"Would you please just shut the hell up for a minute?" Lenox's headache felt like someone was squeezing his skull with a wrench.

Farah quietly complied.

"We're going to Jamaica in a few days. My cousin, Little Floyd, is having his thirteenth birthday," he announced.

"What about work? I just started on that eleven o'clock show," Farah said, worried.

"You told me you had like five sick days left. Plus, they can't tell somebody like you that you can't use a sick day. And if that's the only problem, start packing. I'll call Aunt Joan."

"I guess this means I have to go shopping again," she said, throwing her hands up.

"Um, you know what? Why don't I come shopping with you this time? Maybe I may need a few things, too," he said.

"So I guess I will be meeting all the Whitworths," Farah said, biting her bottom lip.

"Yeah, everyone will be there."

"Well, I'm not from upper-class stock. I can act like it, but . . ." Farah said.

"It'll be fine. I just want you to meet my family since I've met yours. Let's not blow this up," he said, wanting to end the conversation.

Farah walked over to him and sat on his lap. "I'll be ready in a few minutes. Then we can leave to return these things. Don't worry, your family will love me."

Lenox just closed his eyes.

♥

When Lenox walked into his office Monday morning, he was in high spirits. Farah and he were over the Maritza incident and looking forward to Jamaica.

He decided to see George at the Life House and have a talk with him about the exorbitant expenses. He had checked the bank account last week and all the funds were there as expected. The Life House had a small board of directors, only six if Lenox was present. He had been present at the last few meetings and the issues of expenses had come up, however George was quick to excuse the expenditures under the guise of "It's for the children." Today, Lenox wanted to see all the financial records of the last six months.

When he arrived, he went directly to George's office to start their meeting, but George wasn't in yet. Lenox took the time to search his desk. He wasn't looking for anything in particular, but he wanted to find something. At first, he looked with calm, and then he started to look more frantically. In the last folder of the third drawer, he found an unlabeled envelope. In it were receipts, utility and vendor bills, and financial statements. After he went through all the material, he felt sick. He wasn't even angry but dazed. George had been using Life House money to pay his mortgage, family trips, and expensive dinners for himself and his wife. George had manipulated the financial statements for it to look like the extra money was going toward the kids, but it was going to him. Lenox looked out the window and saw George pulling up. He quickly put everything back in its place. He had the urge to kill

George, but his job as a lawyer always prevented him from taking his anger too far.

"What's up, man! I guess you're the early one today. I was stuck in traffic," George said, putting his things down on the couch. "I brought us some coffee."

"No, thanks. I don't have much time."

"Are you all right? I apologize again for being late." George took a seat.

"It's not about that. I'm calling a board of directors meeting for tomorrow morning. I'm very concerned about some things. We don't have the money to keep up with the expenses. It can't be done." It was the truth to Lenox.

"We just had a meeting. How am I supposed to get everyone together so quick?"

"I'll do it. I'll call you later." Lenox got up and left George holding his cup of coffee.

When Lenox got in his car, he called the bank. The account was overdrawn by five hundred thousand dollars. *Shit.* Thoughts that this would not have happened if he spent more time at the Life House came into his head. He had put all his trust into George. He had known George for years and knew how much the Life House meant to him. It was Lenox's refuge from everything else. It was how he wanted to be remembered and seen. Lenox knew he wasn't a well-liked person and that people only liked him for what he could do for them. But everyone at the Life House liked him and the parents always thanked him, even if he couldn't be there every weekend. There was no way he could recover from this. He failed, for the first real time in his life.

"You won't believe what fucking happened today," Lenox said to Farah, who was at work. He had promised himself he wouldn't tell anyone, but he couldn't hold it in any longer.

"What? Something at the network?" she said.

"No, not the fucking network! The Life House. That mother-fucker George ripped me off. He's been taking money from the

Life House to pay for his own expenses. I should have known that man was too lax with my money."

"George? You mean old-ass country George? Come on. He has a family. Maybe you're wrong."

"I'm telling you, I was there this morning and I saw everything for myself. And the bank account is overdrawn by five hundred thousand dollars. So this motherfucker goes in, takes money out, and puts it back by statement time."

"How do you know he's not writing too many checks?"

"He *is* writing too many checks! And it's not for the Life House. It's for him. I saw the receipts."

"Lenox. How could you let this happen?"

Lenox felt like reaching through the phone and grabbing Farah by the neck.

"I hired George as executive director, and it's his job to direct all finances and operations. He let this shit happen. His ass is through!"

"But Lenox, what will this mean for the Life House?"

Lenox hadn't had the peace of mind yet to think about what the larger ramifications would be.

"I have to sit down and see if we can get over this. You know, he wouldn't have been able to keep this up for long. If I hadn't caught him, he would have come to me with a bankruptcy statement in two months and blamed it on the economy or me."

"I support you in whatever decision you make. Just to think I met with him last month and he was smiling in my face and stabbing you in the back. Baby, I'm sorry. Let me call you back later. I have to go on air."

Lenox didn't go to work that day or do anything else for that matter. He stayed in bed and thought about how karma was relentless.

♥

One of the board members was unavailable to meet the next day. Lenox had her make up for the absence via conference call and he conducted the meeting with the other members present.

He did not waste time opening the floor first.

"Take a look at this, George, and tell us what you see." He handed a clueless George a thick manila folder.

George's stubby fingers leafed through the old, wrinkled receipts. His smiling face changed to one of perplexity.

"Can we talk about this—" George said. The members looked at each other, still not sure what the meeting was leading up to.

"You can talk with everyone here. Tell us why the Life House would need two expensive cruises to the Caribbean, furs for your wife, pricey hotel stays, and unexplained cash withdrawals? Should I keep going?" Lenox stood and grabbed the folder from his hands and passed it around to the bewildered board members. Each one read the receipts. Some gasped, others shook their heads.

"I was falling on hard times at home! Please, I can explain each of those receipts."

"This isn't a bank. This a nonprofit organization for children. Not for your profit or mine. George, I'm letting you go. Anyone disagree?"

The room fell silent.

"Please—"

"George, leave now. I'm going to start legal action towards you today," Lenox said, over the animated chattering of some of the board members.

"Like you cared about these kids! You were never around. At least I was always there!" George said, flying out of his chair. Some of the members stood up to calm him down.

"Good-bye, George. And I mean that." Lenox took his file folder and left before the police arrived. Several board members followed him, leaving George alone. Two officers walked in and arrested George. Lenox didn't want to see that part. For the rest of the morning, he locked himself behind the Life House doors and tried to put the pieces back together. He closed the Life House down until further notice.

When he got to work later that afternoon, Margaret handed him a steaming cup of coffee and his agenda for the day. The coffee tasted especially good today, he thought. She always put a pinch of chocolate powder in it. He sipped from the cup as he looked at the city below from his ninetieth-floor window, the television on behind him. He thought about how it would feel to jump from so far. Just when he was getting lost in his thoughts, he heard Derrick's voice.

He listened to Derrick on a national news program talking about how he would fight crime and provide jobs for New Yorkers. He animatedly talked about his years at Harvard Law and how hard he worked as a black man to pay his way through college. Lenox nearly spilled the coffee on his jacket. Derrick was outright lying, because his father had paid for everything. There were several people who helped him to get where he was now, including Lenox. He put his unfinished coffee down and called the DA's office. He made a compelling argument to release Jacob Richard, which worked. He had to relieve himself of the burden, and teach Derrick a lesson. He also sent Richard a message about an interview. He knew Richard wouldn't pass the chance up to set his record straight. He got hard just thinking about it.

Then he called Farah.

"Farah Washington speaking," she said. He could hear her eating.

"I just called the DA's office. Jacob Richard is being released."

"Oh, my God, I can't believe you really did it! Now the shit is really going to hit the fan."

"I know, and just before Election Day."

"This is going to be one of the biggest stories I've handled."

"Exactly," Lenox said. His intercom buzzed. "Listen, I've got to go, but I'll get the guy's info for you." He hung up and pressed his intercom. "Yes, Margaret?"

"Mr. Whitworth, I got your two tickets to Jamaica. Flying first class on Air Jamaica leaving on Friday at eight-thirty in the morning. It's an e-ticket. Is that all right?"

"Perfect. The timing couldn't be better." He meant every word of it. By the time the story broke, he would be in Jamaica.

♥

Later that evening, Seht invited Lenox and Farah to meet after work at the Park Café, an outdoor restaurant in Battery Park.

While Farah talked to a few people at another table, Seht and Lenox got time for themselves. They rarely talked lately. He needed a diversion from George and the Life House matters, and didn't want to bring it up.

"How the hell are you doing this, man? Two women together, and they are not trying to kill each other?" Seht asked as he lit a cigarette.

"To me they are one woman, instead of two. Farah is a partner-in-crime/confidante and Maritza is the one who relaxes me and doesn't need too much but what I give her." They both unwrapped cigars.

"That's some sick shit, man," Seht said, blowing small circles of smoke. "I gotta try that one day."

"I was sure she'd give me hell because of Maritza. But instead, she's calm about it. I just try to make it home before sunrise, but you know how Maritza can get," Lenox said, lighting his cigar. "I know this thing is killing her, but she doesn't show it. And it's not like she asked me to stop. She didn't give me any choices like 'love me or leave me.' And until she does, I'm just going to ride it out."

"Damn, my ex would have ran my ass out of the house a while ago," Seht said.

"She's not like a regular woman. I just hope I don't wake up one morning to a pot of hot grits on my back." Lenox and Seht laughed like sailors as they downed their glasses of Hennessey.

"And you know what?" Lenox said, feeling looser by the minute. "Farah doesn't give a fuck about me anyway. As long as she gets what she wants from me, she can sleep at night."

"Yeah, that sister is strictly about her business." Then a group of attractive light-blonde-haired women strutted by. "Excuse me for a minute, partner," Seht said. Lenox watched as Seht sweet-talked one of the women into giving up the digits. He strolled back over to their table, shoving a phone number in his pants pocket.

"So," Seht said, sitting down. " "Look who just walked in." He held his drink and pointed it to the bar.

Lenox's eyes were diverted to the end of the bar where Maritza sat not knowing he was already there. He watched her sip red wine with one hand and smoke with the other. She carefully flicked her cigarette ashes far away from her Prada bag. He caught her glance.

Passing in between two men who were trying to talk to her, she leisurely walked over to Lenox. She was dressed to impress as usual, he noticed. When she sat down across from him, he caught the scent of baby lotion, and smiled. He remembered telling her how he loved the crisp powder scent of baby lotion, especially between a woman's thighs. She smiled back at him. Of course she had remembered. Everything she had on was delicate and tiny, from her blouse to her shoes. Lenox signaled the waiter over to bring her another glass.

"Damn, you look good enough to take a sip from," Seht said, brushing his shoulder against Maritza's. "A *sweet* drink."

Lenox watched Maritza's reaction.

"Well, all this sweet syrup is in reserve for one man tonight," she said. She scooted her chair closer to Lenox, who had just finished his cigar. "Isn't that right, Ox?" she said, playing with his earlobe.

He took a long, steady drink from her half-finished glass of Beaujolais.

Out of the blue, Farah returned to the table and let an array of colorful business cards fall in front of him. "Here, these are all yours." She sat down next to Lenox with lips drawn in a tight line and greeted Seht but not Maritza.

"Who are all these people? I've never heard of half of these companies," Lenox said, picking up a card. "They give them to you because they know they can't come at me with this shit." He tossed them back onto the table.

Farah just shrugged and cut her eyes at Maritza. Lenox unconsciously moved closer to Farah and Maritza moved closer to Seht. Feeling the tension at the table, Seht signaled for another round of drinks.

"So, man," he said, in an effort to break the silence. "What's up with that building in SoHo you wanted to buy? Figured out yet what you want to do with it?"

"Not yet," Lenox said, laying his chewed-up toothpick in the ashtray. "I'm calling the realtor next week to talk about that. There's some bidding going on."

Maritza smiled as she stubbed out her cigarette. "Lenox, you are definitely doing your thing."

Farah pretended to be interested in the crowd.

"If I get it I may open a small office space. You know, rent it out for commercial use," Lenox said.

"You know, that is what we need. More black men keeping the money in the community. That's incredible, baby." Maritza leaned over to give Lenox a kiss, but he pulled away. Farah got up and left the table.

"I don't know how you can deal with such a moody woman." Maritza scowled, swirling the last bit of wine in her glass. "These American women can be so evil."

"Please, Maritza. You just tried to kiss her man right in front of her. Don't even try to act like it was innocent," Seht said.

"It was innocent compared to what I'm usually kissing," she said, smiling seductively.

Lenox frowned. "Maritza, Farah already knows about you. But whatever we do has to still be discreet just to avoid the drama," Lenox said.

"I'm going for a walk. Want to come?" Seht suggested, standing up. Maritza sighed, got up, and left the table ahead of him.

Farah eventually made her way back to the table. He watched as she sat down next to him, crossed her legs, and casually sipped her drink.

"She's a big flirt. You know how the French are." He placed his lips on her forehead and kissed it. She didn't protest. "Anyway, I don't want to talk about her." He leaned forward. "Jacob Richard will be calling you at my place tonight. I told him to leave a message for you on the answering machine if we're not in. So, I'm sure by the time one of us gets home, he would have called. But just in case, I gave him your work number."

"Is he out yet?" she asked, suddenly interested in the conversation.

"He'll be out officially tomorrow morning, but he won't have time to talk then. He wants to see his family first."

"Of course," she said, in deep thought. "He must be so happy this thing is finally behind him. Ten years in jail for a crime he did not commit. I can't wait to talk to him. I'll make sure I'm home to get that phone call."

Lenox loved it when she got that ruthless look in her eye. He slid his hand under her white pleated skirt, almost touching her thigh, but she crossed her legs, dislodging his hand.

"By the way, what's up with Jamaica?" she asked.

"I knew there was something I was forgetting to tell you. We're leaving Friday, in the morning."

"Oh, so you just forgot to tell me?" She flipped open her Palm Pilot, which she kept snug in her purse. "A girl has to know way more in advance than that, Lenox!"

Lenox sat back in disgust. He picked up his drink. "Maybe I forgot to tell you because I have a lot of things on my mind. You should be happy you're coming, instead of complaining. Meeting my family is a big step," he said.

Farah gave Lenox a kiss on the mouth to show that she was looking forward to it.

"A kiss is a lot better when there's a third person in between," a sultry French voice whispered.

Both Farah and Lenox pulled away to see Maritza standing there. She smiled and took a pull on her cigarette. She sat down next to Lenox.

"Farah, next time, nibble on his right earlobe, he loves that." She flicked her ashes in the tray.

"And I love my ass kissed. Would you like to do that?" Farah asked.

Maritza laughed. "Lenox, should I answer that? I gather she doesn't know me very well."

Lenox placed another toothpick between his lips. "Farah, Maritza is French. There isn't anything she hasn't done yet."

Maritza smirked and shoved his shoulder.

Farah turned up her nose in disgust. "I'm out of here. I need to get ready for the eleven o'clock. I'll see you later," she said, grabbing her purse and standing. But before she left, she leaned down and caressed the hardness between his legs. "Don't stay out too late," she purred in his ear. Then she turned on her heel and left.

♥

Right after she was gone, Lenox accompanied Maritza back to her place. He was in the mood for immediate satisfaction and didn't want to wait until Farah returned home tired from work. They didn't even get inside before she started undressing herself.

"You know that girlfriend of yours is kind of cute," she said, taking off her panties and tossing them aside.

"I only pick the best." Lenox placed a kiss on Maritza's freckled nose.

"I mean, she has a killer body. Her ass is so perfect. And round. I just wanted to touch it to see if it was real." She took out two long glasses from the kitchen counter and filled them with ice.

"So, I guess you wouldn't mind literally kissing her ass," Lenox said, walking up behind Maritza.

"Too bad she's not into threesomes. I think it would be nice. And strangely enough, I think she likes me, too." She filled the glasses with ginger ale and a splash of Pinot Grigio. "She's always staring at me." Maritza sauntered into the living room and laid her naked, petite body on the plush bearskin rug.

Lenox sat down next to her. "I don't know what staring means in France, but here it means a fight."

"Perhaps," Maritza said, shrugging.

"I may have to shut down the Life House," he said, not sure what compelled him to tell Maritza about the Life House.

"Is that a case you're working on?"

Lenox looked at her as if she were crazy. "It's a charity house I founded."

"Oh," she said, clearly not interested. She set her drink aside, then plucked his from his hand and set it next to hers. She crawled on top of Lenox and slid off his tie. He lay on his back. Then she removed his clothes piece by piece, folding them neatly and setting them to the side. The rug felt like a thousand feathers tickling their skin. Maritza got up and set her videocamera on top of the coffee table.

"Do you and Farah tape yourselves?" Maritza looked at Lenox through the lens.

"Farah made it clear that she didn't want to be photographed or videotaped in any compromising position just in case she became famous one day," Lenox said, putting his hands behind his head.

Maritza pressed Play on her CD player and Sade's smooth tunes filled the room. She smiled playfully as she began to undulate sensually to the music. Lenox watched in interest as she got closer and closer. He sat up, making sure he didn't miss one move. She was standing directly in front of him when she bent over and swayed her behind in front of his face. Unable to resist, Lenox grabbed her hips and bit one tender butt cheek. He told her to lie down on the floor as he grabbed the half-full bottle of Pinot Grigio sitting on the ground. He adjusted the lens for a close-up. Then he poured what was left of the wine down her stomach and let it roll down the lips of her pussy, where he licked and sucked the mix of flavors. He readily penetrated her body, smacking her face and calling her slut, bitch, and nasty stripper. With each slap and name calling, she roared with pleasure. For the next hour, they had sex for the camera, outdoing one another each time in performance and orgasms.

♥

When Lenox reached the apartment some time after 2:00 in the morning, there was no sign of Farah. He knew she had come in, because he could see a change of clothes scattered on the bed. He saw a note on the nightstand, picked it up and read it.

> *Jacob Richard called me when I got in.*
> *I'm on my way to meet him for the interview.*
> *I got a camera crew from the job. This is going to be big!*

Lenox crumpled up the letter and let it fall to the floor. She hadn't been thinking about him after all. He stretched out on the bed and fought to stay awake, but in the end, he fell asleep in his clothes. He vaguely remembered Farah coming home, but he had been too tired to move. He promised he would ask her for details in the morning.

*F*arah's story on Jacob Richard made the front page of *The New York Times* and the *Daily News*, as well as *Dateline* and *60 Minutes*. She was thrilled when *Dateline* invited her to introduce the story herself. Almost every newspaper in the country was quoting her interview with Jacob Richard. But most important, she broke the story on Channel 7 first, which gave the station its highest ratings ever, beating CNN and MSNBC.

Lenox convinced Ms. Meyers to let Farah go to Jamaica with him, and the day after she appeared on *Dateline*, they were on the plane.

"Ms. Meyers had flowers personally delivered to me yesterday," Farah told Lenox as they settled into first class. "The card said something about 'good news' when I come back." She watched Lenox closely, wondering if he was holding back on info about *Rise and Shine*.

"Maybe they've finally set an air date for the new *Rise and Shine*," he said. "Katie is still bumping heads with management about money, so it may well be good news." Lenox adjusted his seat to recline all the way back. She recognized the signs of him preparing for a nap, but she wanted to talk.

"Do you know how Derrick is handling everything?"

"I haven't heard from him. He's probably holed up somewhere with his father trying to plot his next move. I'm sure we'll both hear about it when we get back," he said, with his eyes half-closed. "We're on a plane, heading to a beautiful tropical island. The last thing I want to discuss is Derrick."

Farah didn't want to admit it, but it bothered her how he could ruin Derrick's political life without remorse. She was just as much to blame, but Derrick was Lenox's friend, not hers.

Lenox awoke when the flight attendant announced that they were landing. When Farah looked out of her window, all she could see was the blue sea, green mountains, and tiny, colorful houses dotting the landscape.

She felt a shiver race through her. "I love how you can see the entire length of the island from here."

Lenox mumbled something and turned his body away from the bright glare of the window. Farah turned back to the window. She had never been to Jamaica. Traveling to the island, for Lenox, was about as exciting as a trip to Queens.

She didn't let his lack of excitement deplete hers. Farah took out her makeup kit and freshened up her lip gloss. She tied up her hair into a loose chignon when the flight attendant mentioned the ninety-degree temperature.

"Welcome to the island of Jamaica. Have a safe and wonderful stay," ended the message.

Farah enjoyed the way they were able to breeze through customs and how, before the heat even kissed their skin, they were whisked away in a tinted-glass, air-conditioned luxury Escalade.

Ensconced in the backseat, Lenox pulled Farah close to him as they watched the scenery whiz by. He pointed out important places from his childhood, such as the little store where he'd bought his ice cream, the market where he'd shopped for fish with Elsa, and the beach where he and his family would spend their free time. Farah listened to him recall his childhood, something she admittedly knew very little about. The car passed several impoverished neighborhoods with children running barefoot in the street and women walking with large, colorful baskets, usually packed with foods, balanced on their heads. They drove by a crowd of schoolchildren dressed in clean checkered uniforms, which Lenox explained was how all students dressed in Jamaica. The children waved as the car zoomed by.

The scenery changed as they passed the tourist area of Ocho Rios, which held famous resort landmarks such as Sandals and Dunns River Falls. Lenox showed her three guesthouses that his family owned for those travelers who wanted a more intimate stay far from resorts. Guests would pay up to five thousand a week to stay in a plantation-style house along the beach with spectacular ocean views and a cook and maid who serviced their every need. And there wasn't a week that went by without a guest. Farah mentally calculated the amount his family was making on the houses. He explained that the tourist industry was something his family was becoming heavily involved in.

The ride was long, but with Lenox acting as her tour guide, the ride was entertaining. The driver took a turn around a wide circle and commenced up a hill. Farah stretched her neck out to see below which was nothing but water. They drove higher and higher into the hills.

"How high are we going? Everything looks so small from up here." Farah felt a little dizzy. She had always been terrified of heights.

"Everything *is* small from up here," Lenox said. "This is Cherry Hill, my childhood home."

"How did you feel growing up so isolated?" Farah asked, still looking out the window. She wondered how he could have compassion for regular folks, growing up like a prince on a very high hill.

"I hated it. I would always go into town, especially Kingston. When school was over, I'd go down there and play cards, dominoes, or just walk up and down the street with friends. I remember once my mother caught me and whooped my ass from here to the Hill," he said, his eyes sparkling as he relived the experience.

"Who did you go with? Did you have friends in Kingston?"

"I went with Seht mostly. I also learned how to speak patois down there, since that is forbidden in my house. We would just go down there and flirt with the girls. Then when the guys saw us with the girls, they'd plot against us. I was never liked, but Seht had a more comical way of handling things. When word got out about the money we had, everyone wanted to be our friends. So now anytime we went into town, the same people would harass us for money. They'd ask specifically for American dollars."

"Did you give them money?" Farah asked now, watching Lenox's expression.

Lenox laughed. "I had to sneak and take the money from my dad. I thought it was a way to make them like me, but I was only about thirteen or fourteen. So I did it for a few times, but it just became like buying friends. I didn't have any friends when I looked around. Then my parents got suspicious because money was missing. At the time I was old enough for high school, and they sent me away to Andover," he said.

"Well, I can understand your parents doing that," she said. "So now your kids at the Life House, and all the Lyncs parties make up for all the friends you never had."

Lenox laughed again. "Yeah, but I just don't think people *like* me. And it's not that I care what people think, but it always makes me feel I got to keep on my toes and watch people's motives."

"Hey, nobody likes Donald Trump or Puff Daddy. People who don't fit the mold are just not liked," she said. "I never felt people liked me either. Especially women. If I got married tomorrow, Lola would be the maid of honor and my bridesmaid all in one. She's the only girl who I admire."

Lenox laid her head on his shoulder and they continued to look out the window in comfortable silence. Lenox pointed out the perfectly constructed roads and majestic homes. Each home was guarded and gated. Some entrances had large flights of marble steps like the ones that adorn the museums and libraries in New York City. Some even had large Roman-style columns. The gentle noise of landscapers using sophisticated machines to manicure the lawns filtered through the warm afternoon air, but there was no one outside sitting on porches or looking out the window as in Farah's neighborhood in Brooklyn.

They eventually reached Lenox's family estate. It was elegantly set amongst soaring palm trees and a tropical garden. His estate was clearly the largest and, therefore, the wealthiest of all the nearby estates. It was a mansion with three stories, and its length overshadowed the houses nearby. Lenox remained quiet as the driver drove up to the front gate.

The driver got out of the truck to open the door for Farah, but Lenox got out and beat him to it. The driver just patted him on the back and smiled.

Farah looked up at his home, rather impressed. She spotted a lovely cottage to the left side of the house that was dressed in a painter's palette of white, turquoise, and green.

Following her line of vision, Lenox said, "That's the guesthouse. My family always has someone flying in. Mostly politicians from the PNP and artists."

The closer they got to the house, the tighter Lenox held her hand. His hand felt clammy and cold against hers. Farah wanted to ask him what the problem was, but before she could they were facing the large front door. Standing before it, she felt as if she and Lenox were toy soldiers. Lenox's apparent discomfort made her nervous.

He raised his hand, but before he could ring the bell, the door flew open and a woman wearing a light blue apron stood there.

"Lenox!" she cried. "Welcome home! Welcome, babies!" She quickly ushered them in. Farah was sure it was Lenox's mother.

Lenox and the woman hugged each other enthusiastically. Farah stood to the side waiting her turn.

Finally, Lenox turned to Farah. "Elsa, this is Farah. *My* baby," he said, putting his arm around her. "And Farah, this is Elsa, our cook and my second mother."

"What a beauty! And I can tell she has smarts, too, with those looks. Welcome," Elsa said, and gave Farah a hug.

"Nice to meet you, too, Ms. Elsa. Thank you."

"And she has manners! Your parents will like this one." Elsa winked. "Excuse me," she said, and left to direct the driver about where to leave the luggage.

"This place is like something out of *Town and Country* magazine." Farah spun around as she looked up at the antique chandeliers. She walked over to touch a vase of beautifully arranged tulips and orchids, and inhaled their scents.

"My, my, my. If it isn't my only son with a lady friend!" said a chirpy voice from above. Farah looked up and saw an elegantly dressed woman glide down the stairs. She looked as if she was in her late twenties, and she had on the most gorgeous floral wrap dress. Farah especially liked her hoop earrings. At her side was a man with a dimple on the same side of his face as Lenox and a clean-shaven face. He looked the way Lenox would in twenty-five years.

His father approached him with a formal handshake and his mother gave him a light kiss on the cheek, but no hug. Farah waited.

"I want you both to meet Farah Washington," Lenox said. "She is an anchor for Channel Seven in New York. She's one of their aces," Lenox said, proudly.

"Oh, yes, that is where Joan is working now. I'm mighty impressed with such a young lady as yourself being an anchor," Lenox's father said, eyeing Farah as he shook her hand.

"It was something I've always wanted," Farah said graciously, but she felt as though she had a ball of cotton in her throat.

"Why don't we all have a seat in the parlor," Lenox's mother suggested, and everyone followed.

The room was furnished with gold-trimmed white sofas. Lenox and Farah sat on a smaller love seat and his mother and father sat on larger chairs.

Elsa entered the room and walked over to Mr. Whitworth. He whispered something in her ear and she left.

"So, tell me, Farah, how did you get involved in journalism?" Lenox's father asked.

"I actually got into it in college, where I started working for a television network. I did some interviews that got me some notoriety. Are you familiar with the Anniston case?"

"Most definitely," Mr. Whitworth said. "Someone at my firm was associated with that. I do remember a young woman like yourself interviewing the young man. Come to think of it," he said, raising his finger, "your station won an Emmy for that coverage, right?"

"Yes, we did." Farah beamed.

"That's a wonderful accomplishment," Lenox's father said.

"Where did you go to school again? Brown?" Mrs. Whitworth asked.

"No, I went to Columbia."

"Ah, well. Columbia is good, too." But Mrs. Whitworth's tone didn't sound convinced.

Elsa came back with glasses of lemonade. Farah silently thanked Elsa's good timing.

"Sweetie, it's a shame how we've attacked them like this. Why don't you two go upstairs, unpack, and relax. We'll see you for dinner," Mr. Whitworth said, getting up.

"It was nice meeting you, Farah," Mrs. Whitworth said. Farah shook their hands. Lenox kissed his mother's cheek and his parents retreated to the patio.

Farah was anxious to get upstairs and rest so she'd be more prepared for small talk during dinner. She took her glass and followed Lenox upstairs.

"Here we are," Lenox said, opening the door and allowing Farah to enter before him.

"It's beautiful," she murmured.

Farah peered out the window, overlooking the rear of the house and the ocean. She looked down and saw Lenox's parents talking animatedly on the veranda. It looked as if there was a storm brewing, but she didn't mention it to Lenox for fear that it would change his good mood.

"Where do your parents sleep?" Farah asked, walking up to him.

"They sleep right next door," Lenox said. "But don't worry about us getting caught, because I can hear them coming up the steps."

Farah made some space between them. "What? So you mean we have to sneak sex and listen out for creaky steps?" Her eyes opened wide without blinking.

"No, silly." Lenox stroked her face. "You think in a house as big as this that we'd have to sneak and do anything? You haven't seen half of this place. My parents sleep all the way on the other side of the house. And the staff sleeps on the first floor."

Farah nudged Lenox in his stomach and he lowered her onto the bed.

"Let's forget unpacking. We can do that later. Sherry will iron whatever you need her to," he said in between kisses on Farah's cleavage.

"Who's Sherry?" she said, gripping his shoulders.

"One of our maids," Lenox said, sucking on her neck.

"Of course," Farah said, spreading her legs, and showed Lenox just how happy she was to have an entire floor to themselves.

♥

For dinner, Farah followed Lenox's lead and changed into more formal wear. He wore a matching tan linen pants and jacket. She opted for a conservative but stylish yellow-gold A-line dress that fell just above the knees.

Dinner began at exactly 7:00. Mr. and Mrs. Whitworth were waiting at the bottom of the steps for them. Farah was praying that she wouldn't trip on the winding stairs.

"Everything all right, dear?" Mr. Whitworth said, bending his head to look Farah in the eye.

She smiled. "Wonderful, Mr. Whitworth."

"Well, let's eat! Somebody told me Elsa outdid herself this time," he said. Mrs. Whitworth and Farah walked into the dining room ahead of them.

Farah paused when she saw the length of the table. It was laid out for a party of ten. It was covered with sterling silver platters giving off delectable smells. Everything was prearranged, right down to the fresh-cut flowers that sat in the center of the room. The room looked as though it hadn't been used in a long time.

"What a lovely dining room." Farah said to Mrs. Whitworth.

"I know, we only use it on special occasions. So I hope you and Lenox feel special." Mrs. Whitworth walked to the end of the table.

Lenox pulled out a chair for Farah and Mr. Whitworth did the same for his wife.

A small group of servers came around and helped them to the first course. Farah knew it was going to be a long evening.

"So, Farah, how did you and Lenox meet?" his father asked.

"Lenox was working on my contract for the network. After a few phone calls, we decided to meet for dinner. We clicked instantly," Farah said, smiling at Lenox.

"I gather you've met my sister, Joan," Mrs. Whitworth said. She neatly cut her jerk chicken.

Farah answered carefully. "Ms. Meyers is an interesting woman. She's really helped me grow at the network." Farah immediately put a spoonful of rice and peas in her mouth.

"Farah left out the best part, but . . ." Lenox looked at Farah and smiled. "Farah will be co-host on *Rise and Shine* when the new format airs."

Mr. Whitworth nodded. "When's the wedding, Lenox?"

Lenox cleared his throat.

"We haven't even been together a year," Farah replied. "There's still some things we need to work on. But it's definitely an option we're looking at. Right, Lenox?"

"That's right, baby. We're looking at our options," Lenox said, concentrating intently on dinner.

Mrs. Whitworth gave Farah a wink she wasn't quite sure how to interpret.

After dinner, everyone moved outside onto the veranda. Lenox and Farah sat on the same bench he and Joanne had sat on last summer. They made polite conversation and watched until the sun disappeared from the horizon.

♥

Just before dawn, Farah woke Lenox up with a little early lovin'. Pulling the cover away, she moved between his legs and began slowly licking the Whitworth jewels. He hardened in her mouth, and when he reached down and played with her hair, she knew he was fully awake. After he came, she kissed her way back up his body.

"Let's go down to the beach before the sun rises, please?" she asked.

"All right," he simply said. She watched him get up and go to the bathroom.

"Ready?" he said when he came back into the bedroom dressed in a new pair of shorts.

Farah slipped into a sundress, and within minutes they were walking down to the private beach.

The sound of a rooster crowing in the distance broke the morning silence. They sat on a flat spot on the edge of a cliff to get a good view of the rising sun. The water below looked like platinum.

To speak would have ruined the magic of the moment. Farah soaked up the tranquility and let it sooth her like a balm. In the distance, they saw small boats getting ready to catch fish for the morning market. Just before they were about to doze off, the light from the break in the sky woke them up. They walked down to the beach and went skinny-dipping. Farah dipped her head in the warm water and watched the horizon. Lenox did, too. They splashed and fooled around until they exhausted themselves.

♥

Family members began pouring into the Whitworth estate for Little Floyd's birthday party at around 2:00 P.M. One by one, they gathered outside by the shimmering pool and well-manicured garden area. Farah was excited and couldn't wait to meet the rest of Lenox's family, but she could tell from his funky mood that he wasn't looking forward to it at all.

"It's a damn shame. You think for a kid's party you'd see kids playing games instead of adults drinking and hollering," Lenox said, standing by the window, with one hand against the wall. "I don't see anyone arriving with gifts."

Farah walked over to the window as she clipped on her pearl earrings. "Isn't that your father and Elsa standing over there by the jerk chicken pit? They look very . . . comfortable with one another."

"Elsa and my father have a special relationship. They grew up in St. Mary together. She's like a sister to him," Lenox snapped.

"They don't look like brother and sister to me. I mean . . . look at how he's touching her."

"Okay, okay. You can put down your reporter's notepad," Lenox said, sitting down on the powder blue couch. He massaged his temples.

"Is your dad fooling around with Elsa?"

"Fooling around? Elsa has always been the love of his life. My father and my mother just have a relationship built on convenience."

She saw a brief flash of pain on his face, but it disappeared just as quickly.

Farah stopped brushing her hair and sat down next to him.

"I don't need a therapy session. We have people waiting for us," he said.

"I just don't understand how you grew up knowing your father and mother never loved each other. I didn't have to live with both of them and see that," she said, looking at him.

Lenox was quiet for such a long time that Farah thought he wasn't going to speak. "My parents had to learn to love each other," he finally said. His voice was so low she had to strain to hear him. "And even then, it seemed hard. When I was young, I swore Elsa was my mother. It wasn't until I was about age four or five that my mother took me to the side and told me I should start calling her Mommy."

"You thought Elsa was your mother?" Farah asked, shocked.

Lenox sighed. "It's really complicated. My mother was always off in Europe with her artist friends. Or at least that was what my father used to tell me. And Elsa and my father used to be together and we'd all do things like a family sometimes. I'd even see Elsa and my father doing their own things. Things *adults* do."

"God, Lenox, how did you live like that? Seeing your dad in bed with another woman? Being all confused about who your mother was?" Farah shook her head in disbelief.

"Elsa acted more like my mother and seeing her and my father share those 'intimate' moments made it seem even more so. None of us have ever talked about it. We all just lived together. And I know my mother tried like hell at one point to get Elsa replaced, but my father wasn't having it."

Lenox stood and shook off the wrinkles in his pants.

And I thought my childhood was weird, Farah thought. She stood up and put her arms around him and gave him a kiss on the cheek.

He hugged her briefly, then released her, and said, "We should get downstairs." Farah took one last look in the mirror before they left to join the party. She stood side by side with Lenox as he greeted everyone. Mechanically, he went from person to person, offering up the same greetings over and over again. Many wanted to talk and catch up, but Lenox politely moved on. He was obviously a fixation for everyone. He even made his older aunts and cousins blush. There were some unknown faces of a few younger women, around Farah's age, who eyed Lenox hungrily. And Farah eyed them back. However, she didn't want to spend her time playing the ever-watchful girlfriend. She wanted to get to know Lenox's family. With her cooking skills, she couldn't get to a man's heart through food, so she thought his family was the next best thing.

"Aren't you the young lady who was on *Dateline* breaking that story on that awful politician?" said a middle-aged man with a Barry White voice. "That man should really step down from the race."

"Yes, that was me. It's our biggest story in New York right now," Farah said, still holding Lenox's hand.

"Tell me, how were you the first to get that?! By the way, I'm a senior correspondent for the BBC. Martin Cambridge." He gave her hand a wild handshake.

"Nice to meet you," Farah said, looking at Lenox for an answer. But his attention was already taken by a couple standing next to them. "I was at the right place at the right time." She shrugged. "You know how it goes."

"Yeah, I do. And I can't blame him for opening up to you. I would want the first woman I see when I get out of jail to be as beautiful as you, too." He snickered, stealing a peak at Farah's cleavage.

"Thank you. Listen, it was nice talking, but I'm just going to get a refill of the rum punch." Farah excused herself and filled her glass up with the sweet-and-tangy drink. Standing away from the crowd, she observed everything from afar. Little snippets and words from conversations transmitted through the air. She still hadn't seen Little Floyd or any children. She watched Lenox talk to a man who had his arm around him. Lenox handed the man his business card. She knew it was the one with his answering machine number on it.

Lenox kept his "real" business cards at the office. He kept his hands in his pocket, which meant that he wasn't relaxed. He always hid his hands when they were clammy and wet.

At last, Little Floyd came in with his family and a few friends. He and his friends immediately ran to the huge swings and slides that were put in especially for his birthday party. Farah and Lenox walked toward each other through the crowd, each reading the look on the other's face.

"I'd love a big, juicy cheeseburger right now. With some barbecue sauce on it," Lenox said. "And a nice cold Heineken."

Farah laughed. "Listen to you, sounding like a New York boy." She took a frog leg from the food table behind them. She bit into it. "Tastes like bad chicken," she said. The cheeseburger idea was sounding good to her now, too.

Later, a seven-tier cake was brought out on a wheeled cart and everyone sang "Happy Birthday." It was the size of the wedding cake she imagined she would have one day. Little Floyd did not seem one bit impressed by the size or the people. He just wanted to play on the swings. Farah watched him play and remembered her younger days that were spent alone indoors waiting for her mom to come in from work.

Night descended upon the few people that were still hanging around. Some light reggae music played as Farah sat with Lenox's mother in front of the house. She still hadn't been able to talk to his father, but one bird in the hand was good enough for her.

She was impressed with Mrs. Whitworth's sophisticated knowledge of politics and history. Farah had already labeled her a flaky artist and felt bad at her quick assumption. Lenox must have definitely gotten his smarts from his mother, Farah thought. She listened to Mrs. Whitworth talk about the early days of Winston Churchill and British rule over Jamaica. It wasn't the most interesting conversation for Farah, but it was informative.

"What do you think of the Mexican artist Frida Kahlo?" Farah asked, trying to show her interest in art.

"She is one of my favorites. I loved her mind," she said, looking at Farah.

"I have a painting of Frida and Diego in my house. I got it because of the power of that painting. Frida looked so tiny and delicate next to a big monster like Diego."

"And he *was* a monster. He used to have affairs with all kinds of women. And he hated children. I think that is why he married her, because she was barren. She wasn't the most beautiful of women. She was hairy and her eyebrows connected."

"What's remarkable to me was their relationship," Farah said. "They hurt but loved each other. They divorced and then remarried. If you read her poems about him, she was intoxicated."

"It's one of those strange relationships in life we can't explain. They fed off of each other's weaknesses and built on each other's strengths. If it wasn't for Diego, she wouldn't have been readily accepted into the high-profile arts world. He made her," Mrs. Whitworth said.

She nodded in agreement. "I want to love like that. Unconditionally," Farah said.

Lenox had been talking to a young woman just outside the house gates. Though Farah's attention was on his mother, she was counting every second. She managed quick glances in the young woman's direction, but she was turned sideways. The woman was dressed in a neat, tailored pant suit and a medium-length shag haircut. Farah noted she was attractive, which sent the red flags in her head waving. She then noted the woman looked more than attractive. She looked like a beauty queen. Farah's instinct told her to get up and introduce herself to Lenox's new friend. She quietly prayed that Lenox, on their last night in Jamaica, wasn't pulling one of his "other woman" stunts on her again. She couldn't stand to be embarrassed in front of his family.

"Farah, I'm no psychic, but I can tell something is bothering you. Is it Winston Churchill's involvement with Nazi Germany?"

Mrs. Whitworth chuckled at her own joke. "Or is it Lenox talking to that young lady?"

Farah stuttered. "Oh, no, I—I was just wondering if I—I—"

"We're both girls here. I know how you feel. I bet you want to know who that is. Right?" she asked, casually drinking her wine.

"Yes. Who is that?" Farah asked, trying to appear calm. She was afraid of the answer.

"Nobody you should worry over. That is why he is talking to her outside the gate, dear. It's little things like that you have to notice if you plan to be with a Whitworth man." She sighed. "I might as well let the cat out of the bag. The girl's name is Joanne. She and Lenox had this thing going on for about a year or so. But it's been over for a while. She was just crowned Miss Caribbean. It's probably the best thing that happened to the girl."

"He never mentioned a Joanne." Farah's felt her stomach muscles clench.

"Farah, he's not supposed to tell you. My husband and my son are two of a kind. They think they have everything under control. But I assure you, that is one you don't have to worry about. The last I heard, she was engaged. And she's probably here just to wish Little Floyd a happy birthday," she said. "Even though it *is* a little late."

They sat in silence and watched Lenox and Joanne like two owls sitting on a branch. Joanne left when a car approached to pick her up.

In the middle of the night, Mr. Whitworth and Lenox took Farah and Mrs. Whitworth's spot on the front porch. Farah stayed in the bed and heard peals of laughter and the clapping sounds of dominoes being played out her window. Lenox didn't go to sleep that night and neither did his father. She didn't plan to ask Lenox about Joanne. Their flight to New York in the morning was an early one and she didn't want to ruin the last few hours they had left in Jamaica. She had bigger issues on her mind, and Maritza and Derrick were the top two.

Chapter 12 ♥ **Farah**

When Lenox and Farah reached the apartment, Lenox's voice mail was inundated with messages from a desperate Derrick. With each passing day, he was dropping in the polls and there were only a few weeks left before elections.

Eventually, due to Derrick's father's hiring a big-time publicity firm, a veil was pulled over the controversy. Derrick's camp made Jacob Richard look like a jealous foe and even forged psychiatric papers to prove he was delirious. It worked. Derrick won the race for congressman by the slimmest margin in New York State history, but his family reputation was permanently stained.

When Farah got to work, she found a bouquet of about fifty red roses on her desk. She sighed to herself as she picked out a rose from the bunch. It wasn't from Lenox, she thought, because he stopped doing things like that months ago. She sat down and read the card.

Dear Rise and Shine *co-anchor,*
I'll have my TV turned on bright and early next Monday. There's nothing better than a young, fine sister smiling at a brother in the

morning, and she ain't asking for shit! (Smile) See you at the launch
party.

Love you,

Lenox.

The tears welled up in the corner of Farah's eyes and blurred the words on the paper. Each drop smeared the blue ink, making the neat cursive lines into a sloppy mess. Her hands shook. It had finally happened. She had reached the pinnacle of broadcast journalism. She was now the crown jewel of Channel 7.

Farah held her hand to her chest to control her breathing. She talked to herself to calm down and exhale. Before she could get out another breath, the phone rang.

"I suppose you saw the flowers from Lenox. He wanted you to hear it first from him," Ms. Meyers said.

Farah sniffed. "His flowers are lovely. I didn't expect it this way. Thank you, Ms. Meyers."

"Congratulations, Farah. You've been doing an excellent job. While you were in Jamaica a lot went on here. As you know, we have been in a contract battle with Katie for the longest time. It hasn't been extended. Obviously," she said, dramatically. "Let me just say a lot of the higher-ups thought it was time for a fresh face. They were grooming you from the start, so it seems."

Farah realized the difference in Ms. Meyers's tone. She seemed gentler and genuinely happy for her.

"I'm stunned, relieved, excited. . . . There's so many feelings inside of me right now."

"Thank Lenox. He pushed for your two-and-a-half-million-dollar contract. I mean, he gave the boys upstairs no other choice. You're free until you go back on air as co-anchor of *Rise and Shine* next week. I must go, but I'll see you at the launch party on Friday night."

Still holding the phone in her hand, Farah allowed Ms. Meyers's words to sink in. She hung up and dialed Lenox's phone number. But she put the receiver down. She felt odd about something, but couldn't figure out why. Then it hit her that this man had changed her entire life. It was the Derrick story that had sent her over the top. She felt indebted to him and ever more dependent. She picked up the phone.

"It's Farah," she told Margaret.

"Hello, Ms. Washington, but Mr. Whitworth is not in the office now. May I leave a message?"

"Is he in a meeting?" Farah asked, disappointed.

"I'm looking at his book, and he's pretty clear today. Maybe he's out getting you a gift for your wonderful promotion! Congratulations, by the way."

"Thank you," Farah said, her mind filled with thoughts of Lenox with Maritza. They had just gotten back in town! She had hoped their trip to Jamaica would bring her and Lenox closer together.

Farah hung up and dialed his cell phone. It automatically transferred to his voice mail. She tried his other cell phone, but again she got his voice mail.

She sat there with her mind racing until her phone rang.

"Lenox?" she asked, picking it up on the first ring.

"No, this is Sandra Brown calling from *TV Guide*. Congratulations on your being co-host of *Rise and Shine*. We just received the press release," she said, talking rapidly into the phone. There was a barrage of voices in the background.

"Thanks so much! What can I do for you?" Farah straightened herself up in her chair for good news, she hoped.

"You're our cover story for next week. Can we arrange a time to meet? I also need some time to shoot some photos of you." Farah could hear the urgency in Ms. Brown's voice. "Wednesday at ten?"

Farah didn't bother looking at her Palm Pilot. "Sure, that's fine with me. We can do the interview here, if you'd like."

"Sounds wonderful! This story is going to be hot. You are the youngest and the first African-American female anchor of *Rise and Shine* in its forty-year run!"

She forced a smile into her voice. "Thanks again, Ms. Brown. This is the cover I've been dreaming of."

The two shared a few more kind words and hung up.

Farah opened her office door, and a pile of confetti came raining down on her. Then she heard the applause. Everyone was standing outside, including Sam, Pete, and her six o'clock and eleven o'clock casts.

She lightly brushed the confetti away from her jacket sleeves and welcomed Sam's hug. "How long did you know about this?"

"A little birdie told me this morning. You know how things happen overnight around here," Sam said, looking as flawless as ever.

Pete and the rest gave Farah their hugs and handshakes. They all did seem happy for her. The happier she became the more she wanted to talk to Lenox.

"Front page, baby. New York *Daily News* got Phyllis Sherman writing about you already. She called you 'the face of a new era in morning news.' Not a bad start."

Farah grabbed the paper from Sam, who stood there beaming. Her shaky fingers jumped from page to page until they stopped to read every line of the article.

"And she called me a 'sexy siren.' Oh, no! The last time a female anchor was called sexy all hell broke lose. But I ain't complaining," she said, closing the paper. She put it in a folder, which would be the start of many articles about her career she would collect.

Sam went off to a meeting and Farah was left alone again. She called her mother and Lola to tell them the good news. Her mother, especially, was ecstatic and nearly dropped the phone. Farah spent at least ten minutes convincing her not to come to the *TV Guide* interview.

♥

When Farah got home, Lenox was already there, watching TV in the living room. She saw small white specks of dust and a red-rimmed small plastic bag on the kitchen table. It was the first time he'd brought coke home to her knowledge, but she felt it was out of place to tell him what to bring home to his own place.

"Where were you all day?" she asked, throwing her handbag on the kitchen table.

"I had to go to Westchester to meet a new client," he said. "Come here. Congratulations," he said, walking open-armed into the kitchen.

"You could have told me. I got the flowers, but I would rather have talked to you." She put away her annoyance and wrapped her hands around his waist. She squeezed the smoothness of his gray velour Sean John suit that draped his body. It was the one she bought him a few months back. "Thanks for pushing the contract. And for getting them to put me on *Rise and Shine*," Farah said, like a timid student thanking her teacher for passing her.

"You deserve it. And you *finally* got what you wanted." He laughed. He picked up the plastic bag and shoved it in his pocket. "Thanks to Derrick's story."

"I think them seeing me on *Dateline* and *Sixty Minutes* made them a little nervous that another network would snatch me," she said.

"I wouldn't go that far. But you did well." He patted her on the back. "And the launch party is all set for Friday. James is helping me out with that. There's gonna be music, food, cameras, an eight-foot-long cake. And my baby at the center!"

"Lenox, why don't you lie down and get some sleep." Farah was concerned at his behavior. He looked at her as if she was speaking another language.

"I have to go back to the office." He abruptly packed up his things. He took the small plastic bag out of his pocket and tucked it inside one of his briefcase pockets. A look of worry passed over Farah's face as she stood against the sink. She worried that he might be caught with the coke by police. It would ruin his legal career. "I'll call you tonight. We'll celebrate tomorrow," he said, leaving the kitchen.

Farah sat in the den and ordered in from the Chinese restaurant.

She ate and watched the *Bernie Mac Show*. In the back of her mind, she felt Lenox was with Maritza and not at work. She tried to block it out by laughing at every silly joke on the show. But it wasn't enough.

This was the happiest day of her life, and her mind was not on her future but her present. Then the phone rang, interrupting her dinner.

"Hello. Who's speaking?" Farah said, balancing the phone between her ear and shoulder. Her hands were occupied with a hot carton of chicken and broccoli.

The person on the line was silent, until she heard someone shuffle around with the phone.

"Is Lenox there?" Immediately Farah recognized Maritza's voice.

"Lenox is not here now, Maritza. What do you want?" Farah asked, trying to remain in control.

"Oh, I'm sorry. There's my bell. Thanks, Farah." The line clicked off. She called Maritza's number back, but the line was busy.

Farah stuffed a spear of broccoli in her mouth as she wondered if she had just dreamed what happened. Did Maritza just call her house and try to make her feel like a fool? She was fuming. She spit out her broccoli and called Lola.

"Are you calling for advice on how to spend two and a half million dollars?" Lola asked jokingly.

"I think I got a handle on that one," Farah said. She didn't want to rush into talking about Maritza. She was trying her best to block things out. "I'm trying to just focus on next week. I need something to wear for the launch party and the *TV Guide* thing."

"Why do you sound so down?"

"It's Lenox," Farah said. "I wanted to be with him tonight and celebrate, but he's out."

"With Maritza?"

"I guess. His 'friend.' And I don't want to say anything else about it because I don't want to sound ungrateful or overpossessive. He probably even fucked her, but to tell you the truth, I don't want to even get into that with him." Farah swirled her fork around in her chicken and broccoli as she listened to Lola.

"Girl, you got what you wanted. Go up to his face and kick his ass!" Lola blasted.

"I met Maritza. And the girl is just a straight-up tramp, even though she comes off classy. What I don't like, too, is that she uses that coke shit and gets Lenox all involved in that. Seht is into it, too."

"Don't sit there and try to act like Lenox is an angel. I'm sure that man been snorting coke since he started getting wet dreams."

Farah felt like defending him, but she didn't want to argue.

"Just leave him. What can he do now?" Lola asked.

"I can't just leave him. The devil you know is better than the devil you don't know." Farah threw the rest of her Chinese food in the garbage.

"I haven't heard something so real in a while. Just don't let that Maritza get out of hand. You know what I mean," Lola said. She promised to call later and check up on things.

Farah fell asleep and it was the first time since she was single that she felt completely alone. Instead of the sound of Lenox's snores greeting her when she woke up, the emptiness of the apartment stared back at her. She didn't sleep and her puffy eyes showed it. She threw on some sweatpants and went to the office. It was early and she wasn't supposed to be in, but she had some calls to make.

Brian Lester was a former FBI agent whose card she had in her Rolodex. Sam used him to help her get the 411 on her ex-boyfriend before they became engaged. She found out he had a criminal record and dumped him. A few years ago, Farah interviewed him about a ten-year-old murder case he solved. He was an older man in his sixties and had retired since then. After the interview ended, he gave her his card. At the time, she didn't need it.

"Brian? Can I speak to a Brian Lester?" Farah said, reading the faded print on the card.

"Yes! This is Brian here." He coughed profusely until he regained his composure.

"Mr. Lester. This is Farah from Channel Seven. I interviewed you a ways back about that murder you solved. Remember, it was so big it created a new law," she said, trying to rekindle his memory.

"The Logan murder. Ah, yes. The Logan law. What a crock!" he shouted. "And I remember meeting you. A man never forgets a pretty woman." He laughed and coughed at the same time. "What can I do for you? Need a recommendation letter?" He roared with laughter at his own joke.

"No, I'm doing quite fine. I heard you retired," she asked, cooling her Starbucks Tazo chai tea.

"I'm an old man now. Instead of catching criminals, I catch fish," he said.

"Well, I was hoping you can do a pretty woman a little favor." Farah wasn't sure if she should have gone on with the small talk, but she wanted to get to the point.

"Sure! Whadda ya need? Snapper or bluefish?" Again, he laughed at his own dry joke. "Just kidding, what do you have for me, kid?"

Farah exhaled. "Good! Well, I just want to know if you can find out some info on this woman. Her name is Maritza Dubuisson," Farah said, as she read from the piece of paper she used when she copied Maritza's name and phone number from the caller ID.

She began to read off Maritza's age, place of origin, and a few other sketchy details. Mr. Lester said all he needed was Maritza's phone number to get what information was missing.

"I need to know just where she is from exactly and what jobs she's had. You know, basic things."

"So the old man is acting up, huh? Don't worry. I'll take care of that. I was tired of smelling like old trout anyway." He coughed once more. "I'll give you a call in a day or two." Farah hoped he wouldn't drop dead by then.

The newsroom was already bustling and it wasn't even 9:00 A.M. yet. Farah threw on her cap and tried to make a discreet exit. She looked like a hot mess, she thought. She walked briskly with her head down until she thought she heard, "Hey, Farah, kiss ass on *Rise and Shine!*" She turned around to see where it came from, but didn't see anyone. She hit the elevator button.

She called Lola's cell phone to confirm their meeting spot at the Nicole Miller store on Madison. When she called, Lola was already there. In no time, Farah marched across town with Lenox's platinum card tucked safely away in her purse. She couldn't beat Lenox, but she could put a beating on his American Express card. At the end of the day, she charged over five thousand for a few things and two pairs of slinky Christian Louboutins for Lola.

Struggling to find her keys to open the door, she put her bags down. Before she could find it, Lenox opened the door from the inside.

He gave her a blank look. He walked back in, leaving the door half-open so Farah could enter.

"Whoa. What's all the bags for? Tell me those designer bags are filled with clothes for the Salvation Army," he said, watching Farah strut by him.

"No, they are filled with clothes I need. I need a new look for my new show," she said, walking into the bedroom. Lenox walked in behind her, and began emptying the bags.

"Why do you need a twelve-hundred-dollar skirt?" He held it up as if it smelled. "Where's the rest of it?"

"In women's clothing, the amount of material does not matter, just the quality," she said, grabbing it from him. She wanted to ask him where he spent the night, but she didn't want him to know what she was thinking. Brian Lester would answer all her questions soon enough.

"Did you use the AMEX or the MasterCard?" he asked.

"I don't know. They both looked the same way," she said with an attitude. She cut her eyes at him, as she began putting the clothes away.

Lenox looked through the bags for the receipts. He pushed to the side the clothes she had folded.

"You know all the financial problems I'm having with the Life House and you go ahead and spend money like this? I can't even pay the Life House bills." He handed her a receipt. "Five thousand dollars on six pieces of clothing? And two pair of shoes? Where are the shoes?" he asked, looking around on the floor.

"They're around here somewhere," Farah said, knowing he'd flip if he knew she'd bought Lola shoes.

"You're missing a couple of people to be buying clothes like this. Beyonce and Kelly," he said counting his fingers.

"I don't have to be in *Destiny's Child*, but I will take their advice and become an independent woman if I have to," Farah said, avoiding his glare. "Next time, I'll use my own money."

"I'll hold these, until you pay me—Ms. Independent. Have a good night!" Lenox took the clothes.

He slammed the bedroom door leaving Farah amidst the empty bags.

The front door slammed, which meant Lenox was gone. His Range Rover was still parked across the street, which meant he might have just gone to the bar downstairs. She used the time to call her voice mail at work, and a message from Brian Lester was waiting.

"Mr. Lester. It's Farah," she said, speaking low.

"Hi, Farah! Has anyone ever told you there is a song about you, but it's called 'Sarah'?" he said. "It's a great song. It's not that old, ya know."

"I know, Mr. Lester, but I really want to know what you found."

He blew his nose before he started. "Seems like this Maritza was born in France. Is twenty-four years old. Was arrested in 1997 and 1998 for drug possession. But mysteriously she was never charged with anything. Then in 2000, she was charged with forging checks. But the charges were dropped," he said, sniffling. He paused to blow his nose again.

Farah's eye twitched.

"She used to be a stripper. At least, that's all I have for her work history. She moved to New York City last month. Strangely, all her bills are listed under a Lenox Whitworth. Her phone bill, too . . ."

Farah couldn't stand it any longer. "Do you have an address for her?"

Mr. Lester paused. "Hmmmmm. How do I know you aren't planning to do something crazy to this young lady?" he asked with concern.

"Because I just signed a multimillion-dollar contract with a network and I'll be on the cover of *TV Guide* next week. I'm not the likely profile of a killer," she answered back.

"Well, since you put it that way. She lives on East Twenty-third and Grove Street in Gramercy Park. Apartment Fifteen A. Nice area. But there's somebody else's name on the lease. Same guy from before. Must be her dad," he said, alluding to something more.

"It's my boyfriend whose name is all over those papers," Farah snapped. "Look, Mr. Lester, I have your address on the back of this card. Is it okay if I send you a check, or do you want cash?"

"How about a dinner date?" Before she answered, he said, "Okay, okay, I'll take a check." They both laughed.

After she hung up, she took her checkbook out of her purse and wrote out a check for five hundred dollars. She sealed it in an envelope and promised herself to mail it off first thing.

Lenox turned the key in the doorknob just after she hung up with Mr. Lester.

"Baby, look. I have no right to use up your card like that. I guess I was a little angry at some things, but I'll make it up to you," she said, reaching for his hand.

"Yeah, okay," he said, facing away from her and taking out a bottle of beer from a brown paper bag. He opened the bottle and walked past her to the living room. They stayed in that night and watched TV together. He was uneasy, however. There were still some bad vibes in the air. But Farah had it all under control. She was tearing up inside about Maritza and the news she discovered. It took all her power to hold in everything she wanted to say, but she wanted to keep him at bay about what she was planning. She realized this was a matter she needed to handle woman to woman.

♥

At the end of her *TV Guide* interview and photo session, Lenox called. He invited her for lunch at the Four Seasons and said they needed to talk.

"I'm closing down the Life House for good," he said, as they sat in a quiet corner of the busy restaurant.

"What? Why? I thought you were spending all that time there trying to keep it open."

"After what happened with George, I just don't want the burden of it anymore. I have no more time to contribute to it. I'll just sell the buildings." Lenox folded both of his hands under his chin.

Farah watched his saddened eyes. "I think you have helped enough kids in that neighborhood. And who knows, maybe one day you can have your own kids to fill that void."

"I also have a lot of explaining to do and I'm sorry if I caused any confusion for you. I've just been really feeling messed up lately."

"About what? You seem well enough to spend the night out," she said, her suspicions seeping through. She purposely avoided Maritza's name.

"Sometimes I just need some room to think. Since we've been back from Jamaica I feel closer to you. My family really liked you and I liked the way you handled yourself, not only with them but with me overall. I'm not the easiest person to understand. You're tough on me, but you know when to ignore me and the things I do. That had me tripping for a while until I saw you change, too. You got that *Rise and Shine* role, but you're still here with me. Anyone else would have left by now." He smiled.

"I'm still here. I didn't think I would be since things haven't been exactly easy. But Jamaica made a difference for me, too. I'm not going to let anyone get in the way of us. And don't let yourself get in the way of us, either." She smiled, pointing at him.

"I really want to try to make this work between us," he said. "I've never met anyone quite like you, Ms. Washington." He grinned.

"And I have *never* met anyone like you, Mr. Whitworth," she said, meaning every word of it. "You've made your way down to my bones. I couldn't shake you if I wanted to."

He looked down at his empty plate as if he was embarrassed, and then his brow wrinkled with thought, changing his look to sadness.

The waiter came over and poured their glasses of chardonnay. They toasted their future. Neither one knew exactly what that entailed, but the intention to make it work was there. Farah felt it was even more urgent now to get to the bottom of things with Maritza. Maybe Maritza had Lenox cornered or stuck him with the bills on purpose, she wondered. She made herself believe that.

"I've also been thinking about not doing those Lyncs parties anymore. As of today," he said.

"I thought that was your thing. Your ego boost."

"It was, when I was single. But now I just find it distracting. The office, the Life House, and the parties are enough to wear a man down in a day. I'm just ready to cut off a lot of those extra things that kept me busy," he said, drinking his wine.

What Lenox said sounded like sweet music. She thought those parties were magnets for man-hungry women, and with Maritza around, she didn't need any other women to worry about.

"If that's what you want, I'm with you. I think it was time for a change anyway. Those parties were stews for trouble," she said. "Can I ask you something?"

He nodded.

"Do you love me?"

He scratched his goatee, which he had recently let grow back in. "Farah, I never told a woman I loved her before. I feel I love you. I do feel it, but it's hard for me to say it. But . . . I *do* love you. You had my back when I needed you. Some women would have ran if I had come to them with that Derrick mess. But you rode that story to your benefit instead of your downfall. I respect that."

"Thank you, baby," she said, and leaned over and kissed him. Her stomach felt light the way it did when they first made love. She let her hand slide over his dimple and over his lips. His aftershave filled her nostrils. She didn't say she loved him back, but she did and he knew it.

The waiter returned with their meal. For Farah, it was the beginning of a new start with Lenox. And at the finish line, she hoped he'd still be there.

♥

The day before the launch party had arrived. It was where Farah would be officially crowned as the "new queen of morning television" as noted by her *TV Guide* story, which hadn't hit the stands yet.

Lenox went into work for half a day. Farah had a late-afternoon hair appointment with Patrik, her Jamaican hair stylist and finally some time to pay a visit to Maritza.

She took the Range Rover and drove down Madison till she hit Twenty-third Street. The building was right across the street from an art gallery and a park. She sat outside in the car and counted to twenty. She was losing it, she told herself. She scoped the building out and saw a heavily staffed concierge desk. The last thing she wanted was to be questioned. Then she saw a back entrance, which was open for package deliveries. Double-parking the car, she thought about everything Mr. Lester had told her.

When the UPS man rolled the last package in, she walked in behind him. No one bothered to ask. They were too busy sorting through the stacks of boxes.

Farah hurriedly pressed the elevator button, and it opened suddenly. She tried to remain sane, and told herself she wouldn't yell or threaten Maritza. It would give Maritza too much power and make her appear insecure. There was more at stake than another woman stepping on her toes. Farah was fighting for her relationship, her future, and her security. She believed that in the right circumstances Lenox would be a good man and could be a good husband. Lola's words about her needing a man pierced her thoughts, her mother's complaints about her not being able to keep a man, and her own fears all combined into a big chain around her neck. And she wasn't going to let Maritza ruin what was the most satisfying time in her career and life.

"Who's there?" Maritza asked, looking through the peephole. She was talking over some loud music that sounded like Prince.

"It's Farah, Maritza. Can we talk for a minute?" she said, in her best fake-happy voice.

The door flung open. "Farah! So nice to see you. Come on in," she said as she held a glass of juice in one hand.

"Sit, sit. I heard you knocking, but I was playing Prince. His music will never go out of style. Want a cigarette?" she said, lighting one.

Farah watched her give the lighter a quick flick as she held it to the cigarette. "Do you always smoke so early in the morning?"

"It helps me calm down. I know smoking is so 1980s in America. I can't even sit in a decent restaurant here without people making a fuss," she said, blowing the smoke in the opposite direction. She sat on the same couch as Farah. She wore a loosely tied purple robe, which looked similar to one Farah had in black.

The apartment was a duplex with a bedroom downstairs. It was much smaller than Lenox's, but was well kept and decorated. The furniture felt brand-new and the paint smelled fresh.

"I'm really here to talk about Lenox," began Farah. "I don't want to argue. I just want to know what you want from him." She held her head up high and prepared to hear what she didn't want to believe.

Maritza placed an ashtray that already had three lipstick stained cigarette buds on her lap.

"Well, what did he tell you?"

"I want to hear from *you*," said Farah.

Maritza parted her lips as if she was about to say something. Instead, she stuck her cigarette between them and turned her eyes to the floor.

"Okay, let me make this easy for you. When was the last time you were with him?"

"Just a few days ago," said Maritza, taking a slow drag from her cigarette.

"What about this apartment and everything?" Farah's voice was rising.

"He pays for it. He told me to come to New York City and he'll take care of everything until I find a role. He and I met years ago and have never lost contact."

"Maritza, what is it that you really want? Is it an acting job? Because if it is, Lenox can't get you that. If it's a man, *he's* already taken. And if it's some money, then get a job," Farah said. She saw herself gaining more leverage over Maritza.

Hearing what Maritza had to say was important. She didn't want to hear herself talk, because she would walk away knowing nothing new. Maritza blew the smoke in Farah's direction. Farah whisked it away with her hand.

Maritza put out her cigarette and lit another one. "He told me you were like a blood-sucking leech. That you were a nag and all you cared about was your career. How you were using him for your own interests. He even told me that you were gaining weight and were getting fat. Basically, you weren't doing your job," snapped Maritza. Her eyes were red and tired, as if she too, had been under some stress.

Farah maintained her cool. *I got this*, she kept telling herself.

"Lenox and I talked about that. And we're over that now. Just do yourself a favor and go back to France. Lenox and I will pay for your ticket," said Farah.

Maritza walked to the kitchen and turned around. "I don't plan to go anywhere! You're stuck with me."

Farah face became hot and itchy. She jumped off the sofa and followed Maritza. "Are you out of your fucking mind?"

"All your high-and-mighty talk means nothing. Lenox and I are planning on being together. He said after you got your show, it was over between you two!"

"If you think I'm going to let your ass fuck up what I've tried so hard to maintain, going through all kinds of bullshit, you must be high!" Farah followed Maritza back into the living room.

"Did he tell you he bought us tickets to go back to St.-Tropez next month? A woman should always know her man's whereabouts." Maritza reached over the wall unit and pulled out two first-class tickets. "Don't worry, it's only for one week," she said, waving them at Farah.

Farah snatched them from her and saw that they were clearly Air France tickets with Lenox's name on one.

"How do I know you didn't buy these tickets yourself, without his knowledge? If this is the best you can come up with, spare me!" she said, throwing them on the ground.

"And here! These are your man's dirty drawers!" A pair of Lenox's Calvin Klein briefs came flying in Farah's direction and hit her in the eye.

It was the breaking point for Farah and she lunged at Maritza from behind, knocking them both to the floor.

Maritza ground her lit cigarette into Farah's arm. She grabbed a handful of Farah's hair and dragged her across the rug, kicking and screaming. Farah kicked Maritza in her shin and freed herself. She punched Maritza in her face so hard she heard her thumb crack. As Maritza backed away holding her bloody nose, Farah took off one of her heels and slapped Maritza across the face. This time, Maritza became disoriented for a few seconds. Farah hit her again with the shoe and busted her lip. Still standing, Maritza charged at Farah. Farah pushed her so hard she stumbled back on the steps that led to the kitchen and collapsed.

That's when everything stopped. Farah, out of breath, saw spots of blood on the carpet and Maritza lying still.

Maritza murmured something under her breath. And Farah was beside herself. She turned around to leave and ended up opening the wrong door. Turning around again, she felt a guilty pleasure seeing Maritza bruised and motionless on the floor. She wanted her to remember this pain the next time she thought about Lenox. Her feelings of wishing Maritza dead scared her. Still frantic, a tape sitting on an end table with the initials ML caught her reporter's eye. She grabbed it instinctively and ran out of the apartment.

As she ran to her car, Farah knew she couldn't go home. *What if Maritza was seriously hurt?* she thought, starting the car. She took a few deep breaths. She had a big night coming up and she couldn't afford to let anything ruin it. So she drove to Brooklyn to get her hair done for the big network bash, as she originally planned.

When Farah left Patrik's apartment, she drove to Manhattan to drop off Lenox's car. In the car, she turned on the radio's jazz station to help her calm down. If she were to speak to Lenox, she had to keep a steady and even tone. She didn't want to give him any clues to what she did today. Inside, she wanted to kill Lenox herself. She drove with one hand, while she wiped tears with her left. She cried uncontrollably as Maritza's words echoed in her head. Farah had a plan and she wasn't going to let her strong feelings get the best of her.

"Hi, it's me. Got a minute?" said Farah, as Lenox picked up the other line.

"How about two minutes. I'm on my way to a meeting. Everything okay? I thought you'd be busy all day," he said, concerned at Farah's edginess.

"I won't be coming home tonight. I'm going to drop the car off in the lot and go uptown with my mother. She needs my help in getting ready tomorrow," said Farah, dying to hang up.

There was some silence on both ends.

"Where are you?" he asked.

"I'm almost home, but I'll see you tomorrow," she said.

"Did something happen today, Farah?" he asked.

Farah didn't know how to respond. *Did he know?*

"No, everything is cool. I'm just still in a daze trying to get ready for tomorrow. I can't wait." Lenox seem satisfied with her response and Farah was satisfied with her decision to stay away from him.

Since Lenox told her she could hold the car, she skipped Broadway and headed to Amsterdam Avenue to her mother's.

As soon as she saw her mother, she burst into tears. They sat on the couch as Farah played back the day's events. She told her mother everything.

"Don't worry about it. You did the right thing confronting this woman. But the only thing I'm concerned about is you. Have you spoken to Lenox since?" her mother asked. She made them two cups of tea, and put a slice of apple in Farah's cup.

"Yes," Farah said. The tea helped the pain in her chest.

"That girl is probably lying about Lenox going to leave you for her. She's probably just jealous of you. I wouldn't worry. You didn't curse him out, did you?" asked her mother, looking at her from the corner of her eye.

"No! I didn't. That's all you care about is Lenox. What about what he's done to me?!" yelled Farah, looking at her mother's startled expression.

"I, I, was just asking because it could make things worse. You don't want to jump to mess things up further with him," her mother said.

"Me mess things up? You know what, Mom, I am really tired of you acting like I'm the reason why men don't stay with me!"

"Well, they don't, and that's a fact! If you could just calm your nerves and let things develop, instead of looking for problems, you could be married by now!"

"You seem more concerned about me marrying than I am. I'm really beginning to think this is more about you than me!"

Farah's mother got a worried look on her face. "I just don't want you to be alone, Farah. You know, I raised you by myself. I was single for nearly twenty years before meeting Oliver two years ago. Do you know how hard that was for me? Doing everything on my own? I don't want you to go through that. I'm trying to help you!"

"Well, well. You were single for twenty years? It didn't look like that when I saw a different man's face around the house every three months! And don't even try to act like you were there taking care of me. You were busy about town trying to do *your* thing!" Farah pointed in her mother's face. "The only place for affection in our house was in your bedroom with your boyfriends."

"What was I supposed to do? I needed companionship too, you know," said her mother.

"You had me. I had no companionship. Instead of watching you in the kitchen, I had to hear you fucking in the room next to me. I was fourteen. That was the last thing I needed to hear! And some of those men were just low-lifes," said Farah. One of her mother's boyfriends had even tried to hit on her, as she thought back, but she didn't want to bring that part up.

"I'm sorry, Farah," said her mother, holding her chest.

"One thing I know for sure. I don't want to be like you," said Farah. She had never opened her mouth to her mother like that.

"I was doing what I had to do to get things fixed around the house, get bills paid, get some extra money to pay for all those damn dance classes and fancy camps you wanted to go to!" said her mother, defending her motives.

"You're still doing the same thing, Mom. You're still alone, no matter how you look at it. How long will this one last? Oliver is married to another woman. And you are *not* married," she said, her voice steadier. "I want to be married someday."

Farah's mother sat there holding her mouth and her stomach. She looked as if she was about to ball up and cry. Farah's face was already wet with her own tears. She put her mother's head on her shoulder.

"Mom, I'm trying hard to make this one work. But I've run out of cards to play," said Farah.

After a while, her mother lugged herself to her bedroom. Farah lay down in the guest room. The tape she took from Maritza's apartment was still in the bag. She decided she wanted to get all her misery over with in one night.

She dusted off the VCR in the room and inserted the tape. It was what she expected. Maritza and Lenox having sex the way she and he did. Intimate, hard, sweaty sex. Sex that Farah thought she had only shared with him. They had done things that he and Farah hadn't even tried. She couldn't bear to watch more than a few scenes before she stumbled to the toilet and threw up.

*I*t had been almost a year since Lenox slept alone. He stayed on his side of the bed as if Farah was next to him, and tried to sleep. Awake for most of the night, he wondered about her.

He didn't want Maritza to stay in New York because she was sure to destroy his relationship. The lunch he and Farah had at Tavern on the Green meant a lot to Lenox. It was the first time he had truly been in love. Not that Farah was more beautiful, sexy, or intelligent than any other woman he'd been with, but she was simply different. She was like an extension of himself, and his interests. Farah encompassed more than just the ambiguous little title of "girl-friend." Her aggressive nature appealed to him, and her conniving ways aroused him. He knew she was the type of woman to stand by him, even if it was at her own risk. The day she first accepted his invitation for dinner blew his mind. He wasn't sure if he had first fallen for her at the restaurant or when she seduced him in his apartment. He didn't mind that she was using him at first. If he had been a woman, he would have done the same thing, too. If he only understood one thing about Farah, it was that she was a hard woman to grasp. At times, her independence and sharp edges sprouted to such a point that Lenox felt that she could leave him anytime she wanted. However, she withstood a lot of pain, allowing her insecurities to seep through. She showed Lenox one thing no woman ever did, and that was loyalty. Even if it was more a loyalty to her career than him, it still impressed him.

Just before 9:00 A.M., he called Farah's mother house, but there was no answer. He thought perhaps they were preparing for to-night's launch party. He dragged his tired body into the kitchen and opened the refrigerator. Luisa had done the shopping, and the refrigerator was filled with enough to eat. But he didn't know what he wanted. If Farah were home, they'd have gone out for breakfast or cooked something together. He hated the time-consuming chore of cooking. Instead, he made a cold bowl of Grape Nuts cereal. Eating, he noticed that his hard-on hadn't gone away. It had been only two days since he and Farah had sex and three since he and Maritza had. He was so hard that it was hurting. Leaving his cereal half-eaten, he went to the bathroom. His navy boxers dropped to his ankles. He simultaneously jerked himself off over the toilet and thought of Farah in his favorite—her tight jean miniskirt. He looked down on the bowl and squeezed out his excess juices. It was be-ginning to feel like a regular morning, he thought as he smiled.

After he showered, he finalized the papers that would close down the Life House officially. Last week, he wrote individual cards to each student and their families and thanked them for their participation. He even wrote his home number, in case any of them ever needed anything. Farah had mailed them. He also returned the money to the hundreds of donators. That task was the hardest of all.

He called for his car to be driven around to the front of the building. He had stopped parking it across the street months ago, since Farah made that comment about his parking skills. Once in his car, he called Maritza, but she wasn't home. He thought it was best if she went back to Lyon as soon as possible. And he wanted to tell her today. After a few more tries, there was still no answer.

He drove to her building and used his key to get inside the apartment. He didn't knock. When he walked in, the apartment smelled like day's-old garbage. He frowned as he looked at the dirty dishes in the sink and the books and clothes scattered on the floor. After calling out her name a few times, he realized that she wasn't home and that something had happened. Maritza was one of the neatest, cleanest people he knew. She wouldn't walk out and leave any place looking so bad, he thought as he searched the apartment for a note.

The mail lay on the table unopened, which meant Maritza had probably left the place overnight. Lenox felt a queasy feeling as he put together Maritza's disappearance and Farah's not coming home last night. He shook his head as he laughed. There was no way, as he looked around, that Farah could have visited Maritza. He knew Farah was gutsy, but not insane.

The only other person who would know Maritza's whereabouts was Seht. Lenox held his breath as he called him.

"What's up, man. Listen, I'm at Maritza's place. You seen her?" Lenox asked.

"No, man. Actually, I'm tied up—literally—with this chick here. . . ." Seht said. Lenox heard a woman laughing in the background. Then the phone clicked off.

It rang again. "It's Coco. She's here giving me a little back therapy. Did something happen?" said Seht.

Lenox didn't want to ruin Seht's good time. That would have been a serious cock-blocking gesture, and that wasn't his style. "I was supposed to meet her. That's all. She probably left ahead of me."

He snapped his cell phone shut and left. Something was awfully wrong and he didn't like it. He hated feeling that he had no control over a situation. There was lightning striking around him, and he didn't want to get struck by surprise.

The gym was the only place that would occupy his busy thoughts. He immersed himself in lifting weights and cardiovascular exercise. They were both part of his regular program, which no longer included picking up women at the gym. But he wasn't blind. In between his repetitions he stole peeks at women using the thigh machines and the jiggling behinds on the treadmills. One even gave him the eye several times and asked him to help her with the weights, but Lenox was a traditional alpha male, and took pleasure making the first move. He felt secure and comfortable knowing he was a man with a woman, not one lost in the search for one.

He was sure that by the time he went back to the locker room to get dressed, Farah would have called. And she did. She left a short message that confirmed that she was busy all day. Just as he thought.

He called her back when he returned to his car.

"You miss me?" he asked, feeling strangely vulnerable.

"Yeah, of course I missed you. I missed you so much last night I was sick. Just wasn't used to sleeping alone." Lenox was pleased to hear her voice, but noticed a twinge of anxiety.

"Are you nervous about tonight?" he asked.

"No. I waited too long to be nervous about this," she said. "But I do have a surprise for you tonight."

"Is that right? Is it five feet eight inches, with honey brown skin, and long wavy hair? And with a pair of breasts that can hold a pencil in the cleavage?" He felt his erection growing as he drove.

"I missed you. And I just bought a little something to show you I'm grateful. Lenox, I really want to start new. Just want to put all the pettiness behind us. Lola's honking her horn." She hung up before he could agree.

What she had planned would be something Lenox would never forget. Fortunately in her business, bad publicity was always good publicity.

In no less than a minute, Maritza called Lenox.

"Did you come by the apartment?" she asked.

"I was there this morning. What happened?" said Lenox.

"Did you see the mess? Did you see everything?!"

"I saw that the place looked like somebody doesn't like cleaning."

"I was damn near killed! That girlfriend of yours came in here yesterday ranting and raving. She attacked me and I fell on the steps in the kitchen. I spent all night groaning, so that my neighbor next door came and took me to the hospital."

Lenox was speechless.

"So, what do you have to say? Why didn't you warn me about her?" barked Maritza.

"I didn't even know she knew where you lived. What did the hospital say? Were you hurt badly?"

"I said the girl nearly killed me! She busted my lip and nearly broke my nose. When I fell, I bruised my back. I could barely walk!"

"What did she say? What did you tell her?" Lenox eyes darted rapidly in front of him.

"All kinds of things. She told me to go back to France. To stay away from you. She even offered to pay for my plane ticket!"

Maritza's cursing words turned into a hum as Lenox replayed the last conversation he had with Farah. There was no hint that she was angry, just busy. Lenox nearly hit the car in front of him when he heard Maritza shouting.

"What the hell are you going to do? You seem to care more about her than us!"

"What else happened?"

"She just left and left me laying there helplessly in pain. The girl is crazy! She was fighting for blood or death."

Lenox wasn't sure how to react. He didn't even know that Farah was the fighting type. She seemed as though she would be too worried about facial scars and messing up her hair to get in a fight.

"Just sit tight. I won't be able to stop by because I have to do some things. I'll handle Farah. We'll talk later."

"I have a third call-back from that casting director from *The Agents*, that new Broadway show. He said this may be it for me.

Too bad I have to wear a whole tube of concealor on my left eye."
She paused for sympathy, but there wasn't any. "So I won't be in."

"Congratulations," Lenox said, not sure if it was appropriate.
"I'll call you soon."

Lenox checked his watch and saw that he only had less than an
hour to get ready. Farah was supposed to be meeting him at the
party. He was tempted to call her and settle the matter, instead of
letting it fester. But he, too, was good at this game.

♥

The *Rise and Shine* party was the talk of the town. Everyone who
was anybody in journalism from Barbara Walters to Walter Cron-
kite crowded the ballroom of the Waldorf Astoria. The tabloid gossip columnists and photographers were fluttering around the room
like butterflies. The party also brought out an eclectic mix of previous *Rise and Shine* guests like Jimmy Carter, Martha Stewart, Hillary Rodham Clinton, Russell Simmons, Brian Lester, and the little
girl who lost both legs.

Lenox arrived with Seht and his date, and Ms. Meyers and her
much younger female companion. They were all dressed hand-
somely. Lenox was in a tailored, delicately pinstriped Italian suit
that he had especially made for this event. He wore the gold ini-
tialed Cartier cuff links that Farah had bought him. He spotted
Farah graciously standing at the center of a circle comfortably con-
versing. The glow on her face lifted her out of the room. She was
obviously the star of the moment. He suddenly felt out of place and
uncomfortable. Farah would usually be by his side picking up the
slack from conversations he did not feel like finishing with people.

He waited for her to give him eye contact, but he seemed the fur-
thest thing from her mind. Casually, Lenox made his way across to
the side of the room where Farah was posing for pictures. He stood
by the photographer, with his hands balled up in his pockets and
watched her pose to the side, to the left, holding a plaque and roses.

"Mr. Whitworth! Nice to meet you," said a man who Lenox had never seen before. Lenox accepted his handshake.

"Everything is going so smoothly. Are you waiting for your chance to take a picture?" the man said, pointing to Farah.

"Who are you?" Lenox asked, perplexed.

"I'm just the coat check guy. I'm just trying to get to know everyone here. Do you have a business card?"

Lenox looked away, back at Farah who was still busy.

"I don't have any cards on me. How did you know my name?"

"You're Farah's man. Everybody knows that by now," he said, walking away to his next pursuit.

Finally, Farah acknowledged Lenox. He looked for any signs of uneasiness, but she showed none. She signaled for him to join her in the pictures, and he did. They posed together, smiling and hugging, with Ms. Meyers and executives from the network. When they were done, he took his spot on the side again, while some more people posed with Farah.

"Excuse me, but are you here alone?" Farah's mother smiled flirtatiously as Lenox turned around. Lola smiled, too.

"I'm not now." He laughed, giving Ms. Washington and Lola a hug. "Where's Oliver?"

"Oh, he has the most awful case of the flu," Ms. Washington said. "We have him quarantined in the den. We don't need Farah coming down with anything on her new show. I thought she told you?"

"Told me what?" asked Lenox.

"About Oliver."

He wondered how much Farah had told her while she was there last night. The idea that Ms. Washington knew more than he did about the Maritza situation bothered him.

"I hope he feels better," said Lenox. He noticed how Ms. Washington and Lola were acting strangely.

"And you. How are you feeling?" Lola asked. Lenox couldn't

believe that the women were almost as good as Farah when it came to hiding things.

"I'm fine. Why do you ask?"

"Just asking. You look a little tense," Ms. Washington said.

"But you still look handsome as ever. I swear you look like you can play Morris Chestnut's double!" Lola said, laughing. Ms. Washington and Lenox only smiled.

Lenox waved Farah over. "I'm always tense if I feel like I'm being left in the cold about something," he said to the two of them. Then he looked at Ms. Washington. "You wouldn't know what that is?" he asked.

"I spoke to her and she was awfully upset yesterday. She's way too caught up in this right now to even confront you about it here," whispered Ms. Washington. "So just enjoy the evening. I'm sure by tomorrow she'll be ready to face the facts. You know how we women can bury things, hoping they'll just go away," she said.

"Hey, I'm just going to run to the ladies' room. I'll be back," Lola said, excusing herself.

"What did she tell you last night?" Lenox asked, turning to Ms. Washington when Lola left.

Ms. Washington was about to answer when Farah joined them.

"What's up, you two?" she said, giving them both kisses on the cheek. "Where's Lola?"

"She's over there talking to the photographer," Ms. Washington said.

"I have to keep an eye on her. I don't want any drama from Chris," Farah said, looking at the crowd of celebrity faces. "I'm so crazed in here. I don't know how I am going to keep up with all this."

"With me, honey. Isn't the mother supposed to take a few pictures with her daughter on a night like this?" Ms. Washington put on her shades and playfully threw her hair back.

"As a matter of fact, we should take some now, before I make my speech," Farah said, adjusting the strap of her red-and-gold dress.

"What about my surprise?" asked Lenox, tugging Farah by her elbow. She was about to turn away and leave again.

"Do you really want me to slather your body in honey right here?" Farah joked. "The gift is in the back room. I'll give it to you privately. It's very personal. I'm gonna take these pictures with Mom, then make my speech, and then give you my undivided attention," she said, putting her finger in his dimple.

He felt like a student who just got his teacher's approval.

He entertained himself with a straight shot of Hennessey. He started with one shot and ended with three in a row. Feeling more loosened up, he engaged himself in small talk with the esteemed guests.

"Lenox, I just need a moment before the evening ends," Aunt Joan said as she passed by alone.

"I have one now, what's up?" Lenox happily excused himself.

Ms. Meyers and Lenox went outside of the main ballroom area, where there were fewer guests. She appeared relieved to have a moment alone.

"I don't know how much longer I can keep us this charade. Did you know she had the nerve to request approval of the guest list? And today, she called for a bigger dressing room with a bathroom. No one has a dressing room like that! Katie never asked for those little things. A ten-million-dollar raise, maybe, but that was it," she said, throwing her black-and-gold-trimmed silk scarf around her neck. "And her agent. He's really starting to get on my nerves, too."

Lenox wanted to keep the evening light. He didn't have any brain energy to tackle his aunt's complaints.

"She's the star of the network's bread-and-butter show. And if you want to keep her, you have to treat her right. I know she can be a little superficial and self-absorbed," said Lenox.

"And that's the side of her you fell in love with?"

"I fell in love with her being who she is. Instead of being what I wanted her to be." Lenox shrugged.

"Let me put it to you this way," she said, pointing at him. "If you and she ever end this *thing* you call a relationship, give me a call, I'll be happy to replace her. I put her on for you, and I'll take her off for you."

Lenox raised his eyebrows. "I haven't thought about that part. And hopefully, I won't have to take you up on that offer." He filed his aunt's words in his mind as he glanced at Farah walking to the stage with Adam and his wife.

"Seems like they're ready to start," he said as he escorted his aunt to their table. It was just a few feet away from the stage.

The room turned into quiet mumbling as the music stopped and the guests took their seats.

Charles, the president of the network, took the podium. "Good evening, everyone. Welcome to our launch party for *Rise and Shine*, which is not complete without honoring our new star Farah Washington. Welcome to you as a permanent member of the *Rise and Shine* family," said Charles, turning around to Farah and applauding. Everyone gave Farah a standing ovation while she stood and politely nodded at individuals. She was nervous, and it showed. Lenox felt proud to have Farah and planned to show how proud he was when he got her home.

"She came with us heavily armed with a stellar background and an Emmy award. She's still our youngest anchor in the last ten years of the network. And with that lovely face, smile and talent was brought here to Channel Seven. . . ." As Charles took the room down memory lane regarding Farah's career, a short film played on a screen showing various people at the network, including Ms. Meyers, giving Farah accolades and well wishes.

". . . Without further ado, here's Farah Washington," said Charles, handing the mic to Farah.

Lenox stood up from his chair and gave a few hollers in her

direction. So did her mother, Lola, and Sam. Ms. Meyers stayed seated, but clapped nonetheless.

The room quieted.

"Thank you to everyone. Almost everyone here has played a role, big or small, in this day. By the time I finish reading the names my Champagne will be flat," she said, holding up her flute. There were a few laughs in the room, which helped her relax.

"Every young person dreams of being on TV or being famous. Some want to be a famous Hollywood actor or singer, others want to win the Nobel Prize or Pulitzer. As a child first seeing *Rise and Shine*, I knew I wanted to be on that show. Not as a famous guest but the one who gets welcomed into millions of American homes every morning. There are some people who have written to me and said their days don't start off right until they see *Rise and Shine*. And I can relate to that. My life hasn't felt right until I was able to accomplish that childhood dream." Farah paused for emphasis. "I do want to thank God for this day that I prayed for every night. I also want to thank my mother for keeping me focused on this goal, even though sometimes I felt like truly giving up. My crew from six o'clock, we've been through it all. It was during that show that I knew I wanted to be on TV forever at any cost," she said, turning her attention to Lenox. "And to my man, Lenox Whitworth, for being there in the trenches and fighting for me. It wasn't always easy to get here, but I'm going to make every moment last."

The crowd stood up and applauded Farah even louder. She stepped to the mic again, "I do have something I want to show everyone. Please be seated." The screen above blacked out. "Here is a tape that I came across which shows a man and a French whore. It's not the *Moulin Rouge*, but the theatrics are just as eye-catching. The man in the tape belonged to a woman who would stand by him at all costs, who looked up to him, and who endured many nights of heartache to be with him. Roll tape," said Farah.

Lenox thought about getting up, but couldn't even feel his legs.

He was shocked to stillness. Ms. Meyers sat erect with her eyes opened as wide as her mouth. The room filled with bursts of gasps and whispers. Farah had her back turned to the crowd as the room watched the twenty-second tape, which felt like an hour to Lenox. It was the last tape he and Maritza had done together. It showed his face clearly and Maritza bucking wildly with her behind in the air.

Getting a surge of adrenaline, Lenox flew from his seat. He made his way out of the room. Farah was no longer onstage. Charles took the podium to distract from the matter.

Lenox was sweating and his whole body seemed to be shaking. He raced backstage, but Farah was already gone. One of the technicians told him she left in the direction of the parking lot.

He ran outside to the street and caught up with Farah walking briskly as she turned the corner.

He called for her to stop. She didn't and he ran up behind her. He yanked her arm and pinned both her shoulders against the cement wall.

"What are you trying to do? Ruin my life? You know how many people saw me in there?! I swear I can break your fucking neck right now!" he yelled, shaking her hard.

"I can't believe you moved that tramp here to be with her! Having sex with her. Lying to me!" Farah slapped Lenox with her handbag. He took her handbag and threw it over his back. He let her go.

"What about going back to France with her? She showed me the damn tickets. What? Were you just going to disappear and tell me you were in Jamaica instead?!"

"What tickets? Now you are talking crazy. Your conniving ass probably had this all planned."

Farah shoved him on the side of his forehead. He didn't move.

"Fuck you!" she said pushing him repeatedly. "You nasty dog! You kissed me while you had her pussy on your breath! You better thank God I didn't catch you red-handed!"

Lenox backslapped Farah so hard blood trickled down her cheek. Her earrings fell to the ground.

"Don't you ever threaten me!" he yelled. She kept her face turned away. He caught her wrist and twisted her arm behind her back. Her face was up against the cement wall. "I guess you gonna leave me now, huh? Then go ahead," he said, whispering in her ear. He let go of her arm. Farah wasn't crying and held a straight face even though her left side was raw and red.

Farah looked around for her earrings, but they were no place to be found. Everything that she was holding in began to show. One tear did run down her face, and she yelled at the stinging pain. Lenox had hit her with his ring finger, which left an open wound under her left eye. He rubbed his face hoping when he removed his hands this evening would be one of his bad dreams. He found Farah's pocketbook on the hood of a nearby car and gave it to her. She snatched it away. She tottered around the corner.

"We have a car coming to get us in an hour. Go clean yourself up!" he said, shouting behind her.

But she ignored him. He watched her walk up the street and felt guilty for laying his hands on her. When he used to spy on his father beating his mother, he promised he would only inflict that much physical pain on an enemy. Instead, he had done it to a woman that he loved.

Lenox hailed a cab and asked him to follow the cab Farah had got in. He followed the cab all the way back to Trump Parc. Lenox saw her get out and walk into the building. Her back was hunched as she stepped slowly. Her glow was gone and replaced by dark eyes. She stumbled as her heel got stuck in a crack on the curb, but she kept moving without looking down.

Caught between going upstairs or getting drunk at the bar downstairs, he chose the bar.

Lenox gulped down several shots of cognac and tequilas. He even smoked a cigarette, something he hadn't done since college. The noise of the bar and the effects of the liquor in his system drowned out his thoughts. From the corner of his eye he saw a few cops walk in, and he ordered another drink. The cops walked toward the men's room. He ordered another drink, but the bartender refused. He gave him a fifty-dollar tip. The bartender made him two more drinks. As the cops left, Lenox took that as his cue to leave, too. He swigged the last of drop of the Hennessey and licked the taste from the corner of his mouth.

The walk to the building next door felt like a walk across town. Jamal, his doorman, offered to escort him to his floor, but he refused. The elevator door opened and Lenox carefully stepped in. The ride nauseated him and he spit up in a corner. He opened the apartment door, and threw his keys on the table. He saw Farah lying in the bed sleeping with her hand under the left side of her face. His eyes scanned the curve of her hips under the sheets, and her breasts slightly exposed. He walked to the bed and pulled the cover over her shoulders. She didn't move and felt as stiff as a rock.

A room he hadn't used in months was the empty extra bedroom on the other side of the apartment, near the den. He slept there for the night.

♥

Lenox's overwhelming thirst woke him early. Slowly walking to the kitchen, he opened up a gallon of apple juice. He finished half of it leaning against the refrigerator and brought the rest back to the room. He heard water running in the bathroom, which meant that Farah was already awake. Just as he was about to catch his second wind of sleep, the phone rang, but he blocked it out. Then it rang again. He lazily got himself back up from the bed to answer it.

He heard someone crying on the other end, and he knew right away it was Maritza. Confused, he didn't know why she was calling so early. He thought they had already handled the matter.

"What is it, Maritza?" Lenox sighed.

"I want my fucking money back!" she shouted into his ear.

"I never told you to buy those damn tickets. All I simply said was that we should go back to France one day. Not anytime soon," he said, unruffled by her hysteria. "You should have known better."

"Oh, I'll show you how much I know," she said with a warning note in her voice.

"I'm going back to bed," he said, exhaling noisily.

"Not so fast. The fucking producer called about the show. He said he is giving the part to someone else! He said something about seeing me having sex on a tape that ruined a friend's relationship."

"Are you talking about David Connelly?" Lenox asked.

"Yes! He said that Farah is a good friend of his and he can't be associated with what happened! I came to New York to start over, to get away! And then you let this happen?"

"Me? I was just as surprised as you were. One minute I'm listening to her thank God and the next minute she's showing a porno tape to the audience." Lenox rubbed his pulsating headache.

"Do you know when one producer cuts you, your name is blacklisted all across town?" she cried. "Lenox, you know I tried so hard to make it here for this to happen! I can't go back to France like this," she whined.

"Calm down before you get yourself sick. How did Farah get the tape, anyway?"

"She must have stolen it when I was laid out on the floor in pain."

"I'll see what I can do," said Lenox, feeling that things couldn't get any worse. "I'll talk to David myself and call you later," he said. But Lenox had no plans to call David. He could only handle one problem at a time.

Lenox and Farah spent the morning and evening avoiding any kind of contact. She had dressed the wound under her eye with an ointment and spent the day sobbing on the phone, in bed sleeping or pretending to be. And Lenox spent his second night in the small room.

♥

The next morning, Lenox confronted Farah.

"We really haven't talked much about last night. Whatever you want to do, let's just talk first before you decide on anything," he said, standing at the bedroom doorway. The room smelled like Vicks and Ben-Gay. Farah was balled up under the covers.

"I don't have the energy to fight anymore, especially after kicking that bitch's ass." She kept her body turned away from him. "I don't know what feels worse, you hitting me or cheating on me."

Lenox felt ashamed. He didn't care what she did with Maritza. The fact that he had hit her hurt him more than she knew. "I'm sorry about this," he said. He walked over to the side of the bed and touched her face. He kissed the Band-Aid near her eye, but she turned away.

"Don't ever put your hands on me again!" she spat. "I'm calling the cops next time."

"There won't be a next time. And after today, you won't be hearing about Maritza. She's going back whether she said she wanted to or not. You should know from what we talked about the other night at the Four Seasons that I want us to be together. To reach another level in this," he reminded her.

She turned to face him. She thought of asking about the trip to France with Maritza. But he kissed her on her lips and crawled next to her into bed.

When the mailman came the next morning, Lenox had a special delivery. It was a notice from Maritza's lawyer, suing him for the cost of the tickets to France. He ripped up the letter and put it in the trash.

arah wasn't ready to see her mother, not with a Band-Aid under her eye. But she felt she could explain things better to Lola.

"Come on in, girl. I'm so sorry. Come here," Lola said as she and Farah hugged. She held Farah's chin and tilted her head to the side to get a good view.

She stroked her Band-Aid, but Farah took her hand away.

They sat down at the kitchen table, where a pound cake and Champagne were waiting.

Farah still hadn't spoken because she didn't know where to begin.

"Is Chris here?" she asked, looking around. She didn't want anyone else to know that she'd been hit by a man.

"No, he's at work. The baby is sleeping," said Lola.

Farah tasted the Champagne. "Tastes like you moved up in the world."

"Did you know they had extra bottles lying around at the party? I am not about to let a bottle of Cristal sit on a table without putting it to use!" Lola laughed. When she noticed she was the only one, she asked Farah, "So, how do you feel now that you know all this about Lenox?"

"What he put me through the last few months hurt a hell of a lot more than this scratch," she said.

"Don't try to act all tough. The man put his hands on you. Isn't that bad enough?"

"It is bad. But just like I didn't mean to knock Maritza unconscious in her apartment, he didn't mean to slap me," Farah said, defending Lenox. Then she stopped to grab a tissue.

"I made the mistake of falling in love with his ass. I can't just leave because of this. I've been through way too much."

"I just don't get it." Lola sighed. "You ain't even married to him to be that devoted."

"I know what it's like to have someone you love walk out on you. My mother left me for years with my grandmother. Lenox is the only person who's ever been there through and through. He's more than my man, but a brother, a father, and a business partner. I can't just walk out on him like that."

"In time, I guess you'll see," said Lola. She understood where Farah was coming from, she had been there.

"And I probably should have handled things differently and not showed the tape," said Farah. "Extreme situations usually cause extreme actions. What I did was extreme."

"Now, *that* I agree with! Even though it did spice up the evening. I think some of those old folks didn't even know that position existed!" Lola managed to get a giggle out of Farah.

"I know David Connelly took the part from her for *The Agents*. I am very happy about that."

"That is what that bitch deserves. Hopefully, her broke ass will leave back to England, where she is from," Lola said, popping a piece of pound cake in her mouth.

"It's France," Farah said. She was tired of explaining.

"And how did she get that part for *The Agents?* That show hasn't even opened yet and tickets are sold out for months."

"Guess. I'm sure Lenox had something to do with that," Farah said.

"So the bottom line is you're staying with him," Lola said. She took out a bowl of fresh-cut strawberries from the refrigerator and sat back down at the table. "Is he going to marry you?" she asked, spooning a few of the strawberries on their plates.

"The topic came up, but we just told each other we were in love last week. I can tell he's not ready for marriage."

"Is the fact that he had another woman on the side a dead giveaway?"

"Yeah, it is."

"Well, I hate to say this, but you are into some ghetto love shit. I didn't think uppity folks like you and Lenox got down like that. Fighting in the street and all. And you staying with him is another ghetto move."

Farah forced a smile. "The fucked-up part is that I love him. Every couple goes through issues. Lenox isn't a dog, he's a wolf. He's smart about what he does, but he's also smart enough to fall back when he's made a mistake."

"Hopefully, he will," Lola said faintly. "But I have to give you the respect of hanging in there. It's easier to just walk away. What you and Lenox can produce together—if you two can get it right—is far greater than what the two of you can do without each other."

"Thanks," Farah said, despondent. "Anyway, I just stopped by to let you know I'm still alive. I need to get my head together for Monday. It's my first day on the show and I can't afford to look like a mess with this scratch on my eye."

Lola listened to Farah go on about the show on Monday. But she knew Farah was really talking above the problem at hand, and was going through more pain than showed. The weight she had gained had been lost, and she was near her normal size again. Too bad, Lola thought, the weight loss was due more to stress than to a good diet.

♥

The *TV Guide* edition hit the stands the same day as Farah's first morning on *Rise and Shine*. It was a cover shot with her sitting pretty with a crown on her head. Her co-host Adam even used the cover as part of the conversation with all the guests. She interviewed an author of a book about her relationship with her daughter after discovering her daughter had AIDS. The interview brought tears to Farah's eyes and the producers loved it. Later in the morning, she and Adam interviewed their first couple for *Rise and Shine*'s "Most Amazing Couples" series.

From the first day, Farah handed the station manager a list of special requests to fill out her mornings:

- Breakfast of one fried egg, French toast of challah bread, and slices of cantaloupe on the side; waffles substituted for French toast on Tuesdays only
- Patrik on the set every day to keep hair fresh and tamed.
- A manicurist to smooth out chips and moisten dry cuticles.
- A massage therapist, for a half hour, three times a week before airtime

The requests left many of her co-workers jealous of the preferential treatment she was receiving. The following month, a story broke that an unnamed network head called her a prima donna and an insecure brat. *Access Hollywood* covered the story, but Farah declined to be interviewed. *Rise and Shine*'s already high ratings soared another 20 percent after the story. A few weeks later, *Inside Edition* ran a similar story about Farah's temper on the set. They reported that she threw a plate at a production assistant after finding out that the French toast was made of regular bread instead of challah. The story was true, but instead of throwing the plate, Farah had just asked for another one. The more stories that circulated about Farah, the higher the ratings climbed for *Rise and Shine*.

The weeks that followed were hectic and gave Farah a dose of the news diva lifestyle she'd always wanted. She was redefining herself apart from Lenox, but she still looked for his approval. Though she would receive praise from her co-workers and staff, she still waited to see what Lenox had to say. He watched the show every morning at work or at home, and sometimes called the studio with constructive criticism. He would suggest that she talk less with her hands, to cross her legs more, to sit on Adam's right instead of his left. Ironically, those were the same suggestions Ms. Meyers had, too.

Lenox had picked Farah up from work for dinner on Friday. He had been trying especially hard to be extra attentive to her. The restaurant hostess immediately recognized Farah and asked for her autograph. She also asked Farah to sign the wall over the bar, which listed the names of celebrities who had passed through. It was comfortably crowded and the small red glowing candles on each table created a romantic mood.

Farah looked up and down the menu. She mentally calculated the calories in an order of salmon with sweet potato hash, sautéed spinach, and a small order of calamari to start. Her appetite hadn't gone away, but she wanted to keep off the ten pounds she dropped in the last month. She was now a size eight. The camera still made her look like a size ten, and she was determined to go back to the size six of her early twenties.

The waiter came and coughed to signal his presence.

"Are you ready?" he asked, looking down at his notepad. "May I make a recommendation for the evening?"

"No, thanks. Could you please just send us a bottle of Beaujolais? This one." Lenox pointed to the wine list and gave him the orders.

Farah placed the table napkin on her lap. Lenox tucked his in his collar.

"Any word yet on when she's going back to France?" she said

with contempt. The waiter came by and presented them with their wine choice. Lenox sniffed the cork. When he approved it, the waiter poured the red wine into their glasses.

"I haven't spoken to her in weeks. She hasn't called me either. I know she is still here, though. She's probably scrambling for auditions," Lenox said, feeling apprehensive. "Her brother is coming into town. He called my office the other day. It seemed like Maritza just needs some company."

"How does her brother have your number?" Farah asked, squinting her eyes.

"I gave it to him. If it weren't for me, she wouldn't have been here. I felt somewhat responsible, so I told her brother to call me if he ever had problems getting in contact with her," Lenox said. "Can we forget about that for a moment?"

She huffed at his question and didn't speak. She watched Lenox in between bites of her own meal, as he forked the macaroni into his mouth. He seemed to have no care in the world. The whole Maritza incident was still on her mind, and bothered her every day. On top of that, she had all the pressures that come with being a star of a newly formatted show. Farah felt that she was the one still suffering the aftermath of his infidelities. She didn't know what she would do if she did not have the daily distraction of *Rise and Shine*. It was the only place where she truly felt appreciated.

Farah put down her fork, not able to drop the topic. "I just can't help but think that you are connected to her in some way. You have her brother's info. You keep in contact with her family,"

"Don't ruin my appetite, please." Lenox said. He calmly resumed eating.

"Kiss my ass! Hopefully, that will put a little tang in your mac and cheese." Farah got up and threw her chair in. She walked away leaving Lenox behind.

She waited outside the restaurant for him to finish. At times like this she had no place to go but back home with Lenox. She could go by her mom's or Lola's, but she didn't always feel like explaining all the time.

The drive to the apartment was uncomfortable and long. Farah busied herself writing reminders in her Palm Pilot. She looked over at Lenox and felt pretty silly for her behavior. They had promised not too long ago to put it behind them and she always dug it back up. She thought about how disappointed he looked. He didn't look angry, but he looked withdrawn. She put her hand on his knee. She knew that he was trying to build her trust back him in. She had let herself get in the way of that.

When they reached the apartment, Lenox still had not said anything. They undressed with a few words being said here and there. While Lenox was in the bathroom, she found the plastic mat she had been saving. She spread it over the bed and dimmed the lights. She climbed into bed and waited for Lenox. They hadn't had sex since the incident at the launch party. When he got in the bed, she handed him the bottle of oil and he lay there confused. She asked him to pour it all over her. He rubbed her body down. He raised her legs, first one, then the other, and positioned them around his neck. He brushed the wet flat of his tongue against "Sheila" and teased her clitoris. He then turned Farah over on top of him in a 69 position. This was only the beginning. They spent almost two hours indulging in those naughty acts few people admit to. Lenox ravished Farah's body with inches of thrusts and rhythmic strokes. At the end, Farah fell to the floor naked, shaking and completely spent. If he couldn't make her feel secure outside of the bedroom, he sure made up for it inside, she thought. She was willing to take it for what it was worth.

At about 2:00 in the morning, Farah felt awful. She wondered how she had lost herself with Lenox. She had never thought she'd fight a woman for a man, accept a man's infidelities, and let herself be hit by one. She asked what was at the end of all this. *Am I ready to go back to being alone? To become another statistic as a single, professional black women?* She fell back to sleep with her questions still unanswered.

The sharp ringing of the phone jolted her and Lenox from their sleep. Lenox picked up the phone and listened.

"What was that?" Farah asked after he hung up.

"It was Maritza's brother. He wants to see if I can get an airline ticket for them for next week. So she'll be gone," he said, slurring his words. He then went back to sleep. Farah took that as a sign of a good weekend.

♥

On Monday, Farah and Adam had their hands full with interviews with two authors, a short lesson on wines of the season with wine expert Matt Rosengarten, a fitness demonstration on the best ways to keep fit in the fall, and a segment on surviving colon cancer.

Once the two-hour show wrapped, Sam walked Farah to her office.

"Don't tell me you haven't noticed?" Sam said as she closed the door.

"Noticed that we're top five in the Nielsen's ratings? I'm really going to notice that when we go back to the negotiation table. I want at least double. This show hasn't been in top five in years!" said Farah.

"That is exactly right. And some people want to take all the credit," Sam said, filing her nails.

"What people?" Farah asked, clicking on fan e-mail from viewers. She hardly had time to read them, but it made her feel good.

"It looks like Adam is getting his pants in a bunch. He claims that ratings jump is something that the network is manipulating to make you look more important than he is."

"He smiles in my face every morning and is complaining about me behind my back? So typical of this business," Farah said, disgusted.

"But that's not it. There is talk that Ms. Meyers had someone else in mind, but gave it to you because you are her nephew's girl-friend."

Sam's comment dug into Farah like a knife wound. She knew her affiliation with Lenox had a lot to do with things, but she didn't want anyone else to know that. She didn't want her colleagues losing respect for her.

"What do *you* think?" Farah asked Sam.

Sam cleared her throat, and appeared lost for words. She kept filing her nails and made facial expressions that said what her mouth didn't.

"Well?"

"I think that you are a gifted, talented woman. And without Lenox or whoever else helped you get where you are, you would have done the same without them."

Farah was shocked by Sam's bitter words. She hadn't seen this side of her before. Farah kept her fingers on the mouse, clicking away. Inside, she was boiling.

"Anyway, I must go. And I have to say, you look a lot better with those few pounds you lost. What are you now, back to a ten?" Sam asked, sounding phony.

"I was a ten. I'm an eight now," said Farah, grinding her teeth.

"I'm sorry, you know how some clothes just make us look bigger than we are. We'll chat later." Farah glared at her as Sam took her last season's Chanel outfit and Prada pumps out the door.

♥

When Farah reached home late afternoon, Lenox had not arrived yet. She spent an hour on her newly bought treadmill and sweated out all her anxiety. As she was stepping, she saw a commercial featuring Adam and herself that promoted tomorrow morning's show. The commercial caught her off guard. She gloated, telling herself that she was one beautiful woman. But looking at the commercial was like looking at another woman, a woman made for camera and lights. She looked in the house mirror before her and saw someone else. A woman who would always be able to get a man, but never keep one. Then Lenox walked in.

"Wait, wait. Keep going. I like the view from back," he said, as he watched her in her purple spandex leggings. She saw Lenox's eyes zero in on her behind, which was something she did not want to lose with her new workout regimen.

Breathless and giddy, she stepped off the machine. She put her arms around him, and gave him a kiss, sweetened with sweat.

"Mmmm. I always like a little salt with my sugar," he said, kissing her wet neck. She opened her mouth wider until their tongues found each other for a moment.

"I need to take care of some things downtown. I'm buying this new building on Hudson Street in Tribeca. It took me months to get this deal done!"

"Why didn't you tell me you were buying a new building? And in the city?! That's expensive." She plopped down on the sofa next to him. She wondered how many other things Lenox was working on that she had no idea about.

"With the money I have from the sale of the Life House buildings. I may be able to buy another one after this." Lenox opened his briefcase. "I had to beat out three bidders to get this. I was the only brother in there bargaining," boasted Lenox.

"They are finally starting to let other people into those deals." He stood in the dining room, and thumbed through the mail. "Going out later?"

"I may just stay here. That workout really killed all my energy."

"I just dropped in to see you," he said, kissing her forehead. "I have some errands to run because of this new building. I'll be back a little later." Lenox turned back around and closed the door behind him. A small voice told Farah that he would be coming back later—much later.

After she showered, she called her mother. Listening to the phone ring, she looked in the mirror at the old wound under her eye. The mark was gone, but still left some discoloration. She reached for her foundation and dabbed some on.

"How's my baby?" her mother asked.

As Farah opened her mouth to answer, her mother said, "Is Lenox there? Tell him thanks for the tickets to *The Agents.* That was a hard one to get."

"Tickets to see *The Agents?* When was this?"

"Oliver and I went to the show last night. He said it was your idea. And we got orchestra seats. They were perfect!"

"I didn't know anything about tickets to any play," insisted Farah.

"Oh, he probably forgot to tell you. I'm sure he is so busy."

"While he was giving you the tickets, he should have explained himself about that videotape at the same time."

"He did," her mother said plainly. The giddiness of her voice was gone and back to seriousness. "He said the tape was old and that the young lady was someone who was out to embarrass him. He was surprised you fell for that. What is happening between the two of you?"

"I really don't know. If this were anyone else I would have picked up and left a while ago."

"I understand, baby."

"We talked, but not too much . . ." said Farah. Her mother jumped in.

"If it gets too much, just leave. You can always stay here, when you get ready."

"Thanks," she said before hanging up. She was shocked by her mother telling her to leave Lenox, but it was a little too late for Farah.

Her mother's words stuck in her head all evening. The hum of the air conditioner rocked Farah's racked brain to a deep sleep of several hours.

The opening of the door ended her peaceful state. She rubbed her eyes, and saw that the time read 3:00 A.M.

"Good morning," Farah said, scathingly. "I see the stray dog found his way home."

"Don't start, please. It's too late. Did Luisa leave anything to eat?"

"All that time out and you couldn't find anything to eat?" Farah said, yawning. "You know what, don't even answer that."

He threw his keys on the dresser.

"We got to talk," he said. "But just listen before you interrupt."

Farah sat on the bed.

"Maritza got a part in *Fourteenth Street*, that big play that has been around for years. She starts rehearsal Monday."

"And how the hell did she get that part?" The nauseating thought that Lenox could had arranged it fell on her. Farah thought Maritza had been blacklisted.

"I told you, she was out auditioning for weeks before this whole thing happened. But she's out of the apartment. Has her own place and can pay her own rent now. She doesn't need my help anymore."

"Oh, so you have it *all* figured out! How about the fact that she nearly broke us up and she's staying now." Farah got up from the bed, and flipped the lights on.

Lenox took off his shoes. "In the morning."

"Lenox, I swear to God. If you deal with her again I'm out of here! And I won't look back."

"Calm down and come here. Just come *here*," he said, calling her with his finger.

Farah stood at the door with one hand on her hip and her left foot tapping anxiously on the floor.

"Will you come here?" Lenox asked again.

Farah walked over to his side of the bed.

"If you were my wife, you'd still leave me?" he asked, taking her hand for her to sit down. "I know we're going through a rough time right now. But I want us to be together. Can't you just believe in that? I made a mistake. A mistake I pay for every day when I think about it. I did right by you before then. Didn't I?"

Farah nodded her head up and down. His large brown hands stroked her tousled hair.

"And I want to do right by you in the future. I want you to be the mother of *our* children. But if this keeps up, we ain't even going to make it to the altar."

"Sometimes I wish we could just be a regular couple. Do what regular couples do, instead of raising hell with each other or other people," Farah said wishfully.

"I've never been anything *regular* in my life. The only regular thing about me is my bowel movements," he said, showing off a smile. He laid her head in his lap, and stroked her hair once more. It made her feel safe and secure when he did that.

She felt herself relaxing with each stroke, and his hand reaching farther down her back. He lifted up her T-shirt and slid his hand over the curvaceous slope of her backside. She wanted to tell him she was tired and wasn't in the mood, but her mouth couldn't open. Farah asked, half-asleep, "Why didn't you tell me you got my mother tickets to *The Agents?*"

"I forgot," he said. He clapped twice and turned the lights off.

♥

Farah watched Lenox carefully for the next few days. In the mornings, they left together. She'd go to the studio and he'd go to the office. A few times, he had even come by the set to watch the first hour of the show, and then head to work. If he wasn't on the set, he'd call after the show to let her know how she did. She watched for any break in his routine eating, sleeping, and showering patterns. Any disturbances would be an obvious sign for her that he was cheating with Maritza again. He ate his dinner in the evening, which Luisa made for both of them, or they'd both go out to eat. He went to sleep about the same time every night, give or take an hour if *Nightline* was showing anything good. He took a shower in the morning too and one in the evenings. As fall wound to an end, things were beginning to settle down and find their place, not only the leaves but also Farah and Lenox's relationship. Farah still had her guard up, but Lenox gave her no need to build a fortress.

Rise and Shine was still king of the morning shows five months after Farah's arrival. Recently, *Extra* did a show on Farah's fashionable style of dress. The show featured her being dressed by Lara, her stylist, and even visited her closet at Lenox's apartment. As a result of Farah's ability to become a household name and stand out from her female morning competitors, she was given a $4-million bonus.

Lenox helped her invest most of her money by recommending top financial advisors. Farah had her money in three Swiss bank accounts and the rest tied up in stocks and other financial assets. She bought her mother a home in the Hamptons where she and Oliver stayed frequently. In the summers, Farah and Lenox preferred the Vineyard, where they both invested in a huge Victorian family-style home of eight bedrooms, seven full bathrooms, four large dining areas, a state-of-the-art kitchen, and a veranda overlooking the Ink Well. Lenox, Farah, and her family savored their weekends on the Vineyard. Farah hoped each weekend would be the one Lenox would propose.

♥

The official close to a Vineyard weekend would be the arrival of Farah at work on a Monday. She fell into her morning routine and read the *Daily News,* while taking bites of her French Toast. Sometimes, she liked to browse just in case there was something she could share with the viewers. And there usually was.

A headline that read "*14th Street* Premiere" caught her eye. The caption read "France Exports More Than Croissants: Young Actress Makes Bright Lights on Broadway." The makeup lady came at the same time, and began powdering Farah's nose.

"Please, not right now. I'm researching," Farah said, her face still glued inside the pages. The makeup lady apologized and promised to come back soon.

She was holding the newspaper so tight, she crumpled the edges. She felt lightheaded and queasy as she had onstage that night at the launch party. The article was about Maritza and her performance as Inga in the lead role in the play. Under the article was a picture of Maritza and Lenox outside the theater.

Farah slammed the paper down. She counted to three and picked up the paper again, just in case she was hallucinating. It was still there.

She glanced at the clock above her mirror and it read 6:15 A.M. She was due on the set in thirty minutes and wasn't even half-ready. Her world wasn't the same as it was when she entered the Channel 7 offices an hour ago. However, in less than an hour she had to pretend her world couldn't be any better.

"Are you ready now?" the makeup lady asked, timidly opening the door.

"Can you just give me a few minutes? I need to just get something done," Farah said, putting the paper in her bag. The makeup lady crept back out again.

Farah swirled her chair back around to the mirror and cried her heart out on the dressing table. Every tear she'd held back over the last year was falling. The tears about Lenox's late nights out, her weight gain, his behavior in France, her battles with Ms. Meyers, her hand in destroying Derrick's reputation, and Lenox letting Maritza into their lives. The pain swelled up in her to let out a loud wail.

"Oh, my God! Damn it! I heard yelling in here. I thought you were being attacked or something," Adam said, flinging open her door. His dressing room was across the hall from hers.

Farah looked up and talked to Adam in the mirror. She managed her shaky smile. "I—I—was just getting out some anxiety. You know, before we go on air. When will they ever make the perfect brand of mascara that won't run?" she asked, playfully holding up the slim tube.

"I have been trying to get them to put some punching bags

around here for years," Adam said. He watched Farah pensively. "Are you sure you're okay?"

"Yeah!" Farah said, in a perky, light tone. Quietly, she wished she could get a machete and stick it through Maritza.

"Okay, see you soon." Before he could close the door, the makeup lady squeezed through.

"Sorry, Ms. Washington, but the producers want you on the set in a few minutes."

"I'm ready. I just had some allergies I needed to take something for." Farah took a tissue and wiped the tears that had run down her neck.

As soon as Farah walked on to the set, the lights shone on her and Adam. She belonged to the rest of the country. The hottest cookbook author and a former presidential advisor replaced images of Lenox and Maritza.

Schoolchildren were usually invited to stop by the set and get a tour. Farah would always welcome them, and sometimes took pictures with them. But after the show, Farah wasn't in the frame of mind to entertain children. She graciously excused herself and hotfooted out of the newsroom. The car that usually waited for her was delayed. Farah hailed a cab and asked to be taken to Lenox's office.

It was around noon, and most of the associates and staff were at lunch. Farah knew mostly everyone there, and proceeded to Lenox's plush corner office. Margaret stopped her.

"Good afternoon, Ms. Washington," Margaret said, quickly swallowing a cookie.

"Hi, Margaret," Farah drawled.

"Ms. Washington, I'm sorry," she said, running around her desk to Farah. "But Lenox instructed me to announce all visitors. Would you mind just waiting a sec while I ring him?"

"Yes, I mind," Farah said coldly, and proceeded down the hall.

Margaret stayed on Farah's heels until they got to Lenox's door.

But he wasn't in.

"Maybe he stepped out when I left for lunch. I thought he was in here," Margaret said, looking around the office. "It *is* lunchtime."

"Fuck lunch! Page him or something. I need to see him!" Farah dropped her Gucci bag on Lenox's office sofa.

"Yes, Ms. Washington." Margaret rushed off to her desk.

Farah waited for fifteen minutes. But there was no sign of Lenox. His desk looked neat and organized, just like his briefcase. And his cologne lightly scented the air. She saw a few suit jackets behind the door and some shoes in the closet. She noticed that was one thing that had changed. He never kept clothes in the office before.

"Ms. Washington, um, Lenox said he'll meet you at the house. He said he'll be working from there this afternoon."

"Did you page him?"

"Yes, Ms. Washington, and he called back from his car. He's on his way home now."

Farah grabbed her bag and flew out the door.

She walked a few blocks to his apartment. As she drew closer, she noted that he once told her he hated working from home. There was no sure way of proving how long he had been home, because from the sound of Margaret, she didn't even know when he had left.

The first thing she heard when she walked in the living room was the buzz of the shower. A smile of contempt crossed her face. A shower in the middle of the day was a bad sign on her list.

"Lenox! Get the fuck out of the shower!" she screamed. She took the newspaper out of her bag.

He came running out with his wet feet leaving circles of water on the wooden floor.

"What? This can't wait till I wash my ass?" he said, wrapping the towel around his thick waist. Normally, Farah would be ready to snap his towel off, but the arrogant look on his face enraged her more.

"This can't wait!" she said throwing the paper down. "Are you trying to get back at me for something I've done to you? Because if you are, you've succeeded."

Lenox opened the paper and saw the picture. He sucked his teeth and threw it on the armchair. "So what do you want me to say?" he said.

"I don't know, but I know I'm getting the fuck out of here!" Farah said, grabbing up little items that belonged to her. She went into the kitchen and grabbed an empty box that sat under the table.

"You already got your mind made up about the picture. Why come to me and ask me about it for?" he said, following her around the apartment as she sprinted from the bedroom to the bathroom.

"I wish I never met you. You are a lying fuck. You go ahead and lay up with that French ho'. All she was doing was using you anyway," she spat.

He blocked Farah's path back into the bathroom. "And you. You weren't using me?" he said.

Farah tried to walk past him, but couldn't. "Yes! I used you to get what I wanted. And was foolish enough to fall in love with you. But now since I paid my dues, I don't want any part in your little love games. I stood by you when no one else was there. You ain't shit!" she said punching him in his chest.

"Now you can finally leave me because you got what you wanted." He held her arms away from him. He pushed her on to the bed.

Farah charged at him with all her strength and kicked him between his legs, but missed his family jewels. His towel tumbled to the floor and he grabbed her by the arm. He showed her the jewelry and the clothes, the expensive shoes that lined the wall of the bedroom.

"I never asked you for *anything* in return for all this," he said, letting her go. "You think getting you on *Rise and Shine* was easy? I had to put my integrity on the line and nearly beg those people to give you a chance. They had Ms. Barbie, blond hair and big tits from Channel Two for your spot."

"I didn't ask you—" Farah started.

"Yes! You did ask me. Every day. A man couldn't come home and get some peace. You were at me every day about Ms. Meyers, the show, the people, the money," he said, pointing at her. "I was going through a lot being overworked with the whole George and Derrick situation, but you never asked. I'll never forget that."

"So what is it? Maritza asks you how your days are?" she asked, looking up at him.

"Maritza is a hell of a lot more woman than you'll ever be. Look at you, almost thirty and have another man leaving you. You can't leave me. Because I made your success," he said. "I want you outta here." He kicked some shoes out of the way and wrapped the towel around his waist.

Farah flinched as Lenox slammed the bathroom door. In seconds, the shower started running again.

She sat on the floor, not knowing what happened. She had come home to leave Lenox, but somehow he'd left her. Her shoulder throbbed from pain. She wanted to cry, but had no tears left.

Taking only her small purse, she walked out. Her money was in her Gucci tote bag, but she wasn't turning back.

As she walked across the park to her mother's place, she still had on her morning suit and Manolo heels. Her shades protected her red eyes from the view of others.

"Jesus. Oliver!" Farah's mother said as she opened the door.

"Come help me get this girl in here! Lord have mercy." Oliver and her mother helped Farah inside the apartment.

"What's wrong with you, sitting by the door and crying like that? Where's Lenox?" her mother asked, looking back outside.

"Lenox, Lenox, Lenox! That's all anyone ever talks about around here," Farah said, grabbing her head. "That man has taken everything out of me!"

Oliver sat Farah down, and said, "Did he hit you?"

"I wish he'd beat the crap out of me one time and just get it over with. Than to put me through all the hell he has!"

Farah saw an unopened *Daily News* sitting on the coffee table. She opened it and showed her mother the picture.

"I know that is the girl from the tape. Why would Lenox go back to such an awful woman? He should know better," her mother scowled. She showed Oliver the paper.

The phone rang and Oliver went to pick it up.

Oliver came back in the room. "It was Lenox. He said to come back to the house."

"Is he still on the phone? Let me talk to him," Farah's mother said.

"He hung up. He said he had to talk to Farah about something," Oliver said.

"I am not going back there. Whatever he needs to tell me, he can reach me on the set tomorrow!" said Farah, feeling out of control. She wanted to shower and go to sleep. She wanted to wash away everything that just happened.

"Baby, you have to go back to the house. Maybe he feels bad and wants to talk to you," suggested her mother. Her mother caught herself. "I'm sorry. Maybe you shouldn't."

"What about me and how I feel? You know how I feel right now?! I want to get as far away as possible from Lenox, from everything!" Farah leaped up from the chair, leaving her mother and Oliver spellbound.

Farah slept on a small single bed that night. In the dark, she could hear the phone ringing and her mother saying that she was asleep. She knew it was Lenox because her mother mentioned him by name each time, as if she wanted her to know.

Tossing and crying, Farah stayed up straight through the night, wondering where she went wrong, and where she could have been better. In the end, she blamed herself. She realized that she was never good at being a girlfriend and probably didn't give Lenox the attention he needed. She thought about all the powerful men and the women they married. Russell Simmons married a model. Donald Trump married a model and an actress. George Bush Jr. married a librarian. Farah was none of the above. For all of his faults, Lenox did stand by her ambition because it equaled his and they reveled in it together. But she was a hard-edge career girl and after Lenox, was afraid she might not meet another man who could handle that.

♥

When she woke up at 4:00 A.M. to get ready for the show, she realized she had the same clothes on from yesterday. She woke her mother and borrowed a gold-trimmed knee-length dress, which was probably too dressy, but everything her mother owned was too dressy.

The set was buzzing with technicians setting up props for the morning show. Farah walked down the hall to her dressing room, but her code did not work. She knocked on Adam's door, but he wasn't in yet. She tried the code again, a bit slower, and the door still did not open.

"Ms. Washington," said one of the technicians, "I think you may want to talk to one of the producers."

Farah spun around on her heel. "Has the code changed?"

But he didn't hear her and walked back out to the set.

Anxious and tired, Farah found Angela, the supervising producer.

"Hi, Farah. I've been put in such an awful position. But because of some differences between you and the network, there have been some changes. We're just going with Adam this morning. I'm so sorry. I got the call late yesterday evening," Angela said, embarrassed and sympathetic at the same time.

"Who called you?" Farah asked, feeling breathless.

"Station management." A technician was calling Angela to the set. She apologized once more and went back to work.

Frozen still, Farah stood there holding her morning coffee. She felt foolish standing in the middle of the newsroom looking too-dressy. Her paranoia grew, making her feel that all the whispers and stares were at her.

She put her coffee on a nearby desk, and turned around to leave.

"Excuse me. I have to escort you out of the building," a six-foot-six bodyguard with a Swedish accent said.

"Excuse *me*! You are in my way," Farah said, walking around him.

"Ma'am, I won't touch you or bother you. I just have to walk with you out of the building. Then you're on your own."

Farah walked over to the phone subconsciously and stopped. She had the impulse to call Lenox. But there was no Lenox to call. She knew he was behind this somehow.

Without making eye contact with anyone, she walked out the newsroom with her head held high. She didn't want to appear like a wounded puppy. The security guard stood comfortably away from her, as she waited for the elevator. They got on it together. She on one side, and he on the other. Farah was blinking uncontrollably to prevent any tears from falling.

The steps of the security guard echoed hers as she walked up to the building exit. She wanted to yell and scream and demand to speak to someone. But she walked out into the cold dawn.

Instead of taking a cab, she took the Q train uptown to Lenox's apartment. She wasn't nervous about taking a chance and finding another woman there, nor was she scared that he'd be upset or even sleeping. Everything had been stripped away from her, and she felt that she had nothing to lose. The fear factor was gone.

She used her key and opened the door. The apartment was silent. She could hear Lenox's deep snore from across the room. When she opened the door, he was asleep on his back. He was on his side of the bed. For a moment, she wanted to pour a pot of dirt into his opened mouth. But she reconciled herself to gathering some things and leaving. She picked up the box that she started packing during the argument. It was laid next to the door. She tried to be fast but quiet. She took a few tops and jeans from the closet and a pair of sneakers she never wore. It was enough to keep her situated at her mother's until she arranged for the rest of her things.

He turned over on his side. Her eye started twitching as she brought her hand to her mouth. She couldn't shake the feeling that she wanted to still be with him. As she watched him sleep, visions of them making love on the same bed flashed before her. Just last week she had lain across his lap as he stroked her hair. One thing she did believe was that he loved her. She accepted that Lenox was a complicated man who loved in a complicated way. She believed in time he would be the man any woman needed. But it would be in his time.

She used one hand to dry the tears that were beginning to form in her already swollen ducts. Her *TV Guide* cover issue was still lying on the floor. She took that with her, too.

Traveling across town again to her mother's apartment gave her the time to think what her next move would be. By noon, she thought, everything would have hit the fan. The media would know she was dropped and the phone calls will start coming in. She realized that she wouldn't be able to work in television again. And strangely, she felt okay about it. The backstabbing and schmoozing was too much for her. She smiled to herself as she thought about taking a new route in her life. She was nine months away from thirty and wanted to start anew. Just last week, she was planning a life with Lenox, and today she was planning on living alone.

Her mother had given her a key to the apartment, and she let herself in. It was 7:30 and her mother was sitting by the TV. Farah carried the box into the living room.

"I'm so sorry, baby. I turned the TV on this morning, and they said you were on a 'special assignment.' Maybe you should have talked to Lenox last night. Maybe he could have stopped this," she said, pointing to the TV, obviously upset.

"It's Lenox's doing, Mom," Farah said, sitting down by her mother. "I hope you can see now that he is not just some bad boy. He's destructive. And he took away the one thing I held dearly."

"Well, why aren't you still there raising some hell? I would call him right now and give him a piece of my mind!" her mother went on.

"It doesn't work like that. It's just wasted energy. I'm so numb right now, you could drop a boulder on my head and I wouldn't feel it. I'm glad this is over." Farah stared at the TV set with Adam grinning.

Her mother stared at her in awe. Farah got up and walked to the window as her mother watched every step.

"I gave Lenox back his investment on the house in the Vineyard a few weeks ago. So I think I'll be staying there for some time. Just to get my head together," Farah said, looking below at the bustling sidewalk.

"It's so dead up there this time of year. If you want to be surrounded by trees and bushes, fine with me." Her mother shrugged.

"I know, since the summer crowd has left, but I need that time. I think I want to be a writer!" Farah burst out.

"A writer? You've never been politically oppressed and you're not gay. What do you have to write about?" her mother said, looking at her as if she were a new person.

"Anything. Right now, I want to try anything. Maybe I'll even go to Spain and stay in Marbella for a while. It's not like I can't afford it. Damn it, I'm gonna buy a car, too."

"Did you and Lenox have your money tied up?" her mother asked.

"We kept separate accounts and I invested well. I have enough money to live on for years to come. I don't have to work another day if I don't want to."

"You mean *we* have enough money for years to come." Her mother winked.

Farah sat back down with her mother.

"I don't want to get you upset. But don't think that because you have money, you don't need a man at some point," her mother said.

Farah felt a rise of anger, but it dissipated immediately. "Can you please give me some time to get over this one?"

Her mother laughed. "Oh, yes, true. But Lenox has to settle down and marry at some point. I just wish things could have worked out better."

"Yeah, me too. I also wish that I could find a pair of those last-season's pink Manolos that were sold out in a day." Farah said cynically.

"I know you're acting tough for me. But I know you, and I know, as your mother, you're dying inside."

"Whatever you say," Farah said, going into the kitchen for some juice.

She spent the next few days lazing around the house. The phone was quiet and no one called, except Lola. Not even Ms. Meyers called.

On the third morning, Farah got up early to watch the show. She scrutinized the set, the guests, and the questions Adam asked. She pictured what she would say if she were there. Farah flipped the channels in between commercials. When she flipped back to *Rise and Shine,* she called her mother into the room.

Her mother came running in. "What?!" she yelled, with her rollers falling out of her hair.

"It's Maritza! He put that tramp on my show! She's on there talking about *Fourteenth Street* with Adam!"

Farah's mother pulled up a chair close to the TV set as they both watched and listened.

"Lenox knew that I'd be watching this. How could he just throw her on there like that? Why does he hate me so much?" Farah cried. "I can't take this embarrassment. I must leave *today*." Farah didn't even hear the words Maritza was saying. She was wearing a short black sleeveless dress that made her look perfect. Her hair had grown, and now reached her shoulders. Farah knew that an appearance on *Rise and Shine* would boost Maritza's career.

"I guess Lenox found a replacement for me already. Just look at her, sitting there like she got an Oscar before or something," Farah said, not amused.

Her mother just stared at the TV set in one of her rare, wordless moments.

The ringing of the phone made her mother jump. When she picked it up, she handed it to Farah.

"It's Page Six," her mother whispered.

"Yes?" said Farah, grabbing the phone.

"Ms. Washington. This is Martin Fitz. How are you?"

"Fine. How did you get this number?"

"It's Page Six, we have everyone's phone number," the guy said in a snobbish tone. "Can you just tell us your side of the story as to why you were cut from the show?"

"No comment."

"Well, what about your boyfriend putting his girlfriend on a show you used to work for?"

"No comment!" Farah yelled. Her mother hung up the phone for her.

All morning calls came in from industry reporters wanting to know the scoop. Farah packed up some things in a small bag, and called Enterprise for a car.

The Vineyard was the only place she could keep her sanity.

Finale

*F*arah turned down several offers to host shows for *Extra!* *Inside Edition,* and *Entertainment Tonight.* She was done with the demands of television. She wanted simplicity and clarity for a change. Even if it meant ending up alone, it was time for her to trust herself and rely on that to get her to her next phase in life. While at the Vineyard, she entertained the idea of writing a book, but her thoughts were still unsettled.

Since Farah and Lenox had broken up, he occupied his time buying and selling. He sold the Life House name to a private organization. In the agreement he sketched out, he had a coveted seat on the board of directors. He rented his SoHo building to a garment manufacturer and a complex of small offices, who each paid monthly rent in the five-figure range.

Maritza was traveling to Europe visiting friends, and Seht was in Jamaica on a consulting assignment. Lenox's nightmares were also letting up, too. He had cut his losses, and felt renewed. But his longing for Farah still crept up in dark, shady images at night.

Lenox had no idea that Maritza was going to be put on *Rise and Shine* as soon as she was. He had spoken to Ms. Meyers about putting her on the show eventually, but three days after Farah being fired was too soon for him.

Almost a year after that show aired and Farah's departure, Lenox still had an incomplete feeling. He didn't even bother dating because he already had his mind made up about Farah. He felt as though he lost a piece of himself without her around to call, counsel, or make love to.

One night, he found himself in bed, still sleeping on his side and looking over on her empty side. He called her mother.

"Ms. Washington, just tell me where she is. I just want to clear up some things with her," he said.

Farah's mother broke down on Lenox's fourth request. "Farah's at the house in the Vineyard. Please don't tell her I told you," pleaded her mother.

Lenox thanked her and hung up. He took the Range Rover out of the lot and drove up to Massachusetts on a rainy Wednesday evening. When he got there, he took the ferryboat over. And an hour later, he was at the door.

He knocked on the door hard and impatiently. He hoped that she was inside, because he wouldn't know where to look if she wasn't. There was a luxury rental car out front, which had Farah's name written all over it.

Farah expected his visit since her mother was never good at keeping secrets. When she opened the door, she waited for him to speak. She was dressed in a simple ankle-length dress. He hadn't seen her with a skirt that passed her knees before. Her hair was wrapped in a bun, and she had no makeup on, but a pair of chic reading glasses. Her new look intrigued Lenox.

He smiled and could tell that she wanted to, as well. But the hurt she still felt stopped her.

She stepped to the side. And let him in.

"I'm not going to take up a lot of time. I just wanted to come here and tell you my side of things," said Lenox, rubbing his cold hands together. He unzipped his leather jacket.

"I forgot about it. It's been almost a year already," she said, putting away the journal she was writing in.

"I know *you* didn't forget. Let me just tell you that once word got out that you stormed out of the building when you saw my picture in the paper, Aunt Joan called. I was a little angry since you and I just finished fighting and I told her I wished I had never gotten you the job. And she took that and ran with it, cutting you off on the spot," Lenox said.

Before she responded, she took a mental picture of him. He looked weary. He had dark circles under his eyes that showed he wasn't getting much sleep. He had grown a thin beard, which made him look more distinguished and older. The attraction she'd felt for him was still there. She wanted to feel his thick lips over her body again. He still got to her. She snapped herself out of her trance.

"You know, I just want to forget this ever happened. I want to forget I ever met you. That we ever shared anything. Unlike Hillary Clinton, I'm not riding on your power train anymore," she said.

Lenox cautiously sat down.

"I loved you. I mean I *love* you," he said. "Maritza is in Europe and that part of my life is over. I really want to settle down with you. If you want, I can stay here for a while. And we can start over."

Farah chewed on a bagel. "*We* don't exist anymore. Lenox, things are still too fresh. Look at me! I've been totally changed by this. I'm sorry, but I officially bow out of this one."

"I want to marry you."

He moved close enough that she could feel the heat from his body penetrate hers.

"Lenox, don't do this. Sex is not going to fix this," Farah said, gently pushing him away.

He backed away.

"We're made for each other," he said, taken by the truth of his words.

Lenox's lips finally reached Farah's mouth and she didn't withdraw. Their mouths locked as Lenox hungrily reached inside. Farah turned her face, and said in his ear, "I have a one-way ticket to Spain for tomorrow."

"Marbella?"

"Yes," she said, regretting that she gave that away. "And I need to get a lot of rest, so please leave." He knew one-way ticket revealed that Farah had no intention of coming back to him.

"I'm coming too. I can go right now if I had to." He stood up.

"Please, sit down," she said, patting the space next to her. "Look, I've missed you, too. I just feel that we probably had too many odds against us. I can't believe I gave you that much power over my life. I'm ashamed."

"I stopped the parties and the Life House to give you all my time and attention. I'm sorry if it didn't seem that way," he said. "We can start something new."

"Only God knows where the story will end for us, Lenox. If it hasn't already." She wanted to tell him to leave, but he was like the drug she needed to relieve the dull pain of sadness she'd felt since they've parted.

Lenox took out a small box. He slipped a nine-karat platinum ring on her finger.

Farah just looked at the ring. She wanted everything he did, but wasn't going to fall this time getting it. She held her hand out. "How can you do this? We haven't even discussed this." She searched for the exact words. It wasn't easy for her to apologize to anyone. "Things definitely didn't start like they ended. I was using you in the beginning, but now I need something different."

Lenox turned the lamp off next to them. "You know what they say. If you can't be used, you're useless."